I0655188

© 2015 Steve Rowe and Linda Rowe

www.steverowebooks.com

88 Ice House Street is a work of fiction. The names of individuals, places, events or corporations have been used strictly in the interest of creating a document of fictional entertainment and most are products of the author's imagination.

Cover design and photography by Allan Forest

ISBN 13:9780994098511

ISBN 10:0994098510

To Linda, my wife and best friend

and to our family.

Donovan "Doc" O'Connell and business school classmate Bev Patterson develop a unique strategy to get Bev's half billion dollar inheritance out of Zimbabwe, where currency restrictions prohibit the transfer of large amounts of capital.

Their plan involves a resort/campus in Zimbabwe, a five-star hotel in the USA and offices in Hong Kong and Silicon Valley. Thailand and Cambodia provide the backdrop for a mysterious kidnapping that threatens to destroy Doc's plans.

A fast-moving tale of international business and adventure. A "feel good" novel intended to entertain with alternating elements of mystery, love and liberal doses of humor.

"Steve has captured interest from the opening page until the end.

He uses wit, humor, intrigue and suspense to keep the reader entrenched in the story.

Doc O'Connell travels the world and we travel to far off places with him.

A great read to be enjoyed by all."

~ Vicky Forest

88 Ice House Street

A Doc O'Connell Novel

By Steve Rowe

Acknowledgements

A very special thanks to my long time friends, Pat and Griff Tripp for their long hours of editing work. Thanks as well to my brother Chuck Rowe and my wife Linda Rowe for their editorial assistance. Thanks also to my good friend Tom Lau for his review and comments regarding the Hong Kong portions of the book. Thanks to my friends and family who provided encouragement and support to keep me motivated during those long cold winter days spent writing. Thanks to my talented brother-in-law, Allan Forest for his excellent work in design and photography for the cover.

In Chinese numerology, the number 8 is a symbol of prosperity and is considered the luckiest number.

CHAPTER ONE

They say that you never hear the one that hits you. It may be true, but you sure do feel it. Donovan O'Connell was walking crouched over to make himself as small as possible, stepping in mud that stuck to his boots and made him wonder if his leg would come up out of the slop. His last thought was that Pete West, the Drug Enforcement Agency guy closest to him had gone crazy and decided to drive his rifle butt as hard as he could into Donovan's upper back. There was an explosion of pain followed by a total blackout.

He learned later that another Drug Enforcement Agency member, Bill Wong, nicknamed Jungle Bill, had fallen on his unconscious body. He used his highly camouflaged jungle fatigues to take away the assailant's ability to see him for a second shot.

Fortunately, the snipers followed a strategy of retreating quickly into the dense jungle after hitting one or two of the group. When the gunman realized that he wasn't going to get another shot at Donovan he made his getaway.

In the silence of the Cambodian jungle, the group is made up of specially trained members of the United States Drug Enforcement Agency (DEA) and the Royal Canadian Mounted Police (RCMP). Known as the Anti-Drug International Task Force (ADIT), with a mission to shut down the flow of Asian drugs to North America.

Jungle Bill got his nickname as a result of his unique ability to add jungle leaves, vines and other flora and fauna to his camouflage combat uniform. He would disappear by blending into his surroundings. As commander of this field expedition, he called the team to draw near for a conference.

The six team members gathered around Jungle Bill while the medic, Jose did his best to deal with Donovan's wounds.

Bill said, "Ryan, call for an evacuation chopper. Give them our coordinates and tell them we'll send up orange smoke from our position at the clearing a half a mile due west of here."

"Aye Skipper, what destination should I specify?" Ryan asked.

Bill considered this briefly and said, "Tell them we have one man shot and critically wounded. We'll need transport to the nearest hospital with operating facilities."

Bill said, "Al, you take the point, Mike, give Jose a hand with Donovan, Ryan, keep on the radio and the rest of you watch our six. Keep the noise down, let's move."

The group walked slowly towards the clearing when suddenly a thwacking sound followed by a large flying wood chip testified to the fact that the sniper was back. This time however he got unlucky as his flash suppressor failed, and two ADIT team members at the rear of the column could clearly make out his position high in the trees about 200 yards to the rear. Ralph's M4 and Brian's UZI fired at the same spot at the same time, and the sniper fell out of the tree like a stalk of bananas.

Donovan was losing blood fast as the team waited for the evacuation helicopter. Jose was doing the best he could to stop the blood loss; however, the nature of the exit wound was such that all Jose could manage was to slow down, not stop the bleeding.

Jungle Bill said, "Ryan, what's base saying about the helicopter?"

Ryan finished his discussion with support and said, "The chopper is ten minutes out, ETA 2:45."

Bill said, "We'll wait here at the edge of the clearing and stay under cover of the tree canopy until we hear the approach of the bird. Ralph stand by to make orange smoke at my signal." Ralph acknowledged the command and began to prepare for smoke release.

Typically Jungle Bill hated helicopters. He didn't mind flying in fixed winged aircraft where there was the possibility of gliding to an emergency landing. But he knew that a helicopter without power would be about as graceful as an elephant going over a cliff, and this made him very nervous.

When Bill had been recruited by the DEA fresh out of a Doctorate program in international economics from Harvard, he hadn't figured on spending much time in helicopters. He had seen himself as an expert on world economics, who when required to do so, would likely travel first class commercially if not in one of the agency's private jets.

Born in Shanghai with a Chinese diplomat for a father and an American English professor as a mother, Bill had always felt more comfortable with books and computers than guns and grenades.

As Chair of the English Department at Shanghai's Fudan University, Bill's mom, Barbara, with the aid of an Amah from Hong Kong, raised Bill in the ways of Chinese and American high society. When Bill was eight years old, he was fluent in Mandarin, Cantonese and English and had mastered several musical instruments.

All of this academic, upper-class training did Bill very little good when up to his waist in mud and swamp grass on the edge of a jungle clearing.

Bill said, "Jose, what's Donovan's condition?"

"I've just changed the pressure bandages and wrapped him as tight as possible. I fear he has extensive internal injuries." Jose replied. Just then, a report came in from the chopper and Ryan indicated that they were about 2 minutes away.

Bill said, "First check the perimeter for snipers then release the smoke and prepare to head for the chopper."

The large medevac chopper set down with the noise and turbulence associated with these ungainly contraptions. Bill ushered all his team on board and Jose strapped Donovan into the stretcher. As the aircraft increased power and began to lift off, Bill willed his stomach to remain calm and tried to put on his idea of a commanding officer's face.

Throughout the trip from the ambush point in the jungle to the chopper, Donovan continued to bleed, albeit more slowly and remained, mercifully in a coma.

The helicopter landed at Bumrungrad International Hospital in Bangkok, and a doctor rushed Donovan into the intensive care area for preliminary assessment.

"Special Agent Wong," the doctor addressed Bill formally, "my name is Frank Anderson. Mr. O'Connell has suffered severe internal trauma as well as significant blood loss. He remains in a coma, and I feel it's best to leave him that way for now. I'll take care of the urgent aspects of his condition. He'll need several surgeries and a lengthy recuperation period. I suggest he be made ready to travel then flown to Seattle General Hospital, the nearest US major medical facility best equipped to deal with his surgical needs and recovery."

"Thank you, doctor," Bill said. "I'll make arrangements for an agency aircraft to take him to Seattle."

Donovan O'Connell was born of Irish parents from Killarney, who moved to Canada when Donovan was two years old, settling in Corktown, Toronto's large Irish neighborhood. While Donovan played hockey and baseball well, he excelled at football where he could use his height, weight, and speed to his advantage. At seventeen years old, several university football teams, including two from the USA were scouting him.

He finally settled on a football scholarship from the University of Western Ontario in London, Canada due primarily to his desire to play football under UWO's excellent coach, Bob 'Scotty' Lawson.

Donovan also recognized that to achieve his long-term career goals in international business, he would need academic credentials from one of the best schools in the country for business studies. Completing his bachelor's degree in just three years, he stayed at Western and enrolled in the four-year combination MBA and law degree selecting the international options where available.

Donovan liked girls and girls had always found him attractive. With the exception of time spent with a few male friends, primarily classmates or teammates, Donovan was almost always in the company of young ladies who enjoyed his combination of good looks and sense of humor. He discovered early on that girls like to laugh and liked boys who made them laugh. While his quick wit pleased the ladies, his humorous antics caused him some difficulty with coaches and professors keeping teams and classes focused.

While he enjoyed female companionship, he avoided any long-term relationships, focusing instead on his studies and sports. He wanted to travel and to build a career in international business, which, in his mind, precluded any long-term attachments for many years to come. Throughout university, he had formed a close friendship with Bev Patterson, a brilliant young lady from Alberta and had been in the same study group with her both in business school and law school.

Their academic skills complimented each other. Bev was a wizard with numbers, computers, finance and accounting. Donovan excelled at sales and marketing, advertising, public relations and human resources. Together they made a formidable team.

A month prior to graduation, Donovan was surprised to receive a call from Jim Elliott, who introduced himself on the phone as an executive recruiter from Ottawa. Jim said he had a position that might be of interest to Donovan and that he would like to meet with him. He said that he couldn't discuss the opportunity over the phone but assured Donovan that he would find it very attractive. They agreed to meet on Saturday for lunch at Chantel's, London's top restaurant.

The mysterious Mr. Elliott intrigued Donovan, and the intrigue grew as he tried to find information about him online. No executive search firm in Ottawa, Toronto or Montreal had ever heard of Jim Elliott. Saturday was three days away, so Donovan put aside thoughts of the meeting to focus on final exam preparation.

On Saturday Donovan approached the maitre'd at Chantel's and said, "My name is O'Connell, and I have a lunch meeting with Mr. Elliott."

"Certainly sir," the maitre'd responded, "please follow me."

He led Donovan to a private room at the back of the restaurant with only one table. As he approached the table, Donovan extended his hand and said," Mr. Elliott, I'm Donovan O'Connell, pleased to meet you."

As they shook hands, Mr. Elliott said, "Please call me Jim, what would you like to drink?"

Donovan noticed that Jim was having a martini but ordered a soda water for himself. "You don't drink Donovan?" Jim said.

"Sometimes I do" Donovan replied, "however following lunch I have to be back at the books with finals starting in two weeks."

"Of course," Jim replied, "how soon we forget. It was only eleven years ago that I was in your exact position, finishing up my law degree at McGill and fighting for every mark. I suppose you're wondering why I've asked you to meet with me today and knowing how busy you are with studies, I'll get right to the point. The topics we'll discuss are highly confidential and are covered by the Federal Secrets Act.

As such, I'll need you to read and sign this document that is your agreement never to reveal to anyone the things we discuss today."

Jim handed a one-page document to Donovan, who was apparently surprised by this requirement for secrecy and legalities at this stage of the discussion.

Donovan took the paper and read it over. It was a straightforward oath not to reveal anything said today under threat of serious legal repercussions.

"What if I don't sign this?" Donovan asked.

"Then I've wasted a lot of time and money so we had better hope that lunch is worth the trip."

"Maybe I should have had a martini," Donovan said as he reached for the pen and signed.

"I was banking on your inquisitive mind, figuring that you would sign if for nothing else, to find out what this offer involves. I also judged that, after the fact, you would fully appreciate the serious nature of our talk and would not reveal our discussions with or without the document. When I said before that I had spent a lot of time and money so far, I wasn't referring to my trip from Ottawa. The trip cost is the tip of the iceberg. We've spent considerable time and money exploring your background from many different angles before making the call to arrange this meeting. We know just about everything there is to know about you including who your girlfriend was in grade four and at least where we think you want to go career wise.

If our information is accurate, you have a keen interest in the international side of business, love to travel and to study new cultures. As part of your university education, you've become fluent in Mandarin and Cantonese and are presently studying Spanish as a hobby. Is there anything that we've left out?"

"No that's a pretty accurate summary of my career ambitions," Donovan said. "I do have a desire to travel, meet new people and enjoy a bit of adventure. So if your position involves spending a lot of time in an office on Bay Street, then lunch may well be all you'll get for your troubles."

"You've never heard of my organization. Officially, it doesn't exist. They finance us out of secret funds through the RCMP and we are referred to as Eclipse Software. We report to the head of the RCMP, who reports directly to the Minister of Justice. Eclipse is a front company, theoretically developing high-level software for business, governments and military customers internationally. The guise allows us to maintain offices in Ottawa and to travel freely as software developers."

While he'd heard of cloak and dagger operations engaged in covert activities, Donovan had associated this with the CIA and its various tentacles around the world.

"This is the first time I've heard of undercover operations backed by Canada," Donovan said.

"We've been organized to deal with any potential threats to Canada. We focus for now on stopping the flow of illicit drugs. We might in future see our role expand as new threats develop as surely they will."

"Why me?" Donovan asked.

"Our research people are very thorough; probably the best Canada has to offer. They were instructed to look into upcoming graduates in law and or business who have demonstrated leadership skills and an interest in foreign cultures and who have maintained an excellent grade point average. You qualified under all these criteria."

"Assuming I'm interested, what would the job entail?" Donovan asked.

"Despite the secrets act agreement you signed, I can't go into a lot of details until you're on board. I can say the job I have in mind for you will involve extensive travel throughout Asia.

You'll study the Asian drug operations, particularly as they apply to Canada and the USA and determine who the key players are and how

to best thwart their efforts. You'll work closely with the US Drug Enforcement Agency as part of an operation we call the Anti-Drug International Task Force or ADIT for short. Let's order lunch before we go on. The Veal Marsala is the specialty of the house."

With the lunch order taken, Jim continued to tell Donovan about the job. "Your day to day activities will include meeting high-level government officials and senior business executives across Asia and conducting research into the various drug operations in the region. There will

be an element of danger involved; however, we will try to keep this to a minimum."

"Tell me about the danger part. Will I constantly have to be looking over my shoulder?"

"No, for the most part, you'll be seen as a Canadian software executive traveling on company business. You'll stay in the best hotels and frequent places catering to the senior business and diplomatic circles in the countries that you visit.

Most of the job will involve networking at events sponsored by various Canadian and American government and business groups."

"You make it sound like a dream job. Rubbing shoulders with high society and traveling around a part of the world that has always fascinated me," Donovan said, "I'm waiting for the other shoe to drop."

Jim felt that the meeting was going well, so he decided to have a glass of wine with lunch, after all he didn't have to hit the books. He simply had to strap on the Gulfstream jet and head for Ottawa and a long weekend at the cottage. "For the most part, you'll be operating in the main cities. Occasionally, it'll be necessary for you to participate in remote jungle operations to disrupt drug supply lines and to destroy processing facilities. In these instances, you'll be accompanied by DEA agents and depending upon the nature of the field trip, elements of the US and or host country military."

Just then, a light tap on the door announced the arrival of lunch, so Jim took a break from job talk to allow them to enjoy their meals.

Donovan had been working so hard at his studies, ninety to a hundred or more hours a week that he'd almost forgotten what time off was. He promised himself at least a month off after finals to sit on his deck and relax with a couple of good books.

"Let's talk about training," Donovan said, "how does one prepare for this type of work?"

"You would initially be sent to the Depot, an RCMP training facility in Regina and go through their cadet training for new members. Six months later, upon graduation from this, you would be sent to the DEA training facility and several US military training bases for specialized preparation for jungle operations. Our relationship with the DEA has been one of close cooperation and they're able to open doors to a lot of specialized US military facilities including Rangers and Seals training when required."

As they finished their lunches, Donovan said he was very interested in exploring this further and would like to give it some thought. He explained that he would like to get through final exams, take a holiday for a month, and then give Jim his answer.

"Can't do it I'm afraid, if you are to join us, I'd need a response by one week from today. The Minister wants you on the next RCMP training program, which starts three weeks from now.

You'll have time to finish your finals, but you'll be reporting to commence the first phase of your training in Regina three days later.

The further training as arranged by the DEA is all planned to follow in a logical sequence from the conclusion of the RCMP training and will take another four months. Then you will have a two-week break before reporting to Ottawa for further training in diplomatic skills.

Think about it over the next week Donovan. Think of the free education you'll receive in Asian studies, the cultures you'll become familiar with and the senior business and government contacts that you'll make across the region. It's like earning a doctorate in Asian studies with a wealth of high-level experience thrown in."

CHAPTER TWO

Suddenly Donovan was aware of distant voices but they weren't speaking to him, rather they were speaking to each other. He was aware of total blackness and the faint soft noise, sort of a hum that emanates from some electric machinery such as older television monitors and computers. He slowly came to the realization that the darkness that surrounded him may be because his eyes were closed. He decided to open his eyes, and the first site he saw was a lovely blonde woman with eyes the color of a Caribbean Sea lagoon.

"Please tell me you're not an angel," Donovan said in a dry, scratchy voice suffering from a long period of silence.

"No, I'm Lilly, a nurse, and I've been watching you closely today as your vital signs were changing indicating that you might be coming out of the coma."

"Lilly, I have a few questions for you. For instance where am I, how long have I been here and what is wrong with me?"

You've been in a coma for three weeks since arriving here at Seattle General Hospital. Dr. Fulton will fill you in on your condition and prognosis. I've called him, and he's on his way in."

"You're telling me that I've been in a coma for three weeks. So two more questions, are you free for dinner tonight, it's been a long time since I have had real food and can you get hold of a pair of Seahawks tickets?"

Lilly smiled and said, "I may not be an angel, but I usually have to know someone for longer than five minutes before agreeing to a date."

"Ok," Donovan replied. "How long is a reasonable amount of time? We could put it off until tomorrow. Shall I make reservations?"

Lilly said," Get some rest and talk to Dr. Fulton, like you, he's Canadian. He took medicine at Queens University, but as he says, they made him put it back."

"I heard that nurse Lilly," Dr. Fulton said upon entering the room. "Let's let our patient come back to consciousness slowly before introducing him to our peculiar brand of levity. Mr. O'Connell, I'm Tom Fulton please call me Tom and if it is ok with you, I'll call you Donovan."

They shook hands and Tom drew up a chair to the bedside. "Donovan, you have been through a rough time. You were hit in the back by a large caliber bullet, which entered very near your spine and passed through you just missing your heart. That's the good news. The bad news is that the bullet took out part of your right lung and fractured three ribs before exiting your chest.

You have had two surgeries since arriving here, and we have one more to go before you are done. You will need at least two weeks recovery following your next surgery depending on how it goes. We've been waiting for you to come out of the coma before dealing with the next surgery. I'll confer with my colleagues, but I think we can look at doing the next operation in three or four days. As I said, you have been through a lot but should be fully back to normal once we're through with the surgeries and recuperation period. Any questions at this point?"

"Yes," Donovan replied, "what restaurant would you suggest I take Lilly to for dinner?"

"It's good to see that your sense of humor is working, I am afraid that it will be a week or two before you can venture out for dinner. I tell you what, you get well. Then my wife, Lilly and I will take you to dinner at El Gonzo's, our favorite restaurant. For now get some rest and I'll see you tomorrow."

Lilly gave Donovan some water and a pill to help him get some sleep. She drew the shades to block out the bright sunshine and to make sure he was comfortable, then headed to the nursing station.

Early the next morning, Lilly was back with Jenn, a beautiful brunette, in tow. "Good morning Donovan, I'd like you to meet Jenn the physiotherapist who is going to get you mobile again."

"Hi Jenn," Donovan said, "will I be able to dance at my daughter's wedding?"

Jenn asked, "When is your daughter's wedding?"

"I don't have a daughter yet, and I can't dance, but I have lots of time to practice."

Jenn got Donovan up and, on very unsteady feet, got him to walk the fifteen steps to the bathroom and back.

" Ok that's enough for today, get some rest and tomorrow we'll try to walk to the shower room."

"Ladies, can I sit up in the chair for a while, I'm a little tired of the bed?"

Lilly said, "No problem, you'll be having visitors later on, and they'll be pleased to see you up."

"Visitors, who are they?"

"I don't know other than they must be well connected to get in to see you this early on. Normally at this stage, we wouldn't permit anyone but immediate family. You'll know soon enough."

Donovan clicked on the TV to the CNN channel to get caught up with events in the world since he had been out of it. Shortly lunch arrived and already the hospital food was predictable and boring. He started to look forward to dinner with Lilly and Tom Fulton. Whatever El Gonzo's is, it has to be better than this. He thought.

He had barely finished lunch and was working on his second cup of coffee when the door opened. In walked Jungle Bill and Jim Elliott bearing smiles and gifts of flowers, a wrapped gift, and a fruit basket.

"What's with fruit and flowers, you couldn't

find any chocolate cheesecake?" Donovan said as he extended his hand to greet his friends.

"There'll be time for cheesecake in a couple of weeks," Jim replied, "Dr. Fulton says he thinks you'll need about two weeks of recuperation following your surgery. He has agreed to allow you to recuperate elsewhere if you're doing well after a week of observation. Bill here has arranged for you to use a DEA safe house in the Bahamas, and I've arranged for a Gulfstream jet to get you there. The house is fully equipped and staffed, and we'll have a nurse on call to keep an eye on you."

"Try to find me a nurse who is similar to Lilly without the good doctor trailing along," Donovan said.

"Forget about taking a turn for the nurse, it's time for you to heal and get back to work, we have a lot on our plates," Jim said.

"So what's with the wrapped gift?" Donovan asked.

Jungle Bill replied, "It's a little something the guys on the team for the Cambodia incursion put together, open it up."

Donovan opened the box and found it contained a set of scrubs and a stethoscope.

"The guys have decided that you're spending so much time in hospitals that they are awarding you the nickname 'Doc,' derived from Donovan O'Connell," Bill said.

Despite what Jim has said about not chasing nurses, the guys felt that you might be able to walk around in your scrubs with the stethoscope around your neck. That way you can get to know a few of the nurses better and acquire telephone numbers for use later."

Jim said, "I like the nickname 'Doc'...it suits you, and I know that telling you to stop chasing nurses is like asking a hooker to give it away. As a condition of your early release following the next surgery, Dr. Fulton has requested that I speak to him before attempting any meetings for the first three weeks after your operation. For now, get lots of rest and build up your immune system and strength for the surgery. If you need anything here is a cell phone with my numbers programmed in."

Jungle Bill said, "Well Doc, Jim and I are going to have to head out. I'm giving him a lift to Ottawa in a DEA jet and then heading to Langley for a meeting in the morning."

"So long Doc," Jim said while shaking hands. "Good luck with the operation and let me know how you are doing by phone as soon as you are able."

Once the guys left, a new nurse, Vicky, stormed into the room and admonished Doc for staying out of bed and for letting the visit last so long. Doc could see a contrast between sweet, soft-spoken Lilly and Vicky, who came on like a drill sergeant with an abscessed tooth. Doc found himself back in bed and taking a sleeping pill Vicky produced like a magician pulling flowers out of a thimble. He tried to watch a little more television however he fell asleep.

One of the perks of this job was having access to the private jets maintained by both the DEA and Eclipse Software, the cover name for the special agency that Doc joined. The nature of the job called for frequent travel. Often on short notice. Also, the level of secrecy associated with the work, meant that Doc and the ADIT team periodically needed to meet with senior level individuals in unique and often remote locations. The meetings were such that to ensure secrecy in some locations; the jet would land, take on the person or persons attending the meeting and then immediately take off again. The meeting would be held in the sky, free of observation and listening devices. Following the meeting, the plane would land, usually at a different, and where possible, private airport to keep watchers from tracking the passengers as well as departure and landing details.

Doc had been cleared to travel by Tom Fulton.

Doc took Tom, Lilly and Vicky to dinner at El Gonzo's, and they dropped him at the airport for his flight to Nassau.

Doc bid farewell to lovely Lilly with a hug for her and a salute for the drill sergeant followed by a hug.

The sun was setting over the blue Caribbean waters so clear, that as the Gulfstream descended on final approach, Doc could see the ocean floor. The flight from Seattle had been long but comfortable. Jim had sent his secretary out with a company credit card to the top stores on a shopping spree to get Doc equipped for a couple of weeks in the Caribbean sun. She had the duffel bag placed on the jet prior to its leaving Ottawa for Seattle to deliver Doc to Nassau.

Once the plane taxied to its designated place, a white SUV drove up to the descending stairs. A young DEA special agent, Sam Burgess, welcomed Doc to Nassau and helped him load his duffel bag into the vehicle.

The safe house was everything Doc could have hoped for and then some. From the outside, it was a sprawling 6,000 square foot upscale beach house with a luxurious swimming pool that abutted the private beach. Inside it was a lovely five bedrooms, six bathrooms, home. It had floor to ceiling glass windows overlooking the deck surrounding the pool. The deck had stairs leading to the private beach. Sam showed Doc around, introduced him to Sarah, the cook, and housekeeper and Tony, a cheerful giant who fulfilled many roles including driver, butler, bartender, maintenance man and bodyguard.

Sam explained, "Besides Tony, security on the site is very tight. It includes video surveillance of the grounds, around the clock patrols by armed security guards with dogs, and various other measures to make trespassing very difficult if not impossible. Over the years, we have been lucky in that the security has not been tested. No one on the island knows that we own this property. It's registered in the name of a doctor from

Dallas, who died forty years ago. Now I'll show you the basement."

The basement was a two level mix of business and pleasure accessed by an elevator. On the first level, the pleasure aspect included a full bar, in a library setting. It featured a billiards table that looked like it was rescued from an ancient, very exclusive, London men's club. The room, furnished in tropical rattan, reminded Doc of Raffles in Singapore, his favorite hotel. A twenty seat media room with a TV screen the size of some small countries and a well-equipped gym rounded off the fun level.

The second level basement floor contained the business end of he structure. These included a well-equipped business center, a state of the art communications center providing dedicated lines to Washington and Ottawa and secure encrypted capability around the world.

There was a detention room, more like a three-star hotel than a prison cell and a confer-ence room with seating for twelve.

Completing the tour, Sam led Doc back to the elevator and suggested a cool local favorite drink, crafted by big Tony be delivered to poolside.

"The cook, Sarah, is excellent; we lured her away from one of the finest restaurants in the islands. She worked in the US for several years as well as studied at fine gastronomic schools in France and Italy. Since you are the only guest at present, she will plan her menus to include your favorite foods. There is a wealth of fresh fish

in the lagoon so feel free to tell her about your favorite foods. A cautionary note, you should regularly exercise to offset the calories you will take in. I am afraid you will find the food exceptional and put on a few pounds if you are not careful."

As Tony appeared with the beverages, he explained, "These are my concoctions and are of course rum based. I hope you enjoy them. As you walk around in the house, you will see discreetly placed buzzers such as the one at this table. Whenever you want anything simply push the button and I will get it for you. I have put away your clothing and toiletries in your suite.

I was out in the lagoon this morning and caught some very nice looking lobsters. If you wish, I can have Sarah prepare some for your dinner when you are ready."

"Thanks, Tony, for everything and the lobsters for dinner sound fantastic," Doc said. As Tony left the deck, Doc turned to Sam and asked, "Have you heard anything from Jim or Bill as to the plans for these two weeks?"

" Bill and Jim have spoken to your Doctor in Seattle although I haven't been told more than that. I do know the emphasis is on assisting your recovery through a lot of relaxation. They'll probably be in touch tomorrow so for tonight relax and enjoy. Just let the staff know if you want anything. Tony will drive you anywhere you want to go however I'd suggest that you stay close to home at least for a few days.

Sam headed for home after they had finished their drinks. Doc opted for a pre-dinner swim and decided on the pool over the ocean.

He put on the swimsuit Jim's secretary had included in the duffel bag. He made a mental note to tell her that he was more of a boxer guy than a speedo guy.

Refreshed from his swim, Doc thought he would try out the discreet buzzer and ordered a fruit punch on the rocks to sip on in his suite while he changed for dinner. Tony delivered the drink promptly and asked if seven o'clock would be appropriate for dinner. "Thanks for the drink and seven would be fine for dinner." Doc replied. The two hours until dinner would allow time to catch up on emails in the business center as well as the latest world news on CNN.

The next day Doc slept in until eight o'clock, which was late for him. He had found a breakfast order card left on his room door the night before and had ordered a full breakfast including tropical fruit and corned beef hash for delivery to poolside at nine. Prior to breakfast, he decided to take a quick swim in the lagoon and headed down to the beach. Tony followed him to the beach and sat on an overturned rowboat while Doc swam.

Doc came out of the water and, as he dried off asked Tony, "Are you a lifeguard as well?"

Tony replied, "Sometimes we get a shark or two in the lagoon despite the shark net we installed so I try to keep a watch when we have guests in the water."

"Have you ever had to save a guest from a shark?" Doc asked.

"Only once so far, two years ago," Tony answered.

"What did you do?" Doc asked.

" Under this boat I keep a loaded device I invented which is a combination spear gun and bang stick. When I saw the shark nearing the guest, I swam out and first tried the bang stick hoping to scare it away. However, despite the bang, it persisted in approaching, and I was forced to use the spear to kill it. I hate killing things for no good reason but in this case it was a matter of self-defense and protecting the guest."

"Well I appreciate you sitting here," Doc said but you know that old joke about why sharks don't attack lawyers….. due to professional courtesy."

While Doc enjoyed breakfast poolside, he received several calls including one from Dr. Tom Fulton asking how he felt.

Tom was monitoring Doc's vital signs via a new app, which fed a constant stream of data from Doc's cell phone to the computers on Tom's desk in Seattle.

Jim called next, and Doc said, "I had a nice chat with Dr. Fulton this morning, and he seems satisfied with how things are going with my recovery so far. He has authorized me to have the odd drink so I'm drinking every second one."

"Yes and this is good but we have to keep an eye on things," Jim replied. "If all is well I'd like you to plan a week in Ottawa before you go back to Asia."

"Alright Jim, there are some consular officials that I want to get together with as well."

"Ok, get lots of rest and we'll talk later in the week."

"Bye Jim, I'd like to say 'wish you were here' but I'm kind of glad that you're not."

"The phone for you sir, it's Mr. Bill Wong on line two."

"Thanks, Tony, the sun is over the yardarm so how about one of those special drinks of yours. By the way what do you call the drink?"

"I call it a Nassau Nightie Remover."

"Perfect Tony, well named."

"Jungle Bill, how is it going?"

Bill said, "I'm well, more importantly how are you? Your friends in Asia have been asking about you, and I told them you were on a combination business trip and vacation in the states."

"Where are you calling from Bill, the connection isn't that good."

"I'm in Jakarta and you know what communications are like from here. I was thinking of joining you for the weekend to fill you in on what's happening here."

"That's a good idea. Why don't you come on Friday and we can have a nice long weekend in the sun?"

Bill said, "Sounds like a plan, pick up any nurses yet?"

"No, not yet but I'll see what I can do for the weekend. I have a female classmate, Bev, from business and law school working at the Canadian High Commission in Jamaica, which serves the Bahamas. I'll give her a call and see if she has any suggestions for places to meet some ladies in Nassau."

"Ok see you Friday and tell Tony to have a good stock of ingredients for his Nassau Nighty Removers."

As Doc hung up with Bill, he called Bev in Jamaica.

"Hi, Donovan, its good to hear from you again, where are you?" Bev was an upbeat, terminally happy individual and her voice reflected this. She was the head of the class at law school but after a few years with a Bay Street, white shoe law firm, she decided to sit the civil service exams. She aced the exams and ended up in the consular service, presently working in the Jamaica office.

"Hello, Bev its good to talk to you as well. I'm having a bit of a holiday staying at a friend's place in Nassau for a couple of weeks. I figured you wouldn't last too long in the big firm; you're too cheerful for a place like that where somber attitudes are a condition of partnership. I'm expecting a good friend for the weekend and wondered if you could direct us to the hot spots for singles in Nassau?"

Bev said, "I get a lot of requests for assistance from Canadians visiting the Caribbean, but this is the first time someone has asked me to help them meet women. It's good to see you haven't changed much. I'll tell you what; I'll come over there on Saturday with my roommate Linda. She has been trying to convince me to get away for some time, and we'll show you the best night spots."

"That's terrific, I'll book you rooms at the Atlantis, and it'll be great to get caught up."

CHAPTER THREE

Jungle Bill arrived late Friday afternoon and he, and Doc we're sitting at the in-pool bar under a waterfall and enjoying a couple of Tony's Nassau Nightie Removers.

"I've booked rooms at the Atlantis for our visitors from Jamaica," Doc said. "The cover story is that I'm here on a two-week holiday staying with a friend in a small condo, and you've come for the weekend. Thus the lack of space at the friend's place."

"It'll be interesting to meet her roommate," Bill said. "It kind of feels like a blind date situation and I haven't had much luck the few times I've tried that."

"Knowing Bev, I don't think her roommate will be an old ogre. As I said, she's a very upbeat person with a great sense of humor. She would probably choose to room with someone similar in outlook."

Tony approached and said,"Mr. O'Connell, phone for you, a Mr. Jim Elliott."

"Hi, Jim, what's up?"

"I've been talking to Dr. Fulton and he seems pleased with your progress. I just thought I'd say hello and see for myself."

"I'm feeling much better already; Bill is joining me for the weekend. I have a friend with the Canadian Consul office in Jamaica, arriving tomorrow to introduce us to the delights of Nassau."

"I've been thinking about your Ottawa visit. If you're up to it, let's plan on two weeks starting a week Monday. It'll give us a chance to get caught up and review plans for the next quarter. You should then spend a few days in Washington with Bill and the DEA people. Have Bill organize it.

Let me know if all this works and I'll make arrangements for you to meet some people in Ottawa. For one, the Minister wants to have a "coffee" as he puts it. Enjoy your weekend and don't engage in any exercise that might strain your surgery."

Friday evening was spent enjoying a poolside bar-b-q. Saturday morning, they arrived a little early to pick up a car for the weekend. Doc had Tony drop them at the Lynden Pindling International Airport for the ladies arrival from Jamaica. Tony had, as requested, reserved a Jeep convertible, which Doc felt would help set the informal mood that he envisioned for the weekend.

Bev hugged Doc with the intensity of old friends who've shared a common, life changing experience together, in this case, business and law school and lived to tell about it. Bev greeted Bill with the cheerful demeanor Doc had warned of and introduced her friend, Linda. The four of them proceeded to the car rental area and loaded the carry on luggage into the Jeep. Since Doc had suggested informality for the weekend, everyone was dressed in Caribbean casual outfits and ready to do nothing but relax.

The weather cooperated and except for the daily four o'clock shower, all signs of which were gone by four fifteen; sunshine was the order of the day.

"How about we get you both checked in and then we can have lunch at poolside and decide what we would like to do?" Doc said.

"Sounds good," Bev said, "the poolside Fish Hut restaurant has the greatest jumbo prawn bar-b-q in the world."

Over lunch, the group got to know each other although Doc felt sorry about having to lie to Bev about his real occupation. Bill was a little more used to living a double life, having been undercover for two years longer than Doc. Also, Bill had spent more time with family and friends where he had to stay alert regarding his career.

Bev said, "Where did the handle 'Doc' originate? Did you take one of those matchbook doctorate degrees since we last talked?"

"No" Bill interrupted, "Let me explain. A few of us, good friends of Donovan's, were on a fishing trip and decided that Donovan O'Connell was too long a name. So we used his initials D, O, and C to come up with the nickname Doc and it took. "

"Yeah it's a good thing my first name is Donovan instead of Charles, Doc said, "Or I'd be in big trouble trying to explain my nickname to people."

The laughter was interrupted by the arrival of their waiter with the bill.

"Let's go someplace where there's dancing tonight," Linda said, "I love to dance." The group agreed, so dancing was put on the agenda. Bill said he would like to spend some time and money at the casino, and this idea met with approval from Linda.

Doc said, "What about you Bev, are you still a tennis player?"

"I think I can still give you a run for your money Doc."

Bill and Linda weren't tennis players, so they decided to hit the casino for a few hours after lunch while Bev and Doc played tennis. They agreed to meet back here at poolside at five o'clock. After two sets, Bev and Doc went to the tennis bar. They ordered an unusual tropical fruit drink that took the bartender five minutes to make and had a slight hint of cinnamon and some other exotic spices from the islands.

"Doc it's coincidental that you called me when you did. I have a situation that I've wanted to discuss with you and was thinking about trying to track you down."

" Go ahead Bev, what's on your mind?"

"First, here's a dollar. If you accept it, as you know, you have taken a retainer, and I am now your client, so anything said between us is protected by client-attorney privilege." With some surprise, Doc took the dollar and placed it in his pocket.

"Go ahead Bev, your secret is safe with me."

"Let's move to that table at the end of the terrace so we can have more privacy. I'm sorry to be so melodramatic however I think you'll understand once I tell you what's on my mind." They moved to the private table and Bev was about to start her story when along came a very animated Bill and Linda.

Obviously excited, Linda said, "We won the Super jackpot on the slots almost $10,000 USD."

"No, we didn't win, Bill said, you won!"

"But it was with your encouragement," Linda replied, "so we should share it."

"No way, it's yours."

"Well, all right. However, all expenses for the weekend are on me."

Bev gave Doc an expression that said they would continue their attorney-client talk afterward while Linda summoned the waiter to order a bottle of her favorite champagne, Cristal 2002. "You should also bring another bottle on ice as this seems to evaporate quickly in this heat, it must be the vintage."

All agreed that a swim before dinner was in order particularly following the Cristal. It was nice to see that Bill and Linda were getting along so well. Doc had felt that they would, but you never can tell if the chemistry will be right or not.

Bev made dinner reservations at her favorite Nassau restaurant, Tuscany Rose. They decided to leave the Jeep in the parking lot in favor of a cab, given the likelihood that the evening may involve more celebrations over the casino win.

During the evening, Bev continued to look for an opportunity to talk privately to Doc. However Jim, and Linda stayed close. As the night wore on, and the dancing started, the combination of noise and drink caused Bev to give up on her plan to talk privately to Doc until tomorrow.

The casino managed to get back about a thousand dollars between the four of them. Linda insisted that she was supplying the capital and subsidized their losses out of her earlier windfall.

Around two a.m. Doc and Bill left the ladies and got a cab back to the house with the promise of a late brunch at the hotel poolside restaurant tomorrow.

"So what did you think of Linda?" Doc asked as they headed home.

"She's a great person," Bill replied. "We got along well and had quite a bit in common. I'm going to try to get to Jamaica in the next few months to see her again. What about you and Bev?"

"It was great to renew acquaintance with her, she is a lot of fun and just as terrific as I remembered her. I think we'll always be good friends, but that's likely all we'll be."

Doc couldn't tell Bill about Bev's thwarted attempt to confide in him, taking Bev's request for confidentiality seriously. Tomorrow he would try to find a place where he and Bev could talk in private.

The cab driver said, "I think we're being followed by an SUV that has been trailing along about four cars behind."

"Go around a few blocks heading away from the address we gave you and see if we lose it," Bill said.

Taking the next right-hand turn, the driver sped up for two blocks and turned left without signaling. He then turned right into a laneway and raced to the next street, turning right once again and heading back to the street they were originally on. After a few blocks the driver said, " It's still there, it's a tail."

"Driver, we've changed our minds, take us to the Hyatt, and we'll try our luck at their casino," Bill said.

Whispering to Doc, Bill said, "As soon as we get out at the Hyatt, stay close and follow me."

The Hyatt was still jumping at this hour with lots of traffic leaving and arriving. So it was easy for Doc and Bill to get lost in the crowd as they made their way through the main entrance to the hotel and rapidly through the casino to a rear stairwell.

"In here," Bill said and led Doc into a janitor's room he unlocked with a code on a keypad. Once in the closet, Bill tapped into another code on what looked like a large bank vault and opened it to reveal an assortment of tools of the undercover trade, indeed not tools for maintenance men. Bill told Doc to put on the electrician's coveralls and grab a toolbox.

Bill used his cell phone to call Tony, "Sorry to

get you up at this hour but we have a tail and need a pick up at the Hyatt."

"I am on my way, be there in ten minutes," Tony replied. Bill also put on the electrician's coveralls and a cap. He offered a cap to Doc. Bill opened the "toolbox" and produced a jar of brown stage makeup which when applied to their hand and faces made them look a little like local black workers if you didn't look too closely.

Bill said," Just in case, take this Sig Sauer and three spare clips, I have an Uzi in the tool box."

"Who is after us?"

"Probably not pros, just local hired hands. I'll have Tony's guys check it out tomorrow, Bill said. Tony will arrive in a white panel truck with "Island Electric" signs on it. If we head down now we should meet him just as he arrives, we don't want to be standing around looking like a vaudeville act."

Tony was right on time and after a quick walk across the loading ramp, the two "electricians" were in the van and Tony was on the way back to the house. As they drove, Doc couldn't help looking for a tail, which, fortunately, didn't materialize.

"We're going to have to tell the ladies about our adventure, at least the part about being followed," Doc said. "If it is one or both of them that are being watched, they should know about it."

Bill said, "Let's call them in the morning and suggest a change of brunch plans but hold off on mentioning the tail incident until Tony looks into it. Tell them to bring along their carry-on bags and after lunch we'll deliver them to the airport for their flight. Tony, do you know a good restaurant on the beach?"

"Yes, I have just the place. I suggest that I accompany you as the driver, and I'll have a few of my guys in a car following us in case we pick up any unwanted company."

Brunch went off without a hitch. No sign of being followed, but it was comforting to know that Tony and his men were on the job, watching for any potential trouble as we enjoyed lunch. Linda suggested that we order a round of the great Canadian hangover cure; Bloody Caesars and all Canadians agreed that this might be in order.

Jungle Bill had to confess that he had never heard of this concoction. Bev explained that the drink was similar to a Bloody Mary but made with clam juice, which gave it a unique spicy taste.

Doc said, "I don't think I can handle any more seafood, so I'm going for the Black Angus burger." Bill decided on fried clams and the ladies chose the house salad.

"This has been a great weekend, thanks for inviting us," Bev said. "Yes, thank you," said Linda. "Bev and I needed to get away from the office for a bit and this turned out perfect. Plus meeting the two of you and hitting the casino jackpot made this a weekend to remember."

Bev suggested a walk on the beach after lunch, and she and Doc walked slowly allowing Bill and Linda to get out of hearing range. "Doc I want to talk to you about the situation I'm involved in where I can use your help. I'll give you the basics today, you can think about it and we can discuss it again later. Are you planning to be anywhere in the eastern US in the next couple of weeks?"

"Yes, I expect to be in the Washington DC area in about three weeks time."

"Ok, once I tell you about this, all I ask is complete confidentiality on your part as well as your famous ability for developing creative solutions to complex problems.

If you decide that you want to get involved, call me and we'll arrange to meet on your Washington trip."

Doc said," There is a quiet little resort not far from Washington in Virginia, where we can meet and discuss this in total privacy. I can book a small cottage with a sitting room fireplace and a dining area, so even meals can be eaten in privacy. Everyone will think we're honeymooners and leave us alone. Do you still like horses?"

"I love horses, I used to have one as a girl, she was dark brown and I called her Cocoa. Do I see things, or are Bill and Linda holding hands up there?"

"It looks as though they're getting along well. Bill told me that he thought Linda was great and that he would try to see her again."

"Well, well maybe we've started something between them. Linda also told me that she thought Bill was a very nice guy, and she hoped to see him again. She describes him as a gentleman, easy to look at, easy to talk to with a good sense of humor. However, let's not invite them to Virginia. In fact let's not even tell them we're meeting there. That's assuming that we are meeting there,"

Doc said, "Tell me about this mysterious situation that you're involved in before the lovebirds decide to join us."

"Ok, it's somewhat complicated but I'll try to explain as best as I can. As you'll see, for obvious reasons, I didn't want to commit any of this to paper or to talk about it on the phone.

As you know, I was born in Zimbabwe. I left there at two years of age as my family moved to Canada initially settling in northern Alberta for reasons that will become apparent as I explain. My father's relatives had been in the diamond mining business for generations and were quite well off. We've had a family history of enormous wealth, mansions, expensive cars, polo ponies, and servants. My father decided to leave home and moved us to Canada as he searched for opportunities in diamond mining in the north. He was unable to take much money with him when we moved, so our lifestyle in Canada while comfortable, was substantially more middle class than we had known in Zimbabwe. My dad and his brother inherited the family business in Zimbabwe when my grandfather passed away. It was in a mature stage and managed by my uncle, Dad's older brother. Dad studied geology in the UK completing a bachelor's degree at Oxford and masters at Cambridge. He then did his doctorate at MIT and some postdoctoral work at UCLA, Berkley. I think in part due to his international education, and partly because he was bored with the high life in Zimbabwe, he made an agreement with his brother, and we left for Canada.

Under the terms of the agreement, dad and his brother were to be equal partners in the family business and his brother would be paid a significant annual salary for running the company. My father's share of profits was to be banked in Zimbabwe awaiting his return.

Here lies the crux of the matter. One may only take out of the country tiny amounts of money under Zimbabwean law. The rest of the profits, by far the lion's share, had to remain in the country.

My father and mother died a few years ago. Dad never did have much success in the northern Canadian mining business beyond a series of well-paying jobs. These kept us going along with the small amount that my uncle was able to send us annually. My uncle is now terminally ill himself and not expected to last very long.

He sold the business to a South African mining conglomerate and now sits on an enormous amount of cash that he can't get out of the country. As my uncle never married, I'm the sole heir to this fortune, however, to enjoy it, I would have to move to Zimbabwe, which I would not want to do.

So here is my problem. You're talking to a very wealthy woman with no cash or access to it. The task for you is to figure a legal way for us to get this cash out of the country."

"How much cash are we talking about?" Doc asked.

"In the neighborhood of $350 million US," Bev replied.

"Wow, that is quite a neighborhood," Doc said. "You said that you wanted a legal solution as opposed to an illegal one. There must be mercenaries out there that could figure out ways to smuggle the money out."

Bev said, "There are smugglers who have approached me, but I have no interest in breaking the law and then constantly having to look over my shoulder. You were always the most creative guy in business and law school. I think you might be able to come up with a solution that will get the money out."

"I'll think about it and get back to you next week."

CHAPTER FOUR

By the time we crested a dune and caught up with Linda and Bill, they were kissing. They were so wrapped up in each other's arms that it was hard to see where one ended, and the other began.

Doc said, "Whoa are you two going to announce your engagement or what?" They laughed and looked a bit sheepish as we headed back to the car, but Doc noticed that they continued to hold hands all the way. It seemed to him that a Jamaican holiday was in Bill's future and the not too distant future at that.

Doc thought, I'll have to get him to pick me up some Blue Mountain coffee. He had heard that Jamaican Blue Mountain was considered to be one of the finest coffees available, and it was the coffee served at the White House.

As they approached the car, Tony took Doc aside and told him that the previous evening's tail was courtesy of the Canadian High Commission in Jamaica and had been dispatched to keep an eye on the ladies. The men were agents of a local Nassau security firm under contract to the Canadian High Commission. They're retained to look out for individuals visiting Nassau in whom the Commission has an interest.

Doc quickly filled Bill in to make sure that he didn't say anything about the tail incident that might worry the ladies as they returned to Jamaica.

—

They said their goodbyes at the airport and Bill and Linda kissed good-bye rather more passionately than Bev and Doc's brief kiss on the cheek.

As they drove back to the safe house, Tony said he had his people return the rental Jeep and tried to pay for the ladies' rooms only to find that Linda had taken care of it. Back at the house, Bill and Doc sat at poolside and talked about the meetings that were coming up in Ottawa and Washington.

"You know what I am going to miss most about Nassau? Doc asked.

"I can't imagine," Bill said.

"Tony and his Nassau Nighty Removers, Sarah, this great beach house and the pool."

"I'll miss the proximity to Jamaica and Linda," Bill said.

"Yeah, you kind of fell for her rather quickly this weekend, it caught me by surprise."

" I fell for her when we were alone in the casino yesterday. If it wasn't for Bev, I'm not sure that I would have come home last night."

"So when are you going to Jamaica? I have a small shopping list for you."

"Linda and I talked about it; we're going to try to meet at a resort near Montego Bay next month. She has a week off then, and I'm due for a week's leave before returning to Asia. We'll swim in the ocean and enjoy fabulous seafood."

The next day Bill headed for the airport and

home. Doc decided to stay on for a few days, sit by the pool and let the staff spoil him while he thought about Bev's situation. He went for long walks on the beach and rented a sailboat for a day to cruise around by himself. At least he thought he was by himself. He didn't see Tony in the cabin cruiser that just stayed far enough away to be out of sight but close enough to be there quickly if needed.

On Thursday, he thanked the staff profusely and Tony drove him to the airport for a late morning flight to Ottawa.

"Have you ever been to Canada Tony?" Doc asked.

"No sir, Mr. O'Connell, but I would sure like to see it sometime. I have a cousin in Toronto who keeps inviting me up."

"I tell you what Tony, I have so many air miles that I'll never get rid of them. When you're ready to come up, call me at the number on this card, and I'll send you a ticket. I have a cottage on the St. Lawrence River just south of Ottawa. You're welcome to invite your relatives there and enjoy some great boating and fishing."

"Why that is very generous of you sir."

"Oh and Tony, forget about the Mr. O' Connell and Sir bit when we're not in front of uptight bosses. You call me Doc, ok?"

"Yes Doc, I will."

On the flight from Nassau, Doc sat next to an interesting guy in first class. When flying commercial, the rules call for him to fly first class or the highest class available. The theory and this had proven to work on many occasions, was that he stood a much better chance of meeting senior executives and high-ranking civil servants than if he flew economy.

The interesting guy waited until the meal cart was coming their way, and when Doc closed up his laptop he introduced himself as Crawford Ward. He said, "I notice that you work a lot while flying."

Doc replied, "Hi Crawford, pleased to meet you. Yes, I guess I've been buried in my laptop since we left Nassau. It seems that I get my best ideas when I fly, drive or take a shower."

"That could mean that you're particularly sensitive to the ions changing in your environment. I'm an industrial psychologist and have done some research into this phenomenon. In each case where you notice an increase in creative thought, the positive ions in your immediate environment are being bombarded with negative ions.

The net result for ion-sensitive individuals is an increase in brain activity, generation of more creative thought and enhanced problem-solving capability. The impact of ion change is of interest to me because I'm doing some post-doctoral work on methods of improving workplace output, and this ion issue forms part of my study. You might benefit from investing in an air purifier for your office that features an ionization option. Be careful, however, because some people who are highly sensitive to ion changes report difficulty if they put the appliance in their bedroom. The increased brain activity caused by the ionizer can result in vivid nightmares or dreams that encumber sleep."

Doc took a taxi to his studio apartment, cleared out his mailbox and grabbed the keys to his Mustang. It had been so long since the car had run that Doc wasn't sure it would even start. However, it did start, and Doc was headed south out of Ottawa to his private hideaway on the Saint Lawrence River outside Brockville. The riverfront cottage had been in his family for generations, and Doc loved the place. When his parents died, he didn't inherit much except for this cabin. It was the one place he truly relaxed. Putting his fishing gear in the boat, Doc spent ten minutes trying to get the old engine to start before abandoning the motor idea in favor of the aging wooden oars.

He wasn't going far. About a quarter mile off shore, there was a small island, more like a large rock, with a weed bed that was usually good for a few perch and maybe the odd bass. He got comfortable in the boat and waited for his first fish. Forty-five minutes later, Doc had four fish. Three perch and a good-sized smallmouth bass, which, along with the salad fixings he bought from a roadside stand outside Ottawa, will make for an excellent supper.

He returned to the dock, tied up the boat cleaned the fish and put them in the cabin refrigerator. Taking a cold beer out of the fridge he went to the screened porch to do his next favorite cottage thing after fishing....nothing. That's not quite right, he thought. He couldn't help but revisit Bev's situation.

He decided tomorrow he would go to the marine supply store at Mallorytown Landing and buy a new outboard, maybe one of those sleek, four stroke Honda jobs if they have them.

The following morning, he rose early, dove off the dock and swam for twenty minutes. He decided to drive into Brockville and buy an air purifier with the ionizer to test Crawford's theory. He plugged it in at the cottage and forgot about it. Next he drove up to the marine store and picked up the Honda outboard. He put it on the boat and took it out for a test run. It started first try and was so quiet compared to his ancient Johnson that he wasn't sure it was running half the time.

The new motor is one purchase that was long overdue he thought.

He spent the day fishing, sitting on the porch and reading. He noticed that while reading his thoughts kept going back to his talk with Bev and wondered if the ionizer had anything to do with it. His meal of freshly caught fish and the salad was terrific. As is his custom, after dinner, he stretched out on the porch hammock and fell asleep until the morning sun reflecting off the river woke him up.

Doc decided that he would tidy up the cottage and head back to Ottawa later in the afternoon. He wanted to get to bed early and be fresh for tomorrow's meetings, which would include one with the Minister of Justice himself. Not that Doc was necessarily in awe of Ministers in general, but this one, Robert Plante was a very hard working leader. He was well respected by virtually all of the people connected with justice in Canada and worldwide. His staff was intensely loyal and would follow him anywhere. There were some rumors about a possible run for the Prime Minister's office at some point. Doc felt he had the charisma and experience to pull it off.

Doc didn't get to spend enough time at his condo to feel at home here, it seemed more like a large hotel suite. When he wasn't in Asia, he spent a lot of time at the cottage and only came to Ottawa when government business called for it.

As he showered in the morning, Doc reflected on Crawford Ward's ion theory. He thought; I bought the machine, showered at the cottage, drove to Ottawa and am showering now, so I've certainly changed the ions around me frequently. I've come up with one promising idea, but it needs a lot of flushing out. I can't be sure if Crawford is right just yet. Well, I'll keep the appliance plugged in here at the apartment and see what if anything develops.

One of the things that Doc loved about his job is that because of the constant international travel required of him, there were hardly ever any messages for him when he arrived in the office. No one ever expected him to be there. As a consequence, he could usually get a lot accomplished in his little room. In this case, there were a few messages involving invitations to events in Asia, which his secretary had answered and entered into his calendar. She always assumed he would attend the events, so it was up to him to let her know otherwise.

One message was from Bev, which he decided to get to later since the other message was from his boss, Jim Elliott, who asked that he call him as soon as he got in.

Doc called Jim and said, "Good morning boss, what's up?" Jim told him to come right to his office, so Doc decided to call Bev later.

Doc was never much on offices, but he thought that if he were in a job that required his presence in one on a regular basis, he would like to have one like Jim's. It was a good sized space with lots of leather furniture and floor to ceiling mahogany bookshelves populated with enough books to keep a small Oregon paper mill town in full employment for years.

Jim stood and shook hands with Doc saying, "Welcome home Donovan, it looks like the R &R did the trick. Want coffee?"

"Yes please, I'm afraid all this lazing around by the pool has got me so relaxed that it was tough to get up this morning, so I had to forgo coffee."

"Help yourself, I've sent out for some muffins."

"Were you able to get a meeting time with the Minister?"

"That's the rush for us to chat now. He can see us, but only briefly, at ten fifteen this morning and I wanted to go over a few things with you before we see him."

As Doc took his first sip of coffee, he said, "Ok, its good to get a heads up before I take off again for Asia next week."

A light tap on the door and a pleasant aroma announced the arrival of the fresh muffins.

As they started into their muffins, Jim said, "There are a few things the Minister has indicated he wants to discuss. Our progress in reducing drug imports is tops on his agenda. We will cover the effectiveness of our new program for getting you invited to all Canadian sponsored events throughout Asia. One other thing that you and I so far haven't touched on involves relocating you to Asia."

The shocked look on Doc's face gave away his surprise at receiving this news.

"Where did this come from?" Doc asked, "It's the first I've heard of it."

"I know," Jim replied. "I'm sorry to have to drop this on you so abruptly." The Minister is going away today for a three-week European tour, and he wants this dealt with before he gets back. He has come up with this idea for several reasons. First, he feels that you would be more effective if you lived in Asia and felt part of the environment instead of a frequent visitor. Second, he thinks, and I have to say I agree, that relocating there would considerably reduce your time spent flying back and forth to Ottawa, freeing up more time for you to spend intelligence gathering. It would also be better for your health. You are spending so much time flying which takes away from the time that could be profitably spent in healthier pursuits."

"I appreciate your concern for my health and agree with the benefits of living in Asia and thus feeling more like a resident than a visitor. I guess I just need some time to process the idea. Is this negotiable or a done deal?"

"I think you'll find that the Minister has strong feelings about it. As you know, reduction in drug traffic into Canada is a high priority of his having lost his oldest son to a drug overdose. That being said, I know he holds you in high regard so I think you might be able to persuade him if you work at it. What's your first reaction to the idea?"

"I'm spending most of my time there as is and I can't see that changing anytime soon. Our efforts to gather intelligence and work with the DEA are going to take years to be effective despite the progress we've made already. As a bachelor with no family left, I'm free of those concerns. If the Minister is that set on the idea, let's give it a try. If it doesn't work out, we can always go back to where we are now."

The meeting was more relaxed than usual, and the Minister offered coffee, which both Jim and Doc accepted. The Minister was pleased with the results of the Asian operation. He was happy that Doc agreed to try the relocation idea and wished him well. Within fifteen minutes decisions had been taken that would significantly impact Doc's life forever.

After the meeting, he returned to his office and called Bev. "Hi kid how is it going?"

"I'm glad you called Doc; there've been some developments in my situation. My uncle is not expected to live out the next few months, so I'm going to take a leave to visit with him. Any news on your front?"

"Yes, a few things we can discuss when we get together. I have a preliminary idea for you. So if we meet next week at that Virginia resort I told you about, we can catch up and do some planning. In the meantime, I'll do some research on my idea. I have meetings in Washington on Wednesday and Thursday. Why don't you fly in on Friday and I'll pick you up at the airport?"

"Alright," Bev said, "I'll get a flight reservation and text you the details."

Doc spent the next few days dividing his time between meetings with his colleagues and visits with the Ottawa-based Asian diplomatic community. He decided to keep his apartment in Ottawa as an investment and a pied-a-terre for when he returned for head office visits.

His next-door neighbor had a key and kept an eye on the place whenever Doc was away. In return, Doc would bring her gifts such as silk from Thailand, beautifully carved Indonesian art and Selangor pewter from Kuala Lumpur. He spoke to her about his transfer, and she agreed to continue to condo sit for him. Eventually, she would have one of the largest collections of Asian artifacts in the nations' capital.

Having taken care of business in Ottawa, Doc decided to spend the weekend back at his cottage on the St. Lawrence River and then drive to Washington on Monday and Tuesday spending the night about half way. He loved this trip and would be able to give the car a good work out, enjoy the scenery and do some serious thinking.

Jim was overjoyed that Doc agreed to the move to Asia. He decided to let Doc choose where he wanted to live in Asia and had been more than generous in negotiating the terms of his living allowance. His expat package would allow for very comfortable accommodation anywhere in the region and included a cook/housekeeper; several club memberships as well as a car and driver. So as he pointed the Mustang south and crossed into the US, Doc had a lot on his plate to consider. He had to decide where to make his base in Asia, and how to best handle Bev's situation. Also, his schedule was filling up between the Canadian sponsored functions and those that Jungle Bill had lined up through the US diplomatic channels.

CHAPTER FIVE

As Doc cruised down Highway 81 south to-wards DC, he decided to stay in Scranton. It was early enough in the day that he could do the 500 miles all the way to Washington, but he didn't have to be there until Wednesday morning. So he decided to stay over at a boutique hotel in Scranton PA, about half way. The hotel was not large, 50 rooms. It had a great steakhouse and an Irish pub that usually provided some friendly conversation, a game or two of darts and fre-quently some good Irish music. Across from the hotel was a great park with paths along the river that were terrific for deep thinking. Over the years, Doc had become friends with Sean O'Leary, the hotel owner. He was also a Mus-tang aficionado, with a 1965 convertible, a 1967 fastback and a year old Shelby Cobra that passed everything except gas stations.

Doc gave his cell phone the command to call Sean. He answered on the third ring, "Good morning, O'Leary Arms, may I help you?"

In his best Irish brogue, Doc said, "Top of the morning to you to Sean, have you got a room, a steak and perhaps a jar of Laphroaig available for a road-weary wanderer?"

"Donovan me boy" Sean came back with his Irish accent, "Even if I had to evict me Ma to free up a room, you always have one here. If you're free, let's have dinner and get caught up. How about darts at six, we can start cocktail four hours then?" "Perfect," Doc replied. As he ended the call, he remembered that Sean had always felt the term "cocktail hour" was a time reference to start drinking, not the length of the event.

While he was in a communications mode, he called Jungle Bill to confirm the Wednesday and Thursday meetings and to set up dinner with him Tuesday evening. He then called Bev. However she wasn't available, so he left her a message that he was on his way to DC and still thinking about her situation. Doc wasn't sure that it was a result of the exposure to the ion machines in his condo and office, or maybe the ion changing influence of the motion of the car. Perhaps none of the above but he was getting an embryo of an idea for Bev's situation and wanted to think about it some more. He found the perfect place to think. A tourist attraction comprised of a forest of old growth trees.

He parked the car and stretched to loosen up then started to walk through the woods. After about an hour's walk, he found himself back at the car. He bought a coffee and sat on a park bench to decide what to do. Finally, he called an old friend, Brian White in Silicon Valley hoping to bounce some ideas off him.

They had roomed together for two years at Western and enjoyed each other's company.

Brian ended up marrying Kristen, a breathtaking beauty with haunting eyes and a quick wit. Doc had dated her in his second year of

MBA and had introduced her to Brian. Kristen was in pre-med and planning to be a veterinarian. Brian had started his software development company about five years ago. It wasn't any dot com money generator; however Brian managed to live quite well and enjoyed a very upscale lifestyle.

When the call went through Brian came on the line and said, "Donovan, it's great to hear from you. Are you in the area?"

"No, I'm clear across the country," Doc replied, "but I was wondering if I could pick your brains for a few minutes?"

"Of course, shoot," Brian said. They talked long enough for Doc to get some helpful input on his embryo of an idea, and Doc said, "Thanks, Brian I know you're busy so I won't keep you. If this project I'm researching moves forward, I'll come out there and take you and Kristen for dinner. Do you two still have that beautiful Black Lab, Tao?"

"Oh yes, we still have Tao, Kristen would sooner part with me than Tao."

"Please give them both a hug for me."

Doc decided that he would go ahead to O'Leary Arms and make some more calls from his room.

Brian had given him quite a few good leads. Doc felt that if he could reach some of the people Brian suggested he contact, he'd be able to fill in most of the blanks for his idea before meeting Bev on Friday. The embryo was growing.

He arrived at the hotel by mid afternoon and was greeted warmly by Shannon, the lovely front desk agent from Killarney. As usual, Shannon upgraded Doc to the hotel's Emerald Isle suite. Shannon asked for his car keys as Sean always had Doc's Mustang lovingly detailed by the hotel's maintenance lady Jo, who also babied Sean's pony cars. The suite was large with an oversized bedroom with en suite, a bar area, and private dining room. An important feature for Doc was the workstation with telephone, computer, printer and good-sized desk in a quiet little den area off the living room. The den had a door with a programmable lock. So the guest could make up an entry code and close and lock the room. Guests could leave their work at the desk should they wish to keep it confidential from room guests and service staff. Doc plugged in his ionizer and closed the den door to allow the machine to do its thing.

While looking forward to seeing Sean and enjoying his Irish wit, Doc was glad that Sean was out of the hotel so he could get to work on his phone calls and do a little online research.

He was pleasantly surprised by both the number of people who were available to talk to him and by how forthcoming they were with helpful information. Apparently Brian White had called ahead opening a few doors and was held in high regard by these contacts.

He managed to speak to five people today and left messages for three more. He changed into his walking gear and headed across the street to the path along the river. He had acquired a great deal of information in a very short time frame and needed the solitude of the river walk and the fresh air to help him process it. Years ago in business school, he had developed the habit of taking long walks in serene locations as an aid to analyzing the overwhelming volume of case material that was the trademark of Western's business school.

To keep track of his ideas and analysis generated by these lone excursions, Doc bought a small handheld voice recorder. He'd made a point of carrying one with him ever since. Over the years, the technology had improved but the device was still priceless.

Case analysis, business problems, personal issues or anything else that called for recall, could benefit from this device.

As he walked the path, Doc took in the fresh air smell of the clean, swift-moving river, the sound of the birds in the forest and the beauty of the flowers and trees around him.

Doc could understand why Sean had decided on this location for his hotel. The natural beauty of the immediate surroundings was almost too much. The visitors to this area, particularly the guests in Sean's hotel, would get a sense of peace and well-being here that would encourage extended stays and frequent returns.

The incredible natural setting and the excellent job Sean did renovating the old castle-like structure made it into the beautiful hotel it is today. One of the hotel industry's most prestigious membership groups, Relais & Chateaux had admitted the hotel as a member.

Doc used the voice recorder as he thought about the conversations he had today with Brian White and his contacts. The idea was beginning to fill out nicely. The main thing Doc wanted to learn was how to take new software products to market. It was the one part of the puzzle that had the ability to make or break the whole idea. Thanks to Brian, Doc had spoken to several well-placed individuals with extensive experience in software marketing. It turns out that while there are many people involved in this aspect of the business, only a few are considered true industry leaders. These are the people Doc was trying to identify and to establish at least an introductory contact. Doc now had two good contacts and hopefully, following the return calls tomorrow, he will have a few more.

Back in his suite he listened to his messages. He made it a habit of turning off the phone when he was in a thinking mode and only turning it on at periodic intervals to collect messages. He had messages from Jim, Jungle Bill and Bev. He called Jim back first.

"Hi Jim, you called."

Jim, a little out of breath replied, "Yeah, I was just in a video conference call with the Minister, his DEA counterpart and a few others. And I had to run up the hall to get your call. I wanted to speak with you before you get into the Washington meetings." Jim paused to catch his breath. Doc knew better than to interrupt Jim when he was on a roll so just waited patiently for him to continue. Jim said, "Some news that will impact on your work in Asia has developed. The head honchos have decided that senior intelligence agents such as you and Bill will no longer participate in excursions into the vicinity of the drug production, storage, and shipping facilities. US Special Forces who have specialized training in Asian jungle combat will handle this aspect of operations. Teams of Rangers and Green Berets are being dispatched to a secret base in the region and will commence operations shortly."

"What's this all about Jim and why didn't the Minister bring this up at our meeting last week?"

"The Minister is on the road, somewhere in Europe. He probably hadn't heard anything about this until today's conference call. It seems to be a DEA driven idea ironically due, at least in part, to your recent injury. The theory behind it is that people such as you and Bill, along with your South American counterpart, are too valuable as intelligence gatherers to risk in combat field operations. I know that this is a significant change to your previous methods. However, you'll have to agree that the idea of keeping you out of harm's way makes sense. I didn't want you to be blindsided, and I wanted you to be able to think about this prior to your Washington meetings."

Great, Doc thought, another thing to consider. How the hell did life get so complicated? What happened to the swim-up bar and a few of Tony's Nassau Nightie Removers?

"Ok Jim" Doc said, "thanks for the heads up. I'll talk to Bill about this. We're having dinner tomorrow to prepare for the meetings so I'll put this on the agenda. On the surface, it makes sense to leave the combat ops to the specialists and for Bill and me to remain focused on the senior level contacts normally found at cocktail parties and country clubs. The only shooting we have to worry about there is our golf shot."

Bill was next on the call list. "I guess you've heard about the changes that our bosses dreamt up today," Doc said as soon as Bill picked up. "Hello to you too Doc, how goes it?"

"I'm ok, camped out at O'Leary's and looking forward to dinner with Sean. So what's your reaction to the new marching orders?"

Bill said, "It came as a total surprise. Ordinarily moves such as this are preceded by hints or rumors, but in this case it's as though they just discussed it and made the decision today."

"I think that's what happened. No consultation or discussion with us, just a done deal handed down from on high," Doc said.

"We can discuss it some more tomorrow over dinner once we've had the opportunity to digest the news," Bill said. "My first reaction is that while I'll miss the adventure, we're probably of more use to the effort in the boardrooms and embassy events than we are in the jungle getting shot at."

"Have you made any attempt to get Shannon out on a date yet?" Bill asked.

"No, I don't think that'll happen, she knows Sean and I are close friends and probably won't risk her job by going out with me."

"Don't be such a wuss," Bill replied, "give it a try. The last time we talked about her you seemed all eager to attempt to get a date. All she can say is no and you've heard that before."

Bev had left her cell number, and since it was after office hours, Doc tried it.

"This is Bev, "She said when answering her cell. In the background, Doc could hear the distinctive beat of Reggae music and conversation commensurate with people having a good time. He heard higher than average volume, faster than normal talking speed, and a lot of laughing.

"Don't tell me I've interrupted a big date."

"No such luck," Bev replied, "it's girls night at the Junkanoo Lounge, so we're getting tipsy on Appleton's rum and telling each other how neat we all are. How are you doing, still on the road?"

"Yeah, I'm having dinner with my old friend Sean and looking forward to some good jokes, a few drinks, and an excellent dinner. I'll be off tomorrow late in the morning. I have some calls I hope come in first and they may call for access to some office equipment so I'd rather take them here than on the road. Have you organized a flight for Friday?"

"Yes, I'm on United Flight 108 arriving at one o'clock. Is that ok for you?"

"Perfect, that'll get us into the resort in Virginia before dinner. I'll have some things to discuss regarding the situation you're facing. In fact, I'll have a lot of things to discuss, so you better be ready for a mainly working weekend. That's one of the reasons I'm waiting for calls in the morning."

"I'm looking forward to Virginia; I was thinking about the horses you mentioned, let's do some riding we can't work all the time."

"Already taken care of my dear. I also took the liberty of booking you a spa treatment, massage, pedicure, mud bath, facial, the whole nine yards so yeah we can't work all the time. See you Friday."

On his way down to the pub, Doc bypassed the main floor and rode the elevator to the parking level. He wanted to see if Jo, the maintenance lady, had a chance to work on his car. When Doc saw the car, he was amazed at the job Jo had done. The car looked as though it had just driven out of the showroom. Doc went to Jo's office to thank her. She had left for the day, so he went to the front desk. Shannon was just finishing her shift as Doc approached the desk.

He said to her, "Hi Shannon, would you do me a favor and arrange to have a dozen long stem red roses sent to Jo's office with a thank you card from me?"

"Red roses are Jo's thing," Shannon said with a trace of Irish lilt, " she just loves them."

"I know, what are your favorite flowers?"

"I'm an orchid fancier. My Da had a green-house full of them back home, so I grew up surrounded by them. If I walk by a display of orchids, even today, I get a flashback to home just from the smell of them."

Doc said, "Speaking of home, I'd like to talk to you about southern Ireland when you have time. I'm considering a trip next year and would like some advice."

"Why not talk to Sean about it then?"

"Ah you know Sean, he's full of malarkey. I want a woman's perspective. I'm coming back through on Monday, how about we go some-where nice for dinner, and you can help me plan my upcoming trip to visit the land of my ances-tors."

"This sounds like a wee bit of malarkey you are spinning yourself, Donovan O'Connell. Is it a date you're after?"

"You've caught me I'm afraid. Yes, I've been trying to think of a way to ask you out for some time now but was afraid you might feel uncom-fortable since I'm a friend of the boss."

"Don't be daft Mr. O'Connell. I work for Sean but who I choose to date is strictly my business."

"Please don't call me Mr. O'Connell, call me Donovan or by my nickname Doc."

"Should we go on a date then, Doc it is while

we're out. However as long as I'm on this side of the front desk and you on the other, it will be Mr. O'Connell."

"Does that mean we can go to dinner Monday evening?"

"No, it means I'll think about it and let you know Monday when you arrive. Speaking of which, I'll reserve your suite if you wish."

"That's a very good idea and why don't you think about where you might like to go for dinner Monday, you know, just in case you agree to go out with me. Since you're off work, how about a drink in the pub while I wait for Sean?"

"That I can do, go ahead in and order me a glass of Pinot Gris, I have to finish clearing the till."

Shannon felt a little lightheaded. She asked herself, what had brought this on? She had been attracted to Doc for several years but never thought he found her attractive. To her, Doc was a nice guy, a gentleman, good looking, no, really good looking and obviously a successful businessman, who happened to be a friend of her boss. She would admire him as he passed through, but that was the problem; he was always just passing through.

Surely there was no chance that anything could develop between them. She thought of an Irish expression her mother used to say, "May you get all your wishes but one, so you always have something to strive for." Maybe, just maybe, this is the one to strive for....we'll see.

When she entered the pub, it was obvious that she had made a detour to the ladies. Her light red hair, worn up while working was now down and falling below her shoulders. It framed her beautiful, lightly freckled face and highlighted her meadow green eyes. She had done something subtle with her makeup, which enhanced her girl-next-door look, provided you lived next door to the loveliest girl on earth. As soon as he saw her, Doc wished that Sean would call in sick so they could spend the evening together.

Doc was tongue-tied. "Wow he said, you should always wear your hair down, you look lovely."

"Thank you Doc, you don't look so bad yourself. I've had a chance to think about things and decided that I prefer Doc to Donovan. Not that there is anything wrong with Donovan, just that I almost always shorten people's names. It's just a habit of mine. So now that we're not in a work situation, you're Doc, ok?"

"Ok, but you said that you have thought about things, with an 's' so what else have you thought about?"

She said, "Dinner is on for Monday, do you like Italian food?"

"I love Italian food, where should we go."

"I'll make a reservation for eight o'clock. Why don't you come to my place for say six thirty and we can have a drink?"

When Sean arrived, Shannon excused herself

and prepared to leave.

Sean said, "No need to leave on my account. Stick around and join us for dinner."

Shannon said, "No thanks Sean, I have plans for tonight. I was just keeping Doc busy until you got here."

Sean said, "Doc, who the hell is Doc?"

"I am," Doc said, "it's a short form of my initials. Some friends in Canada coined the moniker after I spent some time in the hospital last year, and it stuck."

Shannon said, "Well I'll be off then and let you gents have your evening, see you both tomorrow."

As she left, Sean said, "She's a fine young woman, almost a daughter to me. She's obviously interested in you. What happened between you?"

"I hope you won't mind Sean, I've wanted to ask her out for a couple of years now and finally got up the courage."

"Mind? Why would I mind? I'd be delighted to see you and her become friends."

"I'm back on Monday night, so we're going to an Italian place for dinner."

"Ah, no doubt she will introduce you to the joys of Carmella's. I don't think you'll be disappointed, try the lasagna. Let's get a pair of Jameson's, I've got a great story for you," Sean said as he signaled the bartender to deliver a bottle and two glasses. When Sean poured the drinks, and the appropriate toasts made, Sean said, "So this lad Seamus moves from Tralee to Kenmare and has to find himself a new local. He looks the pubs in town over and settles on one. He goes up to the bartender and orders 3 pints of Guinness. He then takes them to a quiet, corner table and slowly drinks them. The next night same thing, he comes in and orders three pints of Guinness, takes them to the same table and drinks them.

This goes on for a week. Finally one night the bartender says, "Seamus there is no need for you to be ordering three pints of Guinness at once. Guinness is best if poured fresh and I am happy to pour you three, but one at a time. "

"No, you don't understand. I've two brothers, one moved to Australia, and one to America. The night before they left we agreed that whenever we ordered drinks we would order three so that its like all three of us are drinking together." A few weeks later Seamus comes in and only orders two Guinness'.

"Oh I'm so sorry Seamus, did you lose the Australian brother or the American brother?"

"Neither one, he replies, I just gave up drinking."

Doc laughed and raised his glass to Sean, "You always could tell an exceptional story Sean, and I'll get a lot of mileage out of this one at my local in Ottawa."

74

CHAPTER SIX

As always, it was great to spend time with Sean. Doc enjoyed an excellent meal of corned beef and cabbage made the authentic Killarney way, a few games of darts, too much fine whiskey and lots of laughter. Sean knew about a thousand jokes that Doc had never heard and Doc, no slouch himself in the humor department, knew a thousand that Sean hadn't heard. Doc knew that the next morning he was going to be in pain between too much laughter and too much whiskey. It was usually a contest between his head and his stomach, both vying for the leader in the pain department.

The morning came and with it the expected pain contest. Doc called room service thinking that a good Irish breakfast would help cure his ills.

Fortunately, Doc's calls were returned early, so he now had sufficient information to put together a preliminary plan for dealing with Bev's situation. Doc hesitated to think of Bev's situation as her problem. Her having close to $350 million USD is hardly a problem. Doc took orange juice from the mini bar into the bathroom while he shaved and showered.

Refreshed, with most of the cobwebs banished, he dressed for the road in jeans and a T-shirt that read on the front, "If you think I'm sexy, and you want my body" and on the back, "it's reduced for quick sale".

As he finished his breakfast, he called the desk and asked Shannon to prepare his bill.

Shannon replied, "Done and Jo has already brought round the freshly shined Mustang topped up with hi-test, so you are set to go."

Doc took his time settling his bill. He knew he had to get on with his trip to Washington but found it hard to say goodbye to Shannon. He did manage to confirm their date for Monday night. She said that she was looking forward to it. The comment registered somewhere deep inside and, along with the memory of her bright green eyes, sustained his good mood for the rest of the drive.

After checking into the Watergate, Doc made a few more follow up phone calls regarding his plan for Bev. He changed into a pair of chinos, a Tommy Bahamas shirt, a light sports jacket and left to meet Jungle Bill for dinner. Before leaving his room, Doc called down to the concierge and had a beautiful and very rare orchid plant sent to Shannon care of O'Leary's Arms.

Bill and Doc had a long-standing agreement that while in North America, they would usually frequent Doc's favorite steak houses and when in Asia they would enjoy Bill's favorite local cuisine. So tonight it was the Palm Steak House. The dry aged, US Prime steaks were so large that they hung over the side of the plate. They were a challenge to finish and the baked potato looked like an NFL football. Usually when in the States, if a Palm Steakhouse was in the town where he was staying then that is where you'd find Doc.

They ordered their drinks. The young waiter wore an outfit including a white apron tied half way up his chest. He tried unsuccessfully to look like an old waiter. He set menus in front of them and shuffled off slowly, sticking with his attempted old man persona. The Palm had always had a policy of hiring older, very experienced, waiters however they seemed to be dying off, or retiring to Florida to live on the exorbitant tips they had gathered over the years.

Bill seemed to be anxious to tell Doc some news so Doc told him that he looked like he might explode so he should let it out, whatever it is.

Bill said with a suppressed grin, "I talked to Linda today, and we're going to spend four nights next weekend together at a resort near Montego Bay."

"Wow, that's great!" Doc enthusiastically replied. He was genuinely pleased for Bill. They had been close friends and working partners for just over four years and in all that time the grueling pace of their efforts in Asia had taken precedence over opportunities for romance.

Sure there were a myriad of one-night stands but no time to develop a relationship. It sounded as though this may be the start of something long term, albeit also long distance.

"Ok, my turn" Doc announced. "I have a couple of things of interest to share with you including a pending dinner date with Shannon Monday evening. I finally got up the nerve, after all these years, to ask her out and she said yes."

"That's good news but why Monday evening, I thought you would be headed north right after the meetings for a weekend at the Brockville cottage before going to Asia?"

"I'm meeting Bev for the weekend in Virginia" Doc replied.

"Oh that's great," Bill said. "Bev on the weekend and Shannon on Monday, aren't you stepping up to the buffet a tad too often?"

"I'm not thinking of Bev in any romantic way, more like an old friend. We used to see a lot of each other at university and always got along well as friends. We had forgotten how much we enjoyed each other's company until we got caught up in Nassau. She loves horses, so we'll do a little riding, maybe play a round of golf, have a spa visit, and a few nice dinners."

The world's youngest old man, after taking the dinner order, once again shuffled off like an octogenarian turtle. Doc had thought a great deal about how he could explain his meeting with Bev for the weekend. He hated to lie to Bill and thus far hadn't done so.

He had promised confidentiality to Bev regarding her situation and would never even consider breaking this promise. He did, however, need a reasonable explanation for a sudden renewal of their friendship.

If she liked his plan, and it moved forward, no doubt they would be spending a lot of time together. Doc had no idea how much of an understated prophesy this would turn out to be.

Bill had no reason to doubt Doc's explanation. He had witnessed first hand how well Bev and Doc got along in Nassau and was too busy with his newfound romantic interest to pay much attention to them. Although he thought, he would have noticed if they were showing signs of becoming more than friends.

Doc said, "As to other news, my boss wants me to relocate to Asia."

"What" Bill exclaimed. "When did they come up with this idea?"

"I don't know for sure where it originated. Jim said something about the Minister coming up with it to take away some of the time-consuming hours spent in the air between Asia and Ottawa. The Minister feels this would benefit me in at least two ways. It would permit me to have more time to live more of a conventional lifestyle and less like an astronaut. Also, I'd have more time to spend in healthy recreational pursuits and taking care of business in our territory."

Bill said, "What do you think Doc?"

"I've given it some thought and am warming to the idea. They're giving me an excellent expatriate package, and it might be a pleasant change to live in my own place rather than hotels most of the time."

"Where do they want you to live?"

"They've left it up to me; I thought I'd get your input and the thoughts of your colleagues in the meetings before making any decisions."

"What about your condo in Ottawa and place in Brockville?"

"At least for now I'll hang on to the Ottawa place, as you know it's in an up and coming area and will increase in value over time. Despite living in Asia, I'll be required in Ottawa at least on a quarterly basis so I can stay there when I'm home. I can store the Mustang there in the secure underground lot. I'll also keep the cottage. It's been a second home to me all my life, and I love it there. It'll be a much-needed respite from the hectic pace wherever I call home in Asia. Besides it's a home base that is Shannon accessible."

Bill, who was down to earth in almost every way, had one affectation that Doc could never fully understand. He was a wine snob. At some point in his early career, he had taken a sommelier course and had developed a taste for fine wines. Doc knew that red was for meat and white for fish, so he always let Bill order the wine. Bill had insisted that Doc carry a card in his wallet upon which Bill had listed several good reds and several good whites for those occasions when he needed to impress a business contact or a young lady. Tonight, Doc as usual wasn't disappointed. The wine was a smooth tasting Merlot, which, according to Bill, was perfect for the dinner.

Bill said, " We've updated each other on our love lives as well as your relocation plans. The next item for our personal meeting tonight should be to agree on our position on the change in our roles in the crusade against drug interests in Asia."

"Yes I agree, this topic will certainly be high on the agenda of tomorrow's meeting so we should present a unified front."

Bill reached for his coffee and said, "I've had a chance to give it a lot of thought and have discussed it with Pele." Pele was the code name for their South American counterpart despite the fact that he was as English as tea and crumpets. "His feeling is that he does not want to give up the combat patrols. He will probably leave the agency and seek employment that will allow him to pursue the pseudo-military lifestyle. It seems this aspect of the work is that important to him. I see his point of view however I don't share it. Personally I am quite willing to forego the pleasures of trudging through snake-infested swamps in the jungle while under fire. I'm in favor of letting the military specialists do what they do best while I work on getting rid of my slice at the Bangkok Golf and Country Club."

"How much of your change of heart, because I know that you did enjoy the jungle excursions, is a result of my being shot?" Doc asked.

"I have to admit watching you take that hit right in front of me was the scariest thing that has happened to me so far. You were right in front of me. Happily walking along talking about our upcoming reception at the Thai ministry of justice and then in a heartbeat blood was gushing from the wound in your back, and you were flying forward, landing on your face. I was sure we had lost you and we damn near did.

If you hadn't been in such good physical condition, or if the sniper had taken a second shot, you wouldn't be here today. Right at that moment I started thinking that maybe we're not cut out for this line of work. You've become like a brother to me Doc. In fact, you're closer than my brother. He is a bit of a nerd engineer with thick glasses and a pen filled pocket protector in his shirt by Jacques of Wal-Mart."

"Thanks for saying that. At the risk of creating a mutual admiration society, you are my closest friend. I have never had a brother but if I did I'd want him to be like you. Now before you ask me to dance, let's get on with our position for tomorrow's meeting. I have to confess that like you while I've enjoyed some aspects of the jungle patrols; I'm not keen on spilling blood, my own or the bad guy's.

This wound, and recovering from it, has given me a lot of time to think about our role in this business. I agree with you that it's time for us to back away from the tough stuff and trade in our flack jackets for sports jackets."

Bill said, "We can hear them out tomorrow, and then tell them we agree with the change in the modus operandi."

"Sounds like a plan to me," Doc said. "I just had an idea, why don't you suggest that you relocate to Asia as well?"

"The thought crossed my mind. Let's wait and see what the reaction to your move will be tomorrow. They might come up with the idea themselves once they learn of your relocation."

"Good idea," Doc said, "If it comes from them you might be able to negotiate better terms for your expat package; that is if you want to do it."

Bill said, "I need to think about that as well. Unlike you, I do have parents to consider and other relatives. As you know from having spent so many holidays with us over the years, we're pretty close knit."

"That's a good point, "Doc replied. "It's much easier for me with no immediate family to consider and not being close to any relatives."

"Aside from these two topics and the usual reports on productivity and operational costs, is there anything else significant on their plate for these meetings?" Doc asked.

"Not that I have been told. The scuttlebutt is that the executive group in the DEA and the man in the oval office are pretty pleased with our efforts. They're particularly happy with that major takedown in Cambodia, the one you'll always remember from the large caliber generated scars on your back and chest. We put a serious dent in their production facilities and shut down a large part of their business for the foreseeable future."

They decided to forego any further activities in favor of getting a good sleep to help prepare them for tomorrow's meetings. If these meetings follow the usual format, Doc thought, they would commence with the big issues and proceed to the smaller ones. By Friday morning, the agenda is normally pretty clear and allows time for some "blue sky" sessions. These idea-generating discussions are informal in nature, and attendees are encouraged to discuss any ideas that might be of benefit to the overall effort. In the past, some pretty far-fetched ideas have been served up. Some good ideas have been developed as well, including the new plan to have Doc and Bill receive invitations to all events sponsored by both the American and Canadian government offices throughout Asia."

The next morning's meetings started out as Doc had expected but took an abrupt turn when Doc was told that the President wanted to see him and Bill at three o'clock this afternoon in the Oval Office. Doc asked, "What's this all about?"

The Deputy Director Operations or DDO of the DEA, who had delivered the invitation, said, "My administrative assistant got the message from the President's administrative assistant. She didn't elaborate beyond saying that the time allotted for the meeting was from three o'clock to three fifteen." The announcement generated a lot of discussion and speculation in the conference room. Except the Deputy Director, no one else had ever met the President, never mind visited the oval office.

At three o'clock, Doc and Bill were shown into the Oval Office. To their surprise in attendance was the Director of the DEA, the Canadian Ambassador, and the head of the Washington DC office of the RCMP.

The President shook hands warmly with both Bill and Doc and introduced everyone. He asked them all to be seated and said, "The purpose of this get together is to show my appreciation for the hard work being done by these two gentlemen." He motioned toward Bill and Doc and continued, "As you all know, the war on drugs is a very high priority for me both personally and as President. Our joint venture effort with Canada has greatly exceeded expectations, not only my expectations but also those of the naysayers on Capitol Hill. I want you two gentlemen to know how much I appreciate your efforts. I ask you both to stand and accept the Presidential Medal of Freedom with Distinction, the highest civilian award our country has to offer."

The President pinned the medals on each man and shook their hands. The other invitees approached Doc and Bill and congratulated them. The Canadian Ambassador said, "On behalf of the Government of Canada, let me also express our gratitude to you both for your valiant efforts."

At this point, Bill and Doc thanked the President and shook hands with him as the group started to exit the oval office.

Doc said to the President, "May I ask you a question sir?"

"Of course Mr. O'Connell, what is it?"

"What kind of coffee do you serve here? I'm a coffee lover and heard you serve Jamaican Blue Mountain, supposedly the finest coffee in the world."

The President reached for his intercom and said, "Mary, what brand of coffee do we serve here?"

"Why it's Jamaican Blue Mountain coffee, Mr. President."

"Where are you staying?" The President asked Doc.

"At the Watergate sir."

The President again touched his intercom and said, "Mary, send a case of Jamaican Blue Mountain Coffee to Mr. O'Connell at the Watergate."

"Yes, Mr. President right away."

"Thank you very much, sir, I'll enjoy the coffee and think of this day whenever I have some."

Once out in the hall, the Director of the DEA said, "Normally we would pose for group photos and have members of the press in attendance. However, due to the covert nature of your roles, we will have to forego these activities and ask as well that you do not disclose to anyone that you have received this award. I'm sorry, but I'm sure you understand.

"Of course," Doc said, "we'll keep these awards confidential." They shook hands with the Canadian Ambassador and the head of the

RCMP's Washington Bureau and headed for the exit.

As they entered the limo under the west wing portico, Doc said, "I don't know about you Bill, but I feel like a drink."

"I agree," Bill said, "I'm buying, driver, please drop us at the Union League Club." Looking at Doc he said, "The Club is a little stodgy, but it has the best selection of single malts in the USA."

Right now, I feel like a double Scotch and a leather wingback chair in front of a giant fireplace in an old-world, luxurious, men's club environment. Political correctness be damned!"

They got comfortably ensconced in a pair of leather chairs, armed with suitable drinks. They sat in front of an enormous fireplace that Bill had asked the waiter to light and had the privacy to be able to savor what had just happened.

Doc went first "Can you believe it, the Presidential Medal of Freedom and a meeting with the President in the Oval Office plus a case of Jamaican Blue Mountain? Who would have thought we would ever see this day happen?"

Bill took a long drink from his cut crystal glass and said, "I never saw this coming. When I heard we were invited to the Whitehouse, I was shocked. I figured the President might have wanted to tell us directly that he was pleased with our success thus far in Asia, given his personal interest in stopping drugs, but I certainly didn't expect a medal. It's a shame though that I can't tell my folks about it. My Dad places a lot of importance on patriotism, particularly as an immigrant, and would see this as a great honor to our family."

Doc said, "It is a great honor. Your father should be proud of the job he has done raising a son whose contribution to the well being of the United States has been recognized by the President. If my Dad were alive, I'd tell him about it."

Bill said, "I'm going home this weekend so I might swear them to secrecy, show them the medal and tell them about it, I'll see. I thought the meetings today went well. I think the Deputy Director was pleased that we agreed to the new combat-free roles for us."

"Yeah, we accomplished a lot today and I'm looking forward to tomorrow's session. I always enjoy the open dialog portion of these meetings. We don't have opportunities like this to share ideas, no matter how obscure, with our colleagues and bosses in Canada. I'm going to try to get Jim to incorporate something like this in our meetings."

Doc said that he appreciated the group's input to his move to Asia. The Deputy Director liked the idea, and both Doc and Bill felt that he might suggest a similar move for Bill. " After today's input where do you think you want to live?"

Doc said, "The consensus amongst your colleagues seemed to be either Bangkok or Hong Kong. Bangkok because it's closer to the drug production and distribution activities and Hong Kong due to its concentration of large international government representation as well as the fact that it is the business hub of Asia."

"That's what I got from the meeting as well, Bill said. Which city makes the most sense to you?"

I think Hong Kong might be the better choice. It's farther away from the production and distribution areas but given our new marching orders, it might be easier to meet the right senior government and business people in Hong Kong.

"I'm going to head over there next week, prior to our scheduled events and take a look at Hong Kong as a place to live. I've always enjoyed visiting the city and have some good friends there so it might make sense when you add in the business reasons to live there."

The next morning's meetings were interesting although the brainstorming session was not as long or productive as those in times past. Doc and Bill said their farewells, planning to meet again at the Mandarin Oriental Hotel in Bangkok two weeks from Saturday. Doc headed back to the hotel, checked out, and drove to the airport to meet Bev's one o'clock arrival.

CHAPTER SEVEN

Despite all the international travel Doc had done, he hated airports. He hated getting to an airport, hated being there and hated leaving one. As far as he was concerned they were like hospitals, a necessary pain in the ass. It's bad enough Doc thought, to have to go to an airport to catch a flight, but going to an airport just to meet a flight is crazy. Under normal circumstances, he refused to go to airports to meet people, but these were not normal circumstances, and Bev was special people.

As she came out of the gangway, Doc remembered that she had this incredible suntan, courtesy of living in Jamaica, in a deluxe condo with a great pool. He gave her a friendly hug and made the usual inquiries about how her flight was, how her uncle was and how Linda was.

"What do you think about Linda and Bill getting together next week at the resort near Montego Bay?" Doc asked.

Bev replied, "I hope it works out. I'm afraid that they may be moving a bit too fast having just met, but I guess we'll see. Linda's a great lady and a good friend, and I wouldn't want her to get hurt."

Doc said, "Bill's a gentleman in every way. He's honest, hard working, loyal and a real gentleman. Besides he's also a gourmet cook with a good sense of humor, so I think she'll be

---

well taken care of."

The drive to the resort in Virginia was relaxing. They'd managed to beat the rush hour leaving the city and were driving through some of the most beautiful countryside in America.

Bev said, "I'm so looking forward to this weekend. Between some problems at the office and worrying about my uncle, I've had a hectic week to say the least."

Doc said, "Well let's try to relax as much as we can while still getting our work accomplished. I'd suggest cutting out the work part and just relaxing, except that I have to be in Asia for a month, and I don't think you want to wait that long to get started."

"No, you're right, I want to get on with this project right away so let's work and relax as you suggested. My uncle is nearing the end I'm afraid. I'll go to South Africa a few days after I get back to Jamaica. If I get word to come urgently, I'll go directly from here. I've already cleared it with my boss and Linda can cover for me on the projects we have underway."

After checking in, Doc and Bev were shown to their cottage, a cozy two-bedroom fieldstone place with a front porch and three gables in the roof. It was nestled in a grove of maple trees offering a lot of privacy.

Along one side, a small private swimming pool and hot tub were strategically located to provide privacy for those choosing to go without swimsuits.

"Let's open some wine and sit on the porch where we can look out on the white horse fence and pick out which horses we'll ride tomorrow," Doc said.

"Good idea, I'll change into my riding clothes while you open the wine."

Doc went into his room and changed into his jeans. He poured the wine and found the appetizer tray he had pre-ordered chilling in the fridge. He set these out on the small porch table and checked out the horses while waiting for Bev.

"Ok, do we look like horsey type Virginians or what?" Bev asked as she came onto the porch with a document in her hand.

"No, I look horsey, you look beautiful. You should wear jeans and cowboy boots more often."

"Before we get started, I want you to read and sign this agreement. I want to get this part of our relationship in writing before you reveal anything to me about your idea." She handed Doc the document and walked down to the white fence near the horses while he read it over.

When she looked back at Doc, she could see that he was finished reading and was sitting there with a dazed expression on his face.

"There is no way I can agree to this Bev; your lawyer must be out of his or her mind to have drafted it. They should be disbarred. You told me that your uncle's fortune was around 350 million USD. You're offering me half of it.

I could never accept that from you."

"Look Doc, we're old friends who like each other and trust each other. I have no one else on earth, with the possible exception of Linda that I value as a close friend. You and I are alone in the world. Once my uncle goes, I have no other living relatives. FYI, it wasn't my family lawyers that drew up that agreement; I did it. Don't forget, I'm a lawyer just like you. Remember those papers we worked on together at business and law school?"

"What if you don't like my idea of getting the money out, then where are we?"

"We're in the same place; you'll just have to come up with another idea. Doc, you've always been the creative one. You'll figure it out. Here is a pen, sign that agreement and become my partner."

"What about my career? I was just in the middle of being relocated to Asia, probably Hong Kong."

Bev replied, "As we get funds out of Africa we'll be in a position to invest in a lot of different businesses. You should stay with your present career until we need you full time in our company. Personally, I think Hong Kong would be an ideal base for us for many reasons including its terrific attitude about taxation. As Canadian residents there we'll have one of the world's lowest corporate and personal tax rates while operating in a dynamic society. We'll be adjacent to China with all the opportunities that will occur as that economy comes out of the dark ages and, believe me, it's coming out. Now sign the document. I called room service when I went in to change, and they're bringing over a bottle of chilled Perrier-Jouet 2006 to celebrate our partnership. I also told them to bring dinner menus."

Doc said, "I'm still in shock over this Bev. Are you sure you're acting in your own best interest?"

"I need you Doc. I can't manage this amount of money on my own. I need someone I trust unequivocally, who will always stand by me and cover my back. Besides, knowing us, we'll soon have this money invested and making more money than we'll know what to do with."

Just then, the waiter arrived on a bicycle balancing a tray with the $200 bottle of champagne in an ice bucket.

"Shall I open it for you sir?" the waiter asked.

"Best ask the lady it's her party."

"Sure, go ahead and open it for us please," Bev said.

The waiter asked if they would like to order dinner now or call it in later. They decided to phone when they were ready.

"Ok Doc, enough dillydallying, sign the agreement, I'm dying to find out what you have in mind."

Doc reached for the pen and said, "Alright I'll sign. I'd be a fool not to. However, ironically this agreement is like a marriage with no prenup. So

I want a clause in the agreement that if you ever want to end our relationship you may do so simply by saying so to me without the need for any more lawyers. God knows the two of us lawyers are enough. The breakup settlement will be that I get half of whatever profits we make after you take out your original investment in full. In that way, I get rewarded for my efforts, and you get your original investment returned plus fifty percent of the profits that we earn together."

"Agreed," Bev said, "I'll write that in as an additional clause while you pour the champagne."

With the document finally signed, Bev raised her champagne glass to propose a toast saying "To my best friend and partner."

They had a sip then Doc raised his glass in a toast, "To my new partner. Thank you for your trust, your generosity and particularly your friendship. May we enjoy new prosperous adventures together."

"Wow, I thought you were going to make a speech there for a minute. Now before we get tipsy, let's order dinner and get some business done."

With the dinner order taken care of, Doc lit the fireplace, and they got comfortable in easy chairs.

Doc said, "My plan is somewhat complicated, so I think it best for me to simply lay it out, answer questions and let it ferment in your mind over night. Once you've had a chance to sleep on it, we can go through it in more detail in the morning and see if you think it's worth pursuing. The challenge was to find a legal method of getting the capital out of Zimbabwe, so devious means were not considered. I also wanted a way to proceed in an orderly manner, one step at a time so as not to risk all of the capital in one failed attempt."

"That's great thinking. I was concerned that if the plan called for one large transaction of some sort, we would run the risk of losing it all," Bev said.

Doc resumed explaining his plan. "In Zimbabwe you'll inherit a mansion and a large tract of land, the family's ancestral estate am I correct? Tell me what you know about it."

Bev said, "The mansion is truly magnificent and quite ostentatious. It is a palatial, 60,000 square foot structure with 60 guest rooms with en suite bathrooms plus four, two bedroom apartments. There are forty other rooms including a formal dining room, a grand ballroom, a theater, a billiard room, two libraries, and four bars.

There's an enormous gym with every instrument of torture the personal trainer could think of, a business center and an indoor-outdoor swimming pool. Of course, it has all the support rooms such as staff quarters, kitchens and pantries. It's a classic design sort of like those you would see in movies depicting the large plantation mansions in the southern US with wide screened-in balconies and large columns on the front. The grounds include six tennis courts, riding stables, a twenty-car garage for my uncle's car collection, a trout pond, a nine-hole golf course, a landing strip and a helicopter pad. The property it all sits on is 1,900 acres. I have a picture book about it which I'll send to you, but you'll have to come over and see it."

Doc had been listening intently and hadn't noticed his jaw dropping as Bev delivered her narration on the building and grounds. "Wow," he said, "it sounds perfect for what I have in mind. What condition is it in?"

"It's in mint condition. My uncle has been a fanatic about four things: the business, the estate, his thoroughbred horses and his cars. He has always entertained a lot in the tradition of British nobility, with elaborate weekend long events and lots of guests. In many ways, he had the place functioning like a resort hotel. As I mentioned, he didn't have any other family except me, and he liked having lots of people around, the more, the merrier.

Labor is so cheap in Zimbabwe that he has a staff of seventy-five. He has always treated them well, providing excellent accommodations, food, and fair wages. The staff hardly fluctuates, and they know how good they have it compared to other estate workers, so they perform their jobs enthusiastically. When an opening does come up, the human resources manager has a stack of applications to draw on."

"What dollar value have you placed on the estate when you estimate your inheritance at $350 million US."

"I haven't included the value of the property or any assets on it such as cars and horses at all, the $350 million is the cash and securities in the bank. It's virtually impossible to estimate the value of fixed assets in Zimbabwe as it changes, often drastically, with economic and political conditions. The nature of the property is such that when we do go to sell it, the market will be pretty thin even at the best of times."

Doc said, "I've made some preliminary contact with several people well placed in the software industry and, at least so far, I haven't run into any reasons why my idea wouldn't work. The idea is that we use the mansion and grounds as a sort of resort-style campus. We equip it with the world's most advanced computer system and staff it with a team of computer graphics specialists and other hi-tech support staff

We then go to the software hot spots like Silicon Valley, Seattle, and Vancouver and recruit the best software developers we can find.

Our ideal candidates are ambitious, imaginative visionaries with a strong desire to become wealthy entrepreneurs. We offer them luxury accommodations, gourmet food and beverage, a five-star resort lifestyle and access to the world's best support people and equipment. They move to the campus, live there free of charge and spend their time developing computer games, apps and whatever software they want. When they get something market ready, they send it to our office overseas by modem.

We market it and split the revenues with them fifty-fifty. This way we use the money in Zimbabwe supporting the software development but keep our share of the profits from software sales working for us in other business investments around the world."

A discreet knock on the door and dinner was served. Once the waiter left, Bev was anxious to continue the discussion, so they worked as they ate.

She said, "Do you see the development process as a team effort where all the developers work on one project, or would it be independent developers each working on a separate project?"

"I've envisioned individuals working independently, however, if a group wanted to collaborate on a project, we could handle that. I think we would incorporate a separate company as a joint venture between our business and the developer or developers as the case may be. The company would own the software. The profits from the sales would be shared as to fifty percent for us and fifty percent for the single developer or divided among the team of developers where they choose to collaborate. To avoid any legal battles, I think we would stipulate that in any collaborative situations, the developers would be equal partners with each other so there can be no misunderstanding."

"I agree, we don't want to set ourselves up for a host of legal problems down the road. So in a sense then, we would be an incubator for independent start-ups. What happens when the money in Zimbabwe runs out?"

"We can decide then to move our software development activity in Zimbabwe somewhere else and convert the property into a Relais & Chateaux resort. Or continue to fund it from our profits if we wish to stay in the software development business there."

"What if the software developers we attract are unsuccessful at producing any marketable product?"

"We can minimize this risk by carefully selecting developers that come highly recommended to us and giving them a finite time to produce after which they would have to leave."

"Doc, I have to say that this is a fantastic idea! I knew you would put your creative mind to work on this, and you sure have. Thank you."

Doc put another few logs on the fire and revived the flame.

He said, "I think we can start this project with say a dozen developers and grow it as we find good prospects. It's possible for us to handle a large number of people as we could if necessary add additional accommodations. The basic infrastructure as you have described it, suggests that our incubator is very scalable."

Bev said, "Let's get some sleep, this is a lot to

process and I want to give it some thought that I'm sure will lead to more questions. I believe we have an excellent foundation on which to build a strong company."

The next morning they decided to go to the main lodge for breakfast just to get some variety of surroundings. The lodge was every bit as impressive as the cottage with 30 foot vaulted ceilings, generous use of large logs and a stone fireplace that Doc could have walked into without ducking his head. Over the fireplace, the biggest moose head they had ever seen gazed down at them, its eyes seeming to follow them as they moved through the dining room.

"I'm glad there are no stuffed heads in our unit," Bev said.

"I kind of like the moose head, it gives the place a woodsy feel."

"Must be a man thing, I can't help but feel sorry for the poor animal."

'I'm starving," Doc said. "I'm not sure if it is the country air or the intense conversation of last evening, but I think I could eat a horse....or a moose for that matter."

The waitress was a cheerful young lady and wasted no time getting to them, coffee pot in hand. She said, "You'll love our coffee, it's the best in the world. Comes from Jamaica."

I could tell a story about that Doc thought, but kept his thoughts to himself while he had a cup. They looked over the menu.

"I'll have a small bowl of fruit, a nonfat yogurt, a slice of dry whole wheat toast and a cup of green tea please," Bev said.

Doc said, "I'll have the breakfast steak, rare, two eggs over easy, hash browns, a pancake with maple syrup and sourdough toast with jam. And you're right, this is terrific coffee."

Bev said, "After breakfast we should walk around the property and get some exercise before we go riding. You're going to need to walk that breakfast off. Must be a man thing."

"What do you want to do for lunch?"

"Lunch," Bev exclaimed, "you just ordered a full days worth of calories!"

"Between the walk, the horseback riding and the resumption of intense discussion I'm antici-pating, I think I'll probably be ready for lunch when the time comes. I'll order a lunch basket, and we can take it with us on our ride. There must be a place to picnic nearby."

After breakfast, they walked around the re-sort's ample grounds and stopped at the stables to look over the horses.

"We're booked to go riding later on," Doc said to the stable hand, "can you recommend a nice place to stop for a picnic?"

"There is a waterfall and pool about four miles that way," he said pointing south. "The trail runs right through it and it's a good ride for beginners. Should be pretty private today, I don't have any other guests booked."

"Pick us out a couple of gentle horses would you? We're not exactly beginners, but nowhere near experts either." Bev said

As they continued their walk, Bev said, "Getting back to business…"

Doc cut her off, "Oh here we go, it's a good thing I had a substantial breakfast."

"I've been thinking about some aspects of the idea that we should discuss. Not that we have to make any decisions this weekend, but just so we have as much out on the table as we can, to be able to think this through."

Doc said, "Good idea, let's treat this weekend as a blue sky session where we try to come up with all the variables that will impact our new business. Then we can think them through independently and be prepared to make some decisions when we next meet."

Bev replied, "There's a good place to start, where and when should we next meet?"

"I have to go back to Asia in two weeks and I'll be tied up there for another three weeks at least. I have vacation time coming so why don't we tentatively say we'll get together in five weeks."

"That works for me," Bev said. "Let's meet at the mansion in Zimbabwe, so you can check it out for yourself. We can spend a week or two there if you want and get on with some real decision making."

Doc said, "That's an excellent idea. I can get some more research done, and we should be able to develop our business plan while we're there. Let's agree on two weeks there, which will allow for a bit of relaxation as well. I'm going to start using this voice recorder to keep track of ideas and things that we need to discuss. I'll transcribe the notes and send them to you as we progress."

"Communication is going to be important given your upcoming travels in Asia and the probability that I'll have to go to Zimbabwe to deal with my uncle, particularly if he passes away. I'll set us each up with a secure email account that we can check daily and keep each other updated on developments."

"That probably makes more sense than depending on phone calls given the time zone differences we'll have to deal with."

"Re your possible move to Hong Kong, you might want to consider basing our incubator company there for many reasons. Not the least of which is that you will be able to keep an eye on it. If Hong Kong is to be our base of operations, you should see if there's an international law firm and an international accounting firm with offices there and in Zimbabwe. If so, we might be able to have them bill us from their Zimbabwe office and accept our payment for services through that office.

Some of these firms have offices to rent to clients with full secretarial services. We're going to need an office and secretarial services to get started. Once operational, we'll need a base to have the software product sent to electronically. Check it out and if you think it appropriate, meet with them in Hong Kong and we can meet

with them when we are in Zimbabwe to establish a relationship."

"Ok, let's change into our horse riding clothes,
pick up our lunch basket and hit the trail."

CHAPTER EIGHT

Bev rode with more confidence than Doc, who didn't have anywhere near as much experience with horses.

"The highest and best use for horses in my opinion is achieved at the racetrack," Doc said. "I'm glad we're not going too far because I think I may walk a little bow legged for a while."

"You'll get used to it Doc. We'll have lots of opportunity for riding when we visit Zimbabwe. In fact, I have just the horse for you. He's called Midnight and has a beautiful black coat that's so shiny you can almost see your reflection in it. You'll love him and in no time you'll become an avid rider."

They arrived at the waterfall and pool and tethered the horses to a waterside tree where they could drink freely. The stable hand had been right on with his suggestion. The pool was crystal clear, blue water that shimmered invitingly in the noon sun and there were no other people around.

"It was a good suggestion that we wear our bathing suits under our clothes," Bev said. "Let's jump in and wash off the trail dust before lunch."

The swim was refreshing and helped Doc stretch out his riding legs which felt as though they were in a permanent wishbone shape.

They spread the picnic blanket and unloaded the lunch of cold chicken, salads, bread, cheese, fruit and a chilled bottle of Pinot Gris.

Doc said, "I knew I'd be hungry again despite that great breakfast. Between walking around the resort property, the barrage of new thoughts and discussion on our partnership, the ride, and the swim, I'm almost ready for another course of moose, but I'll settle for cold chicken."

"Maybe you can order moose for dinner."

"I think the only moose you are going to find on the menu here is the chocolate variety and spelled a little differently."

After lunch, their bathing suits had dried enough that they could put on their riding gear and set out.

"Let's go a few more miles up the trail," Bev said. "There is a place where this trail intersects another that, according to the resort map, will bring us back to the resort by a circuitous route with a change of scenery."

They rode along enjoying the fresh forest air, change of scenery and conversation. Suddenly the horses seemed to sense something and began acting strange and hard to control.

From behind a rock, the largest black bear Doc had ever seen stood up and growled loudly. Bev's horse, nearest the bear, reared up fast on its hind legs, which caused Bev to lose control and tumble to the ground.

Her horse took off running, leaving Bev on her backside on the ground. Doc reacted fast, jumping from his horse and running towards Bev and consequently the bear, thinking he would put himself between her and the bear. He read somewhere that the best thing to do when confronted by a bear was to raise your hands over your head and make yourself look larger, then back slowly away. As he was a foot taller than Bev, he figured the additional height might help the looking bigger strategy.

The bear, however, hadn't read the same article that Doc had and didn't seem to care that he looked bigger. He started walking slowly towards them.

Doc was in front of Bev and facing the bear still holding his now shaking hands high in the air. He started slowly walking backward hoping that Bev had stood up and was walking backward as well.

The bear seemed to be picking up speed and didn't appear to have any intention of stopping.

Bev suddenly came around Doc with two softball size rocks in her hands. As she headed toward the bear, she started banging the rocks together as hard as she could. The sharp noise startled the bear, and he came to an abrupt stop, turned around and ran off into the woods.

Doc drew his first breath since seeing the bear and said, "Where the hell did you learn to do that?"

"In Zimbabwe we sometimes encounter large predators while riding, or on a photo safari. Our guides will often use whatever is at hand to make loud noises that cause the animals to want to get far away. I bet that bear will run for miles."

Doc took Bev in his arms and gave her a long hug. "You saved our lives," he said.

"No, we saved each other. If you hadn't jumped off your horse and got between the bear and me, it probably would have attacked sooner, preventing me from grabbing the rocks."

"Now we have a different problem, no horses and a long way to the lodge so we'd better get on our way."

They walked for twenty minutes or so when a jeep came barreling up the trail from the direction of the lodge. The stable hand, Mark stood on the brakes bringing the Jeep to a halt a few feet from them. As he jumped out of the Jeep, Doc saw a hunting rifle between the front seats.

"What happened?" Mark asked. "I knew you were in some trouble when your horses came racing into the stable without you."

Doc explained as they got into the Jeep, and they started back towards the lodge.

"We don't get many bears around here and those we do get seem to be shy around humans. Yours is the first contact we've seen in three years, guess it's time we started warning riders to be bear aware."

"Probably a good idea Mark," Bev said. "We were totally surprised and lucky that it decided to go away."

Bev suggested a drink on the porch would be

a good way to calm their nerves.

"Don't forget your spa visit at four o'clock," Doc reminded her, "but I guess a drink might relax us a bit."

Doc went into the cottage, changed into dry clothes and poured Bev's wine while she went to her room and changed into a dry outfit to wear to the spa. He fixed himself a double Scotch on the drinks table and brought the drinks to the porch.

"What are you going to do while I'm in the spa?"

"I booked a massage, then I think I'll go into the billiards room and see if I can get a game. After that I think a nap is in order. What do you want to do about dinner, room service or dining room?"

"Your call, think about it while I'm covered in mud and decide, I'm easy either way."

They finished their drinks and walked leisurely over to the spa. Doc said, "Call me when you're ready and I'll come over to walk you back, it'll be starting to get dark."

"That's sweet of you but not necessary. Don't forget I grew up in northern Alberta and spent some time on safaris in Zimbabwe in my youth, so I'm pretty tough and can handle myself around wildlife."

"I just saw you in action," Doc said, "the next time I'm attacked I sure hope you're around."

"Bear encounters notwithstanding; I'm going to hate to leave tomorrow. It has been productive and relaxing as well," Bev said.

"I've given some thought to your idea of meeting at the mansion in about five weeks. I think it's a good plan, we can decide on a particular date as we get nearer to it. Between now and then, I expect we're going to be busy. You with your uncle's situation as well as your job, me dealing with my meetings in Asia and looking into where I want to live. Then there are the other issues around getting our company started that I want to give some attention to. I think that when we next get together we'll have a lot to talk about and a lot of serious relaxing to do."

"I think we're on the same page. Once we get the money out of Zimbabwe, we'll both be rich enough never to have to work again if we so choose. I can't see us just retiring at our age and spending all our time goofing off. My thought is that we develop a working relationship that includes both work and good times."

"I agree wholeheartedly. I once saw a cartoon that showed a headstone that read, 'Here lies Bill Jones; he wishes he'd spent one more day at the office' "that's not for us, let's develop a balance between work and fun."

The evening was spent enjoying a gourmet dinner in the lodge's dining room. "This is my style," Doc said. "Fine dining in blue jeans and cowboy boots, the best of both worlds."

"You and I have always preferred casual to formal dress. Remember that time at business school when we went to the Dean's reception in our running gear?"

"I was amazed they let us in," Doc said.

Without planning, the conversation was re-laxed and non-business in nature. Each sensed that they would be very busy dealing with the myriad of issues that their new relationship had generated and wanted to spend these last few hours just enjoying each other's company.

The next morning they checked out, and Doc drove Bev to the airport to get her flight to Jamaica. Doc then headed north for his return to Ottawa with a stopover at O'Leary's Arms and, hopefully, Shannon's arms as well.

Sean was working the front desk when Doc came into the lobby. Turning on his Irish brogue Doc said, "Well if it isn't the world's largest leprechaun."

"Doc me old son, as me Da used to say, "You're as welcome as a case of Jameson's at a seven-day wake."

Doc said, "Sure, and you're still full of the best that O' Brien's bull could fertilize the clover with. Why are you detracting from the luxurious décor of this beautiful establishment, where is the lovely Shannon?"

"She had the gall to ask for the afternoon off to prepare for some special occasion this even-ing. I have no idea what it is that's such a big deal."

Doc said, "I hear she may be having dinner with some visiting dignitary."

"Well I hope it's worth all the effort, I'm getting bored with this paperwork and dealing with all these people that think $400 a night should get them something special."

"Can you get someone to take over the desk for an hour or so? I'd like to talk to you about a situation I'm involved in which could mean business for you if you're interested?"

"I'm always interested in talking business, even more so if you're involved. Let me get Anne to take over here for a bit while we talk."

Anne, the hotel's accountant, and the assistant general manager had been with Sean for twenty-five years, through several businesses. Most were successes and a few failures.

Fortunately for both of them the successes had outweighed the failures by a considerable margin and rumor has it that Anne's a millionaire several times over.

Still she works for Sean and probably will as long as he remains active in the business. When Anne came out of her office, she gave Doc a friendly hug in greeting and chased them off to the pub for their chat.

They went to Sean's usual table, a quiet one in the corner by the fireplace. Regulars knew that Sean conducted most of his business from this table and tended to stay away from it out of respect for his privacy. It was understood that if Sean wasn't using the table, it was available for patrons. But if regulars were seated there when Sean came into the pub, they tended to vacate the table. Despite Sean's efforts to encourage them to stay where they were. Sean was a great believer in customers first. He ingrained in his newly recruited staff an old saying he had picked up somewhere, "In the hospitality industry, the answer is yes.....now what's the question?" All new recruits were given a T-shirt, which read, "Sweat the small stuff." Sean was a fountain of sayings.

Before they had been in their chairs for a minute, Pat the bartender arrived with their drinks.

Sean said, "Well Doc, what are you up to now and how can I fit in?"

Doc took a swig of whiskey and savored the musky taste as it warmed its way down his throat. He always particularly enjoyed that first swallow at the end of a busy day. Although he had been mostly driving, he had been able to do a lot of thinking and preserved some ideas on his voice recorder.

He started to develop a list of those people that he wanted to be part of this new venture with Bev. He decided on the drive that Sean if he wanted, would figure prominently in their plan.

Doc said, "Sean I'm going to talk to you today about a deal I'm working on that will have a role for someone with your experience. At this stage, however, it's very confidential, so I ask you as an old friend to keep this conversation strictly between us. For now, I would like you to think about it. We should be over the requirement for confidentiality in three to six months at which time you can tell whomever you want. I would like you to let me know as soon as you have reached a decision. If you are on board, I would want you to start planning while we wait out the confidentiality period."

"Ok Doc, you can count on my discretion, lay it on me."

"I'm in the very preliminary stages of a rather large deal. The details of which don't pertain to your involvement directly, other than the need for us to be able to host about sixty guests in a five-star resort-like environment.

In a sense, this would be a hybrid between a hotel and a very posh university residence for individuals who would be staying with us by the year. I want the ultimate resort experience complete with the finest food and beverage, outstanding service, the best recreational amenities and a terrific variety of entertainment. I want these guests to be extremely comfortable and highly motivated to stay with us for many years."

Sean said, "How do you see my involvement? Do you want me in as an investor?"

"No, there is no need for investment, the deal is financed. I see you originally as an advisor on the redevelopment of the property and then as head of the management company under contract."

"Have you commissioned a hotel feasibility study yet?"

"No, I don't see any need, we won't be looking

to sell rooms to the marketplace. Rather we'll have a captive market so to speak."

"Sounds like an hotelier's dream. You mentioned that you wanted me to consult on the redevelopment, which suggests that you already have a location. Is it an existing hotel that needs a makeover to come up to five star standards?"

"It's not exactly a hotel, more like a huge old mansion that requires conversion to a resort."

"What budget do you have for the renovation?"

"That is one of the things we need you to tell us. I think it is safe to say that we have the capital to do whatever you think necessary for us to achieve our five-star resort goal. I know that as you think this through, you'll have more questions. Let's get together for an early breakfast and discuss this a bit more. Other thoughts we can handle by phone over the next couple of weeks. Think also about the general terms of a management contract. I see it as an arrangement whereby we pay all operating expenses and a fixed annual management fee. There are examples out there to review. Such as the residential palace of the Sultan of Brunei, which at one time had a management contract with a leading US hotel chain, Hyatt I think, to manage the 1,800-room facility. We are talking a much smaller property, but the idea is the same."

"The key for me is going to be the location, I don't think I could handle something located far away."

"That's something we'll have to discuss as it's located about as far away from Scranton, PA as you can get. But don't let that put you off. Once you get it operating the way we want it, you can put in a five star experienced general manager and oversee him or her from here."

"Ok, I'll keep an open mind and sleep on it tonight then we can reconvene for breakfast before you head north. Shall we say seven a.m.?"

CHAPTER NINE

When Shannon opened her door to greet Doc, he was once again amazed at how beautiful she looked with her red hair down and her sparkling green eyes. They gave each other a friendly hug and a kiss on the cheek and Doc handed her a bottle of her favorite Pinot Gris, a large box of candy and a dozen long-stemmed yellow roses.

Shannon said, "What is it they say about being aware of Greeks bearing gifts?"

"Well, I'm going to be away for a while so I thought I should take care of upcoming occasions such as your birthday and Valentine's Day. Besides I'm not Greek, and I don't have any wooden horse out here."

As he entered the apartment, he was impressed by the décor. It was an eclectic mix of well-preserved antiques and some contemporary furniture including a beautiful leather couch and matching chairs. Everything seemed to go together as if the work of a professional interior designer. Overall the impression was one of tranquility and comfort, lived in yet tidy.

Doc said, "Your place is beautiful and somehow not what I expected. That isn't to say that I didn't expect it to be beautiful; I did, but not in this way."

Shannon poured two glasses of wine, set out a plate of appetizers and said, "What way is that?" She sat on the couch and Doc opted for one of the overstuffed leather chairs.

"It is difficult to pin down, it has an almost old-world charm. Did you have it professionally decorated?"

"No, about ten years ago I took a two-year diploma in interior design at night school. I went to Ireland on holiday and found most of the furniture in Dublin. My parents bought it for me and shipped it over. When Sean bought the hotel, he hired me to do the décor."

"You did the interior décor of the hotel?" Doc exclaimed!

"Yes, the whole place including the restaurant and pub. I went to Dublin and bought the pub décor from a tavern that was being demolished. I had it loaded into shipping containers and brought here."

"You have an incredible talent for decoration. I have a place on the St. Lawrence River near Brockville, Ontario in the Thousand Islands. It's a fantastic location, very relaxing and peaceful. It's only about an hour drive from my Ottawa office, so I go there quite often. I'm thinking about having some work done; it needs some structural work, a new roof, electrical and plumbing upgrades and I might add another bedroom and bathroom.

I don't want to tear it down and rebuild, although that probably makes more sense. The cottage has been in my family for a long time, and I don't want it to change to the point where it doesn't look like my old cottage anymore.

Maybe at some point you could come up, look it over and give me some ideas."

"I love going to Canada; I'll come up, as you say, "at some point" and have a look at it. But you have to promise me some boating and fishing on the river."

"I have a pretty full work schedule this year, so I probably won't get into the renovations until next year. But that doesn't mean we can't get the planning done for the interior decor whenever we want. In fact remember that trip to Ireland we discussed on my last visit, well I do want to do that trip next year. If we can get the interior décor planned, maybe you can accompany me and help with sourcing the furniture."

"We'll see Doc, next year is still a bit away yet so let's see what happens."

Doc refilled the wine glasses and proposed a toast, "To the world's prettiest interior designer."

Carmella's Restaurant produced authentic Italian cuisine such as Doc had not seen anywhere. The food was exquisite, the service prompt and cheerful, the music, lighting and décor all blended in perfect sync so that the overall result was a memorable evening.

Carmella had sent over a beautiful Italian red wine that, of course, Doc didn't recognize, couldn't pronounce and thoroughly enjoyed. Carmella came to the table, and Shannon introduced Doc to her. When Doc complimented her on the meal, Carmella said, "Part of the credit for your experience belongs to Shannon. She was our interior designer, and we get lots of compliments on her work."

Shannon blushed and said, "Now Carmella, I've told you before that if you embarrass me in front of friends, I'll stop coming here."

Carmella said, "What's to embarrass, you did a magnificent job, and we are proud of you and our décor."

Doc was somewhat taken aback when they asked for the bill, and none was forthcoming.

When the waiter brought dessert, he said in broken English, "Dinner is compliments of Carmella."

Doc, perplexed, looked at a smiling Shannon and said, "What, you knew we wouldn't get a bill?"

Shannon said, "When Carmella wanted to open this restaurant she didn't have much money, so I did the interior décor plan for free. I was even able to talk some of the trades and some of the other suppliers into doing a contra deal in return for meals.

Over the years, she hasn't forgotten that and told anyone who'll listen about it. You would be amazed at the volume of referral business I get from Carmella's customers. Depending on how busy we are at the hotel, I do those projects that I find interesting, maybe one in five, just to keep involved. I never do a project in the summer when tourists at O'Leary's overrun us."

When they arrived back at Shannon's apartment, Shannon invited Doc in for a brandy and coffee. "Why don't you build a fire while I get the drinks," Shannon said.

Doc had the fire started nicely by the time Shannon came back in the room. Standing in front of the fireplace they clinked glasses and Doc said, "A toast to a long and happy relationship."

"I'll drink to that," Shannon said.

Doc put down his brandy and took Shannon's glass placing it beside his on the mantle. He moved close and touched his hand to her face.

He brushed his lips against hers, and they folded together into an embrace as gentle and loving as either had ever experienced. Their kisses became deeper and more urgent, their bodies crushed even more closely together.

"I've wanted to do that for years," Doc said as he gazed into her emerald eyes.

Shannon stared back and said, "So have I."

Still staring at each other realizing that they had crossed a significant line they slowly unraveled and picked up their brandy.

"What brand of brandy is this?" Doc said.

"It's called St. Agnes XO. It's my Dad's favorite, he still loves a cigar and brandy, so I keep it in stock for when he visits. Why do you ask?"

"Because I love the way you taste after drinking it." Again Shannon blushed.

"Let's sit down," Shannon said. "We need to talk about the elephant in the room."

"There's an elephant in here? Must be a little guy."

"I need you to be serious for a moment. What I have to say is very important to me. I think a lot of you and wish we could spend more time together. I think if we did, it could eventually lead somewhere. For now though, all we have is this drive-by opportunity. Don't get me wrong; I understand that you are an international businessman and that your travels will only bring you here sporadically. But that has implications for me. I would love to spend time with you here when your business brings you this way. I'd like to visit you at your cottage and even go to Ireland with you, but I am not prepared to have sex with you on this basis. I know you'll think this strange at my age however I'm a virgin and plan to stay that way until I meet the man that I'm going to marry. Even then, the first time we make love will be on our wedding night. Can you live with that arrangement?"

Doc couldn't believe what he had just heard, but Shannon was so sincere that he knew she wasn't joking. He took a healthy draft of his brandy. And said, "It will be difficult, that's for sure, but I want more than anything to have a relationship with you even if we don't make love until our wedding night. So yes, I'll live with that arrangement. Now have another sip of brandy and give me a kiss."

"I have a better idea, bring the brandy and join me in bed. Even though we don't make love, I still want to sleep with you and wake up in your arms."

"I'll have to sneak into the hotel early to mess up the bed in my room or we'll be the talk of the hotel."

"You can use my passkey, go in the back door and go up the service elevator undetected if you go around five. Now get out of those clothes and pour me another brandy while I take a shower, or do you want to wash my back?"

The next morning at five o'clock, Doc left Shannon sleeping and took a cab back to the hotel. As Shannon had suggested, he used her key to get into the delivery entrance and took the freight elevator. He made it to his room unseen, stripped off his clothes, set the alarm and fell into bed for another hour. He hadn't had time to reflect on what happened at Shannon's last night or to consider what these new developments in their relationship meant.

He would have time to think in the car inspired by the ion changing, during the drive to Ottawa. He arose at six forty-five, showered and dressed quickly to get to his breakfast with Sean.

Sean was already at his usual table when Doc strolled casually into the room. He didn't want to raise any eyebrows by having Sean suspect him of staying over at Shannon's.

"Good morning Sean, you're looking bright-eyed this morning."

"You are looking pretty good yourself considering your feast at Carmella's and no doubt late hours spent with Shannon."

Good, Doc thought, he doesn't suspect that

anything is going on between him and Shannon. In fact, there isn't anything going on. Well, maybe half a thing.

"Yes, we had a lovely evening. Dinner at Carmella's was fantastic, and Shannon, of course, was excellent company. If it's up to me, we'll be seeing more of each other."

"I am glad to hear that, she is a one-of-a-kind Colleen, and I would love to see her have you as a close, long term, friend. If nothing else, it might bring you back more often, thus making a significant contribution to my pub revenue."

They ordered breakfast, health conscious one for Sean and hi-protein for Doc, who will leave shortly and drive mostly non-stop to Ottawa.

As Doc tasted his coffee he asked, "Well any more thoughts or questions re our talk last evening?"

"Just a few. In no particular order, what about timing?"

"Once you have thought this through, and we draw up a consulting agreement and a management contract, we can get started right away. You provide me with the key points as to your timing and fee proposal. I'll go over it with my associate and draw up formal documents for your lawyer's review and your signature. Depending on how fast you get back to me I expect we could have everything agreed and signed within two weeks. Then you can get started with the consulting phase of your work. I think you would need to be on site for at least two weeks, maybe longer, examining the property in detail and determining what we need to bring it up to five-star status. We would schedule meetings with the architects and building contractors during this period. Then you would need to submit your recommendations to the architects, the builder and me. We would call a general meeting of all parties on-site to go over your report and plan a final budget of both money and time to complete the project. We have a local firm of architects and engineers as well as a local building contractor that we will use. So if we are fortunate and everything goes as planned, we could accept our first guests in four to six months."

"Do you want or need Relais & Chateaux membership?"

"No, not at this point. Having said that, I want this property to qualify for it from the outset and to continue to be managed and maintained as though it were a part of this prestigious group. You never know what will happen down the road."

"What would you think if I were to put Anne in as GM?"

"I would be delighted. Her experience here working with you all these years would more than qualify her for the position. But would she go, and if she did, what would you do without her?"

"I think she would go. She is too young and driven to retire even though she can afford to whenever she wants. She's ready for a new challenge, and we had even discussed her moving on to a GM position with a Relais & Chateaux property elsewhere. She has resisted offers from several Relais & Chateaux members as well as a few members of The Leading Hotels of the World group due to our long and mutually rewarding working relationship. Putting her in the new property would achieve both the goal of finding her a new challenge and keeping us working together."

"It sounds to me like you've given this some serious thought."

"I have and I want to give it a bit more thought before making my decision. Can I call you tomorrow?"

"I tell you what, if you decide to come on board in the next few days, I'll come back down on Friday, stay the weekend and together we'll get things moving. Once you decide, you can talk to Anne about it so she can have a chance to put her questions together for discussion over next weekend."

"You wouldn't have any ulterior motives for racing back down so soon would you?"

"Who me, no way. It's all business. I simply thought the car could do with another workout, and I'd bring it here so Jo can work her magic on it."

"Ok old son, I am ninety-five percent ready to sign on, so look forward to a call tomorrow and have a safe journey home."

Shaking Sean's hand Doc said goodbye and went to his room to get ready to go. He called down to the desk to have his bill prepared, and his car brought around. He was surprised that the night clerk was still on, then remembered that it was only eight o'clock and Shannon started at nine.

Doc called her at home and asked if she had the coffee on and was it all right for him to stop by for a cup on his way out of town. She said the coffee would be ready when he got there. When she hung up, she called back to the hotel desk and asked Dave the night clerk if he could cover for her for an hour.

She greeted Doc at the door with a deep kiss and hug and said, "What a pleasant surprise, I didn't think I'd see you again this trip."

"I stopped to say goodbye. You were sound asleep when I left at five, and I didn't want to disturb you. I guess I needed to see if last night really happened or if it was just a beautiful dream."

"Funny I was just thinking the same thing."

"What did you conclude?"

"Let me show you," she said as she drew him close and kissed him until he thought he would suffocate.

"Does this mean that you'll see me again next weekend?"

"What," she exclaimed! "You're coming back so soon?"

"There is a strong possibility; I'll let you know

by phone. That is of course if you want to see me again so soon."

"Please call me as soon as you know, I'll need time to put together the ingredients for the dinner I'll make for you. When do you want to get together, Friday night, Saturday night, Sunday night?"

"Yes."

He kissed her goodbye and reluctantly pointed the Mustang north while placing a call to Bev. She was in her office and picked up on the first ring, "This is Bev."

"Hi, kid how are you doing?"

"Hi, Doc, it's good to hear from you, just what I need, a friendly voice.

I'm well, but my uncle isn't. I'm awaiting a call from the Doctor in Zimbabwe and may have to go over right away, I'll let you know."

"Do you want me to go with you, I could take some emergency leave?"

"No, I'll be alright, this has been coming for so long that I'm getting used to it. The doctor says that he is in and out of a coma and is just being kept alive by life support systems. He's enjoyed a grand life and is ready to go."

"Ok, if you need me you know how to reach me. On another note, I have lined up a consultant to help plan the mansion renovations and to take over management of the property when it is ready to go."

"Doc that is great news, way to go. It'll be nice to have something positive to think about while I'm going through the next few days."

CHAPTER TEN

As Doc headed north on US 81, he called Bill to check in with him. "How is it going Bill, any news?"

"Hi Doc, no news, not much happening. I have been doing some more research on potential contacts in Asia and have identified some people that we should try to meet. I'm having the appropriate US government embassies invite them to upcoming events. How did your speed dating weekend go with Bev and Shannon?"

"Bev and I had a great time, did some horseback riding which she loves; me not so much. We ran into a bear on the trail and Bev scared it off using two large rocks that she banged together. Scared the crap out of me. We had some gourmet dinners and relaxing time at the spa, overall, a great weekend.

Shannon and I hit it off at dinner. I think over time, it could develop into something very special."

"What the hell does 'very special' mean?"

"I haven't had time to process it fully yet. I know that some barriers came down between us and that we have both agreed to see each other more often. We've overcome the issue of her dating a customer of the hotel and friend of her boss. Sean has given his blessing in his inimitable style, and I think already sees himself at our wedding either as my best man or giving her away. As they say, it's early days, but I feel good about the start we've made. She is one lovely lady not only to look at but also as a person. I may go back down again next weekend to spend some time with her."

"I thought you were going to spend next weekend at the Brockville place doing some serious fishing."

"I'll see how it goes and decide later on in the week. What about you, isn't this the week that you're meeting Linda in Jamaica?"

"Yes, I'm on a flight to Montego Bay with a transfer by resort bus to the Jamaica Inn at Ocho Rios. It looks like a beautiful place online, Linda's been there before and thinks it's terrific so we should have a good time."

"I'm sure you will, pass on my regards to Linda; she's a sweetheart."

"Will do, see you in Bangkok next week."

Doc pulled in to get a coffee and decided to stay off the phone and to use his car-generated ion changes thinking about Bev, Shannon and his return to Asia. He didn't need to think much about the balance of this week in Ottawa. Unless something big happens, it should be relatively routine, lunches, coffee meetings, dinners and cocktail parties with lobbyists, Asian government consular officials and a few prominent Canadian business people with interests in Asia.

As he by-passed Syracuse, NY, he decided to change plans and stay over at the Brockville place then head up to Ottawa early the following morning.

At the cottage, Doc checked his new secure email site and saw that there was a message from Bev saying that she received the call from the doctor in Zimbabwe. She had left already and would contact him with an update on her uncle's condition as soon as she arrived.

He decided to head out fishing. On his way, he ran into his neighbor and friend Gary Morrison. Gary had lived next door since Doc first remembered coming here. Along with his Dad, Gary had taught him much about the river including how and where to fish it for best results. Over the years, Gary had become sort of an unofficial caretaker of Doc's cottage. He was mechanically inclined and knew his way around carpentry and a little plumbing. He wouldn't touch electrical, fearing that any mistake in his work could result in a fire. Doc liked Gary a lot and was happy to have him as a friend and neighbor. Doc could relax as he traveled knowing his cottage was in good hands.

"Hi Gary, what's new?"

"Hello, Donovan, not much new around here. My arthritis is having one of its flare-ups, but I guess that's to be expected. Your cottage has been mostly fine. I had a little trouble with a leak in the roof but fixed it up.

That account at Beaver Lumber that you opened for me sure works well when something needs fixing. Some teens drove down your driveway. I think planning on swimming off your dock or maybe taking your boat for a ride. I went out to see them carrying Old Thunderclap, and they decided that some other place might offer better swimming."

Gary named the new Mossberg Persuader 12 gauge shotgun that Doc sent him on his last birthday, "Old Thunderclap".

Gary had a key for the Ottawa condo and periodically took his wife Barb there for a few days so she could go to parliament and see the politicians in action. She loved politics; Gary loved the big screen TV and well-stocked beer fridge in the condo, so it worked out just fine.

"Come look at the new motor I bought us for the boat." Gary's boat had succumbed to old age a few years back, so Doc had insisted that they share Doc's boat since he was hardly ever at the cottage these days.

"Wow it's a beauty," Gary said admiring the shiny new Honda.

"Yeah and it's a four stroke, no more mixing oil."

"That'll be much easier, thanks, Doc."

"Why don't you go to the boat show in Toronto and see if there's a fishing boat that you think will be good for us.

If you see something say around 18 feet, get Pete down at the marina to order one in, deliver it, put it on my account and give this one to the sea cadets."

"Are you sure Donovan, don't you want to see it first?"

"You know more about fishing boats than I do

so you pick one out. Make sure it's a good one with all the bells and whistles and don't try to skimp to save me money."

Gary had other plans, so Doc took the boat out to his favorite weed bed and casted his fishing line just short of the weeds. He sat back, relaxed and kept one eye on the line.

He got a few hits but no keepers and decided to pack it in for the day. He had hoped that Sean might have called today and kept checking the cell phone for incoming messages but to no avail.

The next morning he left the cottage at five o'clock and was in the shower at the condo by six thirty. Refreshed, he dressed in a business suit and headed for his office with a short stop to pick up a coffee and croissant to go. He had a few phone messages from Asia, but due to time zone differences, he would have to wait a few hours to call them back. He spent the morning on the phone with various Ottawa-based Asian diplomats and was heading out for a luncheon at the Consul for Indonesia when his cell phone rang.

The screen showed that the call was from the O'Leary Arms, and Doc didn't know if he wanted it to be Sean or Shannon. It was Sean.

"Hi, Doc, have you got a minute?"

"You bet, what's up?"

"I've decided to accept your offer and to proceed with the agreements. I'll work with

Anne, and we'll be ready for some serious

discussions on the weekend. We'll also have the terms of the consulting agreement and the management contract."

"Oh, that's great Sean. It's a big load off my back having you with me on this, and I'll see that you are well compensated. Anne as well if she decides to come on board."

"I'm going to have dinner with her this evening and will tell her all about it. Unless it's located on the far side of the moon, I'll bet she's on board. By he way where is it located?"

"It's in a fantastic mansion in Zimbabwe."

"Zim what?"

"I'll give you all the details on the weekend and we can finalize the agreements for review by your lawyer."

"Ok, I'll have my lawyer standing by so he can read them over once we have them done. I'll also have my secretary available all weekend to type up the documents. I want everything done so I can get started while you're cavorting around Asia."

Doc was now running a bit late, so he took a taxi to the luncheon. After lunch, he returned his Asian calls and then called Shannon at the hotel.

"Ok its on, I'm coming down Friday and returning Monday morning."

"Oh that's great news Doc, I can hardly wait to see you."

"Likewise, why not make us a reservation for dinner. I'll probably get in around five or so, and Sean will want to have a drink, so let's make it for eight o'clock."

"Want Carmella's again or would you like to try something else? There's a good seafood house, 'The Galloping Oyster' that just opened and is getting rave reviews."

"I'm leaving it in your capable hands. I loved Carmella's, but I wouldn't want to go there if she doesn't let me pay the bill. I'd feel like I was taking advantage of her generosity, and that's not my style. It's great if she comps your dinners when you go there alone, but if I'm along, we pay."

"Ok, I'll talk to her. If we're going to be seeing more of each other, it would be nice to have Carmella's as our special place and I'd want you to feel comfortable there."

"What do you mean, "IF we are going to be seeing more of each other. There is no IF about it as far as I'm concerned."

"You're right, there is no IF from my side either."

"I'll see you Friday then. Have a good week."

Just then, Doc's cell showed a message telling him to check his secure email. He logged on to the secure site and read a message from Bev.

Hi, Doc: my uncle died today, comfortable in his bed on the land he loved. I made it in time to hold his hand while he passed. He was in a deep coma and didn't even know it was happening. As per his instructions, he will be buried tomorrow in a plot he pre-selected on a lovely hilltop on the grounds.

It will be a very small service, just his employees

here at the property and a few very close friends. His lawyer told me his instructions are to oversee the transfer of all the assets to me right away. They have been working on this aspect of the financial considerations ever since it became obvious to the doctor that my uncle's death was rapidly approaching. So the lawyer has all the documents prepared, and asset transfer will take place right after the service tomorrow. It's safe to proceed now so get Sean going on the consulting and management contract arrangements. I have thought about it, and he is crucial to our business development plan at this time. Keep well, I'll email tomorrow when all is signed.

Best, Bev.

Doc sent off an email to a realtor friend, Art Chandler, in Hong Kong letting him know that he would be in and out of Hong Kong over the next few weeks and would like to view some apartments to lease. He specified that he wanted three bedrooms with en suite bathrooms, a room for a live-in housekeeper or amah and a home office area. In total around 2,000-2500 square feet with a deck and view of the harbor. Doc was thinking that Bev should have her own room for when she visits and Bill will probably stay with Doc when he's in town. It didn't matter if it was on the Hong Kong side or the Kowloon side, only that it be in an upscale building with security. He specified which days he planned to be in Hong Kong but cautioned that business matters might change some of these dates. He told Art that as usual he would be at the Mandarin when he was in town.

He did a little online research and sent off emails to several Hong Kong-based international law and accounting firms with offices in Zimbabwe. He explained that he would be in Hong Kong on four days next week and would like to meet with the Managing Partners of the firms. He then checked out the reputations of these firms with emails going to senior Hong Kong-based executives that Doc had known for several years and trusted to give him the straight goods on them.

Doc was told once that while Hong Kong is densely populated, the business community is close knit so any firm with a bad reputation would be well known.

The next day Doc met with his boss, Jim to update him on current events in Asia and to discuss his plans for the next month. "I'll spend some time finding accommodation in Hong Kong in between trips to business meetings. I've given a realtor I know some specifications, and he'll prepare a list of places to see. One problem with Hong Kong is that real estate, is very expensive, and tends to turn over quickly. So when you find the ideal place, you have to move fast."

"I'm sure you'll find something with the generous housing allowance you've been given."

"I'll let you know how the search is going

once I've had a chance to look the market over. But I agree, I have a pretty good housing allowance so I'll find something suitable. I have a few things to handle here then I'm going to head down to the states for the weekend and be off to Hong Kong on Monday."

"The States, I thought you would be heading to the cottage."

Doc thought about it and figured a female interest would be a good reason for him to be spending time in the States.

He said, "I met this lady in Scranton and we hit it off. I might be visiting there frequently when I'm able."

"Well good for you, I know from experience that meaningful relationships are hard to find and even more difficult to keep when you are on such a heavy travel schedule. But I'm happy for you, it would be nice for you to have someone to come home to."

"Thanks for your positive thoughts. We know it will have its ups and downs, but we're ready to give it a try. See you in five weeks."

Doc went home having done all he needed to do at the office. He decided to leave for Scranton now with a stop over in Brockville. He wanted to talk to Gary about some renovations to the old place and figured he could get them started while he was away.

An hour and a half later he pulled into the

long driveway that went to his cottage. He had called Gary from the car, and he was ready, fishing poles all maintained, gas tank full and the engine warmed up. Doc put his overnight bag in the house, quickly changed into his fishing clothes and headed for the boat.

As Gary expertly maneuvered the boat out of the shed and pointed her towards the weed bed, he said, "She runs great with this new motor. I had her out a few times, even did a little trolling. She trolls real nice, slows right down to barely making way and so silent you sometimes think the engine has stopped."

"That's good to hear, I think it'll serve us well, particularly when we get the new boat. Let's drop anchor and get the rods in the water. There's something I want to talk to you about."

They got organized, and Doc said, "You know that I've been thinking of some renovations for a while now. Well, I think it's time to get on with it. I want to do quite a bit, so it's going to involve several trades. I would like you to take on the role of general contractor. You would deal with the building permit process, oversee the archi-tect, hire and manage the carpenters, plumbers, electricians and drywall people. It's going to be a lot of work so you may want to think about it for a few days before you answer."

"Funny, not two weeks ago Barb and I were talking, and she asked me if I thought that you would do the renovations soon. I told her that I had a feeling you would get to it pretty soon.

She asked if I would do the work and I said no, this project will call for pros, but I'd sure like to oversee the work. So no need to think, I'm in."

"That's good news. I want you to meet with the architect; we'll use Peter Gladstone so get him to send us a proposal. You can fax it to me, I'll sign it and transfer the retainer into his account. As soon as he has the preliminary plans done, send me a copy and send a copy to Shannon O'Sullivan at this address."

He handed Gary a business card from O'Leary's Arms. "Shannon is a close friend and will do the interior design. She may also give advice on the exterior design if so, please see that the trades listen. I'll give her your number in case she wants to talk to you directly. As to the nature of the renovations, I want two new large bedrooms both with en suite bathrooms. Put an en suite in what is now my bedroom. One of the new bedrooms should be large, say twenty feet by fifteen feet. It should have a wood-burning fireplace and be on the end facing the river with a sliding glass door opening onto a deck that will wrap around all the sides that have views. Totally renovate the kitchen. Shannon will design this. Put on a new roof and all new hardwood flooring throughout. Obviously follow the engineer's advice and do whatever needs to be done structurally. We are talking about mostly a new cottage but take care to have it retain its charm. Oh yeah, while you are at it, get rid of the boat shed and replace it with a boathouse.

Be sure that all parties are aware that you are

in charge and that Shannon is your assistant. Between you and me, she may well be the lady of the house one day. That should cover it."

The shocked look on Gary's face was priceless.

CHAPTER ELEVEN

As Doc drove down Highway 81 to Scranton, he turned off his cell phone. The seeds he planted yesterday were bearing fruit today, and his phone calls were mounting up. Rather than trying to deal with all the communication while driving, he decided to press on to Scranton. He was on the road by eight a.m. and thus far was making good time, so he expected to be able to deal with all this communication from his hotel room.

He was glad that he got the ball rolling on the renovations to the cottage, but he wanted to leave the execution of this to Gary and Shannon. He now had a lot on his plate and didn't need to be distracted from the major issues.

Shannon was surprised when Doc came through the hotel door at eleven forty-five. "Hi Doc you must have left early, I didn't think we'd see you until late afternoon."

"Hello beautiful, I wanted to get here in time to buy you lunch, can you get away?"

"Sure, I usually go for an hour, but I'll stretch it a bit today. Do you want to eat in the pub?"

"No, let's go somewhere else, for now I think it best that we keep a low profile at the hotel."

"Give me a minute and we'll go to the 'Hello Deli,' it's three blocks away."

When Shannon came back to the lobby, Doc could see that she had made a stop in the ladies to freshen up and let her hair down, the way he liked it.

"You look super," Doc said as they walked briskly down the street. "Why are we moving so fast?"

"Thank you, you look good too, and you'll see why we are moving fast in a minute."

She led them around a corner and turned sharply into a laneway.

"Is the restaurant down this lane?" Doc asked.

"No but this doorway is."

She brought them into a small alcove where people on the street couldn't see them. "I've been waiting for this all morning," she said as she wrapped her arms tightly around him and kissed him fully on the lips.

"Wow, now that's what I call a welcoming greeting," Doc said when they came up for air.

"That's just a preview, wait until we get home and I have a little taste of Brandy to share with you."

Doc had decided on his way down in the car, that he would get Shannon involved in the cottage renovation for several reasons. She was damn good at interior decoration; she would enjoy the task, and it would give them yet another reason to communicate while Doc was away. Doc's philosophy was to always act quickly to remove stuff from his full plate.

Over lunch Doc said, "I've some business to handle with Sean."

"I know, he told me that he was doing something with you that would result in you being here more often, but he wouldn't elaborate. I got the impression that he was attempting to make sure that I would wait for you if I knew I'd be seeing you more."

"I hope you'll wait for me because you will be seeing me more. Here are two keys, one for the Brockville cottage, and one for my condo in Ottawa. I'd like you to do an interior decorating job on both if you want."

"I'd love to, but I can't guarantee that it will be done quickly because I never let my decorating business overshadow my job at the hotel."

"There's no rush. I think you should first have a look at the two places, take photos and measurements, then think about it and do some planning. The Ottawa condo will be the easier of the two because it's strictly an interior-decorating job. Brockville is a major renovation. I've hired my neighbor and friend Gary as the general contractor for the renovation, but I want you involved in all of it from design to completion, working with Gary and Peter Gladstone, the architect. They are what you would call, 'good ole' boys.' They've lived all their lives there, so they're plugged into the construction side of things and can get a project done on time and budget.

You should approach it like it's your house that you're renovating. I want to feel your presence every time I go there, and I would like it if we could spend a lot of time there together in future."

"I'm overwhelmed. You seem to have a way of doing that to me each time we're together."

"If I can get my business with Sean wrapped up by tomorrow afternoon, why don't we take off for the cottage and spend tomorrow night there so you can get a feel for the place? Sunday we can do some sketching and photography, and I can introduce you to Gary and Barb. Sunday afternoon we can go to Ottawa and spend some time at the condo, and then Monday morning I'll get you on a flight to Scranton as I take off for Hong Kong."

"That works for me; I wasn't planning on doing anything this weekend except spending as much time as possible with you. I'll let Sean know that I'll be back Monday around noon, I don't think he'll object."

"I can guarantee you that he won't object. At some point, maybe after my return from Asia, we should come out of the closet with Sean and the others at the hotel so we can relax more around them."

"I was thinking the same thing. Let's give it some thought while you're away."

After lunch as they walked back to the hotel Doc said, "I've got a lot of work to do this afternoon plus a meeting with Sean. Did you talk to Carmella?"

"I did and she understands completely. She seemed pleased that we might get together. It seems that everyone around here either thought

I was gay or at least destined to be an old maid."

As they approached the laneway entrance, Doc took hold of Shannon's arm and led her to the doorway. She laughed and looked at him with a mixture of happiness and warmth as they kissed.

After checking in, Doc went to his suite and began returning phone calls and reviewing emails.

Sean had left a note saying he and Anne would be available at four o'clock in the executive conference room if that worked for Doc. If not, he should call and set a time. It worked; so Doc didn't have to do anything but show up.

He had emails from the Hong Kong business people he had asked about the law and accounting firms he was considering. They both were highly thought of and passed with flying colors. Doc was very pleased with this news and immediately sent a copy of the email to Bev with the subject bar message "Another piece of the puzzle looking good."

The realtor's email confirmed that he would have suitable places to see next week.

There was an email from Gary with several questions that Doc handled. He also added the news that he and Shannon would be arriving Saturday evening or Sunday around noon depending on how his meetings went in Scranton and, if possible he would like to introduce Shannon to them.

Doc's cell rang and the display showed a call from Bev. "Hi, Bev how are you holding up?"

"I'm ok, but I've been working all through the night to complete the asset transfer. The size of the estate was a little larger than I thought; we now have $417 million USD cash and securities in the kitty. We have to get moving because I worry about having this much capital lying dormant in banks earning little or no interest. I'll feel a lot better once we have it invested in diversified projects in several countries. How are things at your end?"

"Good, as you will see once you get to your email. I've identified a law firm and an accounting firm, both with offices in Zimbabwe. I've vetted them with highly placed Hong Kong contacts, and they both check out. I'll meet with them next week in Hong Kong and, if all goes well, I'll retain them and let you know. On another front, I have a realtor looking for a three-bedroom apartment. My thinking is that you could have one bedroom for your exclusive use so you could set up a home office and leave personal items for when you are in Hong Kong. Does that seem like a good idea?"

"Perfect, at least for now."

"Get some sleep and we'll talk in a few days."

Doc felt that the afternoon had gone well and decided to take a short nap before his meeting with Sean and Anne.

He woke just in time for a quick shower and headed for the meeting room.

As he entered the room, he greeted Anne with a brief hug and shook hands with Sean. He poured a coffee and took a seat around the beautiful circular table that Sean had custom made from old growth Eastern Red Cedar.

Sean opened the conversation saying to Doc, "Anne, and I are anxious to learn more about this development, what can you tell us?"

"Ok you've been patient with me, so I'll fill you in and answer your questions then hopefully we can discuss the terms of our relationship. I am afraid that I must ask you to continue to keep this project strictly confidential. If the agreements are signed, I'd like to head back tomorrow."

Doc got up and refilled his coffee before getting started.

"As you both know, I presently work in international business development for an Ottawa-based software developer. What you don't know is that I recently entered into a business partnership with an old friend from university. She and I did both our MBA and law degrees together.

Recently she has come into a substantial amount of money as well as a beautiful mansion on a 1,900-acre property with all the facilities that one would expect in an excellent resort. The problem is that the money and assets are in Zimbabwe, a country with very strict currency restrictions. I've come up with a way to legally get the money out. First we'll renovate the mansion to five-star standards. Then we'll hire and train the necessary staff to run it at a five-star level. There are presently about seventy-five employees working on the property and in the mansion. We want to give these workers preference in the hiring process, however having said that we will not interfere in hiring or any other hotel-type management decisions. I specify hotel-type management decisions because there will be other management decisions that we may either make ourselves or hire an administrator to make for us. The term for the 'master company' that Bev and I will own is 'incubator.' Our company will help start-up companies grow.

There will be no conflict because, as you will see, the hotel side of the property is distinct from the business operations side, unlike a regular resort. Think of this project as a hybrid, half five-star resort, and half operating business. As a business, it will resemble a very hi-tech university campus, occupied by highly skilled, software developers.

Each developer is writing software that will be the property of independent start-up companies. These companies will be half-owned by the developer and half owned by Bev and I's master company. As each of the software developers, resident at the resort, completes a new software package, he or she will send it via secure email to my office in Hong Kong. We will then market the software worldwide and retain the profits in Hong Kong. Eventually, all my partner's money will make it to Hong Kong this way. Ok fire away, I'm sure you have questions."

Anne went first, "Doc, how will we get our guests?"

"Good point. You won't have to get them; we'll recruit them from various places such as existing software development companies, universities, and colleges worldwide. They'll undergo a vigorous vetting process before being selected to participate in our incubator. I suspect that once word gets out, applicants will inundate us. What a software developer needs is a peaceful place to work and live as well as the latest equipment. We are looking for the exceptionally talented developers that have strong entrepreneurial ambitions. The good ones would much prefer to be in their own business however most of these people are smart enough to recognize that they don't have the training or skills to be independent business people.

We'll give them a full package of development support in terms of food, beverage, and accommodations, with the bonus of living a first class lifestyle at the resort. They will have the latest and greatest computing equipment at their disposal. When they produce, they will enjoy the financial rewards of their efforts through the fifty percent stake they will have in the start-up company. We will provide offices, sales, marketing, secretarial services, accounting, tax support and all legal work required. The developer is free to do nothing but create software and watch their companies make money. Naturally we're hoping that some, if not most of the developers will stay with us and continue to develop software for our shared companies."

Sean said, "Let me get this straight. We will not have any responsibility for getting guests; you'll fill all the rooms by yourself."

"Yes, your job is to run the facility so that it has the appearance and feel of a Relais & Chateaux resort. The guests are to be treated as you would treat a guest here at O'Leary's. I think that if we treat guests like you treat them here, they'll want to stay on and work with us."

Anne, ever the practical finance person said, "What is the operating budget to be?"

"The budget will be up to the both of you to develop. The only input we'll have is to say that we do not want any expense spared.

Remember, your management will, to a very large degree impact the developer's decision to continue with us or to strike out on their own at some point.

The earning potential for the work of these people is astounding, and it's renewable."

"I don't know about you two, but I could do with a wee nip, only two fingers since we're working," Sean said. He went to the wet bar at the back of the room and got the drinks tray he had set up earlier. Doc thought about Sean's comment about pouring two fingers. When Doc mentioned the generous measure he received when Sean poured, Sean's answer was, "I can't help it if I've got fat fingers."

"Anne, would you like something?"

"Sure fix me a Jameson's, I might as well be one of the lads."

"I don't need to ask you if you want a drink Doc, but I do need to cure you of the nasty habit of putting ice in with fine whiskey. It must be a Canadian thing, what with all the snow and hockey and such."

Once they had their drinks Sean said, "I for one now have a much better understanding of the situation, how about you Anne, as GM do you have anything else you need to know?"

"No, not for now. Maybe I'll have some more questions in the morning."

Doc said, "Do you both have time to continue with our discussion of the terms of your agreements, or would you rather do it in the morning?"

Sean looked over at Anne, who nodded signaling a willingness to continue.

Sean said, "As I mentioned to you I would want Anne as GM, and she has agreed, so here are the suggested terms of her contract." Doc scanned the agreement, more of a letter of understanding and handed it back to Sean.

"Agreed," Doc said, "next."

Sean handed the outline of the management contract to Doc. As he accepted it, he asked Sean, "Has your lawyer seen this yet?"

"Yes and he's standing by to make any required changes as soon as we get back to him."

Doc read over the terms and heads of agreement.

"I'm happy with the five-year term, renewable by agreement by both sides. I would like to include a clause covering the employment of existing staff. Most of them have been with the family all their lives and my partner's uncle would have wanted them to stay. How about this, Anne will interview all the staff and determine which of them can be trained up to five-star level. These people will be given jobs in the mansion as Anne sees fit. The others will be given jobs around the property somehow, maybe we can start farming some of our food and or raising livestock.

Let me worry about that part, you determine who works inside, then hire additional staff if necessary. Aside from that, the only other change I want to see is in the remuneration arrangement. You have suggested a fixed fee of $500,000 USD to include a salary for Anne. Also, we pay all operating expenses. I want this changed to a base compensation of $1 million not including Anne's salary, which will be part of the operating expenses. Put in the contract that operating expenses are to cover whatever you two need to make this work at the level we want. Also included is the first class airfare for you Sean when you wish to visit the property. And return first class airfare and all expenses for Anne twice a year for R and R anywhere in the world she wants to go."

"This is most generous of you Doc," Sean said.

"Yes Doc it is a very generous arrangement

for us," Anne said.

Doc went on, "I just thought of an incentive arrangement that I want to include. We will pay a bonus of $1,000 USD per month for each month that a guest stays after they have stayed for one year. So if we have 60 guests, which is our initial capacity, and they all stay on after the first year, you would get an additional $60,000 a month in bonus. You do have to understand, and it will have to go in the contract, that we will be letting some guests go if we feel that they are not performing.

These guests will be replaced. But you need to know about this requirement for them to pro-duce.

"Because, due to no fault of yours, the non-productive guest will not be there after a year. This will not help your bonus situation. Is this clause clear to you both?"

They both agreed that it was clear and Sean said he would have the lawyer draw up the final version for signing in the morning.

"I take it you have plans for dinner Doc," Sean said.

"I do in fact have something planned, a very urgent and important matter to attend to."

"How come you're heading back tomorrow, I thought you would drag things out to spend another evening 'attending to urgent and im-portant' matters?"

"I'm taking the 'urgent and important matters' with me to my cottage, then to my condo in

Ottawa as she will take on some urgent and important renovation work for me."

"Oh I see, when can I expect to have her back?"

"How about Monday afternoon?"

"Get out of here and enjoy your evening, we'll see you at breakfast for the agreement signing. How about here in this room at say eight o'clock?"

"How about we say nine o'clock?"

CHAPTER TWELVE

When they arrived at Carmella's they were shown to their table near the fireplace and Carmella said, "Welcome back Mr. O'Connell and of course Shannon you are always welcome as well."

"It's great to be back, Carmella and I'm looking forward to another excellent dinner. One thing though, please call me Doc. I think being called 'mister' makes me sound old."

"Sure thing Doc. Let's get your drink order going and then there's someone I want you to meet."

Doc looked at Shannon and said. "What's your pleasure in the drinks department this evening?"

Shannon said, "I feel like something exotic, why don't you show the bartender how to make a Nassau Nightie Remover?"

"Will do. Let me take care of this and show him how to pour two fat fingers of Laphroaig while I'm at it, be right back."

Carmella said, "I'm pleased that you both enjoy the restaurant enough to become regulars. I want to introduce Doc to Luigi. I'll go and get him."

When Doc returned, he had a Nassau Nightie Remover in one hand and a generous portion of Laphroaig in the other. He gave Shannon her drink and turned to face Luigi, apparently the chef, according to his attire.

"Doc, this is Luigi, our executive chef," Carmella said.

They shook hands and Luigi said, "We have a unique service for select regulars." He handed both Doc and Shannon his business card and said, "My direct email, phone and fax details are on the back. If you lose the card, just remember my email luigi@carmellas.com. Contact me with any special requests; if possible, give me a few hours notice and I will prepare any dish you desire. I only ask that you both keep this between us as I can't accommodate a lot of people, even our regulars."

Doc said, "Thank you, Luigi, I'm sure we'll take you up on this offer, and I promise not to abuse the privilege."

Left alone, Doc said, "Nice people, it's no wonder you like coming here."

"Yes they've always been good to me and I feel comfortable here even by myself as I usually am. I always get this table, Carmella drops by and talks to me, and they know my favorite dish, so I don't even need the menu most of the time."

"Are you ready to head north in the morning?"

"I'm all packed and ready. I just have to let Sean know that I'll be late on Monday."

"That's taken care of; I spoke to Sean about it at our meeting."

"Oh good, that's one thing off my plate."

Despite the balmy weather, the waiter lit the

wood fire for them, and they stared at it while taking a drink. They placed their dinner orders, and the waiter put a basket of bread and a dish of dipping oil on the table.

"Speaking of your plate, as you know Sean and I are doing some business together and, if you're interested, there's going to be some interior design work required."

"Of course I'm interested, tell me about it."

"There are still a few details to be worked out that I need to talk to Sean about in the morning, but I'm pretty sure that he'll agree with me on this. However, I do think the protocol would be for me to talk to him before saying too much to you. I can safely say that I want you involved in the project, and I insist that everything between us be open and above board. There is, at least for now, a requirement for confidentiality. I want to get this project well underway before any potential competitors decide to copy us. You'll understand all this when I tell you the whole story in the car tomorrow."

"I'm thrilled that you want me involved and will be pleased to work with you in whatever capacity you see fit."

Dinner was delivered along with a bottle of Shannon's favorite red wine, La Cour Pavillon compliments of Luigi.

As they ate and enjoyed the gentle warmth and soft light provided by the fire, Shannon said, "I'm excited to see your cottage on the river. I'm sure the Ottawa condo is lovely, but I have this image in my mind of us diving off the dock. Do you have a dock? Swimming in the river, sipping wine on the porch and getting up early to catch some perch for breakfast. Do you have a fireplace?"

"There is a dock and fireplace, but I want one in the new master bedroom and another outside on the porch. That will be all up to you to decide."

"What about the budget for this project."

"Whatever it takes to achieve the look and feel we want. I say "We" because I want a place that you love and where you wish to spend a lot of time. It's a reasonable distance from here and as you'll see tomorrow it's a pleasant drive with lovely scenery and good roads. Even when I'm away, I want you to use the cottage as if it is your own and go there to relax whenever you want. The property it sits on is about five acres with fifteen hundred feet of waterfront, so it is worth far more than the old building that's on it. I do want to preserve some of the character of the existing cottage, more out of nostalgia than anything else. I never plan to sell the property so it's worth it to create a mostly new home that will last a long time."

Shannon placed her hand on his and looked at him with her lovely green eyes. And said, "That's a very generous offer," "I'll do my best to create a warm and cozy atmosphere at the cottage. It's exciting to have a place where we can escape to and feel that it's our private hideaway."

They paid the bill, and Doc left a generous tip as the service, food and atmosphere was as close to perfect as he had ever experienced.

They walked to Shannon's place arm in arm; Doc said, "I sure hope you have some of that fabulous kissing brandy left. What brand is it again?"

"I bought a new bottle to make sure we don't run out, I'd hate to see you give up kissing me for lack of brandy and it's called St. Agnes XO."

"Have no fear, that's not going to happen. Let's stop at the store where you bought it before we leave town tomorrow, I want to get a case to keep at the cottage."

" Case! You certainly have plans to do a lot of kissing there."

"There is something about the river, country forest smell and the porch fireplace that leads me to think that we'll use up a lot of brandy. Which reminds me, make sure there's a very comfortable hot tub on the porch facing the fireplace and very private. I have a feeling that the Nassau Nightie Removers and good old St. Agnes will work their magic."

"I don't think I'll even have any nighties to remove, but I agree a hot tub will be very enjoyable. I'll place it so that it's open to the stars with a canvas roll out awning that will afford protection from the rain, how's that sound?"

"Perfect, I can hardly wait to sit in the tub with the fireplace burning."

They arrived home and Shannon, without

asking fixed them snifters of brandy and went into her bedroom.

"I've been saving this for a special occasion she said as she came back into the living room in a sheer red nightie that almost matched the soft red of her hair. For this, you don't need a Nassau Nightie Remover. A sip of St. Agnes and a kiss and it will disappear like a Siegfried and Roy tiger."

They awoke in each other's arms at eight o'clock and showered together before heading over to the hotel for breakfast. Doc said, "Give me about fifteen minutes alone with Sean and Anne and I'll come out and get you."

"Sure, I'll go to the pub and have a latte while I wait."

"Doc went to the meeting room and greeted Sean and Anne, "Are the agreements ready for signature?" Doc asked.

Sean handed them to Doc, who looked them over and signed them without any changes.

Doc said, "Ok with the formalities out of the way, it's official, Sean your company now has the management contract to run the property and Anne, you are the general manager.

Have you two given any thought as to who will take over here to replace Anne?"

Sean said, "We've decided to promote Shannon to the position of general manager, that is if you are going to leave her here long enough.

What do you think?"

Doc said, "I think it's a great idea, but she will

need a very capable assistant as I expect that she'll be doing some traveling. For instance, I'd like her to take on the interior decoration of the mansion in Zimbabwe and as I mentioned I'd like her to deal with both my places in Canada."

"Have you talked to her about this?" Sean asked.

"I mentioned the decor jobs on the cottage and condo but nothing about her position here. That's clearly within your purview and, so we understand each other, in our arrangement with the management of the Zimbabwe mansion, my partner and I will not interfere or second-guess your decisions. You two make it work. So if all is agreed, let's invite Shannon to join us so you can fill her in."

When Shannon joined them, they ordered breakfast brought in and filled their coffee cups.

Doc said, "We've made some decisions this morning that impact you and which Sean will discuss with you in a moment. There is a bit of a story behind all this, which I'll fill you in on as we drive to Brockville. Sean, you have the floor."

Sean said, "I've signed a management contract to manage a property that Doc and his business partner have in Zimbabwe. It'll be converted to a five-star hotel, and Anne is going to be the general manager. I would like you to take the position of the general manager here. I know this is all very sudden, but we need to move quickly and confidentially, as Doc will explain on your drive. We also want you to take on the decor of the mansion as we want it done to the same standards as O'Leary's."

Shannon looked at Anne and said, "First of all congratulations Anne on your promotion. You've been a great friend and mentor, and while I'll miss you here, at least we'll still be connected through the management company. Sean, you've been almost another father to me and have given me the opportunity over the years to learn how to run a fine hotel. I'd be proud to be the GM of O'Leary's."

As they finished up breakfast, Doc said, "As you all know, I'll be away in Asia for about four to five weeks. While I'm away, I'd like to see progress being made. I think an initial visit to the mansion in Zimbabwe is a good place to start. There are lots of guestrooms, and excellent food will be available.

A car from the property will pick you up and deliver you to the airport. The car and chauffeur will be available to you while you are there. You just need to arrange your flights. As a suggestion, perhaps you, Sean should go over for say two weeks. Anne, you might want to go with Sean for the first week, and then come back to relieve Shannon so she can go over for the second week. You all can meet everyone you want including the architect and building contractor and Anne you can interview all the existing employees. My partner, Bev Patterson, is there now resting a bit after dealing with her uncle's death. The sooner you could go over the better, so she can make introductions to the appropriate parties. When you know your travel plans, I'll talk to Bev and get her to start the ball rolling over there."

Sean said, "Anne and I will develop a plan over the weekend and discuss it with Shannon on her return. We'll then send you an email with our travel details and outline any other pre-visit questions that we may have."

Doc said, "Sounds like a plan, does anyone have anything else for now?"

Both Anne and Sean said they were satisfied for now. Doc said, "Well ok then, we'll hit the road. I want to pick up a case of St. Agnes XO then we are on our way."

Shannon blushed so that her skin almost matched her hair and turned her face away as she stood up to leave.

"A case of brandy, why would you want that?" Sean asked.

"It's a long story, my neighbor in Brockville loves it, and you can't buy it there," Doc said as they headed out the door."

When they were safely in the Mustang Shannon said with a grin, "That was mean of you to embarrass me like that, I might just punish you by refusing to drink any brandy this evening."

Once they bought the case of St. Agnes, and Doc had the car on Route 81 north, he filled Shannon in on the details of the project. She was an excellent listener and didn't interrupt his thought process, holding her questions to the end.

"I think that about does it," Doc said. "Why don't you hit me with your questions?"

"There are two different but related issues at play here. One concerns business and one is about our relationship. Let's start with business, as it is probably less complicated. First, I want you to know that I appreciate you asking me to get involved with the interior décor of both places in Canada and the mansion in Zimbabwe. Incidentally, we need to come up with a name for the place; we can't keep calling it 'the mansion in Zimbabwe'; it has no connotation of Africa to it.

It needs a name that invokes wild African lands alive with all kinds of wildlife, something picturesque; something that might have been dreamt up by Wilbur Smith.

I'll think about it and get back to you. I know as well that you had some influence over my appointment as GM and for that I am also very grateful. I understand the concept you have in mind and the nature of the property and feel that I can do an interior design job that will fill the bill. I can hardly wait to see the Mansion and start to develop my plans for it with the architect. Any thought or questions so far?"

"No, I think your interior design talent speaks for itself judging by what I have seen at your home, Carmella's and O'Leary's. I look forward to seeing your magic at work both at my Canadian places and the so-called, 'mansion in Zimbabwe'. As far as the promotion to GM goes, admittedly I did play a small part at least by agreeing with Sean's decision, but it was Sean's decision. I wouldn't try to impose my will on his hotel management style."

"Shall we stop for a coffee before we go on to the next topic, I need to pee and don't want that to distract my thought process for the next round of talks?" Shannon asked.

"Good idea, I could use a donut as well."

They came upon a rare sight, a relatively clean and cheerful roadside coffee shop. "I hope they have donuts," Doc said.

After the rest stop and equipped with coffee and donuts to go, Doc said, "Carry on with the next round of your issues discussion. Let's get everything out on the table."

Shannon said, "I want to draw a clear line between our business and personal relationship because they are becoming intertwined in my mind. I want you to understand that we can have one without the other. I mean that I would still wish to work with you even if we were not bed buddies. So let's clearly understand that if you decide that you no longer want to be in a close relationship with me, I would still like to be your friend. I'd still want to welcome you at O'Leary's. I'd still want to work on decorating projects with you. I don't know what your relationship is with Bev Patterson. She's been friends with you for many years. It's all right for you to tell me that your relationship with Bev is none of my business. I guess I'm a little confused. This morning was the first time I heard you mention her name."

Doc didn't say anything for a long time; he just focused on the road. Shannon was starting to think that maybe she had said something that he took the wrong way, but she remained silent as well. After a few minutes, they came to what Doc was looking for, a scenic lookout. He pulled in, shut off the car and got out. Shannon also got out of the car and stood there looking at him.

Doc said, "You're right, Bev and I have been good friends for many years and recently have become business partners, but we are not lovers and never have been. In the MBA program and law school, we found that we worked well together.

In both schools we were in the same study groups and our complimentary skills brought a certain synergy to all the school projects we worked on together. As I told you, she came into a fortune when her uncle died. She is sharing that fortune with me for helping her get the money out of Zimbabwe, so we decided to become business partners and to bring our complimentary skills together to create a new company. I was going to save this next part of the talk for the front porch of the cottage. But since it's pertinent to our discussion, and in the interest of getting everything out on the table, I don't want to wait until we get to the front porch of the cottage.

CHAPTER THIRTEEN

Doc took her into his arms. He gazed into her lovely eyes and said, "I thought you might get the picture when I suggested that you plan the cottage as if it were your own, but let me make it clear. I love you, and I would like to have an exclusive relationship with you. What do you say?

"Even with my no sex until our wedding night rule?"

"It won't be easy but yes, whatever you want, I just want to be with you."

Kissing him warmly again she looked into his eyes and said, "Yes I love you too and want to be with you and with you only."

They returned to the car and headed north again, each lost in their thoughts about the new divide that they have crossed.

Finally Doc said, "What are the rules, do you want me to get you a ring or something?"

"No, just love me and spend as much time with me as you can."

"That's exactly what I thought when I asked you to be with me exclusively. We should live together when we can, either at the Ottawa condo, the cottage or your place in Scranton."

"I agree, let's give up the charade of you sneaking back into the hotel to mess up your bed at five a.m. We want to be together and to sleep together as much as we can. If you agree, I'll speak to Sean about it since he is such a great friend and boss. Let's come out of the closet."

"Yeah, talk to Sean. I know he'll be so happy for us that he'll be planning the wedding. When the time comes, that's not such a bad idea. Right now, we've both got a lot going on but once things settle down we'll consider how we want to spend the rest of our lives, and I hope it's together."

"I agree; I'm at my absolute happiest when I'm with you."

Arriving at the cottage, Shannon was overwhelmed with the beauty of the property, the old cottage and the river full of islands.

Doc said, "It's just like the salad dressing, Thousand Islands. Come on in and I'll show you around."

They did a tour, and Shannon immediately started seeing the renovation plan taking shape in her mind.

Doc said, "Do you have one of those computer programs on your laptop that allows you to do the drawings of the floor plan?

"Yes, it's called CAD for computer assisted design. Let's take some measurements and we can lay out a rough draft of a floor plan before dinner."

They got the tape measure and started by taking the measurements of the existing layout and entering them into the computer. Then Doc told her what he'd been thinking in terms of additions and renovations and Shannon went to work with the CAD program and entered what Doc had been thinking.

"We'll save this as 'Doc's plan 1' if you think it's the way you have been envisioning it."

Doc looked at it, made a few changes and said, "Ok that's it, that is what I've been thinking."

"Why don't you prep dinner while I play with it a bit?"

While Doc was in the kitchen, Gary knocked on the door.

"Come on in Gary, there is someone here I want you to meet. Shannon this is my friend and neighbor, Gary."

"So this is the future lady of the house you were telling me about Donovan, pleased to meet you, Shannon."

At the "future lady of the house" comment, Shannon went as red as Chairman Mao and looked at Doc as if to say with her expression that they would be talking about this later.

"I'm pleased to meet you, Gary, would you like a drink?"

"No thanks Shannon, I just wanted to meet you and see if you two needed anything."

Doc said, "No we're ok, we brought steaks with us for tonight and we'll be heading up to Ottawa around noon tomorrow. Maybe in the morning we can get together, introduce Shannon to Barb and go over the preliminary interior décor and design plans so you can pass them on to the interested parties."

Gary said, "Ok we'll drop by after church around ten if that's all right."

Doc said, "Sure ten would be good, we can go over the plans and do a walk through before we head out. The key thing is that you and Shannon have met so when she shows up or calls you, she won't be a stranger."

Gary said, "Have a nice evening folks, I'll see you in the morning."

Once Gary was on his way, Shannon looked at Doc and said, "Lady of the house, where did that come from?"

"I was trying to explain to Gary that you might, one day, possibly be here a lot and so he should take your thoughts regarding the design and construction seriously as if they came from me. I'm pretty sure I didn't refer to you as the future lady of the house. But so what if I did, frankly as far as I'm concerned, after our talk today, you are the lady of the house. Aren't you?"

"I suppose I am, it just shocked me because I've never been the lady of the house anywhere but at my house."

When Doc looked at the plan that Shannon came up with, he had to agree that it would be nicer than the one he had planned. The best idea she had was to include a master bedroom fireplace that could be seen from the king size bed, the hot tub on the porch and the master bedroom soaker tub in the ensuite bathroom. Doc said, "Now that is ingenious, you know how I enjoy wood burning fireplaces and this design will allow us to enjoy it from three different places. I love it."

After their triple A, thirty days aged, medium rare, rib eye steaks, they spent the evening walking around the exterior and interior of the cottage and discussing the plan. They looked into the boathouse and put together some thoughts for this building. Doc felt that they should make it a doublewide house capable of holding the fishing boat and a 50-foot cruiser in case they decide to buy one. By bedtime, they felt that they had talked everything through. They decided to sit on the porch and enjoy the sights and sounds of the river at night.

"Do you ever go skinny dipping from the dock?"

"Usually I have been here alone, so skinny dipping doesn't often occur to me."

"You're not alone tonight, feel like a dip before bed?"

"I'll race you in," Doc said as he started to undress. Shannon was way ahead of him and ran down the lawn shedding clothes until naked, she ran out the dock and jumped in the river. Doc followed her in and surfaced right beside her, he took her into his arms, and they kissed hungrily.

Shannon said, "I didn't expect the water to be cold this time of year. I'm freezing, let's get out."

As they dried off, Doc asked, "How about a bonfire to snuggle up with?"

"Now that's a brilliant idea, I'll get into some

warm clothes while you build the fire."

Doc had a blaze going when Shannon returned.

Shannon said, "The next time we come up here, let's bring some marshmallows."

"I've got some, wait and I'll get them." Doc went into the cottage and after a few minutes came back with a dozen marshmallows and two long bar-b-q sticks.

Shannon asked, "Where did you get these?"

"I keep some in the freezer and thaw them in the microwave for just such an emergency like this. When you're single and spending a lot of time here by yourself, it pays to use the freezer creatively."

When the marshmallows were gone Shannon said, "Let's see how that bed works for two, I could do with some serious spooning."

When Doc opened his eyes in the morning, Shannon was holding her head up resting on her arm and staring into his eyes. "I've got it," she said, "it came to me in the middle of the night."

"You've got what, Doc asked?"

"I've got the name for the mansion, soon to be campus/resort, in Zimbabwe."

"Well don't keep me in suspense, what is it?"

"Lion's Pride."

"It's brilliant, Wilbur Smith eat your heart out, I love it! It says wild Africa and will appeal to our creative software geniuses. Let's have breakfast at The Village, my favorite little restaurant in town then call Sean to tell him. You tell him, it's your idea. I'll be talking to Bev in a few days, and I'll run it by her, but she always leaves the creative stuff to me; she is a left brain type."

They showered together, dressed and headed for The Village. Doc must have known half the customers and the staff treated him like family. "I can see why you love this place and Brock-ville. It's a lovely community and just the right size for a relaxing cottage type environment, I hope we spend a lot of time here."

"That's the plan. You'll see, if you come up here in two weeks and come into The Village by yourself, they'll treat you like family because they know you're my friend."

They headed back to meet Gary and Barb at the cottage. Shannon and Barb seemed to hit it off right away, and Barb was amazed to see Shannon's computer drawings of the proposed floor plan. Barb said, "This computer design stuff is fantastic, would you show me how to use it when you're back and staying for a week or two?'

Shannon said, "I'd be happy to, it's not that difficult once you get used to it."

Doc, Gary, Barb and Shannon did a walk around and discussed several key issues. Gary had a few questions that Doc and Shannon cleared up for him. Gary asked about a couple of major points and was surprised when Doc deferred to Shannon's opinions. He also was impressed with the instructions Shannon gave him for the rest of the design and construction team. Doc just smiled as Shannon talked to Gary as if she was the lady of the house. Barb could tell as well, that she was going to be seeing a lot more of Shannon from now on.

They drove leisurely up to Ottawa stopping for lunch in a rustic looking diner in Kemptville near Ottawa. After lunch, Doc suggested a quick tour of Ottawa with a drive-by of the major tourist attractions such as the Parliament buildings and the beautiful Rideau Canal.

Doc said, "It's possible to take a boat all the way down the Rideau Canal system and end up right at our dock."

The reference to 'our dock' wasn't lost on Shannon. She still couldn't get over the fact that she and Doc had made a serious commitment to each other although just thinking about it gave her goose bumps.

She looked at him and said, "Let's do that trip at some point when things slow down a bit."

"Good idea, I have always wanted to take a boat up the canal, we'll do it someday."

They arrived at Doc's condo building, and Shannon was impressed with the location, building quality and security, including a doorman. When they'd had a quick tour of the condo itself, Shannon loved it.

She said, "Wow, I wasn't expecting this. I figured you for a small bachelor pad in a middle-class building since you're hardly ever here."

"I hit a downturn in the market, just as I finished university and the developer was having difficulty selling the condos. It was still quite a stretch for me at that time but in retrospect I'm really glad that I bought it. The market has taken off in Ottawa, and it's worth a lot more than when I got in. The quality of the building is such that maintenance is a breeze. I like the security system with the private, lockable garage. And I have a neighbor who looks in on the place now and then and brings in a cleaning service the day before I am due to arrive. So it truly is a lock up and go situation, I never have to worry about it or my precious car, safely locked in the garage."

"What are your thoughts about the interior decor here?"

"I don't have anything specific in mind and wasn't even thinking about doing anything here until I walked into your place and saw the difference between it and this place. Yours is warm and, at the same time relaxing, whereas here I don't feel anything like that. Maybe yours feels warm because you are in it, and it has nothing at all to do with the décor."

"You have a way of saying the sweetest things Donovan O'Connell, just one of the reasons I love you."

"I think the best instruction I could give you is for you to treat this place like it's your own. From now on, as far as I'm concerned, it is your place. So decorate however you like, just try to achieve that same homey feeling I get at your Scranton place."

"You mean our Scranton place, don't you?

After all, if you want me to feel at home here and at the cottage, you also have to feel at home at our Scranton place, deal?"

"Deal. I've just had an idea. As far as this place goes, let's put it third in terms of priority. The cottage is second, and first is Lion's Pride so don't buy any furniture for the cottage or here unless you come across something that knocks you over. Keep tabs on the cottage renovation but let Gary do his thing, I guarantee you won't be disappointed.

Get Lion's Pride done and then we'll take a vacation and furniture-buying trip to Ireland. We'll visit all the quaint little shops in Dublin, Cork, and Killarney and see if we can find pieces that we want for the cottage and here."

"I've arrived at the same conclusion. First priority is Lion's Pride. I think it'll take the Brockville gang a bit of time to get started on the job. I'll go there maybe next week. I'll call Gary and ask him to set up a meeting with the architect, builder and trades so I can make sure that they're on track. Then I'll leave it to Gary. I suspect that I will probably get the heavy part of the Lion's Pride job mostly done in fairly short order if it looks anything like I imagine. The rest will involve overseeing the work and some final touches."

"All this talk about Ireland has got me craving corned beef and cabbage how does that sound for dinner?"

"Sounds good to me as well, can we find an

authentic Irish pub like O'Leary's?"

"Not quite up to O'Leary's, but there is a nice Irish pub that knows their way around a corned beef brisket and they fly in fresh kegs of Guinness daily from the old sod."

"It sounds to me like it could become our local. If they have a dart board, I'll give you a few lessons."

Doc turned on his Irish brogue and said, "You're full of malarkey, Colleen. I can hit a fly at 50 paces."

"That may be the truth you're speaking lad," Shannon replied in her Irish brogue, "but we won't be shooting at flies now will we?"

The pub lived up to their expectations. The food was excellent, the atmosphere was very Irish and they both felt at home there. Shannon won eight out of ten games of darts before Doc conceded defeat and vowed to get some practice in before they meet again. They'd walked from the condo, a pleasant ten-minute stroll, by some of Ottawa's nicest historical buildings. Doc took her home by a slightly different route, taking advantage of another street full of historic buildings.

"I like what I see of Ottawa so far Doc. It is a blend of the old and the new and I love your condo."

"Whose condo?" Doc asked with a distinct emphasis on the word 'Whose'.

"Oops, I forgot, not your condo but our condo."

"That's better. "

When they returned to the condo, Doc said, "You can sit on the deck and gaze at the stars for a bit. I'm going to book your flight home for the morning."

Doc came back from his home office and walking out on the balcony said, "There's good news and bad news. The good news is I could get you a flight in the morning. The bad news is that it departs at six a.m., so we have to be at the airport by five.

More bad news, you have a three-hour layover in Newark so you won't get to the hotel until after one o'clock."

Shannon said, "There's no need for you to drive me to the airport, I can grab a taxi, and you can get more sleep."

"No, I want to be with you for as long as possible, so I'll drive you and stay with you until you board. Besides, don't forget I'm flying to Hong Kong tomorrow, so I'll have lots of time to sleep on the plane. My flight doesn't leave until one o'clock so I'll come back here and take care of a few last-minute details then be on my way. Tomorrow will be the first time I've left on a long Asian trip and didn't want to go. It's the first time I've had to leave someone I love."

"It's called missing someone Doc and I'll miss you a lot. I don't have anyone I love except my parents and now you, who leave me for extended periods. Try to call, Skype or email whenever you can. I know it'll be hard to communicate with our travel schedules but let's try."

CHAPTER FOURTEEN

When Doc got back to his condo, he was aware of a feeling that he had never experienced before. He couldn't quite identify what it was, but he knew that it had to do with the fact that he was here alone. No, not just that he was here alone, but that Shannon was gone, and he wouldn't see her again for five weeks. He walked around the apartment seeing the places where she had been, remembering her happy chatter and longing just to hold her tight and never let her go.

He thought he'd check in with Bev and give her an update as he had a lot to report.

He checked the time and saw that it was eight o'clock in Zimbabwe, so he dialed her number. "Bev speaking," she said in her brisk, official sounding, Canadian Consulate voice.

"Hi kid how is it going, any news?"

"Hi Doc, I was just thinking about you. I'm having a glass of lovely red South African wine and trying to bar-b-q a steak, your favorite, rib eye. But I'm having difficulty convincing the chef that I'm quite capable of doing it myself. I think he may be afraid that if I do my cooking, he'll be out of a job."

"How are the employees handling the loss of your uncle?"

"Better than I thought they would. They haven't been their usual happy selves, but they seem to be handling it a little better each day. What's new at your end?"

"A few things actually. I've signed the management contract with Sean O'Leary and he has appointed a GM, Anne Watson, as well as an interior designer, Shannon O'Sullivan, the same person that did O'Leary's Arms. They'll probably call you in a few days to set up a time to come over."

"Sean already called. He and Anne are arriving on Wednesday. Sean expects to stay for 2 weeks and Anne will return after one week to allow Shannon to come over for a week. These time frames are estimates at this stage until they're able to assess the situation here first hand. I'm going to arrange meetings with them and the architect, contractor, and main trades. Anne wants to interview the employees; she told me of your desire to keep them on, one way or another, for which I am grateful. She also wants to have meetings with the leading executive search firms with hospitality industry experience and my uncle's secretary is arranging that."

"I asked Sean to move quickly in terms of getting over there while you are still available to show them around and make introductions. Both he and Anne are so pleased to have this project to run that they will do anything to help us get it underway efficiently. We've been referring to the place as 'the mansion in Zimbabwe.'

For marketing purposes, we felt that it should have a proper wild African resort name.

Shannon came up with 'Lion's Pride.' What do you think?"

"I think it is super! Thank her for me."

"Speaking of Shannon, there's something I need to tell you. I've fallen in love with her, or I should say, we've fallen in love with each other. I didn't want you to hear about it first from Sean or Anne."

"Doc I'm thrilled that you have finally found someone and I wish you both all the best. Have you popped the question yet?"

"No, we're moving fast but not that fast. We've agreed to have an exclusive arrangement and to live together as much as our crazy schedules permit until we're in a position to do something like getting married. I think it's safe to say that we're both thinking about a permanent relationship in the long term. Aside from her part time interior design business, her full-time position has been the resident manager at O'Leary's and she's taking over as GM this week replacing Anne. I think you're going to get along well with all three of them."

"I'm sure I'll love them all. If they're friends of yours, they must be good people and so they're friends of mine as well. What's the next step in our plan?"

Doc said, "Once the preliminary planning is done, we can go ahead and get started on the renovations side. As part of the renovations, we need to include a state-of-the-art computer system for the software developers.

From a funds availability perspective, it would be best for us to source this equipment in Zimbabwe. I'll talk to my friend in Silicon Valley and get him to suggest a top computer consulting firm. Without revealing the location of our project or the details of exactly what we are up to, I'll get them to design a top-notch system and to develop an equipment list. You can use this information to get quotes from local suppliers. You should also look for the best installer. It would be great if you can get all this done by the time I come there in five weeks. Speaking of five weeks, how are you doing in terms of being away from the office?"

"I was going to tell you. I ended up quitting my job. I explained to them my actual situation and told them I was sorry to leave without any notice. I offered to come back for a month or so while they replaced me, but my boss told me to stay here and be on top of things. He said that Linda could take over for me and they can replace Linda out of Ottawa."

"That was nice of him; he could've made life difficult for you."

"Yeah, he's always been a friend and I'm grateful for his help at this time when I need it."

"Are you getting any rest after all of this?"

"Yes, I'm ok. The staff has been terrific; they treat me like a princess and won't let me do much of anything for myself. I've been spending some time at poolside with a good book and am getting lots of sleep. In a few days, I'll be ready for the visit from the management team and look forward to meeting Shannon. I have to tell her what a lucky girl she is."

"Don't do that, I already told her."

"Have you talked to Bill recently?"

"Not since he went to see Linda. How about you, have you talked to Linda? Should we be dusting off the best man and maid of honor duds?"

"Unfortunately no, things didn't work out for them in Jamaica. I'll let Bill fill you in."

Saying goodbye to Bev, Doc considered calling Bill but wasn't ready to hear his bad news yet. He was still on a Shannon induced high and wanted to think about nothing except her red hair and green eyes all the way to Hong Kong.

There was only one other first class passenger on the Cathay Pacific flight so they had a lot of room, excellent service and a chance to talk. It turned out that he was the senior vice president of a tobacco company heading for Korea after some meetings in Hong Kong. Doc invited him to the Wednesday evening cocktail party at the Canadian Club and he agreed to meet Doc there. Doc didn't have many contacts in Seoul and thought it might be a good idea to develop some. In Asia, you never know when you're going to need someone.

The flight was uneventful and arrived on time. Doc was met by a hotel Bentley and whisked away to his suite at the Mandarin Oriental. He took a long hot shower to help his body start to recover from the flight. Sitting in the very thick bathrobe that came with the suite, Doc called his realtor, Art Chandler, to see what was lined up for the next day.

"Hi Art, how goes it?"

"Hi Donovan, welcome back to Hong Kong. I have four flats to show you, two tomorrow and two the day after. They meet most of your criteria. How about if we see one of them in the morning and one in the afternoon? If you have time we can have lunch at the Aberdeen Marina Club, which is close to the first two suites I'll show you. Are you ok with a ten a.m. pickup?"

"Perfect Art, I'll see you tomorrow."

He then called Bill at his office. His secretary said he was in a meeting so Doc asked him to call back when he could.

Next he called the office of Sir Anthony Kosztyo, Managing Partner at the law firm of Kosztyo, Wong, and Butterton. Of course, he was busy, and as is customary in Hong Kong, his secretary asked Doc where he was staying and how long he will be in Hong Kong.

He said he would be here all week, staying at the Mandarin Oriental and was referred to Sir Anthony by a mutual friend, Kevin James of Jardines.

He then called the office of Lau and Porter Chartered Accountants and asked for an appointment with Dr. Lau, the Managing Partner. He got the standard Hong Kong questions as to where he was staying and for how long. This time he invoked the name of Phillip Waters of the Hong Kong Shanghai Bank.

This tradition of leaving a referral name was in place because senior executives didn't return phone calls without it if the secretary didn't recognize the name of the caller. They were too busy to be bothered with every junior business-person trying to make it into the big league that was Hong Kong business. In addition to being referred by a well-known senior Hong Kong businessman, the other piece of information that helped to get a call back was the name of the hotel that the caller was staying at. The Mandarin Oriental guest had a far better chance of getting a call back than someone staying in a three-star hotel off Nathan Road in Kowloon.

With Doc's referrals and his Mandarin Hotel address, he knew he'd hear back in short order.

Just then his phone rang. He picked it up and said, "Donovan O'Connell speaking."

The voice on the other end said, "Big deal!"

Doc said, "Hi Bill and it is a big deal, how is it going?"

"Some things are good, others not so much."

"Tell me the good news first."

"That group in Thailand bought a software package, the whole ball of wax. Also, we are looking good for a sale to the Malaysian outfit we've been working on."

Making sales were code words for the Special Forces taking down a drug operation as a result of intelligence passed on by Doc and Bill. The reference to "the whole ball of wax" meant that the entire chain from processing the drugs, to shipment to North America had been taken out. It's a grand slam that'll make a lot of people in Gucci loafers at the DEA and RCMP very pleased indeed.

"Wow, finally a jackpot," Doc said.

"Yeah, it appears that some of the sales presentations we made over the last few years are starting to generate sales. Our sales managers are quite pleased with us right now, probably a good time to hit them up for a raise."

"Not altogether a dumb idea. We'll celebrate at your favorite Thai restaurant. Your expense account or mine?"

"I think it's your turn."

"You got it, what's the bad news?"

"Well, things didn't work out with Linda in Jamaica. We booked for four days but left after one night. We simply were not compatible. At first I was upset naturally, we enjoyed each other in Nassau and probably would have in Jamaica if we hadn't tried to get intimate. That was a huge bust, I ended up on the couch for the night and flew back to DC in the morning."

"I am sorry Bill, I was hoping that you would hit it off and maybe become a couple eventually."

"What about you and Shannon?"

"Are you sure you want to talk about it?"

"Of course, how is it going?"

"We've decided that we're in love with one another, have agreed to be exclusive and are moving in together."

"Oh, Doc I am so happy for you both. When you say "moving in together" exactly where are you moving into?"

"Well, we'll be in three different residences. Formerly her apartment in Scranton, formerly my cottage in Brockville and formerly my condo in Ottawa."

"What's with all the formerly stuff?"

We've decided that her apartment is now our apartment, my cottage and condo are now our cottage and condo."

"Boy, you two are serious."

"Serious as an alligator looking for his wife in a handbag shop."

"Is she going to keep working at the hotel?"

"Not only that, she's been promoted to GM of O'Leary's Arms, one of the top three properties in Pennsylvania. Have you still got that jeweler contact you told me about?"

"Yeah, Mr. Lo, my mother's cousin, he has the shop in the Regent Kowloon. Why, do you need a watch?"

"No. I thought I might drop in and look at some engagement rings. What do you think, should I use you like the proverbial friend who sent me?"

"I'll do one better than that. I'll send him a text that you're coming in and are like a brother to me. Give him your business card and he'll give you the best quality products at family prices."

"Ok thanks but tell him I may not make it this

trip because I have a lot on my plate, but will be in to see him at some point shortly. I'm mostly house hunting this week, but I met an interesting guy in first class on the way over. You know how we've been saying that we need to increase our market penetration in China, Taiwan, Japan, and Korea? Well, this guy is a Senior VP of a tobacco firm in Seoul. I've invited him to a reception at the Canadian Club tomorrow evening so I'll try and develop him as a potential customer."

When Doc hung up with Bill, his message light was flashing. He had return calls from both the law and the accounting firm managing partners and decided to call them back as he wanted to arrange the meetings for this week.

"Hello, Dr. Lau"

"Hello, Mr. O'Connell and welcome to Hong Kong."

"Thank you, sir, I was wondering if we could arrange to meet at some point this week. I am a partner in a new company in the software business, and we are opening a Hong Kong office. I have heard good things about your firm and would like to see if your services might work for us."

"Certainly, do you have time at say ten a.m. Thursday?"

"That would work nicely, thank you. I'll see you then."

Doc then called Sir Anthony Kosztyo and had a similar conversation with a meeting arranged for Friday at three.

He decided that he would go for a swim in the hotel's quaint old style swimming pool on the top floor. He loved the opulence of the pool area and the fantastic service provided by the white-jacketed attendants. He always felt like some early day Taipan in this hotel and particularly in this pool area.

After the swim, Doc went for the full spa treatment including, steam bath and massage that he had booked at check-in. After a quick visit to his room, he was off to what in his opinion was the best bar in Asia. The Mandarin Oriental's Chinnery Bar was reminiscent of a London men's club and features a hundred and nine types of single malt whiskeys.

Doc had tried probably half of them over the years and with his move here will no doubt make short work of trying the other half. The thing that always amused Doc about this bar is its location. Unless you know where it is, or asked a staff member, you would have a hard time locating it.

Doc figured that they were trying to keep out the riff-raff like those that were so uncouth as to drink blended whiskey. The steak and ale pie was second to none, and Doc's mouth had been watering for it since his flight lifted off from Canada. While enjoying a two-finger measure of an obscure whiskey that he couldn't pronounce the name of, he had a phone brought to his table and called Shannon. Waiting for the call to go through he thought, "This bartender has thinner fingers than Sean."

When she picked up, he said, "Hi love how are you?"

"Hi sweetie, I'm fine. I just got in from work and have been sitting here, thinking about you and the commitment that we made to each other. It just happened so fast that it's only now sinking in. Remind me again, did we actually commit to an exclusive relationship?"

Doc said, "Well, I did and I thought you did, don't tell me I was wrong."

"No silly, I committed to it as well and I'm thrilled that I did. I love you and miss you already. I have on one of your flannel shirts, and I can smell you on it."

"Oh I'm sorry, throw it in the wash and it'll smell fresh."

"I don't want fresh; I want you. It gave me an idea though. We should put some clothes and toiletry items for both of us in all three places, so we can just pick up and go without having to lug around stuff."

"That's an idea, let's do that when I get back but let's do it with laundered clothes. How did the first day as GM go?"

"Oh, it went fine. Anne is a great mentor and spent the weekend putting together files and comments on how to do everything so I could run the place like a paint by numbers set if I want to. I don't want to, but her precise, "how to" booklet will be a big help, particularly starting

Wednesday when Sean and Anne are going to Lion's Pride.

"They loved the name and have both already ordered business cards for the three of us with, 'Lion's Pride Resort' printed on them. The cards have what looks like a picture of the MGM lion after an all-nighter on the town with a much younger lioness and a substantial supply of catnip."

"I spoke to Bev about us; I felt that I should give her a heads up before Sean and or Anne spilled the beans. She was delighted for us and wishes us well. She wanted me to pass on her thanks for coming up with the Lion's Pride name; she loves it. Have a good sleep and I'll talk to you tomorrow after I look at a couple of flats as they call apartments here. I'm in room 820 at the Mandarin Oriental, my room phone direct line is 852-2522-0820, and I'll be here until Saturday when I am heading to the Mandarin Oriental Hotel in Bangkok. I'll get the number there to you once I check in. Bye, love."

CHAPTER FIFTEEN

Art Chandler was a long time resident of Hong Kong where the average expat lasted about three years before returning home to reality. An American from the Midwest, he had been here thirty-two years. He started off as a cub reporter for the South China Morning Post before graduating to a "talking head" job on TVB, one of the English-language television stations. He ended up with a real estate sales position at Longman's Estate Agents where he had built a successful career over the past twenty years or so. He knew his way around Hong Kong real estate and for many years had been chairman of the Hong Kong Realtors Association. Always prompt, his chauffeur-driven Mercedes arrived at the Mandarin main entrance at ten a.m. Doc was standing outside, enjoying the mass confusion that was the norm for his new home and thinking about how far away this life was from his quiet retreat on the St. Lawrence River.

As Art emerged from the back seat, he extended his hand in greeting and said, "Good morning Donovan, it's good to have you back in Hong Kong. The beautiful young ladies have missed you around the Canadian Club and American Club soirees."

Hello Art, it's good to see you as well. Shall we go in for a coffee or do we have to get there early?"

"There is no rush on my part, let's have a coffee and get caught up."

Even though the early morning breakfast rush was over, they had to wait a few minutes at the entrance to the Clipper Lounge before being shown to a table.

They ordered coffee and pastries, and Doc opened up the conversation, "Since we last met, I have had a few adventures and have acquired a nickname to which I've grown accustomed. I've been christened "Doc" by a couple of my eloquent colleagues. Where it came from is a long story, suffice to say they incorporated my initials D, O and C to commemorate a rather lengthy stay in the hospital. So from now on it's Doc, please."

"What caused the lengthy hospital stay?"

"I was accidentally shot while big game hunting. I've since given up this sport entirely. I haven't even shot a game of golf, never mind a deer."

"Just as well, you never could play golf very well. So, you said you were moving to Hong Kong on a company transfer, what brought that on?"

"Our business has been growing steadily particularly in South East Asia.

The general wisdom, thought up by our unwise leaders, is that I could strengthen our presence in Asia by being here more or less full time and spending less time as an astronaut."

An astronaut was a term for Hong Kong

Chinese, who moved their families overseas but remained working in Hong Kong with frequent visits to see their families, some making the grueling trip monthly.

As they finished their coffee, Art said, "Are you sure you're going to need a three bedroom place? As you know, rents here are high compared to back home."

"I want a three bedroom place for several reasons. I've started living with a lady named Shannon back home and she'll be coming over occasionally to visit. I have a business colleague working with me in South East Asia and another in South Africa. From time to time, they'll be working with me here in Hong Kong for brief periods, maybe a week or two, so I want them to feel at home in my new place. We will want to use the flat as a home office while they are here as well so, as you see, I need some space."

"Ok, so three bedrooms it is and preferably a home office space as well. I got this message from your email but just wanted to confirm. I don't want you fainting when I tell you the rents."

"My employer has given me a very generous expat package as an incentive to get me to move here so don't worry so much about the rent, just find me a suitable space."

"Let's head out and I'll show you a nice flat in Repulse Bay, we can continue to talk in the car."

Art said," Repulse Bay is upmarket and favored by senior expats you'll like the area."

Doc said, "I have been thinking about my other needs covered by my package including an amah and car with driver. My thoughts right now are to do without the live-in amah and just get a cleaning service to come in weekly for a day. I love to cook, and I don't know how comfortable I'd feel with a stranger living in a room off the kitchen."

"This may change over time as you get used to seeing other people with live-in amahs. For now why not try your idea of a cleaning lady once a week. If you like, I can get my secretary to source one for you."

"Yes please, let's get the ball rolling on that once we've decided on the flat."

As the Mercedes pulled up to the porte-cochere, the doorman hurried over to open the rear door and welcomed them to Repulse Bay Towers.

Doc said to Art, "Didn't he say towers with a 's'? I don't see any other towers."

"There aren't any. He may be embellishing a bit to make you feel like it's a grander development than it is. Although it is pretty grand."

Doc said to the doorman in Cantonese, " After we see this tower, please show us around the other tower."

The lobby of the building was done up like a five-star hotel and the overall level of quality extended to the building exterior and extremely well maintained grounds.

Doc said, "Very impressive, let's get a look at

the flat."

The flat was a spacious three bedrooms and den with amah's quarters and a large deck overlooking the bay. Everything in the apartment was high quality and very well maintained.

"It comes fully furnished, all you have to do is bring your toothbrush and clothes and move in." Art said.

"I think this is just great, the area is very quiet by Hong Kong standards and it's an easy drive to Central and Wan Chai for business, what are we looking at for rent?"

"The asking price is HK 75,000 a month, about $10,000 USD. Rent includes all expenses, hydro, cable, internet, and a phone line."

Doc said, "Let's talk about it over lunch, you mentioned something about the Aberdeen Marina Club."

Doc had been to the Aberdeen Marina Club on several occasions. He was always impressed with its blend of quality and ambiance and the extensive variety of recreational facilities such as a magnificent swimming pool with swim-up bar a la Nassau.

It has a huge exercise gym featuring every instrument of torture the personal trainers could dream up. There are ten tennis courts, four restaurants, a pub, a formal lounge, mahjong rooms, card rooms for poker, a golf driving range, a bowling alley, and a beautiful 400-berth marina. The whole place had a view of the three floating restaurants, featuring the Jumbo, which was anchored permanently about 200 yards off the marina. The club was owned and operated by the famous five-star, Shangri-La Hotel group. It was a Shangri-La resort property without guest rooms.

As they sat on the deck overlooking the pool and marina Doc said, "I think I'll join this club. I've always liked it and I'd like to spend a lot of time here. What do you say, Art?"

"I've been a member for years and spend a lot of time here with my family. The kids love it, and my wife takes advantage of the classes like mahjong and tai chi also regular exercise and yoga classes. She's been on my case to use the gym. If you join, we could work out together and maybe having a work-out partner would be the motivation I need to get on with losing weight."

"Let me think about that. I get two club memberships as part of my package, why not this place as one and the Hong Kong Club as another?"

Art said, "A few years back I seem to remember some flack in the newspaper about the Canadian government giving memberships to senior officials. They defended the need for a club membership here on the basis that Hong Kong is a hardship post. Now I agree that life here can be stressful, the city was rated at one point as the third most stressful city in the world after Bagdad and Belfast, which at the time were both war zones. I think Hong Kong is a great place to live. I love the hectic atmosphere, the air alive with deals, the people, for the most part, are nice. Overall it's exciting like no other place I've ever seen. I saw a movie where the lead actor says something like, 'You take 5 billion USD here and 5 billion USD there and pretty soon you are talking serious money.' That struck me as the essence of Hong Kong thinking. Stateside a 50 million dollar deal is seen as significant; here it won't get you a returned phone call."

They ordered lunch and had a fruit punch while they glanced over the marina. Doc said, "I've been wondering what to do about transportation. Should I buy a car, take taxis, get a car and driver, what do you suggest?"

"If your package includes a car and driver and you intend to make frequent trips to Central or over to Kowloon then that would probably be the way to go."

"What if I were to buy a car?"

"You could, lots of people do, but they are very expensive, with an import duty of one hundred percent. So your $50,000 Mercedes in Ottawa is $100,000 here. The worst part though is traffic congestion and lack of parking in Central, Wan Chai, and Kowloon. In my case, my car is also my office as I am always on the road, so having a driver accomplishes a couple of things. It allows me the freedom to talk on the phone and to work on my laptop while in traffic. Often there isn't any place to park, so my driver drops me off and either drives around continuously or finds a spot on a side street somewhere. When I want the car, I just call him, and he picks me up. Someone with nothing to do calculated that if all the cars and trucks in Hong Kong were to be on the road at the same time, they would be bumper to bumper and traffic would come to a complete standstill."

Doc said, "You know, I won't need a car and driver because when in Hong Kong, I'll work mostly from home. So I guess taxis are the answer."

Lunch arrived, and they carried on talking.

Art said, "A lot of people use taxis exclusively. They're relatively cheap and efficient. The MTR as you know is an efficient subway and again relatively inexpensive. In your case, I'd suggest taxis or as an alternative I can set you up with a car service that you can call and order a Mercedes and driver."

"What does this service cost?"

"They have two types of cars, a regular Mercedes sedan or a stretch limousine. The regular sedan is $25 USD an hour the limo is $35.

The main advantage of the service is no waiting in taxi line-ups, which at certain times of day can be brutal. The service cars are much more comfortable, particularly when you get caught in long traffic tie-ups. Also, they will bill you by the month, so you do not always have to fiddle with cash."

"I like the service idea. Please set it up."

"Shall we visit the next flat?"

"Sure let's go."

"The second flat is near Stanley in the same general area of Hong Kong, as Repulse Bay is."

"I've been there on one of my trips. I went to Stanley market. Lots of tourists, an American woman, asked me how to get to Chinatown."

They talked as the chauffeur drove, and Doc kept one eye on the scenery.

As soon as they arrived, Doc could tell that this building was not as upmarket as the first, but he kept quiet until he saw the flat. It was a pleasant flat, like the first one, well maintained and had a great view, but Doc preferred the Repulse Bay one.

"How much for this one?" Doc asked.

"They are asking HK 68,000, about 10% less than the first one. The difference here though is that they might negotiate whereas the people that own the first one are very firm."

"I don't know Art, at this point I think I still want to see what else you have lined up, but I am kind of partial to the Repulse Bay Towers. I have a meeting tomorrow morning near my hotel. How about meeting there at noon, I'll buy lunch at Chinnery's then we can go and look at the other two flats?

"That sounds good. As I said before, if you like Repulse Bay, you'll want to move fast, so you don't get scooped."

Art dropped Doc back at the Mandarin. He went to his room, changed into his bathing suit and went up to the pool for some laps. In most major cities in Asia, the smog was so bad that jogging outside was out of the question anywhere near the downtown core. He liked to jog and preferred outdoors to indoor tracks. He made a mental note to ask Art about jogging in Repulse Bay. He was looking forward to seeing the other properties that Art had lined up to show him. But there was something about the Aberdeen Marina Club that was sitting in the back of his mind, just out of reach.

Returning to his room, he had some email to read from Bill, so he took his laptop and went down to Chinnery's to read and to respond. Handling email was so much better with single malt in a crystal glass. As he walked in, the bartender recognized him and said, "Good afternoon Mr. O'Connell, it is nice to have you back with us."

"It's good to be back Carleton, where are we on the list?"

"Let's see, you are at number 47 which is Aberfeldy 21, shall I pour you two fingers on ice?"

"Thanks, Carleton, I'll have it at my usual table if I may."

"Of course sir, coming right up."

Doc was pretty sure that Carleton wasn't Carleton's real name. It sounds like his interpretation of an English butler's name. He knew it wasn't uncommon for Chinese to change their names, sometimes several times. One of Doc's closest friends was a Hong Kong-born Chinese who moved to Canada at one point. Arriving at Vancouver, he was told by the customs officer that his real name was too difficult so he should adopt a western name. He asked the customs agent what the name of the guy who had just passed through immigration ahead of him was. The agent looked it up and said "Puchanski". My friend said he would take it, so for years this Chinese guy was called Tom Puchanski.

After his drink had arrived, Doc sat back enjoyed a sip and read his email from "head office" in Ottawa.

Doc's boss, Jim, was just letting Doc know how happy everyone at the head office was with these great sales taking place in Southeast Asia. "If this keeps up your bonus will look pretty good this Christmas," Jim said.

Doc answered back that he had spoken to Bill about these sales and was looking forward to generating some more over the next few weeks. He updated Jim on his housing search and told him he would talk to him in a few days.

Next he read Bill's email but it was just a repeat of what he had said over the phone, Doc didn't feel that Bill was expecting an answer. Next order of business was to check in with Shannon. He decided to go to his room for the call. He went into the room, sat in the overstuffed leather chair and placed the call. Shannon answered with a warm greeting for Doc, "Hi love, I hoped it was you, I miss you a lot."

"Hi sweetie, how are you doing? I hope I didn't wake you."

"No, I had a busy day and was going to go to bed early but thought I'd give it a while longer in case you called. I ended up drifting off on the couch. What did you accomplish today?"

"I met with my realtor friend, Art and looked at two flats. I loved one, and the other would do, but it just didn't have the same pizazz. I've got two to look at tomorrow afternoon and a meeting with the potential accounting firm for Lion's Pride."

"Speaking of Lion's Pride, Sean and Anne are on their way to Zimbabwe, they're in the air as we speak. It's exciting. My first day as GM by myself and waiting to hear from Sean and Anne about their reactions to Lion's Pride."

"How is the hotel staff taking the changes in management?"

"Amazingly well. Before they left, Sean and Anne called a full staff meeting in the banquet room to tell them all about it. Without me knowing, they turned it into a celebration of my promotion party. Sean had Carmella's cater the food so our kitchen staff could join the party. Carmella's group served the food and even brought their mobile bar. Carmella announced that her restaurant was pleased to cater this event as a gift to honor my promotion. Sean said that was fine, as long as O'Leary's provides Carmella's Restaurant Christmas staff party on the same basis. Everyone agreed. They brought in Champagne and toasted the Lion's Pride management contract and me. The staff asked if there might be opportunities for them to work there if they wanted to. Sean said he would think about that but certainly there would be the need for some training of new staff whether it is done here or in Zimbabwe. It was a super party, and I almost had tears in my eyes, it's the first time I've ever been honored like that."

"From now on you'll be honored like that every day by me. I love you!"

"I love you too, still wearing your flannel shirt unwashed. In fact, I have decided to wear it every evening that I am here alone and only wash it on your return."

"When I get to Thailand this weekend, I was thinking of getting you some Thai silk so you can make a cheongsam. What color do you want, green to match your eyes or red to match your hair?"

"What color do you want to see me in?"

"Truthfully, if it is left up to me I'd rather see you in nothing but my arms."

"Surprise me, see what colors they have and choose what you like, I'm easy."

"Oh no, you're not, too many rules between you and easy."

"Ok I asked for that, good night, I love you."

As Doc said goodbye, he decided to go to Jimmy's Kitchen, his regular steak restaurant in Hong Kong. Jimmy's Kitchen had been in Hong Kong since 1928 and advertised "Real Gweilo

Food." Gweilo being a somewhat derogatory Cantonese word meaning "Ghost man" refers to white-skinned foreigners.

As he enjoyed his well aged, perfectly medium rare, closer to the rare side, rib eye steak, he thought about tomorrow. He would contact Bev to see how things were going with Sean and Anne and then meet with Doctor Lau to hopefully kick off a working relationship with his accounting firm. It should prove to be an exciting day.

CHAPTER SIXTEEN

Sean found the long flight, or actually five flights to Lion's Pride exhausting. Even the first class treatment most of the way didn't make up for 27 hours of flying. He envied Anne because she was able to sleep quite a bit that took away some of the boredom. Sean's secretary had spent two days researching Zimbabwe from every perspective that might be of interest to her bosses. She purchased two iPads and downloaded a massive quantity of information on to them. A backlit screen and the light weight of the devices allowed them to read as much as they wanted, even when the plane cabin lights dimmed for sleepers. She included information about the country; it's economy, political situation, and tourism industry and import issues relating to food, beverage, and hotel equipment. They had instant access to currency converters, maps and everything else they might need to get started on the management contract of Lion's Pride. Sean was so impressed with the work she'd done that he had her prepare iPads with the same data to give to Bev, Doc, and Shannon.

They flew from Wilkes-Barrie/Scranton International Airport to New York where they went with Emirates Airlines through three stops to Harare, Zimbabwe. At Harare, they were met by the Lion's Pride Rolls Royce limo for the fifty-mile drive to the property. The chauffeur introduced himself as Mike. He provided each of them with a cool, moist towel and a bottle of chilled water taken from a cooler in the trunk. He said, "Welcome to Zimbabwe, it'll be my pleasure to drive you whenever you want to go somewhere. Just push the #7 button on your in-room phone or let the concierge know and I will bring the car around to the main entrance, anytime day or night."

They were fascinated with the City and the scenic drive to the property. The limo slowed as it approached the large iron gates supported by two massive stone pillars. The chauffeur pushed a coded keypad on a speaker box, and the gates opened. From the Gate, it wasn't possible to see the main house due to a rise in the terrain. The grounds were exquisitely maintained, the grass like a golf course, the flowers, shrubs and trees attended to by people who took a lot of pride in their work.

As they crested the hill, the mansion came into view, and they both gasped when they saw the structure. It was beautiful and impressive way beyond their expectations. Sean thought immediately of the White House only this one was bigger.

Anne was amazed at the number of staff working on the grounds, and they could only see a small part of the property from this vantage point. She said to Sean, "Wow, is all I can say. Isn't this something?"

"Yeah, pretty impressive, it's a pity we could not have this building and grounds in the right area of the States. What a resort this would make if we could open it to the public."

"From what I see so far, I don't think that we're going to have difficulty attracting and retaining the computer whizzes that Doc is seeking. With our brand of service, gourmet food and beverages and all the recreational facilities we'll offer, these software developers are going to think they have died and gone to geek heaven."

Mike had called ahead, and as the limo approached the porte-cochere, Bev walked down the steps to greet them. Mike jumped out and with a move perfected through many years of practice, was around the car and had the door open for them. As soon as they had stepped out, Bev offered her hand, first to Sean and then to Anne and welcomed them to Lion's Pride. "It's so good to meet you both finally. Doc has told me over the years of your friendship, and I feel as though I know you already."

Anne said, "Likewise, he's spoken of you frequently and the times you had together at the University.

Sean and I can only imagine how much fun it must have been to hang out with him in that atmosphere."

"Yes we had more than our share of laughs and parties, but you know Doc, when the time came for work, he was very serious about it. I confess that I probably wouldn't have made it through MBA and law school without him as a friend and partner. Now let's get you inside, and start your jet lag recovery process."

Sean was curious as to what the jet lag recovery process included but didn't ask, just went along for the ride. As they stepped into the vast foyer, a butler holding a silver tray appeared out of nowhere with a double Jameson's in a crystal glass, no ice, and a chilled flute of champagne for Anne.

"This is step one of the process of rehabilitation. Let's go up to your suites and I'll suggest what we should do next for the jet lag fixer." She motioned to an elevator door that had been cleverly disguised as part of the wall, kind of like that door to the Oval Office that you see in movies. They rode swiftly and silently to the fifth floor. Bev explained that the fifth floor wasn't available to the public. Bev's suite was on five as were several others intended for VIP guests only. As they stepped off the elevator, a young lady in what could have been a flight attendant's uniform greeted them.

Bev introduced her as Sharon, the fifth-floor concierge, "If you need anything at all you can call on Sharon and she will get it for you. She lives on this floor and is available 24/7. Just push the #2 key on your in-room phone."

Sean thought that Sharon must be held in high regard if she has the prestigious job of the concierge on this floor. Bev said, "Before we start working, I thought you might like to avail yourselves of the spa facilities, perhaps a sauna and massage. Then you might like a dip in the hot mineral pool, followed by a nap before I show you around. Depending on your preferences, we can start with the facilities tour today or leave it until tomorrow morning. I know, jet lag and I don't want to rush you. For now I'll leave you to settle in. Sean, you are in Suite 501 and Anne you are in 502. If you decide to use the spa, push the #2 key on your phone and Sharon will show you the way. Once you are both rested, let me know. She handed each of them a very thin small cell phone. These are part of the property's communications network. They work like a standard cell phone sending and receiving outside calls if you wish. Similarly, they can be used like your in-room phone to contact people like Sharon, Mike and many others that you'll meet. Let Sharon know if you want them programmed for your cell phone numbers and she'll do it for you.

There is a directory here that she pointed out to Sean and Anne. Push button #1 to call me. I have just had the Wi-Fi password changed to 'lionspride' all one word. So you should be all set communications wise. Please get some rest and relax a bit then call me when you're ready to meet."

Sean said to Anne, "The temptation to explore the overall property is strong. I guess it's got to do with being hoteliers, but let's take Bev's advice. Let's hit the spa and let them work the kinks out, do the sauna and hot tub bit then take a nap. But first let's give in to temptation and check out our suites quickly." They were impressed with the suites. They were identical in layout and comprised of a bedroom with en suite, a large comfortable living room with floor to ceiling windows offering a spectacular view. They looked over the private deck to the outdoor pool, tennis courts and what looked like riding stables. These attractions were all set in a lovely garden with walking paths joining everything together. The suites also featured a private dining area, a small kitchenette, and well-stocked wet bar. The kitchenette and bar were discreetly located behind a sliding door that, like the elevator door, which impressed Sean in the foyer, were designed to "disappear" from view by blending into the wall. Sean was pleased to see a bottle of Jameson's and two cut crystal glasses set out on a silver tray at the bar.

Similarly, sliding another invisible door revealed a compact office with built in desk, computer, printer, telephone and shredder along with a slide-out, ergonomically correct, office chair.

The décor could be best described as luxurious African. It made use of African woods, locally made carpets over hardwood floors, ceiling fans, and locally produced artifacts as well as some beautiful paintings commissioned specifically for the mansion. The colors were mostly light and cheerful and mounted heads were kept to a minimum although Zulu shields and spears were commonplace.

Anne said, "I think from the look of the suites, Shannon's touch will put the rooms over the top."

Sean said, "I agree, she'll have a lot to work with in terms of décor pieces. People who know what they are doing have maintained the artwork, furnishings and rooms. She is going to love this job."

Anne hit the phone button for Sharon and said, "Hi Sharon, we would like to go to the spa now."

Sharon said, "Yes Madam, please meet me at my desk, and I'll take you there."

They went to Sharon's station, and she said, "Just before we go down, I'd like to acquaint you with a few safety features.

There are four elevators including this one, each located in the middle of the wall that forms the building envelope. There are stairways beside each one. The building has a sprinkler system, and there are individual fire extinguishers located in the kitchenettes. When you come back from your spa visit, I'll show you a few controls for things like the television, air conditioning, bath, and icemaker."

The spa area was breathtaking with a huge indoor/outdoor pool as it's focus; massage rooms, a sauna room, a steam room and the hot tub. The gym was designed so that it extended from the main structure and surrounded on three sides by retractable glass walls. Depending on the weather and desires of the guests, the gymnasium manager could open the glass walls to have most of the gym outside, or he could leave them closed. When the walls were closed, guests could, if they desired, dive into the pool indoors and swim under an opening in the wall allowing them to get to the outdoor part of the pool. Outside there were deck chairs with cushions and folded fluffy towels on each similar to what one would expect at a five-star resort in the Caribbean.

The massages were just what the doctor ordered and along with the sauna that Anne had and the steam bath that Sean had, they were more than ready for a nap. Returning to their suites, they agreed to meet in two hours and get together with Bev.

In his suite, Sean remembered the bottle of Jameson's on the bar and went to the door, opened it and poured a short one to help him sleep.

Two minutes after hitting the bed he was snoring like a buzz saw in an echo chamber.

Anne called his suite at the agreed two-hour point, and Sean answered apparently out of a deep sleep.

She said, "Are you ready to get together with Bev? "she's suggested we meet in the library for drinks before dinner."

"Good, you go ahead down and I'll be along

in a few minutes."

Anne went to the library following directions cheerfully provided by Sharon. As she joined Bev, the butler asked for her drink order, and they sat on twin leather couches facing each other. Bev asked, "Did you manage to get some rest?"

"Yes, I had a grand massage, a sauna, a quick dip in the hot tub and a very nice nap. Great suggestions on your part, thank you. Sean will be right along, I think he went into a deep sleep, and he sounded groggy when I called him."

"There is no rush, but you were right to wake him otherwise he would have made the classic mistake of sleeping for five or six hours then being wide awake in the middle of the night. I understand that the plan is for you to stay for a week, then return home to allow Shannon to come over for a week is that correct?"

"Yes, we're planning to do it that way, however, we've made it, so we're flexible. Should circumstances dictate, I can stay on longer, and Shannon can fly over when I get back, or maybe Sean will return home before me and let Shannon come over. We don't know what to expect so we're purposely keeping everything loose. One of the things I would like to do after we tour the whole property is to interview the existing employees. I want to determine who will be a fit for accommodations and food and beverage positions. Who will be able to do jobs in maintenance and grounds keeping and what training we'll need to arrange to prepare them."

"As you asked, I have had them all prepare resumes with the help of my secretary, and we've had everyone photographed with the photo attached to their resume. My secretary will have placed them in your room by the time we have dinner. She has also had them sign up for a fifteen-minute interview slot over the next three days as you requested."

The managing directors of the three largest recruiting firms with experience in hospitality recruiting will be here to meet you on Friday. I scheduled one for nine a.m., one for lunch and one for three p.m. The fellow coming at lunch heads up the largest of the three firms. All they know is that we are planning a five-star resort."

"That's good work; I'll owe your secretary some nice flowers by the end of this visit."

Just then, Sean walked in, and the butler waited until he sat down and placed a double Jameson's in front of him. "Now that's what I call service," Sean said.

Bev said, "I think you'll find that everyone will be trying hard to impress both of you with their service attitude. They are all keen to stay on here, for many of them it's the only place they know. Many were born here. Anne, we were just speaking about my secretary, well she was my uncle's secretary, but I can vouch for her. She is signed up for an interview, I had thought about having her join us here for a few minutes so I could introduce her. But I decided not to because

Doc and I have agreed that we'll not interfere with your management of hospitality operations and we'll stick to it. A ship can only have one captain and from now on it's you."

"In that case, if I'm captain, here is my first official command. Invite our secretary in for a glass of wine and let us get to know her because we'll be running her off her feet over the next few weeks."

Bev picked up her cell and hit the speed dial for Mona and when Mona answered Bev asked her to come in for a few minutes.

"Now Sean don't you start off interviewing her, I have a meeting set up for that, let's just get to know each other a bit," Anne said.

Both Sean and Anne took to Mona right away. She was everything Anne could want in a secretary and more. By the end of the wine, she said to Mona, "I do want to talk to you some more, but there is no need for an interview. I want you to be my secretary, and that's it. I'm going to ask you to do things that are to be kept strictly confidential, and I feel comfortable after this talk that I can count on you."

"Thank you, Miss Watson. I served this family as a confidential executive secretary for over twenty years. I'll be proud to do the same for you."

After Mona had left, Anne said, "I'm excited to have someone of her quality as my secretary. Coming from overseas, I will need a fair amount of guidance getting to know the business climate and cultural do's and don'ts. And I'll need to count on her to handle what will often be lots of work and to be my eyes and ears with the staff."

Bev said, "Obviously I don't know anything about the hospitality industry and running a five-star resort-style property. But I do have the ability to judge people and good people make the best employees. I look forward to talking to you once you conclude the staff interviews. I have a feeling that you are going to find a lot of people who, with the proper training, will become excellent five-star level employees."

Anne said, "I suspect that you're right, and I'll find a lot of suitable employees already working here. Once I've concluded the interviews and talked to the three recruiting executives, I'll be in a position to identify how many people we'll need to hire. I will then prepare a training plan and start on a timeline for achieving the critical steps towards opening for business. Doc has said that he will dream up something for any employees not needed in the hotel and related operations to keep all people employed. Once I conclude my interviews I can let him know if we are going to have any people for him to worry about."

Bev said, "How about a good old American bar-b-q at poolside later? It's going to be a lovely night, and I thought something relaxing would be better for tonight."

Sean said, "That works for me, I'd like to put on my old blue jeans and rodeo shirt, get into my cowboy boots, and sit back and enjoy the stars and the clear African air."

Anne said, "I have jeans with me but no boots, but the bar-b-q idea suits me fine."

Bev said, "I've arranged for a three-way conference call with Shannon and Doc for six a.m. our time the day after tomorrow. I'm sorry about the six a.m. part, but it works best for the three time zones.

You'll both have time to assess the situation a bit before speaking to them. I've also scheduled a meeting with the architect and general contractor for Saturday morning from nine to noon with lunch following. It'll be an excellent opportunity for the both of you to have input into the design and construction process. I've had the architect busy drawing up preliminary plans with the key word being preliminary. He's a talented individual who has done some hotel design and also work for my family's company, so I know him well and trust him to do a good job. Like all architects that I've run into, however, he tends to get caught up in his ideas and loses track of who's paying the bills. I explained to him that there was a team who will determine how this project is going to go. The team comprises you both, Shannon, Doc and last and probably least, me. Tomorrow morning when you're both ready, I'll take you on a full tour of the mansion, the recreational facilities, and the grounds. I'll answer all your questions and have alerted the management personnel to be available to show you their areas of responsibility and also to answer anything you ask. By day's end tomorrow you'll be thoroughly briefed on all aspects of the property and will have seen it all. Mona will join us all day to make notes for you and to get anything we require."

CHAPTER SEVENTEEN

The following morning Sean woke early and tested room service by ordering an orange juice and pot of coffee. They arrived promptly and were appropriately cold and hot. He had an hour before the breakfast with Anne and Bev was scheduled in the dining room so he turned on the television to the CNN channel to see what Anderson Cooper, Wolf Blitzer and the other talking heads could tell him about today's disasters. He often thought CNN should stand for "Calamity News Non-stop."

The coffee, as expected, was excellent so he poured another cup and took it into the en suite to take care of the morning essentials before dressing to meet the ladies. On Anne's recommendation he had packed his New Balance, long distance walking shoes which will come in handy today for the grand tour.

Anne's internal clock beat by seven minutes the travel alarm clock she always packed. She also turned on the television but chose the BBC news channel for a change. Same old news, but different accents. She looked at her email to see if there were any from Shannon that required her input to situations at O'Leary's.

As she expected, there were no email cries for help, the place would have to be on fire for Shannon to seek assistance. She was dressed and ready for action so she headed down to the dining room a bit early and ordered a cup of Earl Grey tea, which was her favorite engine starter.

Bev and Sean arrived at the same time having shared an elevator so "good mornings" were exchanged and the waitress took breakfast orders. Bev said, "There's a buffet if you like or anything from this menu."

Sean said, "The menu is quite extensive considering that we're the only guests."

Anne agreed, "Yes, do you always have this menu available? What happens after we leave?"

Bev said, "Remember what I said, the staff, including Chef, are all trying to impress you in the hope of staying on, so order anything you like to give them a chance to show their stuff. But in any event, we do always have this menu available; my uncle insisted on it because of the volume of houseguests he always had passing through. I can't see the point in changing it at this stage as we'll be having all kinds of people staying over in order to complete the renovations. Also bear in mind the employee feeding that goes on daily; our kitchen staff are kept busy even when there are no guests in-house."

Breakfast was served, all three ordering different selections from the menu in order to give Chef a chance to show off a bit, as chefs like to do. While waiting for breakfast, both Sean and Anne went to the buffet to look over the available items.

Sean said, "An impressive selection, beautifully presented, just as one would expect at a five-star property."

Anne nodded in agreement, "I tend to avoid buffets personally as my self-control evaporates if the buffet is well conceived, and the food fresh. I want to sample everything, but I appreciate a buffet's value in a setting such as this."

After returning to the table Sean said, "I was thinking that I might sit in, purely as an observer of course, when you interview the chef, executive housekeeper, food and beverage manager and the head of maintenance. Is that ok with you Anne?"

"Of course it's ok, I'd appreciate your feedback on these key positions and in any event you know my motto, the boss isn't always right but he's always the boss."

After breakfast Bev said, "I thought we'd start at the top and work our way down, then deal with the outside afterwards. I assume you'll want to inspect every room?"

Anne said, "Yes please, we want to give the entire place a going over as if we were being inspected by the Relais & Chateaux team and our membership depended on it."

Bev said, "Well if you're ready, I'll have Mona join us, she'll take notes and photos of anything you want. I do have a professional video company coming in the next few days to shoot a complete DVD of the place. I thought it might help with renovation planning and execution and probably Doc could use it when recruiting developers."

They took the elevator to the fifth floor and were met with Sharon's smiling face and the executive housekeeper, Shelly, who would join them for the tour and answer any questions. Bev said, "As I mentioned, this floor is not presently used for regular guests only VIPs. That isn't to say that it has to stay that way. I would want to keep a suite for myself, one for Doc and say six for visiting dignitaries such as you Sean. Anne, I would suggest that you take suite 502, as it's a two-bedroom apartment and since it will be your home, it will give you more elbowroom. Let's start there, so Sean can see it."

As they inspected 502 Bev told Mona to stock the suite with the needs of a full time resident and Anne gave her some ideas for things she would like in the suite, for instance, a bar-b-q on the deck. Suite 502 featured a full second bedroom with ensuite, a den that could double as a home office, a larger kitchen and dining area. The deck was off the master bedroom and continued to the living room and was about fifty percent bigger than the one at a standard suite.

Anne said, "This is a beautiful apartment, I'm going to be quite comfortable here."

After touring the floor, both Sean and Anne agreed that this level should be kept as is, separate from the guest floors in order to provide privacy for Bev, Anne, Doc and the visiting VIPs. The other guestroom floors, 4, 3 and 2 were comprised of 20 identical suites per floor.

Each suite was designed like a studio apartment, with a king size bed and a large, well-appointed sitting area plus a small galley kitchen and wet bar hidden behind sliding doors similar to Sean and Anne's present accommodation. Smaller than the suites that Anne and Sean had on floor 5, they were still generous in size and very comfortable for 2 people. Even allowing for the computer equipment to be installed, it was the general feeling that each suite, with only one guest in it, would provide a luxurious, efficient, space for the software developers to work and live comfortably. Doc's research had indicated that these development types were often marching to the beat of a different drummer. They frequently would work 24 or more hours straight through without even taking breaks for meals in the dining room. Some would work all night and sleep all day; others might work in their suite for a week without leaving it and then spend a week sitting by the pool or in Harare partying.

Thus the galley kitchens would allow them to prepare something quickly if they so desired, 24 hours a day. The compact dining area would allow for watching television while eating a room service meal if they wanted. Doc said that some of these people would be gregarious and outgoing while others could be more like hermits, staying in their suites for days at a time. The design that Shannon comes up with for the guest suites will account for all their idiosyncrasies and hopefully encourage them to want to stay on. It was obvious that the building was mostly concrete with adequate provision between suites for soundproofing. Sean conducted his sound test by turning up the stereo full blast in a randomly selected room then closing the door and entering all the rooms up, down and on all sides and listening. His recommendation was that attention be paid to the doorways, perhaps different doors would be required but the walls and floors were very soundproof.

Sean said, "The guestrooms are more important in this situation than they would be in a traditional resort where, as tourists, the guests would be spending most of their time in recreational pursuits."

Anne added, "Right and another major difference is that we're trying to encourage our guests to stay with us, hopefully for years instead of weeks, so it will be a different sort of challenge completely."

After half the rooms had been inspected, Mona took a call and announced, " Lunch is ready when you are."

Bev asked, "Are you ready for a break? We can continue to talk over lunch if you like."

"Sounds good to me Anne said, I'll just go to my suite and check email to see if Shannon needs anything and meet you. Where are we eating?"

Before Bev could reply, Sean said, "Let's throw the kitchen a curve ball and tell them we'll dine in the kitchen and we are on our way now."

Bev said, "You are a tough cookie Mr. O'Leary but let's do that. Mona let them know that we are on our way down."

As they walked through the kitchen swinging doors they were presented with the full kitchen staff standing at attention across the counter that had been set with a white linen tablecloth, lit candles and place settings for three. A violinist was playing softly in the corner and the butler approached with their favorite drinks on his silver platter. Sean and Anne were really impressed and Sean laughed as he shook hands with the chef who was resplendent in his tall hat, crisp whites with an array of medals signifying his many international awards.

"Bravo," Sean said, "The kitchen is spotless and the setting is beyond anything I could have done myself with such short notice, you are all to be congratulated. But how did you come up with a violinist on such short notice?"

Chef replied, "She is one of our sous chefs."

Sean, Anne and Bev clapped their hands for the entire crew who stood there with beaming faces then served a fabulous lunch, which Bev had ordered ahead to save time.

Over lunch Anne said, "So far I haven't seen anything that would cause concern to a Relais & Chateaux inspector; quite the opposite, I think he or she would be most impressed."

Bev asked, "Why the concern for Relais & Chateaux, you won't need membership in that organization will you?"

Sean said, "No we won't, however we're members at O'Leary's Arms and wouldn't want to lessen our status in the organization. I'm a governor of the US group. There are only three of us and we're responsible to the worldwide group for the reputation of the organization in North America. Anne and I have been living with their strict adherence to the highest standards and we'll just naturally apply these same standards to Lion's Pride. Given what we are trying to accomplish here, I think you and Doc will agree that this is the way to go."

Bev said, "Oh I concur fully. Doc and I have talked about it and decided right off that a part of our strategy is to overwhelm the software developers with quality to keep them with us for as long as we can. Shall we head back and inspect the balance of the rooms?"

Sean and Anne shook hands with all the kitchen staff and thanked each one for a superb lunch.

They went to the third floor and picked up where they had left off. By now both Sean and Anne were familiar with the standard suite layout so the inspections went much faster than when they first started. Around three o'clock they moved to the ground floor and Bev began in the library. It was a classic, mansion type library with the floor to ceiling wooden shelves and the requisite sliding ladder to access the higher shelves. The room, furnished in what Sean calls, "Old English Men's Club" rose up two stories and was brightly lit this time of day by a beautiful African sun, flowing over the magnificent English garden. The cocktail of images: leather bound books, sunlight on flowers streaming in through floor to ceiling windows and the thick, studded leather, over-stuffed furniture, created a room as beautiful as Sean and Anne had ever seen. The chairs were placed in pairs or fours at cocktail tables around the room's centerpiece, a hand carved billiards table custom made of Bubinga wood, a very rare African hardwood. Bev's uncle was a billiards player who loved the game and played at least once a day. He commissioned the top billiards table maker from London to build this table for this room. The carving, done by local artists took nearly a year to complete and depicted scenes of African wildlife.

Coincidentally, a pride of lions figured prominently along one side. Sean, no slouch around a billiard table himself was overwhelmed with the beauty of this piece. Adding to the men's club atmosphere was the inevitable display of trophy heads from a wide variety of African wildlife.

Sean said, "So your uncle was a hunter then?"

Bev replied, "No, other than clay pigeons I don't think he ever shot at anything. He was a gentle sort of man, not the type to sneak through the jungle taking shots at animals for sport."

Anne said, "So did he buy all these trophy heads for décor?"

"No they were gifts from his friends who used

to stay here as a base camp for their various safaris into the wild. I decided just to leave them on the walls and let Shannon decide if she wants them here, elsewhere in the building or given away. I don't care, I'm not a fan of having dead animal heads on the walls but then again, Shannon might want them for the "wild African" ambiance that they lend to this great room."

"Let's move on to the theatre room. The theatre room is a state-of-the-art combination movie and stage production room. My uncle loved to host weekends where theatre groups, often from one of the local universities would put on plays or musicals. In fact we have our own theatre company comprised of some quite talented employees."

As they left the library and walked down the wide corridor, Bev said, "We also have a small but enthusiastic band drawn from our staff that put on concerts offering everything from jazz, big band sound and believe it or not my uncle was a big fan of country and western music. He used to make regular trips to the US on business and often made side trips to Nashville to take in some shows. Willy Nelson, Emmy Lou Harris, Kenny Rogers and many others performed on this stage while visiting on safari. The acoustics in here are incredible, my uncle had the same company that did the Beatles' sound studio design this room."

They moved down the hall and entered a ballroom. Bev said, "This room is capable of sitting

300-theatre style and has access to the kitchen through those doors there. That wall slides back to open up an identical room next door so in all we could host a function for 600 to 800 depending on whether or not seating is required. We have full audio and visual capabilities, a removable dance floor and a movable stage so we can accommodate a broad variety of functions here."

Anne said, "This is excellent for what we have in mind. The rooms can be used for presentations by guest lecturers, group banquets, dances, poker tournaments and I'm sure many other events that our guests will dream up. Doc mentioned that the computer games designers may want to have computer games tournaments once their productions are on the market.

This is a way that they can improve subsequent editions of the games they develop. Doc's sources in Silicon Valley tell us that having a venue for this interaction between developers may end up being a large part of the draw that brings them to Lion's Pride."

Bev said, "You've seen the main dining room and the kitchen so let's move along to the Zulu Pub. The pub is completely done in Zulu memorabilia that was donated to my uncle by the leader of the Zulu people of Zimbabwe. It was designed to showcase the Zulu people and honor their contribution to African society. My uncle was a student of the Zulu people and employed many of them in his mines over the decades. We'll see what Shannon wants to do. If she doesn't want it here, I suppose we could find a home for all these artifacts elsewhere but I hope she'll like the décor and decide to keep the theme. It's sort of a museum in a way and the artifacts are priceless. Over the years, it has been the venue for some great parties. Guests like the historical atmosphere and a chance to learn a bit about these fantastic people. Also it provides an alternative to the formal dining room which some of our more casually inclined guests have appreciated. Nevertheless we'll do what she says."

Anne said, "I think Shannon will love it. She is a big believer in decorating with the use of local furniture and historical artifacts.

She scoured Pennsylvania when she was decorating O'Leary's and wait until you see the job she did there. In fact you should probably come for a visit and get a look at O'Leary's. The website shows it well, but as you know there is nothing like seeing the property first hand. Perhaps we should schedule a progress meeting there for when Doc gets back from Asia, let's put that on the agenda for our conference call. Speaking of conference call, let's have a look at the business center and then we can visit the stables and I'll show you around at least some of the grounds." Bev continued, "The business center is very complete and up to date with all the latest technological advances in communications and computing. It features a twelve person executive boardroom furnished with a custom made table and chairs covered in the finest African leathers but nothing taken from endangered species I assure you. Until my uncle sold the mining company, he conducted a lot of his business from this center.

As I mentioned, Mona has organized the conference call with Doc in Hong Kong and Shannon for six a.m.. There will be juice, coffee, Earl Grey tea and croissants that will be rushed straight from the oven to that sideboard. So no need to fuss, just show up. Mona has arranged a wake up call for us all at five thirty.

Sean said, "I'm anxious to see how Shannon is doing and how things are going for Doc. Everyone's so busy all over the world at the same time. I don't think we've ever had so much excitement happening at once."

CHAPTER EIGHTEEN

They stopped in at the Zulu Pub and ordered fruit punch to go. Bev then led them outside where a driver with a luxury vehicle, much like an oversized golf cart, was waiting. Bev said, "I thought we'd start with a tour of the immediate grounds, a full property tour would take all day unless we did it by helicopter."

She said to the driver, "Robert, please go to the golf course and on the way make a stop at the tennis courts."

"As you can see the courts are clay, well lit for night play and there's bleacher seating available for 200. My uncle never missed a day of tennis unless he was too sick to move from his bed. He loved the game and hosted many tournaments here over the years. On occasion, he would bring in a well-known, international player and invite his tennis cronies for a weekend of semi-private lessons. Let's move on to the golf course.

Robert, take us out on the course about half-way. The course is only nine holes, not for lack of space as you can see, but my uncle only liked to play nine holes and couldn't see the point in having nine additional holes that he wouldn't use. He had the course designed by Jack Nick-laus's outfit. Fortunately, they convinced him to allow them to design it in such a way that it may be expanded to 18 holes. So if you decide the course needs to be 18 holes, we can make it happen. I know we're moving quickly, but I want to show you the stables and car "garage" before dinner. You can see the rest of the grounds on your own, just call Robert here and he'll take you."

The stables held 28 of the finest thorough-breds that Sean and Anne had ever seen. Bev said," My uncle loved horses and often had weekend horse related activities such as riding to hounds. People would come from all over, some riding these horses and some bringing their own. That's why there are so many stalls, to accommodate all the visiting horses. I don't know if you will want them for the use of your guests if so, we'll keep them for that purpose. Only this brown stallion, 'Leopard' is not availa-ble to guests as he's my private horse. This one, 'Midnight', I have my eye on for Doc, but I'm not sure that equestrian activities are going to take up much of his time.

I really haven't any plans for the rest of the horses. If you ride or would like to learn Anne, pick out one and we'll reserve it for your use exclusively.

Anne said, "At this point we can't judge the level of interest our guests will have in riding. As long as we have them let's keep them and see. We can always decide to sell them off later if there is no interest in using them."

Sean said, "I agree. Since they're here let's keep them and offer them as an alternative recreational pursuit. Remember, these software geniuses are a long way from home and in a very different environment than they are used to. It's a long way to Candlestick Park. So I think the more entertainment and recreational activities the better. In an ideal world, they'll work hard, play hard and produce programs over the long term. In fact, I think a baseball diamond and a football field would be great additions for our purposes."

Bev said, "Good idea, I'll put the grounds staff to work on a baseball diamond and a football field right away. When they have their plans finalized, I'll send them to you Sean as an email attachment so you can see if they're on the right track. I'm afraid I don't know enough about these sports to make sure they build them correctly."

Sean said, "That's a good idea. I have some friends in pro sports and I'll run the plans by them to see if they have any suggestions. I thought you had mentioned a bowling alley at one point."

Bev said, "Oh no, I completely forgot all about it, the wine cellar and basketball court as well. They're in the basement and I hardly ever go down there. I'll show them to you right after our conference call in the morning. Let's take a quick look at the car collection, then we can take a break. You might want a nap before cocktail hour."

As they looked over the uncle's collection of antique cars, Bev said, "I'm really not sure what to do with these, how if at all, they would fit in with the plans for Lion's Pride."

Sean said, "They certainly are impressive, no doubt worth a fortune but like you Bev I don't see a fit with the new development. Do you see any use for these cars Anne?"

Anne said, "Not at the moment, but let me think about it a bit. Like the horses, they're here so if we can use them in some way we should do so unless you want to sell them, Bev."

"No, I don't have any plans to sell them so let's just hang on to them for now and see if some use comes to mind."

Both Sean and Anne were still feeling the effects of jet lag and were pretty tired after all the touring they did today. Anne decided to go for a nap. Sean decided to go for a drink in the Zulu Pub. He said, "I saw a dartboard in there so I'm going to do some practicing, I hope you have some decent bar darts. Besides, I've found over the years that if you want to know what's going on, talk to the bartender." Robert delivered them back to the rear entrance and they agreed to meet for dinner at seven, giving all parties a chance to put their feet up and get away from each other for a bit.

When Anne stepped off the elevator Sharon, smiling as ever, said, "Your apartment is ready. I'll just walk you there to see if you need anything." Rather than argue that she was fine, she let Sharon accompany her to the suite. When she entered, she found a bottle of her soon to be favorite white wine, Dry White Wood Bushman Rock, in a chilled copper wine bucket. There were a dozen red roses in a crystal vase and a silver serving dish with a dozen chocolate dipped strawberries all neatly arranged on the dining table. Anne was pleased with the welcoming gifts. They were totally unexpected. She said, "Did you put this together Sharon?"

"Yes madam, Miss Mona called and asked me to get this ready and to send a driver to the store to pick up a list of items she gave me. I have stocked your cupboards and refrigerator in case you feel like eating something in your apartment. So I think you are all set for now, but if you think of anything you need just let me know."

Anne kicked off her shoes and went into her ensuite to fill the Jacuzzi tub with very hot water. Mona had thoughtfully included a bottle of good bubble bath so she added a generous portion, turned on the jets, before slipping off her clothes and getting into the tub.

Sean ordered a double Jameson's and asked for the bar darts. The darts were presented in a velvet lined wooden case and were displayed according to weight. Sean had played a lot of darts in a lot of pubs using bar darts. He had never seen a presentation such as this with different weights available. He managed to keep his surprise from showing as if this is how all bar darts are presented. He usually gets them, thrown on to the bar by the bartender who has taken them from an old beer mug. He was seldom offered a choice of darts and considered himself fortunate if the darts were all the same weight and had matching flights.

He sipped from his whiskey glass and began his regular practice routine going around the board in doubles, then triples then three bull's eyes. After a while, he glanced at the bartender's nametag and said, "So do you like working here Fred?"

"Yes sir, I enjoy my job and get to meet some interesting people. I've served politicians, movie stars, music legends and international sports stars, not to mention a host of others that have passed through over the years."

"How long have you worked here?"

"Just over nine years. I started as a waiter for the first year then moved in here."

Taking another sip and beginning another practice round, Sean said, "What don't you like about working here?"

"Absolutely nothing, Mr. O'Leary," Fred said with a wide grin.

Sean, realizing he had been made, smiled back and said to Fred, "I think we'll be seeing a lot of each other, I like the feel of this room."

Sean went to his suite and opted for a long hot shower followed by a look at CNN to see if he was likely to make it through tomorrow without some major international threat starting world war three.

He dozed off for a bit in the easy chair, a

power nap some called it. He dressed and headed to the dining room at the appointed time to meet the ladies.

Greeting them both, he said, "So Anne how are the new digs?"

"Just great" she replied. "The suite is very elegant and already I'm being spoiled with wine, flowers and chocolate dipped strawberries."

Sean said, "I've come up with an idea to throw a few more curves at the chef. Let's see what's on the menu then order a dish made with the same meat or fish but in an entirely different manner. For instance, if there's seafood offered in a sauce over pasta, and another entree of filet mignon, I'll order filet mignon, Oscar. And you two mix up some other items and let's see how they handle it."

Bev said, "Don't you ever just do something like having dinner without an ulterior motive?"

"Oh sure I do but not when I'm testing the abilities of one of the key parts of the operation. The kitchen is going to be preparing meals for the same group over an extended period of time. For the guest, it will be almost like embarking on a world cruise with food being prepared repetitively by the same kitchen staff. This is going to be a unique challenge, to keep sixty or so individuals happy with their meals. I have some ideas that I'll discuss with chef when we interview him."

They ordered as Sean suggested. The waiter didn't show any sign of concern, only wrote down the off-menu orders and took them to the kitchen.

The butler, as usual arrived with everyone's preferred beverage on his tray at which point Sean said, "No Jameson's this time Walter, I'll have a Caesar, please."

Walter, as he served the ladies said, "Of course sir, I'll be right back."

Walter returned a few minutes later with a large Caesar with peppered rim and garnish that was a plastic sword with olive, pickles and pickled asparagus sections on it.

"Bravo," Sean said, "how did you do this?"

"Fred did it, sir, he keeps up on the latest drinks popular worldwide. He said this is his first Caesar for a customer so if it is not to your liking he will fix it according to your instructions."

He took a sip and said, "Tell Fred....never mind I'll tell him myself." He excused himself and went to the Zulu Pub.

He said to Fred, "This Caesar is perfect, how did you do it?"

"I sent an email to O'Leary's the day before you arrived asking for help from your bartender with any local special drinks that I might get asked for. Brian responded with a list of recipes and specific instructions. At the top of the list, right after the Nassau Nightie Remover was the Bloody Caesar. Would you care to sample a Nassau Nightie Remover sir, I'd imagine they are an ideal drink for poolside served in a tall chilled glass on a hot day?"

"Yes I would like to try one, please have it sent to my table. In fact send three." They all sampled the Nassau Nightie Remover and Bev said, "It tastes exactly the same as those we had in Nassau. And along with this Caesar, originally a Canadian drink, it looks like Doc's been doing some bartender training."

"Yeah, Doc introduced these drinks to Brian, our bartender at O'Leary's, and Fred got the recipes by email. Quite clever of him."

Bev said, "I think you're going to be pleasantly surprised when you interview the employees. There's a lot of hospitality experience here. The former manager who left about six months ago was a Hungarian bear and a tough taskmaster. He trained the staff well. They called him behind his back "the Hungarian Sergeant Major" but they respected him and learned a lot from him."

"What happened to him?" Anne asked.

"He married this lovely South African beauty and they moved to Canada. I last heard that he was running a hotel school in the west."

Dinner arrived just as ordered as if the items had been on the menu. It was delicious and Sean said, "This kitchen is well run. I'm going to give them a final test tomorrow when Anne interviews the chef."

"I thought you were just sitting in, now you're planning to get involved?" Anne said.

"I won't interfere, just a final test of the kitchen, no big deal."

After dinner Bev said, "I for one am going for a quick walk around the gardens then off to bed. The wake-up call will be early so I need my beauty rest."

Anne said, "If you'd like some company, I'll join you for the walk."

"Of course. Bev replied. How about you Sean, would you like to join us?"

"No thanks, I think I'll walk to the library and test out that billiards table to see how she handles with a snifter of brandy in hand. I'll see you ladies at the ungodly hour of six. I never used to think six a.m. existed except as a good time to be rolling in after a night at the local."

Bev had been right; five thirty a.m. arrived early and was no time for decent folk to be up and about.

The three arrived in time to get a croissant and beverage before Mona connected with Hong Kong and Scranton. The high-tech communications system not only provided clear audio but also allowed for the 90-inch screen to be divided into three sections, one for each location.

As Shannon and Doc appeared on the screen, Sean said, "Top of the morning to ya."

They both said their hellos and Bev said, "If it's alright with everyone, I'll act as moderator so we're not all talking over one another."

Doc said, "I think you mean so we are not all trying to talk over Sean who tends to dominate."

"Ok let's go, Shannon how about a report from you, certainly Sean and Anne would like to hear how things are going at O'Leary's."

Shannon said. "All is well, occupancy is up 4% and the average rate is up 7% over the same period last year. No major problems to report in fact not even any minor problems thus far. So all is well in Scranton. On the Lion's Pride front I have been doing some internet research on Zimbabwe in general and the Harare area, in particular, just trying to get a feel for the place before I get there. Speaking of which, is the plan still for you to head home on schedule Anne?"

"I may be a few days later than I thought, but I'll let you know in time to book your flight. Glad to hear all is well, I know you can handle it but I've been in charge for so long that O'Leary's still feels like my baby. I have to admit though that Lion's Pride is already starting to feel like my new home. I'm being treated like royalty by the staff and I'm very excited about the future of the place. I know you haven't seen it yet, but I'm sure that it's going to work perfectly for your new business venture Doc."

"That's good to hear Anne and I look forward to seeing the place soon. Shannon when you go over, how long do you plan to stay? I thought that it would be good if we could overlap our visits there so I can walk the place through with you and offer some ideas."

Sean, Bev, and Anne glanced knowingly at each other, but no one spoke.

Shannon said, "I'm not sure how long I'll need to stay, I won't really know until I give the place a once over. If Anne gets back next week, I'd better give her a week or so to get over her jet lag so I'd probably head over about two weeks from now."

Doc said, "That could work well, I could go there from Hong Kong and we would have a couple of weeks there. We can get a lot of work done in a couple of weeks."

Another knowing look was exchanged between members of the group at Lion's Pride.

Other than that, I have been busy over here, mostly with my regular job but have managed to get a few things done on the Lion's Pride front as well. But they are of a legal and financial nature and don't impact on operations."

Getting the hint, Bev said, "If it's ok with everyone, I think we'll wrap up the operations side and I have a few things to discuss with Doc on the ownership side. Do you have anything further Shannon?"

"No, that's it for now, so long everyone." She knew that she would be talking to Doc later today; they made a habit of trying to talk every day.

Doc said his goodbyes to Sean and Anne, who left Bev alone to talk business with Doc.

Once they were gone Bev said to Doc, "I have some great news and I have some bigger news, which do you want first?"

Doc said, "Give me the great news first."

"Ok, I think Sean and Anne are perfect for this place. Sean has been walking around like a kid in a candy store. He sees the potential here exactly as we hoped he would. Anne is a super-star; she's going to be right on top of this place. The staff she met have all thought she's terrific and they, of course, have passed on the word. It's as though a huge sigh of relief has passed right through the entire employee group.

They both have expressed some great ideas for the place and they've only been here for two jet-lagged days. Our grounds people are already drawing up plans for Sean's ideas to put in a baseball diamond and a football field, we should probably toss in a cricket thingy, what do you call it?"

"A cricket ground. That sounds terrific, what's the greater news?"

"You had better be sitting down for this one. My uncle's lawyer has uncovered some seques-tered offshore money. The banks were instructed not to tell anyone about this until his death. Somehow my uncle stashed away $50 million in a Swiss bank and $75 million in a bank in the Grand Caymans.

So we are not only $125 million richer than we thought, but also we have money, lots of it, offshore where we can use it. On both accounts, I was listed as the authorized signatory so I have contacted the banks and have had you listed as signatory as well. This way you can draw down funds, as you need them to get this project underway. I'll text you the bank details. My suggestion is that you open three accounts in a bank in Hong Kong. Put $10 million in one personal account for me, another $10 million in a personal account for you and $50 million in our company account for working capital. Unless you think otherwise let's leave the balance of the $55 million evenly distributed between the Swiss and Cayman's banks as backup money should we need it in the development process."

"Hey, you're the financial partner in this deal remember, I'm only the creative guy. So whatever you say financially we do."

Bev said, "Don't give me this, 'only the creative guy bullshit' without you this whole project wouldn't happen and I'd still be a wealthy heiress provided I stayed in Zimbabwe."

"I'll open all the accounts at the Hong Kong Shanghai Bank. I have a good friend there, Vice President of Personal Banking who'll take care of details like issuing us credit cards, etc.

They have a system for displaced people like us where we have unlimited credit, unlimited access to ATM machines worldwide and the credit card bills go directly to them for payment. They also have an internationally recognized medical plan. It's like a credit card but when presented it guarantees payment of all medical bills worldwide. I think this is good insurance since we are leading such a nomadic lifestyle. Speaking of nomadic lifestyles, what are you plans now that you've quit your job."

"For now I'm going to stay here until the renovations are complete and then I don't know.

Maybe I'll get a place in Hong Kong and another somewhere in BC. I've always loved BC so we'll have to see what happens. I want to make one decision at a time and I think it's best for me to stay focused on Lion's Pride."

"What about you Doc, have you decided on anything for the future?"

CHAPTER NINETEEN

Following the conference call, Sean and Anne only had time for a quick coffee in private before their first interview, Sean said, "I told you things were okay at home. You shouldn't worry so much, O'Leary's is in capable hands under Shannon's stewardship."

"I know I shouldn't worry so much and I've thought about it. I'm going to basically leave O'Leary's to you and Shannon and I'm going to focus here."

"Good idea, I think you should plan on moving here as soon as you can."

"I agree. There are a few things I need to take care of at home, pack some personal stuff and clothes. I'm going to put my furniture in storage and give up my apartment. The apartment here is beautifully furnished and I have everything I need really, except clothes."

"You should speak to Bev about your wardrobe, I think you'll need to buy a lot of new stuff that's appropriate for this climate. You can expense it to the project and go on a shopping spree with Bev. I'm sure she knows all the right stores. Ok, let's call in chef and see what he has to say for himself." While Anne talked over the standard interview points, Sean went over his resume and employee file, both of which were admirable. When there was a lull in the conversation, Sean said, "I'd like to host a little banquet this evening say seven o'clock. Does that work for you?"

Chef replied, "Certainly sir, how many people are you expecting?"

"I'm inviting all the employees and their families."

"Yes sir, do you have any preferences for the menu?"

"No, I'll leave it up to you."

"Do you have a budget in mind?"

"Yes, whatever it takes to provide a meal that they will still be talking about years from now."

Sean called Mona on the cell phone he was given when he arrived, "Hi Mona, please advise all employees that they are invited to a banquet this evening at seven in the ballroom, spouses and children are also invited. Tell them that attendance is optional. If they can't make it that's fine."

After the chef had gone, Chuck, the Food and Beverage Manager came in. This time Sean was true to his word, he listened but didn't talk. When the F&B manager left, Sean asked, "So what do you think, is Chuck five-star material?"

"No, at least not yet. I think he has the right attitude and can be developed. I was a bit concerned by his depth of wine knowledge. He's ok on African wines but a bit weak on French, Italian and American. I want to send him to O'Leary's to work under Pascal for a few months. Then on to a sommelier course in California so he can get up to speed on California wines which I think many of our guests will favor."

"On the topic of wines, perhaps you should look at the inventory in stock and place orders where necessary. I doubt they'll even have any California product in the wine cellar; you should probably place a large order, which may take some time to get here. I agree with your plan for Chuck, ship him off to Scranton a.s.a.p."

The executive housekeeper, Shelley, was decidedly nervous but had a lot of experience in high-end properties and Anne thought she was capable of handling this property when full of guests.

Anne went through the usual interview small talk and said, "If we had sixty rooms full of people who would be here long term and working in their rooms, what do you think we'd need to do to handle them?"

"I think we'd need to do a laundry service plan which is no problem from an equipment or staff point of view. I suggest that rooms be equipped with laundry bags with the room number stenciled on them.

Guests should be advised to put their laundry bag outside their door at night before bedtime and we'll pick them up, do the laundry during the night and have it at their door when they wake up. Another issue is that the guests will need to put a card on the door handle or press #3 on their phones if they're ready to have their rooms made up. Once they get used to this, it shouldn't be an issue. The challenge for us will be to stay on top of the guest notifications so we disturb them as little as possible. My people are good at that."

When she left Sean asked, "Well what's the verdict?"

"She'll be okay. She was a little nervous when she first came in, I expect that she wasn't planning on you being here and you probably intimidated her."

"Why don't you send her to O'Leary's for a month and see how she does under pressure? She says the right things and has a good resume, but I'm not sure about the pressure of a full house."

"Ok, she'll go to O'Leary's right away."

The chief of maintenance, Johnnie, also looked after the groundskeeper job and was a tough, old, weather-beaten guy who had been around the block a few times.

He spoke with the confidence of someone who actually knew what he was doing and who had been doing it since Colonel Saunders was a private.

Sean once again just listened while Anne did all the talking. Once he left, Sean said, "I doubt there is much around here that he can't fix; I bet he has a machine shop and probably makes his own parts when things need parts replaced. I'll visit his shop on the pretense of seeing how the plans for the new sports fields are coming. If I get a vote, he's a keeper."

Sean left Anne to conduct the balance of the interviews. Personnel issues are her bailiwick, but at least so far, Sean felt that someone in the past had a terrific sense for people because there were certainly some good people here.

Sean called for a burger from room service while he planned the rest of his day. After lunch, he called for Robert, the golf cart jockey. And asked for a more in-depth tour of the property starting at the front gate and taking in all the buildings and land within the area used for mansion grounds. As he was driven around, Sean was interested in observing the employees as they worked. They seemed to be happy, some singing, others whistling, some chatting to their workmates. He had Robert drive the whole golf course slowly and Sean noted the excellent overall appearance and condition.

The greens were like pool table surfaces, the fairways trimmed in the style of a links course, challenging, particularly for the infrequent golfer. He did another quick walk through of the stables and car garage and then went into the maintenance shop. Johnnie greeted him with a smile and a welcome to his world. As Sean expected, the shop was very well equipped in terms of machinery. It's necessary for a relatively remote area where parts were hard to come by and often entailed several flights to arrive. What Sean didn't foresee was the appearance of the place. Johnnie asked if he would like a coffee and Sean said he would love one. Johnnie led him over to a wet bar with a small refrigerator, a sink, a microwave and a coffee machine, one of those that made coffee from little individual cups and permitted a variety of choices. "What's your pleasure, Mr. O'Leary?" Johnnie asked.

"A decaf please if you have it, Johnnie," Sean replied.

"Coming up."

Sean said, "I'm very impressed with the size, machinery and cleanliness of your shop. Is it always like this or is this because of our visit?"

Johnnie handed Sean his coffee and motioned toward the wet bar, "Cream and sugar?"

"No thanks, black is fine."

"To answer your question, we always keep the place clean. Many of us are graduates of the army car pool and learned military discipline particularly about cleanliness at an early age.

We're often called upon to manufacture parts. Some we make for the antique cars where, in some cases, new parts are no longer available at any price. Some we make for buildings and grounds equipment or the vehicle fleet and even down to household appliances. Two weeks ago, we rebuilt Chef's favorite toaster. It may not sound like much, but out here things are hard to come by so we're called on a lot."

"What do you think about the addition of a baseball diamond, a football field, and a cricket ground?"

"Our job is to provide what management needs, always has been, always will be. We'll happily build these projects and anything else you want, we sure have enough land. I've been working on the plans and should have them ready before you go back to the States."

"Thanks, Johnnie that would be a big help."

Sean asked Robert to take him to the employee housing. Robert was surprised by this request but took him there. Sean's eyes opened wide as they crested a hill and the staff accommodations came into view. Robert pointed out a cluster of six bungalows that appeared to be about 1,200 square feet each. And a complex comprised of seventy units. One building comprised of one-bedroom suites for singles and the other building of two and three-bedroom homes for families.

There was a good size pool, a tennis court, a children's playground and another building near the playground that Robert pointed out was the school and infirmary. The bungalows were for supervisory level personnel such as chef, Johnnie, and Shelley, the executive housekeeper, Chuck, the food and beverage manager and Teaghan Walsh, the nurse practitioner. Several golf carts were in the parking lot as were children's and adult's bicycles.

Sean thought this could be a middle-class complex in any decent suburb in the US.

Sean said, "This is a very nice complex Robert, do you live here?"

"Yes, in the apartments for families, we have two girls."

"Are residents happy living here?"

"Very much so, we have satellite television, the internet, a library and a small convenience store. We also have a community center for things like billiards, cards, darts a library and rooms for arts and crafts. Really everything we need."

"I don't notice any private cars."

Robert replied, "No need, we have several large passenger vans that do daily trips into Harare to pick up supplies and take employees into the city for things like shopping, doctor's visits and whatever else they require. Should anyone need a private car, they can sign one out from the motor pool."

"It seems like you have everything that you need in this community. Is there anything else that you want?"

"There has been talk of putting together a soccer field for the youngsters. There is a soccer league for kids in the vicinity and we could probably field a team if we had a field, a coach, and equipment."

"Let me think about it. For now talk to the others and see if a soccer field is a top priority in terms of what they would like to see added to the community. When you have the answer, let Miss Watson know and her and I will discuss it. If a majority is in favor, we'll take a serious look at it. "What do you do about daycare while mothers work?"

"Teaghan, besides being a nurse, took a diploma in early childhood education. She runs the daycare facility along with a mother who works there full time. All our children receive free education including university for those who want to go. Presently we have three children of our employees in University, one in teachers' college, one in science who is thinking of veterinary school, and another studying physical education. In fact if we do the soccer team idea, she could be the coach as she goes to class three days a week and she has been a star player on the University team for two years."

Sean thanked Robert and said he would walk back. From here he would walk through the extensive gardens, pause at the peaceful ponds stocked with exotic fish and come out by the swimming pool. Since it was still a couple of hours before cocktail hour, he decided to walk the inside of the mansion once again. He went into the kitchen, which was alive with preparation for the banquet this evening. Although the pace was hectic, as one would imagine, there was no sense of panic, no yelling. The kitchen was of course crowded with containers of ingredients, but that was the only sign of clutter. The place was still spotless.

He didn't bother Chef or talk to anyone and walked out to the banquet halls. Which were also busy with the staff setting up tables and decorating the room under the direction of Chuck, the food, and beverage manager. Sean asked Chuck to have a podium set up and the sound system ready to go at about seven-thirty. Waiters would pass among the guests serving trays of appetizers and fruit punch.

Sean looked in at the library and wondered if something needed to be done with the room from an interior design perspective. He felt is was close to perfect as is but decided to leave that to Shannon and Anne.

He went up the stairs to check out the stairway and walked the halls of the second floor. He used his passkey to gain access to random rooms to refresh his memory of them. Having inspected fifteen rooms, he took a different stairway up to floor three, looked at ten randomly chosen suites and did the same on level four. He headed back to his suite and decided to go for a swim. He changed into his swimsuit, covered up with the plush bathrobe provided and went down to the pool area. More wide awake this time than when he was in here three days ago just off the plane. He gave the whole area a close inspection, jumped into the indoor portion of the pool and swam outside through the pass provided. He did a few laps for the exercise benefit then climbed into a floating chair to just float around and enjoy the sun. No sooner had he hit the chair and Fred the bartender came out of the Zulu Pub entrance and delivered a fruit punch. Fred said, "here you go Mr. O'Leary, try this, it's made from all local fruit and non-alcoholic."

Sean took a long drink of the ice-cold concoction and thanked Fred. An attendant from the spa appeared and offered Sean a sun hat and a tube of heavy-duty sunblock ointment. She asked him to turn around in his chair and back it against the side of the pool so she could apply the sunscreen to his back.

She said, "We wouldn't want you sunburned for the party this evening sir." He thanked her and applied some more ointment to his chest and legs and drifted away to the center of the pool.

As he drifted, he thought about the progress made so far and what was left to do. He decided that a meeting with Anne was in order and signaled the pool attendant for a phone.

He called Anne and said, "When are you through interviewing for today?"

"In about fifteen minutes, I have only one left today."

"Let's meet in my suite, I want to get caught up and see where we should go from here."

Anne knocked on his door just as Sean had stepped out of the shower. He slipped on the robe, let her in, told her to fix drinks and that he would be right out. A few minutes later, his hair still wet, Sean came out of the bedroom in casual attire and suggested they go out on the deck. Comfortably seated at the teak table under a large umbrella, Sean said, "I did a private walk around and spoke to a few interesting employees. I talked to Robert, our cart driver from yesterday and Johnnie, the maintenance guy. I got filled in pretty good on life here in general and had a look at the employee village.

My first impression is that I know why employees stay here and are concerned that they may lose their jobs over this change in management.

They have what would be, by Zimbabwean standards, luxury accommodation, free schooling through to and including university, free daycare, free medical care and a host of other benefits. They even have their own swimming pool! We need to reinforce the fact that they are all staying on under the new management so I think you should be hostess this evening and I'll remain in the background. I've talked with Robert and he's going to poll the others to see what we could add to make their lot even better. His first reaction is a soccer field and team, but I asked him to get back to you once he has spoken to the others. What do you think?"

"Super idea, it will be an opportunity for them to see that I'm not an ogre and that I'm approachable. In fact, I'll announce a monthly award of $1,000 USD to the employee who submits the best idea for an improvement to Lion's Pride."

Sean continued, "I had an idea while floating in the pool. Let's award use of the antique cars to software developers that are the highest earners and that sign on for a three-year stay after year one. They could each get to select a vehicle for their own use, one that they could, if they want to, wash, wax and generally baby and do minor maintenance as a hobby. They could drive them all they want just like they owned it."

"Now that's a hell of an idea, I'll run it by Bev and see what she thinks. It's a way to put them to use while keeping them in her possession as a remembrance of her uncle."

"It also occurred to me that once the Saturday morning architect and contractor's meeting is over, I really won't have much to do here. Unless something comes up that you, Doc or Bev think I should deal with. Let's see how the meeting goes, but I think that it would make more sense for me to head back and hold the fort and for Shannon to spend more time here than we had planned. I think you three ladies can do the interior design job and brow beat the architect and contractor better than I can. Then you could all meet with Doc when he comes; before you come back to prepare to move."

"Sounds like that would make sense. Let's see how the Saturday meeting goes, but let's get Mona to set up a conference call for Sunday morning with Shannon and Doc to discuss this possible change of plans."

"So how did the interviews go?"

"Better than I expected. With some intense training, I think I can get a lot of our hotel staff from among the existing employees. I'll have a better idea after I complete the interviews to-morrow. I also have meetings with three leading hospitality recruiting firms lined up so tomor-row is going to be pretty busy for me. Next week

I intend to organize the training plan and begin hiring anyone we need from outside."

Sean said, "I'm looking forward to tonight's banquet. We'll learn a lot about the capabilities of our chef and catering staff and at the same time entertain all employees and their families."

Anne said, "I've been thinking of Shannon but resisting contacting her so she doesn't get the idea that I'm "hovering." I have also been wondering how things are going with Doc, he has a full plate."

"I'm going to see if Bev can organize a helicopter to take us on a tour of the whole 1,900 acres of property owned by Lion's Pride. I want to have the full picture before I head home."

CHAPTER TWENTY

At the appointed hour, Doc arrived at the accounting firm of Lau and Porter. He told the receptionist that he had a ten o'clock appointment with Dr. Lau, the firm's managing Hong Kong partner. It was a mid-sized practice by international standards. Due to a merger a little over five years ago, what was Lau and Partners became Lau and Porter. The Porter group was based mostly in Europe but had a few South African offices including one in Zimbabwe. The merger was good for both firms because Dr. Lau had always wanted to diversify from the total commitment he had in Asia and the Porter firm had been actively pursuing a merger in Asia.

Dr. Lau greeted Doc as he was ushered into his spacious corner office overlooking Hong Kong Harbor with a view to the Star Ferry terminal on the Kowloon side. The first impression one got was of a well-established but not overly opulent firm.

"Good morning Mr. O'Connell, make yourself comfortable." He motioned to a pair of leather club chairs across from a beautiful, antique Chinese cherry wood table.

"May I offer you a cup of the world's finest coffee, Blue Mountain from Jamaica?"

"I love Blue Mountain, so yes please."

Dr. Lau pushed a button on his intercom and said one word, "Coffee." He was probably in his forties, well dressed and good looking. He obviously took care of himself as he had an athletic demeanor.

He said, "So you're looking to establish a company in Hong Kong and are interested in having an accounting firm here. Is that right?"

"That's correct doctor, we're a new company and, quite frankly, are uninitiated in Hong Kong business. We have some rather ambitious plans and don't want to make any mistakes as a result of our lack of local knowledge."

"What you need is what we call Guanxi in Cantonese. It means several things but mainly 'contacts' or 'relationships'. Business here is done person-to-person unlike in North America where it is more company-to-company. For instance, if you were a computer salesman selling us Toshiba computers but you changed to selling Dell computers, if we had a good relationship, we would start using Dell computers because we would stick with you. This is Guanxi. That's what I mean when I say we need a firm with local knowledge to help us along."

"What business are you in, Mr. O'Connell?"

"We are in software but before I get into that, can we talk about your firm and the services you provide?"

"Certainly, we provide full service, we handle the usual things that North American accountants do such as bookkeeping, tax, audit, insolvency and general consulting advice pertaining to these practice areas. We also provide corporate secretarial services. This includes company incorporation and corporate registered offices. We are presently the registered office for over 1,300 companies. For some of these clients we handle re-invoicing, where goods are shipped through Hong Kong on route to an overseas buyer. We receive the original invoice from the manufacturer and mark up the prices as instructed by the client, then send along the revised invoice to the purchaser. For some clients, mostly overseas, we receive mail, telephone calls and other forms of communication and pass them on to them. So it's conceivable that a distributor, let's say a shoe merchant based in Seattle, could order his shoes from Asia for shipment to a buyer in say San Francisco and by having us as his registered office, never have to deal with the product after the sale."

"I had heard of this service but never fully understood the mechanics of it."

"We have offices and conference rooms available, with a full secretarial pool for our clients when they visit Hong Kong, I'll show them to you if you like."

"I would like to see them on my way out. One of the reasons I decided to speak with you was because you have offices both in Hong Kong and Zimbabwe. At this stage of our development as a company, we would like to pay our fees in Zimbabwe where we have the bulk of our capital. Can this be arranged?"

"I think you'll find in Hong Kong virtually all

things may be arranged. If you let me know which services you would like, I'll prepare a proposal letter to be issued from our Zimbabwe office and once it's signed and our retainer is paid, we can be underway. But first it would really help if I were to know a bit about what you are trying to accomplish in Hong Kong."

"I don't wish to sound melodramatic however, our business is, as I said, early in the start up stage and we need for now to keep a tight lid on what we are doing in order to put off potential competition. We want to get off the ground running and be well established before anyone else copies our business model. I can assure you that we are honest business people starting up a legitimate business nothing illegal is involved. Our capitalization is just over a half a billion USD."

"I am sure that your reputation is solid Mr. O'Connell or you wouldn't have been referred by our mutual friend at Hong Kong Shanghai Bank."

"The same is true in reverse. It doesn't take me long to assess a person's character so I am ready to do business with you with one provision, please stop calling me Mr. O'Connell, my name is Donovan, my friends call me Doc."

"Agreed Doc if you call me Tom."

"Tom it is, now let's get to work. Have your Zimbabwe office email the proposal letter to my partner, Bev Patterson, at this email address with a copy to me at the email address on my card." He handed Tom a copy of Bev's card. He had given Tom his card when he first came in.

"Bev will pay the retainer directly to that office. Incidentally, Bev and I are equal partners so whatever she says is the same as if I said it.

I'm going to appoint an attorney tomorrow and have him prepare powers of attorney for both Bev and I so we can act on each other's behalf anywhere in the world."

Tom asked, "Who are you considering as your attorney?"

"I'm meeting with Sir Anthony Kosztyo at Kosztyo, Wong and Butterton."

"Good choice, we have worked closely with them in the past and I know they will serve you well. Please give my regards to Anton when you see him."

"I'll do that and it's good to hear that you work closely with them.

As you'll see, our business is going to act as an incubator generating a host of other companies over time, so there will be a great deal of interaction between your two firms."

When Doc left Tom's office he felt good about Tom, the accounting firm and the relationship that they have with the law firm. Tom had already assigned him a part time office and secretary.

Doc was meeting Art, his realtor, at the Hong Kong Club for lunch then viewing a flat at mid levels and one in Kowloon. Since he still had an hour, he used the office in the accounting firm and sent an email to Bev telling her about the appointment of Lau and Porter and the requirement for her to pay the retainer. He also mentioned that they would need a name for their holding company and did she have any suggestions.

His new part-time secretary, Winnie, asked, "Would you like a coffee Mr. O'Connell?"

Doc said, "Yes, if you can get me another one of those Jamaican Blue Mountain coffees."

"Yes sir and I'll make a note in your file that Jamaican Blue is your coffee of choice."

Doc loved this firm already. He walked over to the Hong Kong Club and met up with Art in the Jackson Room. Over lunch Doc said, " We're going to have to stop meeting this way, the meals are excellent but the pounds are adding up."

Art replied, "In my business it's rare that I don't have a business lunch and always in the best restaurants. So I do a couple of things. I watch what I eat, limit my alcohol intake to one beer or one glass of wine and consider it to be my main meal of the day. Dinner is usually a bowl of soup and a salad. I try to walk to as many meetings as possible, but this is often not possible because I am usually taking clients to showings. I do have an exercise room in my condo building and I try to get in an hour a day but again this isn't always possible due to business. You'll soon see that in Hong Kong, once it's known that you're a resident here, you'll probably average three invitations a week to various business functions, usually cocktails from five to seven."

"I'll have to remember that regimen and try to do something similar. My problem is that I love good food and when I look at these menus, my resolve dissolves."

The flat at mid levels was actually very near Art's. It was nice with an excellent view but only two bedrooms and not furnished. It's main advantage was that you could easily walk to the business core of Central and Wan Chai as well as to the Star Ferry which brought you into close proximity to most of the businesses on the Kowloon side. In fact after viewing the mid levels flat, Art dismissed his driver for now and they walked to the Star Ferry for the short, pleasant trip to Kowloon.

The Kowloon apartment had a whole different feel; it was right in the center of things, beside the Star Ferry terminal. The flat itself was nearly twenty five hundred square feet. Walking around the exterior of the building, Doc was aware of lots of kids, apparently the flat sizes drew the attention of expat families with two or more children.

When they left the building, they stopped at the bar in the Regent Hotel Steakhouse for a beer and discussed the offerings Doc had seen so far.

Doc said, "They're all suitable and have different appeals but I think I'm sold on the first one we saw in Repulse Bay."

"Are you sure? I can show you more tomorrow if you wish."

"No I'm sure, one thing though I want a short term lease, month to month would be preferable. This whole move has been thrust upon me so fast that I don't wish to make any long term commitments at this point"

Art took his cell and called the owner of the flat. They exchanged pleasantries and then got down to business. Art said he had an offer to lease on a month-to-month basis at twenty percent below asking price.

The owner thought about it and said that he wanted at least a two-year lease at full asking. Art said that his client would not go for a two-year lease and wanted to pay less than asking.

He pointed out that Doc was a senior professional businessperson who would treat the condo as if it were his own; he didn't have any children or pets and didn't smoke. After some more haggling back and forth the owner agreed to a six-month lease at ninety five percent of asking. Art put him on hold, took a sip of beer and related the deal to Doc who nodded in agreement. Art said a few more things to the owner and hung up.

Art called his secretary and gave her some instructions then hung up and said, "The lease will be ready for you to sign if you want to accompany me to my office. If you give me a check, I'll hand over the keys and you can move in tomorrow if you like."

"Boy things move fast in Hong Kong," Doc said.

"Hong Kong is the embodiment of that old expression, "Time is money."

They boarded the ferry and returned to Art's office. True to his word, the lease was ready, Doc handed over a check and Art gave him the keys.

Art said, "If you like, my driver could take you and my secretary Margaret to the suite, she could give it a once over from a woman's perspective then make a list of things you need and go pick them up for you."

"No, it's too late in the day, I wouldn't want to impinge on Margaret's free time. How about tomorrow?"

"Sure that works, I'll need my car but I'll get a car from the service and send Margaret along to the Mandarin. You could check out and then proceed to the condo and Margaret can do her thing then."

"I really appreciate it Art, I'll talk to you tomorrow."

Doc got back to his room in time to call Shannon. Everything was fine in Scranton. She had heard from Gary and was planning to go to the cottage for two days when Anne got back in order to meet with the architect and builder and see how they were progressing. She wanted to make sure that they had all the input they would need from her before she left for Lion's Pride.

She said, "Did you get the email from Mona re the Sunday morning call?"

"I haven't even had time to check email. I just got in and wanted to talk to you before it was getting too late to call. I had a busy day, got an accounting firm signed up for Bev and I's company. Incidentally we need a name for the enterprise so put on your thinking cap and come up with another beauty like Lion's Pride. I got a condo in an upmarket, quiet part of Hong Kong Island called Repulse Bay. Its relatively new, beautifully furnished and I think you're going to love it when you visit."

They said their protracted good byes and signed off.

Doc went up to the pool for a few laps before dinner.

After his swim he went to Chinnery's Bar. As he walked in, Carleton, the bartender said, "I believe it's number 49, Royal Lochnagar" he poured two fingers and handed it to Doc. He took it to his usual table in the corner and settled in to the club chair to think about things. Tomorrow morning he would check out, move his things to the new condo and, with Margaret's help, stock up with the necessities to make the place livable.

He made up his mind to take a late afternoon flight on Sunday instead of Saturday to meet Bill in Bangkok. He would email this decision to Bill, who wouldn't mind having some rest time after his long flight from Washington. This would give Doc time to settle into the condo, visit with Sir Anthony at the law firm in the afternoon and do something else that has been on his mind; join the Aberdeen Marina Club. He decided to take a taxi over to the Cleveland, one of his frequently visited Chinese restaurants for an early dinner then take a taxi to the new condo in order to have a quiet look around before Margaret picked him up at the Mandarin in the morning.

After dinner at the Cleveland, Doc found a taxi just dropping off passengers and was able to get it right away. The driver spoke good English but Doc spoke Cantonese to him in order to practice his use of the language. When he got to his building the night doorman/security guard greeted him in a friendly but wary manner, as he hadn't seen him before.

Fortunately Margaret had called ahead to let security know Doc had leased the unit in case he decided to go to the condo before morning.

In the suite, he found a bottle of Laphroaig and two Waterford crystal glasses courtesy of Art. He began his walk around in the master bedroom. It was fully furnished even down to bed linens and towels. He tested the bedroom television and found it working fine as did the air conditioning. The closet needed hangers so that would go on his shopping list for morning. The ensuite needed a scale, as he liked to keep tabs on his weight regularly. The guest room closets also needed hangers and all three bed-rooms needed waste baskets. They would need things like toilet paper, Kleenex, shampoo and other toiletries. The kitchen had all the cutlery, pots, pans and other equipment necessary. So unless Margaret came up with some things he may have missed it looked like the kitchen, once it has some food in the cupboards, was stocked. He went out on the deck and watched the fishing junks and western style yachts go by. He locked up, went down to the lobby and asked the doorman to call him a taxi. Twenty minutes later he was in his room, he filled up the tub and called down to the desk asking that his bill be sent up, as he'll check out in the morning.

At nine a.m., Margaret called his room to announce her arrival to take him to his new home.

As they drove to Repulse Bay Towers he told Margaret about his trip to the condo the night before, "Except for food and toiletries, some clothes hangers, waste baskets and a bathroom scale, I think I'm all set."

Margaret said, "Well let's have a look and then I'll go to Park and Shop and stock up on food. Is there anything you want in terms of food?

"Maybe some steaks and chops for the freezer. The rest should be canned as I will be away a lot and there is no sense having anything here that will get spoiled. Get some good coffee and teas, some sodas like coke, some wines and beer."

"I'll take a taxi in case you need the car."

"No you take the car, I won't be going anywhere until mid-afternoon and you'll be back before then. If I do need to go out, I'll get another car from the service in which case once you get the food in the condo, just take the car back to your office and dismiss it."

"Ok Mr. O'Connell, I'm off, see you later."

Later in the morning Margaret came back. Margaret, the driver and the doorman had to make two trips each in order to get it all in. Margaret put everything away, including the hangars and bathroom scale then Doc sent her back to her office with the driver. Doc called the secretary, Winnie, at the accounting firm and asked her to send a large bouquet of flowers to Margaret at her office with a thank you note he drafted and dictated.

Doc made a few phone calls pertaining to his visits next week and took a nap before showering and heading back to Central for his 3 p.m. appointment with Sir Anthony Kosztyo, Esq. of the legal firm of Kosztyo, Wong and Butterton. Sir Anthony turned out to be a down to earth yet gregarious individual. He was tall and stocky, well, but conservatively dressed and the type of person that could intimidate when mad but fortunately today was happy. He had a presence that would stand him in good stead in front of the Chairman of the Board of a large corporation or a judge of the highest court in the land. He seemed like exactly the type of lawyer you would want on your side in any legal dispute. Similar to Tom Lau at the accounting firm, Doc took to Sir Anthony at once. He passed on Tom Lau's regards and said that he had retained Tom's firm as the accounting firm for his new companies. He told Sir Anthony about the same amount of detail he had shared with Tom. Sir Anthony said that he would have the Zimbabwe office of his firm draw up the proposal letter and send it to Bev with a copy to Doc. It was understood that Bev would also take care of paying the retainer. As they shook hands, Doc said, "From now on please call me Doc."

Sir Anthony said, "Please call me Anton."

CHAPTER TWENTY-ONE

After his visit with Sir Anthony, Doc thought he'd chance dropping in on his friend, Phillip Waters, Vice President of Personal Banking at Hong Kong Shanghai Bank.

Doc was shown into Phillip's office and greeted him, "Hi Phillip, sorry to drop in unannounced. But I was literally across the street and thought I'd take a chance that you would have a few minutes to chat."

"I always have time for you, Donovan, how did you get along with my referral to Dr. Lau?"

"We hit it off just fine, he's our accountant as of today, so that's one task off my plate. Speaking of my plate I need to establish some bank accounts and get some money transferred into them. Can you take care of this for me?"

"Of course, whose names are the accounts in?"

"One is in my name, one is in the name of my partner, Beverly Patterson. This document gives you all the contact details for both of us. I want to transfer in ten million USD to Bev's new account and the same amount into mine. Transfer from the bank shown here, it has already been authorized to make the transfer when you contact them, use the code word 'Lion'. I'll also need a corporate account, is that within your purview or do I need to deal with someone in corporate banking?"

"No need to deal with anyone else Doc. We

arrange things in such a way that all you need to do is to tell me what you want and it's done."

"May I use your phone to call Tom Lau?"

"Certainly, I have him on speed dial, here you are."

"Hi Tom, could you please set me up with a shelf company and send the details over to Phillip. I want to transfer some funds to a corporate account and Phillip will need the details to complete the transfer. Can I swing by your office tomorrow morning to sign whatever needs signing?"

"Sure Doc, but if you want, I'll have our runner bring them to your condo in the morning and you can sign the documents there. Who are the shareholders?"

"Issue fifty percent of the shares in my name and fifty percent in the name of Beverly Patterson. I left all contact details with your secretary. List Bev, as President and me as CEO, both of us are the directors. Just fill in any other posts that you require with your people and we'll straighten it all up later."

"Any particular name you fancy?"

"I'll get one to you shortly, for now just use the first shelf name that comes up."

"Let's see, the next name on the list is "Rauno Engineering Inc."

"That'll do, we'll change it later. Anything else you need?"

"No, it'll be done tomorrow morning when you sign the documents. Pass me to Phillip and

I'll authorize the corporate account."

"Ok Tom, thanks, here's Phillip."

When Tom and Phillip were finished, Phillip said, "Do you want the corporate account money transferred from the same bank and how much is it?"

"Yes, the same bank has been authorized to transfer fifty million USD to the corporate account on your authorization. The code word is 'Pride'."

"I'll have our runner deliver a platinum Visa card in your name to your condo with a million USD limit on it. The bills will come to me directly and, if you sign here, I'll pay them on your behalf. I'll send Bev's card by courier along with an authorization card for her to sign. She will also have a million USD limit. Both of you can raise your limits on a phone call to me and the limit is per transaction. This way you can travel freely knowing that you never have to worry about paying your Visa bill."

"Thanks, Phillip but how did you get our cards so soon?"

"I ordered them the other day once we talked on the phone and you told me about Beverly being your partner. I anticipated what you both would require. You'll soon learn Doc, in Hong Kong the primary objective is to make money. We earn money when you do your financial transactions with us. So it's in our best interest to see that you're able to access your financial servicing needs 24/7 and anywhere in the world."

"Man, I wish bankers thought like this in North America."

"No, don't say that. If they did and if you had a reasonable tax system, you wouldn't need Hong Kong."

"When will the transfers take place?"

"Oh they are all done, both you and Bev now have ten million USD in your new HKSB accounts and your corporate account has fifty million USD in it."

"How did you manage that so fast?"

"It's called keystrokes my boy. Now that you are so wealthy, I'd suggest a celebratory drink at The Club, as the Hong Kong Club is referred to. While we are there, we can get you signed up as a member if you like."

"I'm not even going to ask how you can arrange that so fast."

"Oh that's simple, you are being sponsored by HKSB, and membership is, therefore, automatic. Besides if I can get you signed up as we go in, then we can charge our drinks to your new member's account. Sort of a christening you might say."

At the Club, Doc ran into Art, who, of course, knew Phillip so they had a drink together. Doc told Art he had just joined The Club this evening. According to tradition, Doc had to buy the drinks for Phillip, Art and everyone they introduced to Doc. Like sharks sensing blood in the water, several members gathered around to be introduced to Doc and to help break in his new membership account. Doc was made welcome and invited to the Friday afternoon/evening get together of the regulars in the Club Bar.

Doc got Art aside and said, "If you're free let's you and I meet tomorrow for lunch at the Aberdeen Marina Club. I'd like to join and maybe, as a long-standing member, you can get me in."

Art took out his cell phone and called Margaret his secretary who by now was at home. He said, "Margaret, Mr. O'Connell wishes to join the Aberdeen Marina Club tomorrow. Please make the arrangements tomorrow morning. Tell Nick, the membership director, that Doc and I will drop in to sign up just before lunch, say twelve thirty."

The corporate documents arrived by Tom Lau's office courier at nine a.m. Doc went over them then signed them and the runner took them back along with a note to copy everything to Sir Anthony and Bev. He and Bev now officially owned fifty percent each of Rauno Engineering Inc. a registered Hong Kong Company. The firm has fifty million USD in the bank and close to five hundred million USD in reserve in Zimbabwe, Switzerland and the Grand Cayman's.

Doc had a few hours before Art was picking him up so he decided to go for a run in his neighborhood to check it out both for running tracks and air quality. He managed to find a trail that the doorman had suggested and ran for an hour. The air wasn't too bad by Asian standards and the trail offered a variety of forest and ocean views.

When he returned to the condo, he went for a swim in the pool and checked out the tennis courts. Neither facility was getting any action from other tenants.

Art arrived at Doc's condo at eleven forty-five and came up to see how he was settling in. Doc had only been there for two days, but somehow he'd managed to give the place a bit of a lived-in look. They headed for the Aberdeen Marina Club and walked into the membership office at twelve twenty. Nick welcomed Doc as a member and gave him a package of information on the club. Doc signed the necessary papers and gave Nick a check to cover the fees. Nick gave Doc his membership card, which acted as an internal charge card and an access key to the gate to the Marina and the parking garage. Art's driver was standing by to take the documents to the car. Art and Doc went to lunch at the Portside Room, a casual indoor/outdoor restaurant. Nick had offered to take Doc on the new member's tour, but Art said he would take care of it.

Looking out on the boats Doc said, "There is something about this place that I find very enticing, I can't put my finger on it, but it seems to stay in my mind. I feel really comfortable here, I guess this is probably only my third or fourth visit, but I feel like I'm a part of it some-how. It's strange; I didn't get the same feeling at The Hong Kong Club last evening, it's more business oriented. Look at some members sitting here in Bermuda shorts and they don't look out of place despite the very up-market atmosphere. Shannon has to see this; whoever did the décor really knew what they were doing."

Art said, "The owners, the Shangri-La hotel people, know how to cater to an exclusive clientele. They have created an environment that offers both an opportunity to have a formal experience or an informal one depending on your mood. But, in either case, the experience will be an elegant one."

"If you're busy this afternoon, I can show myself around."

"No, I've got the family coming for a swim at 4 o'clock and an early dinner, would you like to join us?"

"Thanks but no on the dinner part. I'd love to see your gang again so perhaps we can have a drink with Lois when they get here then I'll be on my way. I still have some things to do before I go to Bangkok tomorrow.

After lunch Art took Doc on a complete tour of the club and a walk on the marina docks.

Doc asked, "Does anyone live on these boats or are they just for pleasure use?"

"Some people live on board, in fact, there is a large contingent of Canadians living aboard their boats here."

"You know that might be an idea for me. I love boats and grew up on the river, maybe that has been haunting me about this place." Doc noticed a Canadian flag flying from the stern of what looked to be a sixty-foot sailboat. There was a guy in the cockpit doing a repair job on a VHF radio. Doc stopped and said to him, "Excuse me are you the owner of this boat?"

"Yes I am, can I help you?"

"Well, I'm a Canadian and saw your flag. I'm a new club member and wondered if I could ask you a few questions?"

"Only if you come aboard and join me in a beer, my name is Adrian."

"Hi, Adrian, my name's Donovan, friends call me Doc, this is my friend Art."

Hands were shaken all around and Adrian's wife Charlotte came up from down below bearing a tray of beer.

Adrian introduced her and, beer in hand, they got comfortable in the cockpit of this spectacular yacht.

Doc opened the conversation by saying, "I'm just in the process of moving here from Ottawa and love this club. I've been at the club four times now and there is something about it that agrees with me."

Adrian said, "We know how you feel. We've lived aboard here for three years now and are really comfortable with the lifestyle. There are about thirty families living on their boats and a lot of us have formed a close relationship. I guess we're somewhat out of the ordinary types, sharing a rather unique lifestyle."

"I'm thinking about buying a boat, do you

know of any reputable builders?"

"It depends on what you want. Would it be sail or motor?"

"I'm not much of a sailor, probably motor."

"We had our boat built in Taiwan and we're happy with it. There are some good power boat builders there as well."

Adrian went below and came up with a directory of Taiwan boat builders. He handed it to Doc and said, "Take this with you, the reputable companies have been circled in red."

"Thank you, this will be a big help. What about security? I travel a lot on business so the boat would be left a good deal of the time alone."

Charlotte said, "There has never been a problem here. The club provides good security and there is a group of boat boys who work on the boats here as skippers, deck hands, maintenance men and general caretakers. People who live elsewhere and only use them a few times a year for corporate entertaining own many of these boats.

That boat over there, for instance, is owned by a Japanese businessman. He comes here and takes it out for a few hours two or three times a year. The owner has two boat boys whose full-time job it is to take care of that yacht. Since we employ so many of these guys, they have the word out that no one is to bother any boats in this marina and it works."

"How about telephone and other services?"

"There are telephone lines available if you

want one as well as cable television. We use cell phones and have our own onboard television satellite dish so the only services we need are fresh water, electricity, sewage and garbage removal, all of which are provided. There is a Park and Shop grocery store on the side of the Marina Club building where we get groceries and liquor. You said that you are a club member?"

"Yes as of today I am."

"Well for business entertaining the club is fabulous. Not only do you have a wide array of dining alternatives in the facility, we can also order meals delivered to the boat like room service if we choose.

Business clients who visit us for the first time, I'm sure, don't know what to expect from us 'boat people' but I think they usually leave impressed with our lifestyle. How about another beer?"

"No thanks, we had better shove off, but I'm going to give this idea some serious thought."

Adrian said, "Here take my card and if you have any questions give me a call or if you are back at the club, come on down, the beer is always cold here."

Doc and Art walked back to the club and Art said, "It sounds to me like you're seriously considering this idea of living on a boat."

"I am, I can see where it could be a really pleasant lifestyle living in this club with all it has to offer. You'd have everything you need in a high-quality resort atmosphere and whenever you like, you can cast off and do some boating and maybe some fishing, an excellent way to entertain friends and business associates. Look how friendly those folks were, if the rest of the live-aboard people are as friendly, what a great neighborhood this would be. I think Shannon will love it on her visits as well. I wonder how much boats cost around here?"

"While you're away, I'll have Margaret do some research on the Hong Kong pleasure craft industry so you'll have a package of information waiting for you on your return. I'll have her check with Nick regarding the availability of berths and costs so you have some ideas in this regard as well."

"I feel guilty using Margaret for all this work."

"That's what I pay her for and she is well paid. Besides the thoughtful flowers, you sent her were much appreciated. She thinks the world of you."

They returned to the club and caught up with Lois and the kids at poolside. Lois had a big hug for Doc and they sat in the shade of an oversized beach umbrella and ordered Singapore Slings, Lois' favorite drink and one in keeping with the poolside ambiance.

Doc said he should head home and take care of some business communications regarding his next week's activities. Art picked up his cell and called his driver to meet Doc at the main entrance.

"That's not necessary Art, I can get a taxi."

"No it's ok Doc once he drops you off, he'll head home and I'll get a ride with Lois and the kids after dinner. Have a great week and give me a call on your return. We can meet here in the gym for some serious work-out action."

Lois said, "Now that's what I like to hear, it's going to be extra good having you living in Hong Kong Doc if it gets Art moving in the gym."

When Doc got home, he called Shannon who, as usual, was up watching the late news still wearing Doc's unwashed shirt.

Doc said, "Hi love how are things with you?"

"Hi Sweetheart, I miss you terribly. There are a few things happening here. We had a guest die of a heart attack in the Pub, which was really sad. It happened so quickly, he was playing darts and laughing one minute and the next he was dead on the floor. Not even a chance to help him.

I've been a bit down since it happened, but I feel better having you to talk to so let's shift gears and talk about your day."

"I've been busy since we spoke yesterday. I've joined two clubs. The Hong Kong Club is a very formal businessperson's club in Central District and the Aberdeen Marina Club, a more relaxed recreational club. More like a country club with boats. In fact, I'm thinking of buying a boat and living on it at the Marina Club."

"Well, why not. You've always been around boats and the water and it could be a lot of fun.

A little unconventional maybe, but where does it say we have to be conventional? I guess seeing that poor man die right in front of me has had me thinking about life and how short a journey it can be. I'm starting to understand that old adage that you shouldn't put things off until tomorrow because it may never come. There I go getting sad again, sorry I promised myself not to bring you down."

"It's ok sweetie, being there for each other is what we are all about. I just wish I could be there in person so I could wash that dirty shirt before I wash your back."

"I'm not going to wash this shirt until you get back and give me another one. Maybe you should send one by courier?"

"I should go and let you get some sleep, I have to call Bill in Bangkok to organize a few things. Love you."

Doc called the Mandarin Oriental Bangkok to speak to Bill. The operator at the hotel said that Bill hadn't checked in yet, but they're holding a guaranteed reservation; perhaps he should try the call later. Doc left a message that Bill should call him as soon as he gets in.

Doc hung up and thought, "That's odd, Bill was on a flight that was scheduled to land in Bangkok at one p.m. Bill always followed the same routine after the nineteen-hour flight from Washington. He went directly to the Mandarin Oriental, checked in, and went for a Thai massage at poolside followed by a long swim in the pool."

Doc called the hotel back and asked for the GM, Andrew Chang. Andrew came on the line and said, "Hi Donovan, I understand you're coming in tomorrow, I look forward to seeing you again."

"Hi Andrew, listen have you heard from Bill today?"

"No, did you call his room?"

"Your operator said he hasn't checked in yet."

Andrew checked the computer and said, "She's right, we have a reservation of course, but he hasn't checked in yet."

"I am going to check with the airline to see if he missed his flight."

"No Donovan, let me do it I have contacts with Thai Air who will tell me things they won't tell you.

I'll also have a look around the hotel and double check his room to make sure he hasn't somehow checked in without it being recorded on the computer. I'll call you back in a few minutes."

"Ok thanks, Andrew, I appreciate it. I'll wait by the phone for your call. I'm sorry to bother you with this, but it isn't like Bill to change his routine, I want to make sure he's ok."

CHAPTER TWENTY-TWO

After what seemed like an eternity but was probably between five and seven minutes, Doc's cell phone rang. Without even looking at the caller ID, he pushed the button and said, "Hello, Andrew?"

Andrew replied, "Doc the airline says he was on the flight, first class as usual and the flight landed on time at one o'clock. I've checked with the front desk, looked at his reserved room and searched the property. There's no sign of him here and he missed his hotel car pick up at the airport. Our driver says he stood there with the sign bearing his name but he didn't show up. I have instructed the hotel operator to have him call you should he call in and also the front desk personnel have been told to alert me and to give him a message to call you when he checks in. I don't know what else to do at this point. It's probably too early to call the police."

"No don't do anything further, I'll take it from here. Thanks for your help and let's stay in touch."

There are procedures in place to cover virtually all-possible eventualities regarding agents in the field. Doc knew that when a person is missing, the first twenty-four hours are critical to his or her recovery.

In one way he hesitated to implement the procedure for a missing agent this early, but Doc couldn't see what Bill could be doing or where he could be.

It's been almost five hours now without a word from him. Doc had called his cell phone repeatedly but it was apparently turned off or disabled.

Doc felt that he had to do something; his instincts were telling him the Bill was in trouble. He dialed a particular 'panic' number that rang at the office of the DEA in Washington. The agent who answered asked the nature of the emergency somewhat like a 911 call responder would.

Doc said, "This is Jim Anderson, his code name for such emergencies, I need to speak to the Deputy Director of Operations. Without hesitation a phone rang and was picked up by a groggy DDO who said, "What is it?" Doc knew the DDO's home phone was a secure line so he said, "It's Donovan O'Connell sir, Bill has been missing for five and a half hours."

"Who knows about this?"

"The GM of the Mandarin Oriental Bangkok, Andrew Chang."

"Wait a minute until I put this on record mode. Ok there it is, now tell me everything you know at this point."

Doc said, "I called the Mandarin Oriental Bangkok at four forty five p.m. local time and asked for Bill's room.

The hotel operator said that he hadn't checked in as yet but they were holding a confirmed reservation for him. I left a message that he should call me as soon as he got there. I thought about it and couldn't see where Bill could be for almost four hours so I called Andrew Chang who knows Bill and I. He said he would check on things from his end. He called the airline, Thai Air, who confirmed that Bill had been on the flight. He checked with his front desk personnel and the driver sent to pick him up and no one has seen him."

"Are you sure that there is no stop that he might have made on route from the airport, maybe to see a young lady that you don't know about?"

"No sir. Bill is a stickler for routine. He wouldn't divert from his regular routine voluntarily. As to a lady, that wouldn't happen without me being made aware of it. We are very close friends sir."

"I'm taking charge of this Donovan. I'll dispatch a team to Bangkok immediately. You're to wait where you are for a phone call giving you a time to be at the Hong Kong airport private jet terminal; a DEA plane will pick you up to bring you here. I'll divert a plane that's in Taiwan."

"But sir, I should go to Bangkok, I know lots of people there and perhaps I can help in the investigation."

"Absolutely not, while you technically work for Jim Elliott, you're under my command presently and I'm ordering you to return Washington.

If someone has taken Bill or harmed him, they may be after you as well. Also, we don't know for sure that Bill was on that flight, it could have been someone posing as him that boarded the aircraft and he might still be here. No, there's too much uncertainty at this point and we can't risk you disappearing as well. The team I'm sending over is comprised of the best investigators that we have, FBI, CIA, DEA and probably NCIS. No doubt Jim will want to include a top RCMP investigator as well. They don't need you getting in their way. Send me a list, with contact details of everyone you both have met in the region. Meet me in my office when you get in tomorrow. If you hear from Bill call me at 778-769-0952, this is my secure cell. Likewise I'll call you on the plane if anything develops while you're in the air."

"Ok sir but somehow I feel like I am letting Bill down by running away, I sense he's in trouble and we've always had each other's sixes."

"I know Donovan but you have your orders and you're keeping me from taking action, see you tomorrow."

Doc called Jim at his home. He hated to wake him at this hour but he wanted to fill him in and to confirm the DDO's decision to call him back.

After four rings a sleepy voice said, "Elliott."

"Jim it's Donovan, I need to talk to you."

"Wait one minute. Sorry, I wanted to get to my study. Ok what's the matter?"

Doc filled Jim in on events thus far and told

him of his recall by the DDO.

Jim said, "I agree with his judgment, get moving a.s.a.p. out of there in case there is someone after you as well, assuming someone was after Bill. I'll call the DDO and if he concurs, I am going to send our top two RCMP investigators off to Bangkok on the next plane. They can meet up with the US team over there. Keep me copied on any correspondence to the DDO and stay in touch by phone. Once you get here, I'd suggest that you stay away from this office, your condo and even the cottage until further notice. After you meet with the DDO tomorrow, go underground somewhere until we see what the investigation turns up. Now I have to go and get the RCMP guys airborne. Don't worry Donovan, if any team in the world can find him, this is the team."

As Doc hung up with Jim, he was thinking about the power of the word 'If' as in If any team in the world can find him. What if no team in the world could find him?

Just then his phone rang, the caller ID said Mandarin Oriental. Doc pressed the button and said, "Bill?"

Andrew said, "No, sorry Donovan, it's me. We haven't heard anything yet from Bill, should I involve the police?"

"No, but thanks for your concern. I've called our company's president and got him out of bed. We have our own security people who are top notch and he wants them to deal with it. They are first checking to see if indeed he boarded the plane. He wants to rule out a case of mistaken identity. They want me to return to head office tonight to brief everyone. You will probably be contacted for an interview. Please keep in touch while we sort this out. Just cancel our reservations."

"Ok Donovan, if anything comes up I'll call you, in the meantime if there is anything I can do, you know where I am."

Doc hung up and walked out on the deck to think about the situation. His phone rang again and he quickly answered hoping once more that it was Bill. Again, no such luck. It was the pilot of the DEA plane telling him they would be at Hong Kong International's private jet terminal in an hour.

Doc called his car service and ordered a Mercedes sedan. He grabbed a suitcase and quickly filled it; taking everything that would fit because he didn't know how long he'd be away.

He went downstairs and the car was pulling into the porte-cochere so the doorman took Doc's heavy suitcase out to the car and the driver placed it in the trunk.

Throughout the flight, Doc kept going over in his mind where Bill could be. Why would someone take him?

He refused to think that Bill had been killed and kept hoping that his phone would ring or the pilot would call him to the flight deck to take a call. He ate some of the offered dinner while he pondered the situation.

Despite his orders from the DDO and Jim that he get back to North America immediately, and despite the fact that he could grasp their concerns about any potential problem for him, Doc still felt he was deserting his best friend in the world after Shannon. The flight attendant, Angie, a cute girl that Doc guessed was flirting with him part of the way, asked if he would like a drink. He requested a coffee, black. Doc could seldom tell when a girl was flirting with him; usually Bill had to advise him. In any event it was moot because there would be no more flirting with the ladies now that he was with Shannon and with Bill on his mind, flirting wouldn't occur to him anyway. She didn't have much to do, looking after just the pilots and him so she tried to make friendly conversation about her regular Italian restaurant in Washington, hoping he'd extend a dinner invitation. She was a beautiful girl whom, under different circumstances, Doc would have loved to have dinner with, so he felt he owed her an explanation of sorts.

He said, "Angie I'm heading home to ask the girl I love to marry me. Is it still customary to ask her father's permission these days?"

She was taken by surprise but recovered quickly and said, "I don't think it's as common as it used to be, but I think it's an excellent tradition and shows some respect to the father. If you want my vote, go for it."

That seemed to be the end of the flirting. Doc finished his coffee and went into the bedroom in the back of the plane to try to get some sleep.

Due to favorable tail winds, the pilot said they would land in Washington about 25 minutes ahead of schedule. He also told Doc that there was an SUV waiting to take him to 'the head office' as they called it.

Angie fixed him a big breakfast, made to order and including three pancakes, four sausages, three eggs over easy, hash browns, toast, orange juice, no pulp, and several very acceptable cups of coffee. She was a hell of a cook to be able to do something this good in such a cramped galley. If they always flew together, these pilots were going to have weight gain issues that could impact their flight physicals not to mention their heart health. One of the positive things about the agency is that they monitored employee's health, not only pilots but all employees and provided ample time and equipment for exercise.

If a hotel didn't have adequate workout facilities including a pool, it would not make the list of hotels that employees were permitted to stay at when on business travel. Doc thanked Angie and the two slightly overweight pilots for a great flight and went down the stairs to the waiting SUV.

When he walked into the DDO's office, Doc said, "Good morning sir. I take it there are no new developments?"

"Hello Donovan, no nothing to report yet. Our

investigation team is just landing in Bangkok and they'll meet your RCMP investigators at our embassy. The embassy people have set up meeting rooms, communications facilities and sleeping rooms so they can all stay together. There are four embassy SUVs with drivers, a helicopter and a Learjet all reserved for their exclusive use. We've sent a team of Navy Seals to a nearby secret base. They're fully equipped and very mobile either by air, land or sea. So if any muscle is required it can be wherever needed very quickly."

"That was quick sir, I am glad for Bill's sake that we're on top of it. Did you get my list of Asian contacts I sent from the plane?"

"I did, thanks and our people at the embassy are already arranging interviews with them. Of course they won't know the real reason for the meetings to protect your relationship with them."

"What can I do to help sir, put me to work."

"I want you to meet three of our people and brief them in person. Then I want you to disappear until Jim or I call you. We have decided to suspend operations in your area until this case is resolved.

There is nothing else you can do here except stay out of the way. You're too close to Bill and we can't afford to have personal emotions involved."

The DDO called in and introduced the three section chiefs that the DDO wanted briefed and he wanted it done in his office so that he could hear it once again.

After the briefing the DDO thanked Doc and said, "Now get out of here, stay away from Asia, Ottawa and here as well. If anyone is after you, these are the places they would look. If you want, we can fix you up with a safe house somewhere or even a place on a military base. Let's see how this investigation goes and how you feel.

If you see anything at all that gives you concern, you call me and we'll put you in hiding. Are you ok with that plan for now?"

"I guess I don't have much choice now do I?"

"No I'm afraid not. My secretary has been instructed to make your travel arrangements throughout your temporary exile, so all you do is call her and it's done."

After saying goodbye and shaking hands with the DDO, Doc went out to talk to Clara, the DDO's secretary. "What I need right now is a car but I don't want to rent one because that's traceable."

Clara said, "No problem, as she knew Doc spoke Cantonese she actually said 'Mo Mun Tai'.

What kind of car do you want, a Ferrari, a Lamborghini maybe something faster? We have a pool of cars confiscated from drug ops and can probably get you whatever you say."

"It shouldn't be anything too flamboyant how about a Mustang?"

As she consulted the computer she said, "Lets

see what we have here. I've got a brand new Shelby Cobra or a two year old Mustang convertible."

"I'll take the Cobra."

"Done, I'll have them bring it up to the front door for you. I have here $5,000 USD in cash and ID including a passport, a driver's license and two credit cards. Your name is now Jim Brown. The credit cards have no limit and the bills are sent to me and paid by us so spend freely Jim. One other thing, if you need to go anywhere that involves flying, the DDO has authorized unlimited use of agency aircraft, he explicitly said that commercial flying is not permitted until this blows over."

Doc thanked her and asked, "Where would a fellow find a good flower shop, one with lots of orchids?"

Clara picked up the phone and called a nearby flower shop, the one used by most of Washington's Senators and Congressmen. She asked Doc, "How much do you want to spend?"

"I want the finest they have regardless of cost."

She said, "They have a White Ghost Orchid that costs $1,500."

"Tell them to wrap it up for a road journey, I am on my way to pick it up."

"Wow, you must be very serious about this lucky lady."

"What can I say, she likes orchids?"

Doc took the money and ID, retrieved his

suitcase and headed down to get the Cobra. He was pleasantly surprised to see that it was candy apple red with a shine so deep you could use it as a mirror. This car he was going to enjoy; to the extent he could enjoy anything until he heard from Bill. The driving instructions to the flower shop were excellent and soon Doc, the orchid safely and lovingly packed in the trunk, was headed north.

As he drove he thought, so how do I explain my early return home and what do I say about Bill? Often some truth mixed in with a bit of lying can get a person through a tight spot. He decided to say that Bill had disappeared, the company security force was looking for him and the company wanted Doc out of the way in case whoever took Bill targeted him as well. Essentially what happened, the only difference was the 'company' that was doing the searching. Doc would explain away the fact that Bill's plight was not on the evening news, as a request from the government of Thailand that the whole matter is kept secret.

The 'company' agreed to the secrecy request because the Thai government felt it would help them find Bill if there wasn't any publicity and, after all the Thai government was one of the company's larger clients. Yeah this should work.

He called Jim, "Hi Jim, any news at your end?"

"Hi Doc, are you ok?"

"I've been better. It's driving me nuts that I

can't find Bill, I can't even imagine where he is or how he is."

"As far as news at my end, no nothing yet, but it's early days. Our RCMP guys just got to the US embassy and are currently meeting with the rest of the team. I spoke with the DDO after your meeting with him and concur that you lie low until this is resolved. It sounds like the DDO has got you all set with ID and some walking around money. Let me know if you need anything else. I don't even want to know where you are, just as long as you keep your phone handy so I can reach you if we need you or if anything develops."

"Ok I'll take it easy for now, stay out of the way of the professionals and let them do their thing. I think I have the perfect hiding place. I'll be in touch."

CHAPTER TWENTY-THREE

The last thing Bill remembered was getting into the Mandarin Oriental limo and feeling a sharp pain almost like a bee sting in his arm. He started to lose consciousness and felt himself sliding over sideways onto the seat. Perhaps he'd been pushed over by the driver who had closed the door then moved swiftly around the vehicle to take the wheel and drive sedately away from the airport.

Of course, Bill didn't know about driving away from the airport sedately or otherwise, as he was totally knocked out by the drug that the driver had injected.

They drove about five miles away from the airport into a largely abandoned warehouse district, shut down for the Sunday holiday. The driver entered an open garage door that closed after them. The car came to a stop next to a florist's van and Bill was lifted out of the Mercedes and transferred to the van along with his suitcase. Handcuffs were closed tightly on his wrists, duct tape applied to his mouth and a hood fastened over his head. To further restrict movement, he was securely tied with a sturdy rope to a bar running along the side of the van's interior. The warehouse truck door opened and the van drove off while Bill still lay, passed out, in the back. The Mercedes had the Mandarin logo removed from its doors, its original plates reattached, and a good vacuuming throughout. No one could tell the car apart from any of the hundreds of black Mercedes in Bangkok. The van left Bangkok heading northwest toward Nakhon.

Thirty miles short of Nakhon, the van left the highway. It drove for two miles down a rutted farm road cut through the dense jungle until it came to a barn painted green in a clearing overgrown with jungle trees and vines. It would be practically invisible, particularly from the air. When sentries had confirmed that the van was the one they were waiting for, they opened the door to the barn and wheeled out a helicopter that looked like it was a hand-me-down from the Vietnam War.

Bill was starting to show signs of coming around so he was given another injection to put him back out like a light. He was transferred to the helicopter, which lifted off for the flight to Battambang near Tonle Sap Lake in northeastern Cambodia. Upon arrival, Bill was locked in a ten foot by ten-foot cell with a solid steel door containing a square of one-way glass so people could look in and a rectangular pass through for food. The room was clean and had a stainless steel flushing toilet, as well as a sink along with a desk and chair unit, bolted to the wall and floor. There was a shelf about three feet long and a foot wide for personal items. The bunk bed had a reasonable mattress and pillow along with a blanket. A solitary light had been set into the ceiling, which appeared to be about twelve to fifteen feet high. In all it could have been worse; actually it could have been much worse.

When Bill started to regain consciousness he became aware of a throbbing pain in his head, which competed for attention with a terrible thirst and dry throat. He sat up slowly and his head swam a bit while his eyes moved in and out of focus. After a while, this started to pass and he thought he might venture over to use the toilet. He then ran the water and tasted it; not finding anything unusual in the taste, he cupped his hands and swallowed several handfuls of water. He noticed that his suitcase had also been placed in the cell and looked through it to see what had been taken. He was surprised to see that everything was still there including his toiletries.

There was no window, so no way to tell if it was night or day. He had no idea how he got here, why he got here, where he was and how the hell he was going to get out of here. The only thing he knew for sure was this wasn't the Mandarin Oriental, and if it was, he was going to have a long talk with Andrew Chang, the GM about their deteriorating standards

Doc's phone rang as he headed north towards Scranton and he saw that it was Bev calling. He found a safe place to turn off onto the shoulder of the highway and answered the call saying,

"Hi Bev how are you doing?"

Bev said, "I'm great and having a good time with Anne and Sean. We're worried about you though, you missed the conference call and didn't call Shannon last night, is everything ok?"

"Well yes and no. We have a problem; Bill is missing and we fear possibly kidnapped. It's a long story, but I'm ok. I'm back in the States and heading for Scranton to surprise Shannon so don't say anything if any of you speak to her or text her. I'll be there in a couple of hours. Why don't you do the conference call at the same time tomorrow and I'll explain to you all at once? I'm of course worried sick about Bill.

Everything went well regarding our company and finances. You and I both have personal accounts with ten million USD at the Hong Kong Shanghai Bank. We also have a corporate account at the same bank with fifty million USD in it. There are documents for you to sign and a Platinum Visa with a one million dollar limit on the way to you by courier. So we're making progress. I'll wait to find out what's up over there when we talk tomorrow morning ok?"

"I'm so relieved to hear that you're ok. Like you I'm sick over Bill, there isn't any word on him?"

"Nothing yet but our company has a very capable team investigating. I'll talk to you in the morning."

When he got to Scranton, he walked into the hotel, bypassed the front desk and went straight to Shannon's office. The door was closed so he knocked lightly. Shannon said, "Come in, it's open."

Doc opened the door and said, "Hi Red, how goes it?"

Shannon couldn't believe her eyes and for a moment couldn't move. Then all at once she jumped up from her chair spilling it over backward and ran around the desk into his arms. Two staff came running to see if she was all right. She assured them that she was better than all right and closed the door as she gave him the longest deepest kiss she had ever participated in, lack of St. Agnes Brandy notwithstanding. She had a lot of questions and Doc said, "Let's go home and get comfortable, it's been a long, eventful and sad day."

They took Doc's car to their apartment and Doc brought in his suitcase but left the orchid in the trunk. When they were inside, Doc said, "Oh I've forgotten some luggage in the trunk, why don't you change into your comfortable clothes and make us a drink? I'll be right back." He went out to the Cobra, retrieved the orchid and returned to the apartment.

He placed the gift-wrapped flower on the coffee table and waited. Shannon returned with their drinks and asked, "What's this then?"

"Why don't you carefully open it and see?"

Shannon sat on the edge of the couch and gingerly unwrapped the flower. Her eyes went as wide as saucers and she exclaimed, "Oh my

God, a Ghost Orchid! I never dreamed I'd ever own one of these beauties. I love it. The gang at my orchid club is going to be envious. Thank you so much." She jumped up and gave him a big hug and said, "Wait a minute." She ran into the kitchen, took a sip of St. Agnes brandy and returned to give him the kiss of his life.

Doc built a fire, enjoyed a sip of the double Laphroaig single malt Shannon had poured for him and looked at her lovingly for a few minutes.

Once they had calmed down and relaxed a bit, Doc explained what had happened and why he was here. Shannon was a good listener, which came from years of patiently listening to complaints and kudos from thousands of well-heeled hotel guests.

She said, "My God Doc why would anyone kidnap a software sales executive? I've never worried about you being harmed in any way due to your profession."

"You're right not to worry about me being harmed. This is a very rare occurrence; in fact it has never happened to anyone in our firm or even anyone we know at other companies.

We are completely baffled. The company however always errs on the side of caution so they've ordered me to stay away from Asia until they get to the bottom of this.

They've put together a team of world-class investigators. Thus far, there has been no word from anyone."

"You're sure he was kidnapped, that seems to be a forgone conclusion on your part."

"It's the only conclusion I can accept. I refuse to believe that he has been killed. There's simply no reason for anyone to do that."

"Let's go to Carmella's for an early dinner. You need to get some good food into you and we need to lighten up a bit."

"Yet another great idea, you always seem to be full of them."

They were early enough to get their table by the fire and Carmella as usual made them feel like family. They asked Carmella to bring them whatever she suggested along with a bottle of La Cour Pavillon.

They relaxed a bit over dinner, happy to be together and prepared to put all problems out of their minds for the evening.

After dinner Shannon said, "We should probably head home and get some sleep, don't forget we have the conference call in the morning. I'd like to stop by the hotel for a quick look though, is that ok?"

"Of course, I'll buy you a brandy in the pub. I take it you have St. Agnes in inventory."

When they got home, Doc said, "How about a long hot bath before bed?"

"Sounds perfect, fill the tub and light the candles while I fetch a couple of brandies."

Doc was in the tub when Shannon walked naked into the room and handed him his brandy. The sight of her naked took his breath away.

She stepped into the tub and sat between his legs with her back on his chest.

As they molded together, Shannon said, "You're going to have to be slow and gentle the first time."

"I will be sweetie when you're ready on our wedding night, I'll be as gentle as can be."

"I've decided that I don't want to wait for our wedding night, I want you now."

"Doc was so taken by surprise that he dropped his brandy snifter into the bathwater."

"Are you sure? I mean you were so adamant; what's changed your mind?"

She turned around and on her knees looked straight into his eyes. She said with an Irish lilt and a flirtatious look that was reflected in the smile on her lips and the twinkle in her emerald green eyes, "Now Mr. Donovan O'Connell, it's complainin' you are is it? Maybe we should forget the idea and get some sleep, we'd feel better for it in the mornin'."

Doc was out of the bath and had her into the bed so fast that they nearly broke the moan barrier.

Shannon was wrong about one thing. More sleep couldn't have made him feel any better in the morning. Making love to Shannon finally made him feel better than he had felt in his entire life. It just confirmed what he was already suspecting; he never wanted to be without her again.

The conference call came early and Doc took

the lead wanting to get the news about Bill out on the table and all questions answered right off.

He explained as truthful as he could what had transpired and promised to keep all appraised of any developments in the case.

Shannon reported on the status of things at O'Leary's, which was going along fine with no problems she couldn't handle.

Sean said that he was comfortable with things at Lion's Pride. The three of them had met with the architect and builder and made a few strong suggestions for changes. The plans were just about finalized and construction could begin as soon as Shannon could do her thing. In fact, they all agreed that they could get underway as soon as Shannon could give the place a once over and determine what, if any, structural changes would be required.

Bev had hired a helicopter and the three of them had toured the entire 1,900 acres. It helped put the overall site map into perspective in Sean and Anne's minds.

Sean said they had decided that he would return to Scranton so Shannon could go over, as they didn't want her input to hold up the development process.

Bev said, "I have an idea. Is there someone who could handle O'Leary's for a few days?"

Shannon said that the new assistant GM, Donald, could handle things for a few days and Sean agreed. "Why what are you thinking?" Sean asked.

Bev said, "I could charter a jet through the Hong Kong company using my name since Doc's company doesn't want him to fly commercial. Doc and Shannon could fly over on it. We could keep it for a few days then it could take you home Sean and return for Doc and Shannon when they're ready to go back in a few weeks. This way, we can meet here after Doc and Shannon are indoctrinated and deal with whatever needs discussing while we are all together."

Doc said, "That's a good idea, Bev, it'll keep the renovation process moving quicker. Does it work for you, Sean?"

"Yes, it's fine with me. I could take back a few of the staff that you have identified as needing training at O'Leary's Anne. What about you Shannon?"

"Sounds good, I could be ready to leave this afternoon, I just need two hours with Donald to cover off a few details."

Doc said, "Ok Bev order up the jet and have them call me when they have the departure time set. We'll leave from Wilkes Barrie/Scranton International Airport. We'll see you guys in a while."

As soon as they hung up, Shannon called the hotel, told them to track down Donald for a meeting in a half an hour. She then began to pack furiously, hopped in the shower and of course Doc joined her to quickly wash her back. They dressed quickly and Doc drove her to the hotel. While she met with Donald, Doc went into the dining room and had a large breakfast with several cups of coffee. He told the waitress to tell the chef to prepare Shannon's breakfast. He went into the pub and told Brian to put a bottle of Pinot Gris, a bottle of La Cour Pavillon, a bottle of St. Agnes and a bottle of Laphroaig into an insulated travel bag and put it on his tab. He took them down to the Cobra then returned to find Shannon having breakfast in the dining room. He joined her and the waitress automatically delivered a coffee. Doc said, "This coffee tastes much better than what I remember."

"It should, it's your Jamaican Blue Mountain, bloody expensive but the guest comments are great and it'll keep you happy. I had a professor at hotel school that told us that coffee is so important to the guest's perception of the meal because it's the last thing that they have before leaving. So to keep them coming back, make sure they leave happy."

"Is everything ok with Donald?"

"Yeah, he's like a backup goalie when the starter has just suffered an injury, excited about being the starter for a change. I still have a couple of things to do in my office, maybe a half hour, ok?"

"I'd like to make a few phone calls so I'll go to the business center. Meet me there when you're ready to go."

Doc called the DDO and Jim and both reported that the team was turning Bangkok inside out, working in shifts twenty four/seven but so far no breaks in the case. Doc asked about Bill's family and the DDO said, "I called his parents myself yesterday and explained what had happened. I told them that we had the best people on it and that as soon as something breaks, we'll get back to them. They're naturally upset and worried about their son, as we all would be under the circumstances. They asked if they could speak to you and I told them that I'd ask you to call them when we next spoke."

"Should I call right now or give them time to process it?"

"No, call them now. I think hearing your voice will give them some comfort."

Doc hung up and then called Mr. and Mrs. Wong at their home in San Francisco. Doc said, "Hello Mr. Wong, how are you and Mrs. Wong doing under the circumstances?"

Mr. Wong said, "We are apprehensive and sad. Bill's mother has times when she just breaks down and cries. She is terrified that Bill won't come home."

"Please don't think like that. Some of the best people, highly trained investigators, are on the job as we speak. I've just checked with the head office and I'm told that the investigators are working day and night, I'm confident that we'll have news soon."

"We appreciate you calling Donovan, you have been a great friend to Bill over the years. It gives us comfort to see that you are on top of things. Please let us know the moment you hear anything."

"I will sir, keep the faith and we'll talk again soon."

The charter service called so Doc took the message and learned that the plane would be ready at Wilkes Barrie/Scranton International Airport private plane terminal for a 4 o'clock departure.

Bill still had no idea what was going on. When they put him in the cell, they must have removed his watch so he didn't have any idea what time it was or how long he had been there. He sat on his bunk and tried to figure out who had done this and why, but nothing came to him. There was a movement at the door and a tray slid in through the food slot. The food was definitely Asian but not too spicy and actually quite acceptable. It was accompanied with a pot of tea and a bottle of water.

Bill ate the entire food not knowing if or when he might see any more. He drank the tea but saved the bottled water for later.

He passed the tray back through the slot in the door, keeping the teapot and cup as he still had about half a pot of tea left. In a few minutes, a second tray passed through the slot, this time with a Tom Clancy novel, "Executive Orders". Along with the book were a pad and ballpoint pen. On the pad were the words, 'If thing wanted put here no question.'

Bill printed, 'Want to talk to boss please' and slid the note back.

CHAPTER TWENTY-FOUR

The Gulfstream private jet was spacious, luxurious and fitted out for long haul travel including a private bedroom with a shower. Doc was glad he remembered the St. Agnes brandy. If you are going to join the mile high club, do it in style! The flight was mostly smooth, the food was good and you certainly couldn't complain about the company. Shannon was not only beautiful beyond words, she was witty and an excellent conversationalist. They sat and talked for hours. Shannon said, "I've thought of one idea for your new company name, "Software Conceptions Inc." It came to me the other day as I was thinking about what the purpose of the company really is. I know it's an incubator, but I didn't much like the name "Incubator Inc." sounds too much like a chicken ranch."

"I like Software Conceptions Inc., you're right, as usual, it's much more sophisticated than Incubator Inc. Let's send a text to run it by Bev but I'm sure she'll like it, then I'll text it to our accountant, lawyer and banker in Hong Kong. Of course, there is always the possibility that it might not be available, but they'll find out quickly. Brilliant work once again Miss Creativity."

Doc called the flight attendant Rosemary and said, "Rosemary, my lovely creative partner here just came up with another gem for our company.

I think this calls for a glass of the Pinot Gris I brought aboard and a double Laphroaig on the rocks to celebrate this linguistic achievement."

Shannon said, "Couldn't you just say, "We want a drink, please? I thought you were going to deliver the bleedin Gettysburg Address."

They took their time over dinner, after all it wasn't like they had anywhere else to go and Rosemary was able to create some very decent steak and lobster dinners with Crème Brulee for dessert. Shannon said, "I'm going to have to see that you get plenty of exercise after and pointed towards the bedroom door. Now that I've tried it, I kind of like it. Besides it's my duty to see that you get lots of exercise so you can live a long time to be an incredible father to our children."

"It's funny you should mention children. The other evening I was out on the deck at the Hong Kong condo and a young family with two kids passed by across the street, laughing it up with ice cream cones in their hands. I have always enjoyed kids but never really thought about whether or not I'd ever want to have any."

"Well don't keep me in suspense, what did you decide?"

"I think I would like kids at some point once I am tired of all the traveling. What about you?"

"Oh yeah, definitely, kids are a high priority for me."

"Ok then, they are a high priority for me also. How many shall we have?"

"Five."

"Five? Where did you come up with that number?"

"I don't know. Ever since I was a little girl, I always planned to have five kids one day."

"All right then Shannon O'Sullivan, you drive a hard bargain but five it is. Boy, we're going to need a big house."

"Where do you think this big house should be?"

"I am going to leave that entirely up to you. You decide where home for us will be; you design it and get it built entirely to your specifications. Just make sure there is a man cave where I can lock myself away when the five kids get too raunchy."

"No, seriously, where do you think we should call home?"

"I am serious my lovely colleen. I haven't had a place I'd call home in so long I forget what it's like. My old cottage, oops excuse me, our old cottage on the river is about as near to a home as I can remember. In the long term, my home will be anyplace that you and our five kids are."

As the hours passed, Bill walked the floor, did some push-ups and read. Finally another tray with food arrived. It must be dinner he thought. One way to keep a rough idea of time passing is to keep track of food deliveries, assuming they made the deliveries on some sort of regular schedule.

Again the Asian food was good, the tea was

hot and there was another bottle of fresh water. Again he ate all the food but saved some tea and the bottled water for later. As he hadn't received a reply to his earlier note, he once again printed the words 'Want to talk to Boss' and placed this note on the tray before passing it back.

He laid back and read for what seemed like an hour or so then jet lag overpowered him and he fell into a deep sleep.

When he woke, it must have been morning because the tray was back, this time with a western breakfast of scrambled eggs, sausages, hash browns, and toast. Coffee was served in a thermos carafe with individual creamers and sweeteners on the side. As Bill had his first cup of coffee, he thought, it's as though I am being held captive in a two-star hotel, hell of a way for them to get their occupancy numbers up.

He thought he would try another communication; obviously they weren't going to let him speak to the boss at this point. He printed the one-word 'shower' on the paper, put it on the tray and passed it back, keeping the coffee carafe, creamers, and the bottled water. A while later a note came back through the door with a pair of handcuffs and a black hood. The note said, 'on hood, on cuffs, no talk.' He did as he was told and the door clanged open, someone took him by the arm and led him forty-two paces to the right after leaving the cell.

They came to their destination and the cuffs were removed as he was gently pushed into a room. A door clanged shut behind him. He took off the hood and saw that he was in a small room with a shower in the corner. On a shelf, there was a bar of soap, shampoo, and two towels. He undressed, put his clothes on the peg provided, turned on the shower and stepped in. They let him stay for as long as he wanted. Once dried off and dressed, the handcuffs came through the slot with the same note as last time, 'on hood, on cuffs, no talk'. Once he was ready, the door opened and he was led back to his room. His cuffs were removed and he was gently pushed into the cell.

It seemed strange to Shannon to sleep in a bedroom on a plane. It was nice to be spooning naked with Doc after some very erotic sex with round one in the bed and round two in the shower. It certainly beat dozing off in the seats in commercial aircraft so she wasn't complaining. In fact she thought, I could get used to this. Little did she know.

But regardless of the luxury accommodations, 20 hours of flying takes a toll on you.

Bev, Sean, and Anne went to the airport to meet them. After welcoming hugs all around, Bev said, "Ok let's get you two started on my soon-to-be-famous jet lag cure."

They drove to the mansion that's now Lion's Pride, both fascinated with the beauty of the countryside.

The first sight of the building and grounds offered the typical "Wow factor" response that overcomes all first-time visitors.

As they entered the grand foyer, they were greeted by Walter, the butler with a pair of Nassau Nighty Removers courtesy of Fred from the Zulu Pub. They all retired to the Library Lounge to make small talk with everyone asking about Bill. Unfortunately, there was nothing new as yet on Bill's situation. Bev said that the spa was waiting to pamper them and, if they wished, they could have a nap before cocktail hour. Bev said she'd like to speak to Doc for a moment so Anne took Shannon off to the spa and Sean headed off to parts unknown.

Bev said, "I wasn't sure how you wanted to handle sleeping arrangements so I've put Shannon into a suite adjacent to your two bedroom apartment. It so happens that the suite and your apartment have inter-connecting doors in case you ever need a third bedroom or for whatever use you wish to make of the door to the suite. Shannon's a lovely person; of course you already know that. She and I are going to be good friends. I sense it. I don't want you to think that I'm interfering in your relationship and, in fact, you may elect not even to give it to her, but I have a gift for you." She handed Doc a small velvet covered box.

Doc opened it and gasped out loud. The box contained the most beautiful diamond Doc had ever seen. Bev said, "This diamond and its twin are considered to be the finest diamonds ever mined in Zimbabwe. They're called the "African Twins" and have been in my family for generations. I'm keeping one in case I ever get married and as a family keepsake; this one is for you, the one person on earth that I care most about.

If it ends up on Shannon's hand, I'll be jubilant, but as I say, that's up to you; it's yours to do with as you wish."

"I can't thank you enough for this. We'll think of you every time we look at it. Is there a jeweler here that you trust to have it set in a ring?"

"Yes, we have a jeweler that has served our family for nearly fifty years."

"Would you arrange to get it set for me? What do you think, platinum? Perhaps a temporary setting so I can give it to her now and she can go to the jeweler to choose what she wants?"

"Platinum would do nicely, I'll tend to it right away. Now go have your spa and nap; I'll see you later."

While everyone was busy, Bev had her chauffeur take her into Harare to her jeweler. She presented the diamond and asked if he would put it in a temporary platinum setting so it could be given to the lady right away. And then she would come in to pick out what she wants in terms of a permanent setting.

She explained that time was of the essence and he agreed to have it ready by tomorrow afternoon.

Doc was amazed at his two-bedroom apartment with an inter-connecting suite. He was even more amazed when he saw that the inter-connecting door was open and Shannon was fast asleep, naked on the king size bed in his, no make it their, bedroom. He decided to ask Shannon to marry him tomorrow and, if she said yes, to announce it to the group. He already had Mona contact the O'Sullivan's, Shannon's parents, to invite them to Lion's Pride as a surprise for Shannon. They accepted and would be here tomorrow evening in time for the surprise engagement party at which point he would ask Shannon's father for her hand. Mona had dispatched the private jet to Cork Airport and the O'Sullivan's were very excited to learn that they would be visiting Africa and on a private jet no less. They will be the talk of the Killarney Senior's Recreational Club.

Mona, at Doc's direction, had spoken to chef about doing a dinner party tomorrow with drinks and hors d'oeuvres at seven o'clock. Dinner is to be served for seven people at eight o'clock. Menu up to chef but spare no expense. Mona arranged for a four-piece band and a harpist for the dinner period.

When Shannon awoke, she left Doc sleeping and went to the fridge in search of some fruit juice.

She dressed casually and came out on the deck to take in some of the sights and smells of Africa.

She loved Lion's Pride at first sight and

looked forward to using her decorating skills to make her mark on it. She felt Doc's arms encircle her waist as he spooned her and kissed her neck. She turned and kissed him passionately pulling him as close to her as possible.

He whispered in her ear, "There is a bottle of St Agnes in the bar, how about a wee nip and then let's see if that big bed is any good for exercise purposes?"

"I never thought you'd ask." She replied and took him by the hand back into the bedroom.

Afterward as they dressed to go meet everyone Doc said," I'm sure glad we tested the exercise capabilities of that bed and found it suitable."

"Suitable….I'll say, if it were any more suitable, it would've taken a Chiropractor to get us untangled!"

The room phone rang and Sean announced that the drinks were starting in the Zulu Pub so they'd best get mobile or they may run out of Laphroaig and Jameson's before they get there.

Doc sent Shannon on ahead so he could check with the head office on the latest developments regarding Bill. The DDO was in a meeting so Doc said he'd call again tomorrow, Jim was in and Doc said, " Hi Jim any news?"

"The team thought they were on to something, an informer agreed to tell them where Bill is for $2,000 US. They paid and followed up but found they had been conned, I guess there is a lot of that going on over there."

"Word must be on the street that there are investigators from North America in town. Informers will come crawling out of the wood-work, particularly now that they know we'll pay. Expect the price to go up, the calls to increase in frequency and the bullshit quotient to grow exponentially."

"I'll pass that on to the team. It sounds like you are far away."

"You don't want to know, but I assure you no one could find me here. Maybe I should go to Bangkok, I might be able to vet the informers or ferret out some better quality leads."

"No Doc, our decision still stands. We can't afford to lose two trained agents at the same time. Wherever you are stay there; or at least stay out of sight."

Doc was very frustrated with the lack of progress in Thailand and, as time passed, was growing more concerned about Bill's well being. If it were a kidnapping, usually a ransom demand or some group claiming responsibility would have been forthcoming by now. It was difficult for Doc to stay focused on Shannon and Lion's Pride with all the uncertainty surrounding Bill's disappearance.

Doc had a quick shower then headed down the hall towards the elevator. Seated at a desk in the elevator lobby was a smiling young lady with the name Sharon on her nametag. Sharon said," Hello Mr. O'Connell, I'm Sharon the fifth-floor concierge, sorry I missed you earlier.

Would you like me to show you the way to the Zulu Pub?"

"That would be nice, thank you, Sharon."

She called the elevator and motioned Doc inside. As they went down to the main floor, they made small talk about Sharon's background and career at Lion's Pride.

The Zulu Pub captured Doc's interest as soon as he entered. He said to the group, "Now this is what I think of when I think of a five-star pub in Africa!"

Shannon said, "Yes I agree and everything is so authentic, not a Lone Star Beer sign anywhere in sight."

Fred was introduced to Doc and handed him a double Laphroaig on the rocks in a cut crystal glass, just the way he likes it.

"Bev, I love my apartment, thank you, and a nice touch having the top shelf of the bar devoted exclusively to Laphroaig Scotch. That could last me all week."

The consensus at breakfast was for a poolside seafood bar-b-q dinner so Bev had alerted the chef early in the day. The group moved outside and sat at a large, teak deck table to enjoy their drinks and dinner.

Bev said, "Tomorrow, I'll show Doc and Shannon around. Of course Anne, you and Sean are welcome to join us if you'd like another tour."

Sean said," I'd like to tag along at least for some of the tour to share some decorating ideas with Shannon since I'm heading back in a few days."

Anne said, "I could use the day winding up my staff training plan and preparing a list of employees that I just can't see working in food, beverage or accommodations. By this time tomorrow Doc, I should have a list for you so you can start to think of alternative ways to employ them elsewhere on the property."

As usual chef Griff, resplendent in all his finery, prepared a seafood bar-b-q that one might expect poolside at the Four Seasons Maui.

Over dinner Doc said, "I'm really impressed with the staff that I've met, the quality of the service and, of course, the building and grounds. I don't know if I'll be able to sleep tonight just thinking about the tour tomorrow."

Shannon quietly asked the waitress to lend her a pen and a slip of paper. She wrote a note "Don't worry about sleeping tonight, we have a bottle of St. Agnes...you'll sleep like a baby once I've had my way with you!"

She slipped the note to Doc below the table. He opened it and laughed despite himself. People wondered what was so funny and he just said, "I'm probably overtired.

I was looking at the platter of lobster tails and an old Irish joke just came to me. Paddy is driving down the road and he passes a pub which has a sign that reads "Lobster Tail and Beer $9.95." "Tunderin Jaysus he says......tree o my favorite tings""

Of course not to be outdone Sean had to tell one and soon a bottle of Bailey's appeared and the liqueur and the blarney was flowing.

Finally Doc said, "I'm jet lagged like crazy, I think I'll hit the sack, I have a feeling it's going to be a long day tomorrow."

Shannon said, "We're on the same time zone Doc I think I'll join you." Then she realized what she had just said and with a beet red face stammered, "I, I didn't mean I'd join you….I meant I'll also turn in." Then she made an effort at saving the embarrassing situation by saying, "I almost forgot to thank you, Bev, for the lovely suite, I'm sure I'll sleep well there."

Through all this stammering, Doc held a slight smile then said, "As long as you are ready now, I'll be happy to escort you, after all we are neighbors."

Shannon said, "That'd be fine, thank you." Saying a fast, good night to everyone, she moved quickly towards the door and away from the faux pas zone."

Doc said, "You should enter your own suite and muss up the bed. It would be a good idea to check for flowers, wine or chocolates in case anyone put some in your room. You'll want to thank Bev in the morning if there are any welcoming gifts in there so she gets the idea that you at least passed through the suite. I'll run the tub and get snifters of St. Agnes lined up."

Doc went into his apartment and thought Shannon my dear, you have no idea; tomorrow is going to be a long day but, hopefully, one of the happiest days of your life.

CHAPTER TWENTY-FIVE

Doc and Shannon came awake with a start as this shrill noise came through an open window. Shannon said, louder than normal, "What the hell is that?"

Doc said as he calmed down, "It was some kind of bird I think, what a racket! I'll ask Bev what it was over breakfast."

Thanks to the bird's timely need to call to its mate, Doc looked at the clock and saw that he also had time to call to his mate before meeting Bev for the pre-tour breakfast.

Doc asked the group, "Did anyone hear that horrible screeching earlier this morning?"

Only Bev had noticed it. She said," That was our famous secretary bird, a rather large and noisy Raptor that doesn't fly and makes a hell of a racket. Fortunately, they're not around here very often. They usually stay away from people. There are a few loud animals in Africa, after a while you'll get used to the noises."

After the screeching, secretary bird-enabled sex, Doc and Shannon were famished and put away substantial breakfasts to fortify them for the tour ahead.

Bev said," A professional team is arriving to-day to make a DVD tour of the property including a fly-over in a helicopter. I chartered a large helicopter in case you two would like to do the fly-over with them.

It's really the only way to fully understand the size and features of the 1,900-acre property."

Doc said, "I'd love to do the fly-over, how about you Shannon?"

"Yes I agree, it'd be a great way to get a handle on the potential for the whole property."

Bev said, "Mona will be joining us on our tour to make notes and fetch anything we need. I'll have Walter, the butler notify us when the DVD team is here so we can meet with them, give them any final instructions and agree on a time for the helicopter. Let's start on the fifth floor and work our way down."

As they toured the rooms, Shannon had her camera clicking away regularly capturing features she would want to modify and decorative items she would probably incorporate into the renovation. She also dictated a lot of notes for Mona to transcribe later. The tour was slower than the one for Sean and Anne because of the attention to building details that Shannon needed to focus on for her study of the property. Sean was uncharacteristically quiet not wanting to disturb Shannon's intensity. Only infrequently did he point out some suggestion where he felt it would add to the renovation. They managed to get the fifth through the third floors reviewed before the DVD makers arrived and Bev said, "Let's talk to the DVD people over lunch. I asked chef to prepare salads and sandwiches at poolside."

When Shannon took a break to call Donald at

O'Leary's to check on things, Doc said to Bev, "Were you able to get the jeweler to put something together?"

"Yes, he'll deliver it this afternoon so relax."

"Relax?...... Relax? I'm as nervous as a chicken at Colonel Saunders' farm."

"Everything will be okay. You should aim for around six o'clock to make your move. The O'Sullivans will get here at six thirty and the party can start at seven. I thought we'd all congregate in the library for a champagne toast and then have the folks just walk in. There'll be a hidden camera capturing all the excitement for posterity. Chef has decided to do the dinner in the wine cellar, something my uncle loved to do on special occasions. It's quite a unique experience and something that Shannon will always remember."

"Thanks for everything you've done for us, we both really appreciate your friendship. I'm going to leave you, Sean and Shannon to deal with the DVD guys and run up to my apartment to make a few phone calls regarding progress on the search for Bill. I'll be back shortly."

Bill had been trying to keep active by walking, doing push-ups and squats. He'd been reading the Clancy novel and was almost a quarter way through it. He'd tried several more times to send a message via the food tray asking to talk to the boss. These requests were never answered.

The tough part was that since he didn't know what was going on, he couldn't even start to think about how and when he was going to get out of here. Even a prisoner jailed for the most heinous crime knew that his sentence had a finite time to it; he didn't even have this much.

The next day there was a note with breakfast that read "eat, shower. good dress, photo, no talk."

After breakfast, the hood and handcuffs appeared through the slot. Knowing the drill, Bill put the cuffs and hood on and waited to hear the door's metallic sounds as it swung open. As before, someone took hold of his arm and led him to the shower room. After he showered and put the hood and cuffs back on, he was led back to his room. The note had said good dress so he guessed that they wanted him to look good for a photograph. This was welcome news. If they were going to photograph him, Bill thought, it must mean that they were planning to contact someone, possibly the US embassy, to initiate negotiations to turn him over to them. Bill couldn't see any other reasonable possibility.

He shaved and dressed in a suit, dress shirt and tie and combed his hair. Without a mirror, he could only guess that everything was in place. When he was ready, he stood so he could be seen through the one-way window and waited. In a few minutes a hood passed through the food tray opening with a note that read' put on hood, no question, no talk, stand at wall, no move or you suffer.'

Interesting, Bill thought; the first threat of possible suffering. He stood against the wall with the hood on. He heard the door open and what appeared to be two people enter the room. Silently one man placed a copy of a newspaper, which turned out to be today's edition of 'USA Today' in Bill's hands so it was just below his still hooded head. Then the hood was removed from Bill and a flash from a camera went off and the hood was back on. It happened so quickly. The contrast between the darkness of the hood and the brilliant flash from what appeared to be a high-powered camera, combined to permit Bill to see a quick view of two people for a fraction of a second. They were in black coveralls with hoods over their heads. Then they were back out the door and it was locked. He took off the hood and glanced at the date on the newspaper that they had either forgotten to take with them or left for him to read. In case they demanded it back, he read the front pages quickly to try to get some idea of what was going on in the world.

He knew that the newspaper was to show anyone looking at the photo that as of this day he was alive. This was known as 'proof of life'. The fact that he was showered, shaved and well dressed would show the interested party that, not only was he alive, he was in good condition. No one came back for the paper so he sat and read it twice, cover to cover.

The next day a motorcycle sped past the US

Embassy and a package was thrown from it towards the guardhouse at the main gate. Immediately a cordon was set up so no one could go near the box and the Bangkok police hazmat squad was called to check it out. It contained only the picture of a healthy looking Bill Wong and a note written in broken English 'we have him, we keep him.'

Doc called the DDO who had still not heard anything. He then spoke to Jim. He expressed his frustration and said that unless something happened soon he was going to have to take matters into his own hands. Jim told him to calm down and give the team some more time. He said, "They've only been there for five days and they're chasing down countless leads. I know what they say about the first twenty-four hours being critical, but there is nothing we can do about that, twenty-four hours have long gone. All we can do now is to keep doing good investigative work until we catch a break. It'll happen Doc."

"Ok Jim I'll give the team a few more days, but don't forget that's my best friend we're talking about and I have no idea if he is dead or alive. At some point, I am going to have to take action."

"Don't do anything rash without talking to me first. That's an order."

"Ok, I'll be back at you in a few days."

Doc went to poolside and met the DVD crew who were about to get mobile. Mona was recruited to take over guiding the film crew around while Bev, Shannon, and Doc continued their tour. Doc took a sandwich and bottle of water to have while he walked. They had just completed the tour of the mansion when the helicopter arrived for the aerial tour. They agreed to do the aerial tour now and resume the grounds tour either when they got back or tomorrow morning. Bev said, "Probably it would make sense to continue the ground tour tomorrow morning, I'm sure you both must be tired between the building tour and the jet lag."

While they were in the air, the jeweler arrived and delivered the ring to Bev. It was stunning, set in platinum, the African Twin diamond was absolutely spectacular, and she could hardly wait to see Shannon's reaction. When the helicopter returned, Shannon decided to go to the spa for another massage and facial and Doc tracked Sean down in the Zulu Pub practicing darts.

Sean said, "Well Doc let's get a drink and toss a few darts while we talk about what you think of what you've seen so far."

Doc ordered beer and Sean had a Jameson's. Sean said, "This lad Fred is a good bartender, but I had to straighten him out about the difference between an Englishman's idea of two fingers of whiskey and an Irishman's. He's got it right now." He held up his glass to show a proper measure had been poured.

Doc said, "I've still got the developed grounds to see in the morning, but that helicopter tour was a real eye-opener. I can see all kinds of possibilities here for future development. I'm no agriculture expert but why not a farm where we raise all our own food for openers?"

"Sure why not, if the land is right for it. While you're at it, why not a winery? This general region produces some world class wines, has for years."

"I'm going to talk to Bev about it and see if she thinks these ideas are worth looking into."

"Any word on Bill yet?"

"No. I just spoke with the people at the head office and I've been told that there isn't anything positive to report as yet. There've been lots of tips apparently but none that lead anywhere. I may just go over there and see for myself. I hate being kept in the dark not knowing how he is."

"I thought your company ordered you not to go over there but to let the professionals handle the investigation."

"They did tell me to stay away, and I've done as they asked, but at some point I'm going to run out of patience."

Sean signaled Fred who promptly delivered fresh drinks and said, "But what about your job?"

"If it comes to a choice between my job and one of my best friends, friends trump jobs. Besides, at some point I am going to give up my current job to work full time on this project with Bev. That's always been the plan. So If need be, I'll resign to go look for Bill."

The phone rang and Fred answered it then passed it to Doc saying, "It's for you Mr. O'Connell."

Doc took the phone and Bev mentioned that she had the ring if he wanted to come by her office and get it. She also reminded Doc that it was near five o'clock and he might want to start thinking about speaking to Shannon before her parents get here.

Doc said, "Well Sean, I am off for a nap before dinner, I'll see you at cocktail four hours."

Doc stopped into Bev's office and she gave him the ring. When he looked into the box its beauty overwhelmed him, but he was even more overwhelmed by what it signified. He was about to take a huge leap, one that he didn't think he would make for many years yet. Doc said, "How many times since we've been friends, have you known me to be speechless?"

"I don't remember ever seeing you speechless."

"I'm so happy right now, so excited about the future with Shannon and so pleased to have you as part of it in such a meaningful way. Do me a favor when the O'Sullivan's get here, bring them to your office for a few minutes and call my cell, I need to talk to the O'Sullivans alone before Shannon sees them."

"Leave it to me."

Doc gave her a hug, said thank you one more time and went up to his suite.

When he got to the suite, Shannon was not yet there. On the dining table was an enormous bouquet of unusual flowers in an array of colors and fragrances.

Next to the flowers, on a silver tray sat a copper ice bucket with a chilled bottle of Cristal in it, a crisp white linen napkin around the neck of the bottle and two crystal champagne flutes. A large platter of homemade chocolates and chocolate dipped strawberries filled out the display.

Doc decided to take a quick shower and went into the master bedroom, stripped out of his clothes and stepped into the shower. The notion that it would be a quick shower was dispelled when the shower door opened and Shannon, naked, stepped in. She said, "My turn to wash your back big guy."

After the shower, they went into the living room and Shannon asked, "What's with all this opulence? are you trying to spoil me or fatten me up? My God these flowers are lovely, I've never seen any of them before and they smell divine."

Doc opened the Cristal and said, "Remember on the plane over here we talked about building a house capable of handling five kids?"

She took a sip of the bubbly and looking him in the eyes said, "Oh yes I remember. It seems to me you said that I could design it and build it to my specifications anywhere I want."

"Yes and I am standing by that idea. I want a home that has your spirit built into it.

Doc reached into his pocket, took out the ring box, got down on one knee, opened the box to show her and said, "Marry me Shannon O'Sullivan and build an elegant home for the seven of us."

Shannon looked at the ring, looked at Doc and burst into tears. Doc stood up and said, "What is it colleen, will you not have me?"

She took him in her arms and said, "Oh yes Donovan O'Connell, but you've done it now for I'll never let you go."

Doc slipped the ring on her finger and said, "The diamond is part of a set of two called the African Twins. They're considered to be the two finest diamonds ever mined in Zimbabwe. They have been passed down from generation to generation in Bev's family. She gave one to us and is keeping one in case she gets married at some point.

"But Doc, we can't accept this, it must be worth a fortune and it's Bev's family heirloom."

"Bev doesn't have any family left with the passing of her uncle. She has always looked upon me as a brother and now, she sees you as a sister. She wants us to be her family."

"I'm honored to be her sister. I know we'll be the best of friends."

"So when and where do you want to get married?"

"I would love to get married near Killarney. There is a lovely little church with a thatched roof, beside a lake in a meadow, in the ring of Kerry. I used to go to church there on occasion with my parents and it would make them so happy to see me married there."

"Then that's settled, now when do you wish to become Shannon O'Connell?"

"As soon as possible. How about two months from now?"

"I like a woman who is decisive, two months from now it is."

"I don't believe this Doc. I've wanted you for so many years and now to think that we are going to be together forever. I have to call my mother, she'll be so thrilled."

Just then Doc's phone rang, "Hi Bev, sure I'll be right down. Can you do me a favor and come up to the apartment for a quick glass of champagne? Great, see you soon."

"What's all that about?"

"Sean is in a heated argument with the DVD producer and Bev wants me to mediate. I'll only be a minute. I thought I'd invite Bev up so you can thank her for the diamond besides I'd like her to be the first to know."

Bev knocked on the door and Doc let her in. She could see right away from the look of Shannon's face that they were engaged.

Doc said, "Bev, Shannon and I want you to be the first to know that we've become engaged."

Shannon was absolutely beaming as she gave

Bev a long hug and thanked her so much for the lovely diamond.

Doc handed Bev a flute of champagne and the three of them clicked glasses. Bev said, "To my best friend Doc and his lovely bride-to-be and soon-to-be my other best friend, Shannon. I wish both of you all the happiness in the world."

Doc said, "I'll run down and see what's up with Sean and the DVD guy. I'll leave you two to chat while Shannon gets ready for dinner. See you both in the Library in about fifteen minutes."

Doc went into Bev's office and saw that Walter had served them drinks and hors d'oeuvres. He said, "Mr. and Mrs. O'Sullivan, I'm Donovan O'Connell."

Mr. O'Sullivan said, "We're pleased to meet you, Donovan, please call us Kevin and Mary."

Mrs. O'Sullivan said, "We feel as though we've known you for years. Shannon talks about you all the time."

Doc said, "I'm sorry to spring this on you without us having the chance to get to know each other longer. But I have known Shannon for almost five years now and I love her very much. I would like your permission to marry her. I promise that I'll adore her all her life and will give her everything she wants including five children."

Mary said, "Oh she told you about the five children has she. It's always been a dream of hers to have five, don't ask me where that came from."

Kevin said, "You're right Donovan, it is short notice. But the way Shannon has always spoken of you to us, gave us the idea that this would be

the reason for the fancy private jet trip to Africa, so my answer is yes. I have always treated her like a princess; if you promise to keep that up, you have our blessing, right Mary?"

"Yes indeed, I am all for it and look forward to seeing these five grandchildren."

"Thank you both, right now I'm the happiest man on earth. Why don't you both wait here until Shannon's in the Library and Walter here will come and get you? Oh and my friends call me Doc."

Doc went to the library and saw that Shannon and Bev had just arrived. Doc nodded to Walter and he went to get the O'Sullivans. Shannon's back was to the entrance to the room as Doc tapped his glass several times in the universal call for attention. He started to say, "Shannon and I….." when Kevin, entering the room with Mary, took the cue and said, "Not without us you don't."

Shannon spun around and shrieked in disbelief, she ran to her parents and hugged and kissed them both. The tears were flowing like Victoria Falls all around; even tough old Sean had some 'dust' in his eye that required a tissue. At a nod from Bev, the band started softly in the corner, the waitresses and waiters appeared serving canapés and taking drink orders and of course everyone started talking at once. When things quieted down, Doc once again tapped his glass for attention.

He said, "As I was about to say, Shannon has asked me to marry her and I have agreed, so you are all invited to our wedding."

CHAPTER TWENTY-SIX

The engagement party went on until the small hours when people, starting with the O'Sullivans, headed for bed. Everyone was thrilled for Doc and Shannon; they made a perfect couple and the wedding in Ireland was highly anticipated by all.

The next morning, a breakfast buffet was served at poolside with champagne and orange juice or Caesars to accompany a wide array of breakfast fare. Shannon was so excited to see her parents and vice versa. They were obviously a close-knit bunch and Doc was pleased to be part of this loving family having lost his own at such an early stage in his life. Kevin O'Sullivan was an avid golfer so they decided to play nine holes this morning. Shannon, Doc, and Bev excused themselves to continue their tour and Anne needed to complete her training plan. Sean wanted to host the golf game. They all agreed they would meet back here for lunch then departed to their various activities.

The tour went more quickly and Shannon and Doc were impressed with all the out buildings, the stables, the car garage, the employee-housing village and the works shed. In the stables, Bev showed Doc Midnight, the horse she had in mind to be his, and Doc loved the horse immediately. Bev showed a chestnut beauty to Shannon and said, "I think this one would be suitable for you, but if you would prefer any other just say so."

Shannon looked around and said," No Bev, this one is great, what's his name?"

Bev said, "Flaming Star, he runs like the wind yet is very well trained and easy to control. Have you done much riding?"

"No, some when I was much younger. I would have probably done more if I'd had the time and opportunity."

"When all the excitement dies down, I'll see that you get proper training by our groom, he's an excellent rider and trainer. Then you and I can go riding together."

"That sounds like fun, I look forward to it."

Over lunch, after the expected malarkey that happens when two Irishmen try to outdo each other at anything had ended, talk turned to Doc and Shannon's future together.

Doc said, "Our business interests are going to require a fair bit of travel at least in the first few years. As well as here at Lion's Pride, we'll need a base in Hong Kong, which will probably be on a boat. We'll be spending some time on the software development-rich west coast, including California, Seattle, and Vancouver BC. We'll need a base on the east coast as well as our cottage on the St. Lawrence River. Shannon and I haven't discussed it in detail as of yet, but it probably would make sense to sell the Ottawa place, particularly once I leave the company to work full time on our business. Incidentally,

Shannon, besides naming this place Lion's Pride, has chosen the name for our new enterprise, Software Conceptions Inc. so a round of applause please for our creative genius."

The group gave her a round of applause and her face went very red as it usually does when she gets embarrassed.

Shannon said, "We're going to do some thinking about our future living arrangements. We've decided to build a family home somewhere; Doc is insistent that I choose where, select the site, design the house to my liking and oversee the construction. For now I'm busy with the Lion's Pride project, the Brockville cottage, and O'Leary's Arms. So I'm putting the house on the back burner until I get a few of these other things off my plate."

Kevin said, "Don't forget Killarney in your travel plans, we're going to want to see these five grandkids often you know."

Doc's phone rang and he looked at the screen then stood up and walked away for privacy.

It was Jim who said, "I'm sending through an email, once you've looked at it call me back where you have privacy." The line went dead.

Doc excused himself, said he had some business to deal with and went to his apartment. He opened the email attachment and saw the picture of Bill. His heart skipped a beat, he's alive Doc thought, oh thank God, he's alive!

Doc called down to the business center and had a magnifying glass sent up. Once he had it, he was able to see the date on the newspaper. Three days ago. Checking Bill over Doc saw that he didn't appear to be mistreated in any way, he didn't even seem stressed. Doc searched the photo for any other clues but couldn't see anything that would help.

Doc called Jim, "This is great news! At least he's alive, that's a big load off my mind."

"Yeah, mine as well, the DDO is also very pleased."

"So obviously by now you have had the forensics people all over this message and photo, what do they say?"

"The message was probably typed on a typewriter as opposed to a computer. They can tell this from the typeface. The photo was probably taken by one of those old, flashbulb-type cameras like you see reporters using in the 1940's and 1950's black and white movies. The grain of the shot along with the relative intensity of the flash suggests that the photo was taken with old, unsophisticated equipment."

"So, if that's it, there aren't any clues here that I can see."

"There is one clue that the forensics people picked up on, the copy of the USA Today newspaper was sold in Cambodia."

"How do you know that? I'm looking at the photo with a powerful magnifying glass and I can't see anything that would lead me to that conclusion."

"No, you're right, it's only faintly visible on

the original photo. There's a chop in the upper right-hand corner bearing the name of a small shop at Siem Reap International Airport in the northeast corner of the country."

"Ok, now you're getting somewhere. What happens next?"

"Our team is moving agents into the area and establishing a base at a hotel near the airport. Their investigation will now focus on this region."

"Ok, I'm going over there."

"No Doc, don't do that yet, the DDO and I agree that the investigation is still best left to the pros. Give it a week then let's talk about it once we see what the team can do on their own."

"I'll give it three days, then I want to meet with you in Ottawa and head for Cambodia."

"Ok Doc, I'll see you in three days, but I can't say that you'll go to Cambodia. I'll call if I hear anything from the team."

Doc returned to the poolside discussion about wedding plans to hear that Shannon had asked Bev to be her maid of honor and Mary O'Sullivan was taking responsibility for planning the details on the Killarney end. Sean said," I have a cousin with an interest in a place called The Dunloe, which is the most luxurious place in Ireland to hold a wedding, and it's just outside Killarney."

Mary said, "of course we know The Dunloe, but the cost Sean will be quite steep at such a grand place."

Sean said, "Not once I get through with my cousin it won't. Besides, the wedding event will be my wedding gift. Mary, I'll set it up and you go see my cousin Bryce when you get home, she'll be expecting you and between the two of you, work out the details. Mind you spare no expense. I don't want to hear that there is no Jameson's because you're trying to save money."

Doc said, "That's very generous of you Sean but are you sure?"

"It's what I want to do Doc, you're one of my closest friends and Shannon, as you know has been like a daughter to me, with all due respect to the O'Sullivans. So let's have a grand party!

You know there was a story going around that one of the earlier Lord Mayors of Killarney wanted to be buried standing up, so when he died, they buried him standing up. After a seven-day wake, he was the only one in Killarney still standing up. As far as I know it's the truth so let's see how many are still standing up after this shindig."

Doc said, "Not to interrupt the party atmosphere, but I was thinking of heading to Ottawa in three days for a meeting there and then to Asia to take care of some unfinished business. I could go via Ireland and Scranton if you'd like and take all you folks home.

Think about it and you can decide later. I'd like to spend a few days just relaxing with my new fiancée and all you people before I go."

Shannon said, "Doc let's go for a walk through

the gardens."

Doc knew what was coming as they joined hands and strolled away through the well-manicured bushes and flowers. Once out of earshot from the group Shannon said, "What's up Doc? And I don't mean to do a Bugs Bunny imitation."

"There's been a development in Bill's disappearance. His captors have sent a photo and note so we know he's alive."

"Oh Doc that's such a relief, what did the captors say in the message?"

They said, "we have him, we keep him."

"What does that mean, didn't they demand money or something?"

"No, just what they said, 'we have him, we keep him.'" There was one clue that the investigators are following up. In the photo, Bill was holding up a copy of "USA Today" showing the front page so we'd know when the photo was taken. It was three days ago. On the paper, there's a faint chop with the name of a shop in an airport in Cambodia. So the search is now focused there."

"So why do you have to go to Ottawa?"

"As you know, my company has wanted me to stay out of the investigators' way and I have done so. But I've had enough, if they don't find him in the next few days, I'm going over there to get my best man back in time for the wedding."

"I'm not going to try to stop you. I know how much Bill means to you and I've seen how frustrated you are with the situation. But do you think that you can accomplish what the investigators haven't been able to do so far?"

"I don't know for sure, but I can't just sit around much longer, I have to do something."

"Just promise me you'll use caution and come back to me. I've just got you and don't ever want to lose you."

"I know sweetie, I'll be very careful and will come back, I promise you, just as soon as I can bring Bill with me. Now let's relax, enjoy the group of friends we've got here and do some wedding planning. If you agree, I'll list the Ottawa condo for sale when I'm there. It'll be one less thing for us to think about. Let's go up to the apartment and look online for houses with six bedrooms in Scranton."

"Is Scranton where you want us to live?"

"It's up to you as I said. I like it there, it's a two-hour drive, close enough to New York City where I'll have to go often on business. We have O'Leary's there and Sean of course and it's only a couple of hours drive to the cottage in Brock-ville."

"I love it there, particularly as a place to bring up kids. It rates high in overall quality of life comparisons with other cities of its size."

They went online and looked at some listings in Scranton to get some ideas. Shannon said, "I think I'd rather build so we get the exact place we want and where we want it."

"I agree, do you know any good realtors in

Scranton?"

"Yes, there's an excellent agent I know from the Orchid Club, Brenda Sopel."

"Ok send her an email, ask her to identify some prime building sites for you to view on your return."

"What should I tell her about price range?"

"The price doesn't matter. Get the perfect lot in the perfect area for your dream home, just make sure it's close to a good school and has a large lot. I'm going to need a lot of lawn to play football with my boys and at least a six car garage with my man cave over it."

"Football with your boys is it? What do you intend to play with your girls then?"

"Well whatever they want, baseball, soccer maybe tennis. Oh yeah, make sure there's room for a large swimming pool and a tennis court."

"So are you designing the house now?"

Doc said, "I could use a little exercise before we go back down to see the gang, how about you?"

"Smooth talker, let me get a swig of St. Agnes."

When they went back to poolside, Anne said, "Doc, we should have a little meeting to go over where we're at, before cocktail hour, could we do that?"

"Sure let me get Sean and Bev then let's meet in the conference room."

Bev was in her office putting the final touches on the DVD project and said she would be free in fifteen minutes. Doc found Sean and Kevin in the Zulu Pub, swapping jokes and playing darts.

Doc said, "Sean, Anne had a good idea that we meet in the conference room for an update in about fifteen minutes, does that work for you?"

"You bet, I'll be there."

Kevin said, "Mary and I are going for a massage at the spa then a short nap so we'll catch up with you later."

Doc said, "How about the Library Lounge at five o'clock?"

"That'd be great, see you there," Kevin said.

The conference, while put together quickly, was worth doing particularly in light of Doc and Sean's impending departure.

Doc said, "Ok Anne let's start with you, how are we on the staffing side?"

Anne said, "Mostly good news to report. Only seven of the employees won't be necessary for hotel operations, maintenance or grounds keeping. Of the others, I'd like to see the F&B manager, the head housekeeper and four of the sous chefs receive some training at O'Leary's. Perhaps they could fly back with you Sean. The rest of the staff, I can train here on the job."

Doc said, " Sounds good, thank you, Anne. The extra employees for now can be put to work preparing the sports fields under Johnnie's watchful eye. I'll speak to him about it."

Sean said, "When we get back to O'Leary's, I'll get the employees you're sending over going with training programs under our staff. How long do you want them to understudy?"

Anne said, "A month should do it under your supervision. And I'll be able to help when I come back with Shannon."

Doc said, "What about you Shannon, having looked things over how long do you think you need here to wrap it up?"

"I don't see the need for any structural changes other than what is required for the computer installation and specialist equipment required by the graphics, audio and visual technicians. And I think the architect and builder have a good handle on that since meeting with them. So I'd say another week should do it for me here, then a week or two at home to finalize things. The builder can start right away as far as I'm concerned."

Doc said, "Great, the sooner the better as far as getting the construction underway. I'm going to visit a friend of mine in Silicon Valley on my way to Cambodia to see if he can recommend a knowledgeable recruiter type who knows his way around software development. I want to get this person on board right away, starting to source potential developer candidates. When I get back from Asia, I have some software-marketing people I want to meet with In New York. Bev, what are you going to be up to?"

"I'm going to call the architect and builder and tell them to get started tomorrow, then I'm going to ride them like a drill Sergeant trying to make Lieutenant. I am determined to bring this project in on budget and on time."

Doc said, "Bev as if you need anything else to think about when I was doing the flyover, it occurred to me that we might want to explore the possibility of a farm. We could raise our own food, or at least most of it and maybe add a winery. These projects, if feasible, would be a way to keep the remaining seven employees gainfully employed in the long term. In fact, we'd need to hire more employees depending on the size of these operations. Think about it. If you decide it might make some sense then hire an agricultural expert to look at the land and to advise us what if anything we should do with it."

"I'll give it some thought but on the surface I don't see any reason not to at least study the idea with the help of an expert. I'll contact some people I know at the University of Zimbabwe; I think they have a faculty of agriculture where we might source a consultant. I like this idea, I'll get on it right away….good thinking!"

Doc gave the group an update on Bill and said he'd, of course, keep them apprised of developments. They agreed that the private jet would depart in three days. It would deliver the O'Sullivans to Cork airport, Sean and the staff bound for training at O'Leary's to Scranton/Wilkes Barrie airport then take Doc to Cambodia via Ottawa and Silicon Valley.

Doc said, "Does anyone have anything else before we adjourn because if not, I'd say it's time for a couple of days of fun in the sun."

They spent their time relaxing; Bev chartered a helicopter and took everyone for a picnic at Victoria Falls, the largest in the world.

They swam in the pool, played tennis, rode horses, played golf and generally had a great few days together.

Finally, it became the time for the party to end and Shannon cried as she said goodbye to Doc and her parents. Doc had left her a used shirt of his to wear to bed. Anne gave Doc and Sean a hug as did Bev and they were off. The flight to Cork was long but smooth and the O'Sullivan's were home in fourteen hours. The overnight trip to Scranton took eight hours and Doc slept through most of it in the private bedroom, which he had offered to Sean. But Sean declined saying he preferred to sit up when flying. After dropping off the Scranton contingent, Doc flew on to Ottawa. He headed for his condo to get reasonably back to normal with a long, very hot shower, a double Laphroaig, and a well-aged, rib eye steak. He was going to meet Jim in the morning and he wanted to be well rested for what he was sure would be a tough battle.

CHAPTER TWENTY-SEVEN

Bill was reading his three-day old "USA To-day" for the tenth time when a tray came through the food door. That's unusual, Bill thought, I've had breakfast and I don't think it's time for lunch. He went to the door and re-trieved the tray. On it was the hood and hand-cuffs signifying a move as well as a note. The note, written in broken English, read 'on hood, on cuffs, shower, dress gode, no talc'. The note was obviously written by a different captor, one with a slightly worse command of English. As he put on the hood and cuffs, he figured that this was probably preparation for another photo. As before, he stood in the middle of the room and heard the metallic sound of the door opening. A captor took him by the arm to the shower room where he had his cuffs removed before being pushed into the room and hearing the door close. He removed the hood, undressed and got in the shower. When he finished, he dried off, got dressed and put the hood and cuffs back on. He was becoming a well-trained prisoner but in any event, he appreciated the opportunity to shower. He was led back to his room where he automatically got out of the clothes he had on and put on his suit, dress shirt, and tie. A few minutes later the cuffs came through the slot and he bent and put them on, then put the hood on.

The door opened and there was the sound of

at least two people arranging things in the room. He was lifted off his feet and placed on what seemed to be a chair or platform of some kind. The newspaper was placed in his hands and positioned to be right under his face.

He felt the hood move a bit as something was placed around his neck. One captor said "no move or die." Bill stood completely still; he felt that the object around his neck was some sort of noose. If they had fastened the end of the rope to one of the pipes on the ceiling and if they kicked away whatever he was standing on, he would hang. Shaking all over, he tried to stay as calm as possible to avoid falling off the raised object that he was standing on. There was the sound of more activity and suddenly the hood was removed quickly followed immediately by a blinding flash and instant darkness as the hood was replaced over his head.

Bill felt some relief as the noose was removed. Two people took hold of his arms and he was lowered to the floor. The door opened, more sounds of activity as objects were removed then the cuffs came off and the door quickly closed. Bill, still shaking from the experience took off the hood, moved carefully to the bed and sat down to gather his thoughts. He tried to process what had just happened. The juxtaposition of darkness afforded by the hood and brilliant light, apparently from a camera's flash, had bright stars going around in his head. He sat still with his eyes closed and let his body come to grips with the fact that he wasn't about to die just yet.

This event was unique in a few respects. First a captor had spoken, "no move or die" in an accent that sounded Vietnamese or certainly from the region. This marked the first time anyone had spoken to him. Second, this was the first time that the mention of death was brought into the situation. On the floor was the paper he had been made to hold, today's edition of USA Today, which he retrieved and read the relevant pages quickly in case they came back for it. There was no mention of him missing which was no surprise, as he knew the agency would put a tight lid on anything to do with a missing agent.

Doc was on time for his nine o'clock meeting with Jim, who had arranged a conference call at nine thirty with the DDO.

Jim said, "Help yourself to coffee and muffins Doc and let's talk about where we go from here."

Doc got his coffee and muffin from the side-board and getting comfortable in one of Jim's leather chairs said, " I've given it a lot of thought Jim. I've sat around doing nothing about Bill long enough now. I have to go there and try to do what I can."

"Doc you know that I would do anything for you and Bill that's within my power, but, in this case, it's simply not possible. I've tried putting pressure on the Minister; he's spoken to the Prime Minister and the verdict is simply that the government cannot interfere with the team of specialists that's in place. The Thai government and now, the Cambodian government have agreed, reluctantly, to permit the original team to conduct their investigations, under their governments supervision, so our hands are tied. Even the US President and you know what he thinks of you and Bill; feels that at this point, the best bet is to leave the investigation to the original team. The DDO and I have spent hours lobbying on your behalf and in preparing for this meeting because we want you to understand that we have done all we can to try to accommodate your wishes."

"Jim, let me say first of all that I appreciate all you and the DDO have done for Bill and I. Let's get another coffee and wait for the DDO's call before we continue. I have a plan, but I think it's best that I discuss it with you both at the same time."

Jim agreed, they recharged their coffee cups, took a forbidden second muffin and talked about cottages and fishing. At exactly nine-thirty, the DDO called and, after the pleasantries, admitted that there was nothing new other than that the team was scouring the area around northeastern Cambodia looking for any clues.

Doc said, "I have a proposition for you both which I think could work. I feel that I can help find Bill if I were on the ground in the region. I have years of contacts and experience that might open some doors to me that are closed to others, including the official team, precisely because they are the official team. In Asia, people do business with people not with companies or organizations. I want to try using some of my people contacts in the search for Bill, but this has to be done face to face.

I have here my resignation, which I'll give to Jim. As of this moment, I am no longer employed by the Government of Canada and, therefore, no longer a member of the task force. Whatever I do from now on, I do like a private citizen. You both have "plausible deniability."

The DDO started to say, "But Donovan…

Doc interrupted him and said, "With respect sir, please let me finish. I'm going to Cambodia, leaving later today as a private citizen, no longer under your command or Jim's for that matter." I will do my very best to stay out of the way of the official team while I search for Bill. If I find….no when I find him, I will get back to you both and turn the retrieval process over to you and the official team."

Jim said, "Look, Donovan, if I accept this resignation letter, I won't be able to hire you back once this is over. As they say, you can't put the toothpaste back in the tube. You are going against direct orders originating in very high places."

The DDO said, "I agree with Jim; despite all you have done for your country and mine, we won't be in a position to bring you back in once you leave. I suggest that Jim destroys the resignation letter and we forget we ever had this conversation. At the very least, think about it overnight and we can talk again same time tomorrow."

Doc said, "Gentlemen, I really appreciate your efforts, but my mind is made up. I'll leave you both with something to think about, however. Once I get Bill back, I'm going to do my best to get him to join me in a private business venture. Whether he joins me or not, I'll start up this business. I'll be continuing to do business in Asia as well as the rest of the world. My proposal to you is that I, and possibly Bill, will continue to look for ways to help you both stem the flow of illegal drugs into North America. We will do this on a volunteer basis and what we ask for in return is access to you both from time to time to get assistance when we might need it. It's understood that we'll not contact you unless we have no other option. I would ask that if possible, you provide us with any business leads or contacts that might help us; for instance, I'd like to keep my access to embassy events open if possible."

The DDO said, "Ok apparently you have given this a lot of thought. What you want is a mutual assistance agreement, that has no particular parameters and that would be aimed at cooperation between your private company and the governments of the United States and Canada, is that right?"

"I don't want an official deal with Washington and Ottawa. I want a handshake agreement with you both as individuals that we will scratch each other's backs whenever we can."

Jim said, "I hate to lose you Doc, and of course I can't commit to anything in writing, but that's not what you are looking for anyway. So yes, I personally will agree to a mutual back-scratching arrangement between you and me with no official sanction."

The DDO said, "My sentiments exactly. Go get our boy back!"

Doc said his farewells and left the building feeling like an enormous weight had been lifted off his shoulder. He headed to his realtor's office, signed the listing agreement on the condo and returned there to determine how to dispose of everything.

He called Shannon and said, "Hi love how're things going?"

"Can you hear the noise in the background? They started this morning with hammers and saws. The renovations are underway, let's hope there are software developers ready to fill the rooms."

"I don't think that will be a problem. I just left a meeting with my bosses and have resigned. As I expected, they wouldn't come off their demand that I stay away from Asia so it's a done deal now."

'Oh Doc, I'm sorry, you liked working there so much."

"I did, but it is time for a new chapter. I can't rest until Bill is found. In any event, the business with Bev will keep me more than busy from now on. Anything else to report on your end?"

"No, I'm making progress on the interior décor and Anne has started conducting training sessions on five-star service. I expect that I'll be coming home next week and Anne maybe a week or two later. To escape the construction noise, she has set up a training classroom in the car garage. Bev and I call her 'the Professor.'"

"I've listed the Ottawa condo. Can you remember, was there anything here that we might want for the cottage or the new house or should I just give it all away?"

"Nothing strikes me as memorable so if there's nothing you want to keep, call a charity like the Diabetes Association and have them pick it up. Be sure to have someone organize a cleaning service to go through the place once it's empty."

"There isn't much I want, just some mementos and some clothes. I'll get my neighbor to box them and have the storage people pick them up. We can retrieve them from storage once we get the cottage renovation completed."

"Do you need to speak to Bev? She's running around with a hard hat on bullying the contractor. She's determined to get this done right. We've become close friends as I thought we would."

"No, leave her to her bullying. I am off to California to meet with my friend Brian White to get his input on some software development recruiters and a few other related things. Then I am headed for Bangkok and Cambodia to get my buddy back."

"Ok Sweetie, be really careful and get back to me as soon as you can. Love you."

"I'll call whenever I can, love you too."

Doc talked to his neighbor, who agreed to look after the donation of everything to the Diabetes Association and to get the cleaning service lined up. He called the pilots and told them he was on the way. They had already handled the refueling and filed the flight plan so it would be wheels up as soon as he got there.

Once underway, he called Brian White. "Hi, Brian are you and Kristen still on for dinner this evening?"

Brian said, "We are looking forward to it. It's been way too long so we have a lot of catching up to do."

"You bet. Did you have any luck lining up some people for me to interview for the recruiting position?"

"Yes, I have two left on a shortlist that was originally seven. I have interviewed them both twice and have had them vetted by my personnel lady. They both check out. You'll see Stanley at 8 o'clock for breakfast and Grant at 10 o'clock for coffee."

"Which one would you hire?"

"I have been thinking about that, I figured you'd ask. I think I'd be inclined to go with Stanley because he has both sales and recruiting experience; Grant has been more on the academic side, recruiting students for the computer software development program at UCLA. I don't think you can go far wrong with either one."

"Ok let's talk about it some more this evening, The Mandarin Oriental Brasserie at seven o'clock right."

"Yes that's right, see you then."

"One last thing before you go, are you aware of any office space available in the area? I'd prefer an executive office with a reception area, in an upscale building that will appeal to potential software developers."

"There's lots of space available in the area. I can have my secretary look into it if you want."

"No, it's ok, I'll have the new hire do it. See you tonight."

Doc checked into the Mandarin Oriental, had a quick shower, changed into a sports jacket with an open neck shirt and headed down to the Brasserie Bar. Brian and Kristen weren't there yet so he ordered a drink and sat at the bar to people watch. When they arrived, Kristen was as radiant as ever and gave him a big hug. Brian looked fitter than last time they'd met and explained that he had started to watch his diet more closely and was now running five miles a day on average.

Doc said, " Boy it's good to see you two looking so healthy and happy. Shall we go to our table or would you prefer a drink here first?"

Kristen said, "My vote is the table, I am famished."

Doc said, "The table it is then." He motioned for the Maître 'd and they were led to a nice corner table with some privacy as Doc had requested.

The waiter arrived to take drink orders and Doc ordered another scotch while Brian and Kristen decided on a bottle of California red.

Once the waiter left Doc said, "First off, let me thank you for all the help you have provided so far. Your assistance has given us a real leg up in getting our new company underway."

Kristen said, "Tell us about it, we're dying to hear what you're up to."

Doc said, "I'll give you the Cole's Notes version rather than bore you to tears. You remember Bev Patterson, my friend from law and business school? Well, she came into a substantial inheritance, that's the good news. All the assets are in Zimbabwe, which has strict currency rules so it's very difficult to get the money out in any meaningful amounts, that's the bad news. She offered to share her fortune with me if I could figure out a way to get the money out of the country. We're creating a software developer incubator in Zimbabwe so we can use the cash to accommodate software developers who will develop programs.

They'll be sent by email to our office in Hong Kong where we'll market the software and share the revenue with the developer. It's a win-win because we get the cash out of the country and the developer gets full development support including accommodation, food and all his or her needs taken care of. They then become fifty-fifty partners with Bev and I. So if they produce, they go from starving software developer with little or no business sense to possibly a wealthy partner with people that understand business."

Brian said, "That's amazing, obviously you've put a lot of thought and money into the idea so far, what stage are you at?"

We have a fabulous mansion in Zimbabwe called Lion's Pride. As we speak, it's being converted into a high-tech, luxury campus/resort to be home to our developer partners while they create. This is where our new recruiter comes in. His job will be to find appropriate software developers, sell them on the proposal, get them to move to our mansion and get to work."

"Will this bring you here more often?" Kristen said.

"Oh yeah, I expect between here, Seattle and Vancouver we should find lots of takers for our idea. The key for us is to identify the ones that have the entrepreneurial drive and want to get rich. We only make money if they make money."

The dinner was exquisite as usual, the company fantastic and Doc finally said, "I hate to call it a night, but it's mid-week and you both have jobs to do tomorrow. I'll meet with the two potential recruiters and let you know how that goes. Then I'm off to Asia. Again thanks for your help."

In the morning, Doc had breakfast with Stanley, a very impressive guy, with that look of ambition and drive that Doc was looking for. He handled the interview well and didn't skip a beat when Doc told him to tell a joke.

He told an old one about a fellow who is playing golf when a funeral procession passed and he stopped, removed his hat and lowered his head respectfully. His mates were amazed and one said, we had no Idea you were so respectful of the dead and he said, "It's the least I can do, we were married for forty-three years!" Doc was impressed with his quick pick up on the unusual request for a joke as well as his delivery. Apparently, a man who can think on his feet. They talked about the nature of the new business, the duties of the position, availability, and compensation package.

Doc said, "I have one more person to see, then I have to be on a plane to Asia right away. I'll make a decision on the plane and let you know. If I offered you the job would you take it?"

Stanley said, "Yes I would, it sounds right up my alley and I like the idea of working with entrepreneurs in a new start-up that's well thought out and well funded. I've known Brian for a long time and have a great deal of respect for him. Since he recommends you, I feel comfortable about the position."

Grant was also ideal for the job although altogether different in style from Stanley. Grant was used to the academic life and relating to students whereas Stanley was more of a sales type. He too said he was impressed with the referral from Brian and that he would accept the position if it were offered to him. Doc told him that he had to head out to the airport but would be in touch by tomorrow.

As the wheels locked into the fuselage, Doc had some tough decisions to make, whoever he chose would be crucial to the success of the new company.

CHAPTER TWENTY-EIGHT

Doc was relaxing and watching some CNN on the plane's television. He thought to himself maybe we should look into buying our own plane. With all the travel, we'll be doing a private jet might make economic sense. I'll ask Bev to do some analysis and see. She just loves number crunching and thank God one of us does. She had insisted that I keep the charter jet for this trip due to the concern about someone possibly being after me.

Doc thought about Grant and Stanley, and it came to him. I'll hire both of them. Stanley as Director of Marketing and Grant as Director of Recruiting.

Stanley could market the Software Conceptions business to attract developers and also deal with sales and advertising of the final product once developers produced something saleable. Grant would devote his time to recruiting developers into the organization. Doc liked this idea and decided he'd sleep on it then call them both tomorrow morning their time.

Doc called ahead and reserved a room at the Mandarin Oriental Bangkok for three days and then he booked at the Intercontinental in Phnom Penh for the next three days.

Doc answered his phone, " Hello, Donovan speaking."

The voice on the other end of the line belonged to Jim Elliott who said, "Hello Donovan are you in the air?

"Hi Jim, yes, I'm 40,000 feet over the Pacific about halfway to Bangkok, my first stop. What's up?"

"There was another communiqué from Bill's captors today. This one arrived by ordinary mail; postmarked Bangkok. It contained another photo. I've sent it as an attachment so open it and we can discuss it."

Doc opened it and was shocked to see Bill with a noose around his neck. He said, "What do you make of this Jim? It looks like they're turning up the heat."

"Yes they are, there was a note with it saying, '$10 million USD in one week be ready or we kick the chair and send new picture of death dance.' "My God! One week is all we have. "

"Doc I'm sticking my neck out a country mile here first by sending this to you at all and second by what else I've done. I spoke to one of our RCMP investigators, no need for names, but he's a friend of mine. He'll contact you with any Intel they dig up. There won't be any names exchanged or conversation, merely a telephone call on the secure line and an intelligence dump. When you find where Bill is, you call my friend back with the location, and he takes it from there. I need your agreement on that or no intelligence dump. The investigators have the muscle in the form of a navy seals team of exfiltration specialists standing by at a secret location. Trust me, you can't do this without them."

"I know I need them to get him out and I will not get underfoot. Unless I call them with a location, they won't even know I was there. I'll travel the Cambodia leg of the trip under a false passport that I can get in Bangkok, and I'll fly commercial from Bangkok so no one can trace the plane."

"Anything else show up on the photograph this time?"

"Yes, two things. One, the chop of the airport news shop was still on the USA Today, so they bought it at the same place. And two, Bill's pants were wet down the front, it looks like he pissed himself."

"Thanks for the heads up, I'll let you know if anything breaks on my end."

Doc checked into his usual room at the Mandarin and called the GM, Andrew. His secretary said he was at a meeting but if it's urgent, she could interrupt him. Doc said, "No, just ask him to meet me at the Poolside Bar when he can."

Doc showered and went down to the Poolside Bar to wait for Andrew. If he was going to get anywhere fast, he knew he had to get connected into the underworld of the region. All his contacts thus far had been with respectable senior government or business people. He couldn't think of any that might have the connections he now needed or if they did have such connections, would share them with him. Doc didn't know if Andrew might be able to hook him up with someone, and he didn't know how much he should tell him. He took another look at the last photo of Bill on his cell phone and decided that he just didn't have time to waste. The wet front of Bill's pants drove the situation home more than words could ever do.

Andrew came by and welcomed Doc back with a sincere handshake. He sat down and ordered a Virgin Caesar. He had stopped drinking alcohol on the job many years ago when, inebriated from too much champagne, he tripped over a well-heeled guest and fell into the pool. Andrew asked about Bill and Doc had to make a decision. He thought again about Bill's wet pants and said," Andrew, Bill's still missing. My company's security team has been informed that he's being held for ransom. They have reason to believe that he's somewhere in Cambodia. Their investigation is continuously running up blind alleys. They've been through the list I gave them of our business contacts in the region."

"I know, they have been to see me three times, but I told them that I just can't think of anyone who would do such a thing to Bill."

"Andrew, I need to start thinking outside the box as they say. I don't think the way to find him lies in talking to high-ranking government officials or wealthy businessmen. I'm starting to believe I need to go underground and find someone with connections to the Asian gangs and other criminals active both here and in Cambodia."

"Doc, that can be very dangerous ground on which to tread. It's very difficult, if not impossible, for a foreigner to get close to these people. They wisely keep their affairs strictly among themselves. Also, they are ruthless. Many would slit your throat just for looking crossways at them. No, I would strongly advise that you stay away from these people completely and try to think of some other way to find Bill."

"I appreciate your advice Andrew, I know it's well-intentioned, but I have to do something, and I have to do it fast or I might lose my friend."

Doc called Shannon and said, "Hi love how is it going?"

"Hi Doc, you sound sad, is everything okay."

"Well it's as good as can be with Bill still missing, I'm not going to feel truly happy until we have him back. One development in the case is that we've received a ransom note demanding ten million USD within a week. Doc decided to spare her the image of Bill with a noose around his neck."

"Would the company pay the money?"

"No, I don't think so. All these big firms that are doing business in areas where kidnapping is common tend to have the same strict policy about not giving in to terrorists. It's hard to accept when it's your friend or loved one that is the victim. But the logic makes sense, in that once word got out that any particular company paid the ransom, their executives would be sitting ducks."

"I know, but it leaves us stuck between a rock and a hard place. I don't see any option but to pay them and get Bill back."

"If I paid them, there's no way to guarantee that we'd get him back, and the entire business community would be up in arms for us having established a precedent. We wouldn't be able to do business anywhere in Asia again. My primary concern is that we might be setting up our colleagues and countrymen as targets. I know Bill wouldn't want that. I've got a pretty full day of meetings tomorrow; I'm going to see if I can catch a break with any of our long-standing business and government contacts. I don't have a lot of faith in this approach, but I have to do something, and that's all I can think of for now. Let's change the subject. How are things at Lion's Pride?"

Things are going well here on all fronts. I'll finish in three days, and then a meeting with the contractor and the architect and I'm on my way to Scranton. I spoke to Gary this morning, and he thinks the Brockville place is coming along well. He thinks another two weeks should do it."

"Wow, that's way faster than the original time estimate isn't it?"

"Yes, he says a large project that the contractor was working on was put on hold. So our construction crew has tripled, and they're making faster progress. I'll get up there as soon as I get home and see how O'Leary's is doing."

"Have you heard from Sean?"

"Yeah, he reports that all is fine other than Donald having a nervous breakdown. I think the GM role is just beyond his capabilities. Best to find out now before tourist season. "

" If there's nothing else, pass me on to Bev if you can. Love you."

"Love you too, here's Bev."

"Hi Doc, Shannon can fill me in on Bill, what's new business wise?"

"I'm in the process of hiring two people, one as Director of Marketing and one as Director of Recruiting. They both come highly recommended by Brian White. Incidentally, he and Kristen asked me to pass on their love; they are doing well and looking great."

"I'd like to see them again. Maybe we should have a grand opening party and have all our friends, particularly those who contributed to our start-up of Lion's Pride and Software Conceptions."

"Good idea but you'll see them before that, I've invited them to the wedding."

"Super, another reason to look forward to it."

"I know you're busy with the renovation but did you get a chance to look into the agricultural consultant?"

"Already done. He is a retired professor from the agriculture faculty at Zimbabwe University and he is starting the consulting project in two days."

"Funny I was thinking that one approach to this might be as a joint venture with the University using our property as a training farm."

"I'll keep that in mind, let's see what he comes up with first."

"How is the construction doing?"

"Noisy, as you can hear and dust everywhere but I'd say we're a bit ahead of schedule at this point."

"All sounds good at your end. Is Anne progressing with her course on five-star service techniques?"

"Yes, she's brought in service supervisors from some major hotels as guest instructors and seems very pleased with the results thus far."

"Is there anything else you need from me?"

"No, I guess that's it, get some sleep and get Bill back."

The next morning, Doc rose early, did some laps in the pool to shake off jet lag, had a light breakfast at poolside then went to his suite. He dressed in business casual for Bangkok's climate and started working the phones. He had gone through his list of Bangkok business and government contacts and began making appointments with those that he thought would be the most likely sources of relevant information. By eleven, o'clock he had lined up seven appointments for the afternoon and tomorrow. He decided to take a walk and have lunch before his first appointment for the afternoon. He walked over to the River City Shopping Complex and picked up a bolt of red and a bolt of green Thai silk for Shannon. The clerk assured him it would be enough to make several outfits in both colors. He had it shipped to O'Leary's marked 'confidential, hold for Donovan O'Connell.'

He went into a small noodle place that he often frequented with Bill and sat at a small window table where he could watch the people and teeming traffic. He sat down and ordered an ice tea and a bowl of Pad Thai noodles. Suddenly a young boy maybe ten or twelve years old ran by him, and threw a box of matches on the table as he passed through the door and disappeared. Doc looked at the matchbox, which was from a country and western music bar called, 'The Neon Moon.' He opened the matchbox and read, 'seven o'clock, alone'. He returned to his room and did some online research on the Neon Moon. He found that it was popular with some of Bangkok's biker gangs. He went to his afternoon appointments but other than the opportunity to renew old acquaintances, he didn't come up with anything useful.

He was apprehensive about going to the Neon Moon by himself. He realized how alone he was. Another reason to get Bill back. He tried to dress down as much as possible, wearing blue jeans and replacing his Gucci loafers with his jogging shoes. A T-shirt he usually wore for jogging completed his best attempt at looking like a tourist. He thought about adding to the tourist persona by bringing along his camera then had second thoughts about having a camera in hand in a biker bar. He slipped off his Rolex and left it, along with his wallet and passport in the safe in his room. He kept a couple of hundred US along with about the equivalent in Thai Baht. He headed out to get a taxi. No limos this trip.

He arrived at the Neon Moon ten minutes early. There weren't many people there at this hour. He sat at the bar and ordered a Singha beer and surveyed the place making use of the back bar mirror and being careful not to make eye contact with anyone. It didn't take long for a tough looking Asian wearing the colors of the Thaicats Motorcycle Club to approach him. The guy said, "There's a tax for being in this bar and I'm the tax collector."

Doc said," How much is the tax."

"Three thousand Baht."

"I think I'll just leave."

"Then there is a six thousand baht departure tax, kinda like at the airport."

Doc could see three equally tough looking gang members watching this conversation while playing pool. It didn't look right; maybe he'd been set up, and the kid in the noodle shop gets paid for luring tourists in to get fleeced. Doc knew that Thailand had a group called the Tourist Police specifically charged with protecting visitors, but he didn't see any in here.

Just then, another tough guy came up and

said, "He is with me D, get lost." D seemed to defer to this new guy and went to join his cronies at the pool table. The new tough guy then motioned towards a door at the back of the bar and started to walk towards it. Doc figured that maybe this new guy was the one who sent the matchbook or maybe he was just taking him into the backroom to rob him. He didn't see that he had much choice. If there were any chance of getting help with Bill's situation, he would have to play along with this fellow and hope for the best. When they passed through the door, they were in a private, cheaply furnished office not meant to impress visitors. The host, as Doc thought of him, motioned towards a chair as he produced two Leo beers from a small bar fridge.

He said, "Your first name?"

"Donovan, who are you and who referred you to me?"

"No matter, what you want?"

"Information about the location of a friend who has been kidnapped."

"Who kidnapped him?"

"I don't know."

"Why kidnap him, for money?"

"Yes."

"How much?"

"They want $10 million US."

"What his name?"

"Bill Wong."

"What country he in?"

"I think Cambodia."

"I ask around, need payout money, $10,000 USD for start."

"How do I get it to you?"

"Get cash, put in envelope be at Jim Thompson House at eleven o'clock tomorrow morning. I find you. What is hotel and room?"

"Mandarin Oriental room 550."

"Ok. I get information; I call. Go out this door, get in taxi waiting."

Doc did as he was told and twenty minutes later was back at the Mandarin. In his room, he sat to contemplate what had just happened. Either he was on the track to potentially finding Bill or he was in the middle of a huge con and would be feeding money into a scam. Regardless at least he was doing something and he had achieved his goal of getting an underground contact, for better or worse. Obviously someone he had spoken to had made this contact happen. He didn't think the boy running by his table in the noodle house to draw him into a scam theory held water. It could happen, but he hadn't heard of it before. He called Andrew and asked if he would join him for dinner.

Andrew said, "I'd love to Donovan, but I have a previous engagement with my wife. It's our tenth anniversary; a major one where we come from and I promised to take her to dinner. I have time to buy you a drink at the Poolside Bar if you like."

"I'll be there, are you ready now?"

"Sure, I'm in my office so I'll just be a minute

then meet you there."

Andrew was off the clock and on his way out with his wife so he joined Doc in a Laphroaig, but only a single, no ice. Doc had his usual double on the rocks.

Doc said," Andrew have you ever heard of a scam on tourists where a young person delivers a message on a matchbook to get someone to go to a bar to be fleeced?"

"Did this happen to you?" Andrew said, "I've not heard of it, and I think I would have since I sit on the board of both the Tourist Bureau and the Tourist Police. We keep close tabs on scams, you can imagine what would be the result if Bangkok were to get a reputation for having tourists conned all the time."

"I'm not sure that I was conned. I was in a noodle house when a young person ran by my table and tossed a matchbook on to it. The matchbook was from the Neon Moon bar and a message inside told me to be there at seven o'clock. I met a guy who seemed to know about me; we talked, and he asked for $10,000 US to see if he could get information for me. If it's a scam, it's a pretty sophisticated one, and coincidental don't you think?"

Andrew said, "I'm not a big believer in coincidences. I think if I were you I'd pay the money and see what happens, after all $10,000 isn't much if it works now is it?"

Andrew left for his date with his wife and Doc thought about their conversation. Normally

Andrew has been quite a conservative guy with a strong accounting background. Not the type to blindly give away money, yet he seemed to be in favor of pursuing this lead. Maybe he knew more than he was saying but in any case Doc would be at the Jim Thompson House at eleven o'clock in the morning to see where, if anywhere, this leads.

CHAPTER TWENTY-NINE

Bill tensed when he heard the food slot open, praying that it would contain food and not a hood and cuffs. When he saw the hood and cuffs, his pulse quickened, his heart sped up, and he began to perspire. So far, life in captivity here hadn't been that uncomfortable. He'd been well treated, given enough food, taken for showers when he wanted and given the newspapers and the Clancy novel to read. However since the last episode with the noose, he'd been living in constant fear of another visit where instead of a photo opportunity, they hung him. The note this time only said, "on cuffs, on hood no talk." Probably not a photo this time as there was no requirement for a shower or to dress well. He heard the usual metallic sound of the door opening then felt the captor's hand on his arm. They led him this time to the left for seventy-one paces then up eight stairs to a landing and up another eight stairs. He figured he must be the second floor, assuming his jail cell had been on the first floor. They then walked sixty paces to the right and stopped. Another door opened, and the captor pushed him into a room. He was made to sit at what felt like a table, and they attached his handcuffs to some chain that was bolted to the floor. The captor standing behind Bill removed the hood and was out the door before Bill could see him or her.

Bill glanced around and saw that he was in a room slightly larger than his cell with green painted cinderblock walls, a cheap, gray, linoleum tile floor, and no window. There was another chair sitting directly across from him and nothing else in the room. He sat for what seemed like an hour listening for any sounds that might give away where he was. All he heard was absolute silence until finally a metallic sound came from behind him as the door was unlocked, and someone walked in. The man had on a hood and was wearing what could have passed for a military uniform from the lower ranks or an auto mechanic's work shirt and pants. He smelled vaguely of cigar smoke mixed with cheap cologne, not a pleasant combination. He sat on the chair across from Bill, placed a pad and pen on the table and stared at him through small eye slots in the hood fabric for what seemed like five minutes but probably was less. He said, "You my prisoner. You write on paper to boss. You say he pay money or you die if no money pay in one week. He wire $10 million USD immediate, no longer than five minutes when we call USA embassy in Bangkok one week from tomorrow at eleven o'clock we give bank account detail. You say you ok, but no want to die."

Bill said," What if I refuse to write this note?"

"We write same note, cut off you right hand to send with note instead, you choice."

Bill could see no harm in writing the note. He knew the agency would not pay the money under any circumstances, and if he played along at least, it gave him another week. He also knew that a full-scale search would be underway and held out hope that maybe they'd get here on time. Once the note was written, Bill was returned to his cell.

Doc drew $10,000 USD in cash out of his account at Hong Kong Shanghai Bank. He put it in a large manila envelope and took the hotel limo to the Jim Thompson House in time for the eleven o'clock meeting. He met the biker and handed over the envelope. The biker said, "I call you at seven o'clock with report. I may have lead and working on it."

For some reason, Doc felt encouraged by this guy and felt that there may be work underway to find Bill. It was the first time Doc felt a semblance of hope since he learned of Bill's kidnapping. Doc met with the three executives he had arranged to meet, and even though he told them of Bill's plight, no one seemed to have any idea of what Doc should do to get Bill back.

After his meetings, Doc went back to his room and thought about calling Jim. But since it was still early in Ottawa and since he didn't have anything concrete to report, he decided to wait until he heard from the biker….if he heard from the biker. He headed down for some laps then came back and ordered room service. He wanted to be here when the guy called. At exactly seven o'clock the phone rang and the man said, "I am in Phnom Penh at payphone in hotel lobby. You go to payphone in your hotel lobby and call this number 866-925-4772, I wait." The guy hung up and Doc went to the lobby. At the front desk, he asked the clerk to check the phone number and learned that it was indeed from Phnom Penh. He called it from the lobby phone. He didn't bother to tell the guy that it wasn't necessary for him to use a payphone as he has a special secure phone, but he didn't want to waste the time. The guy picked up on the first ring and said, "What was place we meet this morning?"

Doc recognized that he wanted to make sure it was him he was talking to and said, "Jim Thompson House."

The guy said, "I have good contact here so came over to meet. My contact having his 'friends' talk to many people in Phnom Penh right now. He says if he find location of your friend he want $1 million USD, I also want same."

Doc said, "If your contacts give me the right location and Bill is there, I will pay the money you ask."

"How do we know you will pay?"

"I will give two cashiers checks that may be cashed by the bearer and are certified by Hong Kong Shanghai Bank to Mr. Andrew Chang, General Manager of the Mandarin Oriental Hotel. He will have instructions to give them to you when I call him. Do you trust Mr. Chang?"

Doc suspected that it was Andrew that put Doc in touch with the biker, and this was confirmed when he said, "Yes I trust him. But we get money if he is where we say, no matter if you get him out safely right?"

"I agree. If Bill is where you say he is, you get paid even if we don't get him out alive."

"Ok you tell Mr. Chang about this and I call him in 1 hour to talk. You be there in room with him."

"Fine you call Mr. Chang's office in 1 hour, and we will be on speaker phone to talk to you. Stay on this phone for a few minutes while I see if Mr. Chang is in."

Doc called Andrew's office and luckily found him in and agreeable to the phone call in an hour. Doc said he would explain what it's all about when he joins him in his office in ten minutes. Doc then got back to the biker and said Mr. Chang has agreed to the call and that they would speak to him in an hour. Andrew's secretary had left for the day so Doc knocked on his office door.

Andrew said, "Come in."

Doc went in, and Andrew handed him a scotch and said "I figured you could use this by now."

"I sure can. Let me fill you in. The guy I met at the country bar looks as though he's honest and on to something. He called me from Phnom Penh and has people there searching for Bill. If they find his location, I have agreed to leave you with two cashier's checks certified by my bank and payable to the bearer for 1 million USD each. These are to be released to him if I call you saying I have found Bill. They get the money if Bill is there regardless of whether we get him out alive or not. Do you agree to do this for us?"

"I will do my part to help Bill but my involvement must be kept confidential, or I could lose my job or maybe even go to jail. I was trying to decide if I should tell you or not and have decided that I will. The biker is the son of my cousin. I have known him since birth, but I wasn't sure if he would be able or willing to help on this; that is why I set up the meeting in such a round about way."

They talked to the biker, Diesel Soon and got everything organized. Doc asked Diesel to call the minute he had anything, no matter what time. He went to his room to call Jim and wait.

"Hi, Jim I'm glad I caught you so early, bet the muffins are still warm."

"Hello Donovan, yes they are still warm, I wish you were here to enjoy one with me. You sound chipper is anything new?"

"Well, there may be some news soon. I don't want to raise any hopes just yet so let's keep this between us, but I've developed an underground contact in Cambodia who is shaking the trees. He is supposed to be well connected there. If he meets with any success, I'll get right back to you."

"Wow that would be perfect, should I tell the DDO?"

"No, not yet, I don't want any more activity spooking anyone. I want to let this guy do his thing and see where it takes us. If they find Bill's location, I'll call you day or night and then you call the DDO and activate the team. I'll wait in the hotel while they do what they do best. Then I want to buy Bill a drink and ask him to be my best man."

"What's this about a best man, are you getting married?"

"Yes, your invitation will be forthcoming. Are you prepared to go to Ireland for the ceremony?"

"I'd go anywhere for your wedding, you know that. Who's the lucky girl?"

"Her name is Shannon; she's GM of the hotel I stay at in Scranton, we've known each other for years but have finally fallen in love."

"Well congratulations and we'll talk again when you have some news."

Doc called Shannon and filled her in on developments. She also reported on the progress at Lion's Pride, and they said goodbye because Doc didn't want to keep the phone tied up in case Diesel called. Doc decided to take a long hot bath and soak in the tub with some soothing candlelight and soft music. He was too wound up for sleep yet and didn't want to leave the room in case the phone rang. Finally after adding hot water three times, he gave up and went to bed and read. He read for about ten minutes and fell sound asleep.

He woke to the sound of the phone ringing

and jumped up to get it.

Diesel said, "We got location. Go to lobby and phone back 886-485-3861."

Doc said he would but instead just used his secure cell for the call.

Diesel said, "My contact has found location and has it confirmed by another party. He is there for sure."

Doc said, "Where is the location?"

Diesel explained exactly where it was even providing map coordinates. Doc thanked him and called Jim, "Jim we've got it, here are the map coordinates: 13 degrees 6 minutes north and 103 degrees 12 minutes east. My sources say he is there, and they have this confirmed by someone else."

Jim said, "I'll call the DDO right now, and we'll activate the exfiltration team, I'll be back to you."

Doc sat back and closed his eyes, "It's out of my hands now, I just hope they find him alive and can get him out, I want this to be over!"

The DDO activated the exfiltration team and provided them with the map coordinates. When he first heard of the possibility that Bill may be in Cambodia, he made arrangements to have satellite reconnaissance focus on the region. He also made arrangements for drones to be on standby aboard a carrier in the Gulf of Thailand for immediate surveillance or combat missions as required. Between the satellite and drones, the team would soon have a clear map of the layout of the compound where Bill was being held. To determine exactly where he was, the seals decided to capture a person from the compound's compliment of thugs.

They dispatched a team of four by helicopter to a position about five miles away from the jungle road into the compound and chopped down a good size tree so it fell across the road. After an hour and twenty minutes, a Jeep came down the road with a driver and a passenger. They stopped to move the fallen tree, and the seals shot them with tranquilizer darts. The seals then cleared the tree and hid the Jeep deep in the jungle. They bundled the two captives into the helicopter and lifted off headed for their secret base of operations about 175 miles west.

The two prisoners woke up with their hands tied over their heads and pulled up in the air so they were forced to stand on their toes or to dangle in the air, a most painful position. They were both naked and staring at a car battery with electrical leads attached that left nothing to the imagination. They would cooperate, or they would suffer unimaginable pain. They both opted to talk.

They were taken into separate rooms and seated at a table with a map of the compound. Independently, they both indicated the same spot where Bill's cell was located. They were told that they would be kept as prisoners until Bill was freed, if they lied and as a result Bill was killed, they too would be killed. They got the message!

Now armed with the information provided by their captives and the maps courtesy of the drones and satellite, the plan was to go by chopper to a suitable clearance in the jungle. The noise from the helicopter wasn't an issue as they set down far enough away from the compound. The seal team would move in during the middle of the night, retrieve Bill, hopefully using only their knives and silenced weapons, and be gone with a minimum of killing. According to the captives, there should only be one sentry on duty patrolling the compound and one guard covering Bill. But at three a.m. he would no doubt be asleep on a cot just outside Bill's cell.

The seal team moved in, arriving at the compound at exactly three a.m.

The patrolling sentry was taken down with a tactical combat Bowie knife across the throat and similarly the guard outside Bill's door would never wake up. The seals were so quiet that Bill didn't even hear them come into his cell until they woke him with a hand over his mouth. They quickly led him out of the compound and through the jungle to the waiting chopper. Once airborne the seal team commander sent a message to the drone commander aboard the US carrier that said, "Mission accomplished, clear to strike." Five minutes later four drones armed with Hellfire missiles reduced the compound to ashes. Losses included a huge drug production facility, a warehouse full of processed drugs awaiting shipment and the quarters of the drug operation's leader and lieutenants.

The chopper headed for the US carrier where Bill was debriefed by members of the investigation team and given a thorough medical examination. Once they cleared Bill, he was flown to Bangkok where Doc greeted him warmly.

Doc said, "I've arranged a full spa treatment, your favorite dinner and time for you to have a good sleep, but first call your folks."

Needless to say, the DDO is anxious to see you at head office. He offered to provide an agency jet to get you home, but I told him I would give you a ride in my plane because I want to talk to you on the way."

Bill was ready for the massage and dinner but was too wound up for sleep.

Doc had advised Andrew to release the checks to Diesel and told him that a retirement bonus for him had been put into a bank account in Switzerland. He gave Andrew the code number that would establish him as owner of the one million USD in the account.

Doc said to Bill," If you're restless why don't we head back now, we can fly overnight, and you can even have the bedroom?"

Bill said, "That suits me, I want to get this whole experience behind me, and that won't happen until I deal with the DDO. Let's hit the road."

On the plane Doc called Grant and Stanley, told them they were both hired and to meet him at O'Leary's Arms in Scranton the day after tomorrow.

He said to Bill, "I know you've been through a lot so if you just want to relax on this flight, that's ok with me. I have some ideas that I wish to talk to you about at some point, but it doesn't have to be tonight."

Doc called the flight attendant, and she delivered drinks.

Then Bill said," Let's talk now, I'm still so excited to be out of that mess, that I won't relax."

Doc started, "Since they captured you I've quit my job. I no longer work for Jim or the DDO. I'm an independent businessman."

"Wow, I never saw that coming, tell me about it."

"The reason that I quit now is that they, being Jim and the DDO, wouldn't allow me to go to Asia to help with the search for you. So I resigned. I told them I was on my way to Asia, promised to stay out of the way of the team that had been sent to find you and to keep in touch. I also said that if I found you, I would contact them to take on the exfiltration part. I was able to hook up with some rather seedy individuals that, in return for some financial persuasion, were able to determine where you were being held."

Bill, surprised said, "So you found me, not the investigation team?"

"I found you, but they got you, sort of a reluctant joint venture. Reluctant on their part, not mine."

"You paid these gang guys out of your own pocket?"

"That's neither here nor there, my pockets have become significantly deeper lately."

"Hence the private jet?"

"This one's a charter, but I'm thinking of buying one. I'm in a partnership with Bev. We're creating a diversified investment company, Software Conceptions Inc, which has started with a development in Zimbabwe where we'll incubate software start-ups. I'll give you all the details later. For now, I want to offer you the position of executive vice president. Name your own compensation package. What's your first reaction?"

CHAPTER THIRTY

Bill said he was very interested in what Doc had to offer, but there were a couple of things he wanted to do before accepting the position. First he wanted to get through his meeting with the DDO. He wanted to see which way the wind was blowing at the office. The DDO can be a hard case at times, in fact, most of the time. It goes with the territory. Bill wasn't sure if he'd be blamed in any way for this fiasco. He knew it cost a lot of money; you don't reposition satellites, move around aircraft carriers and put high-level investigators in the field for free. Then there were the issues around the ransom. After much prodding, Doc had admitted that he had paid the informers $3 million USD out of his pocket. What was the DDO's reaction going to be to all this? Well, he'd soon know, they were scheduled to land in a half hour. The DDO said he'd have a car there to pick him up and to invite Donovan along if he would like.

When Bill and Doc entered the DDO's office, he greeted them and said he is holding the meeting to in the main conference room. He led them down the hall and opened the door, and they certainly weren't expecting the reception that they got. Most of the senior staff of the Anti-Drug International Taskforce was there except those that were out of town. All at once, when Bill and Doc walked in they, rose to their feet and gave them a long, enthusiastic standing ovation.

As it was early in the day, coffee and pastries had been brought in, and the DDO went to a small podium. He said, "I am not going to make a speech, I just want to say how happy we all are to have you back with us Bill. I would also like to thank Donovan for the important role he played in finding you. We were all worried sick since we heard that you went missing and wanted you to know that we missed your smiling face around here. I know it's going to take some time for you to come down from this terrible experience. So I'm asking everyone to back off, don't load you down with work and let you adjust to normalcy, whatever normalcy is in this place! So let's have a coffee and pastries and welcome our friends home."

The DDO asked Bill and Doc to join him in his office when the festivities were over. In the meantime colleagues were shaking hands, patting backs and giving hugs to the two returning warriors.

When things in the conference room died down, Doc and Bill sat around the conference table in the DDO's office for a meeting. The DDO said, "You know you don't get to be deputy director of operations at the Drug Enforcement Agency without having to make a hell of a lot of decisions. When a person is forced to make so many decisions, he is bound to make some wrong ones now and then. Donovan, I have discussed it with the President and Jim has talked to the Prime Minister, and they've both accepted the fact that we made a bad decision in letting you go. They have both authorized me to ask you to come back to the ADIT group."

"Sir I'm honored that you all feel this way. However, I've made other plans that are firm. I've accepted a partnership with an old friend and classmate from university days, and I want to take it up."

Bill said, "I hate to add to the bad news, but I too will be leaving to take up a position with Donovan's new company. I just this second made the decision."

The DDO said, "Jim and I figured that you would go with Donovan but hoped that you both might reconsider if Donovan rejoined the team.

Bill said, "No, we're going to move on, at least as employees. As Donovan said, we would like to have that mutual back scratching agreement so if you accept that, we'll still be working together."

The DDO said, "Yes I accept the agreement wholeheartedly as does Jim. Remember though, should you ever change your minds you know where we are, and you're both always welcome." He reached into his inside suit pocket and handed Doc an envelope with a check in it for $3 million.

Doc said, "I have a Mustang Shelby Cobra that belongs to the agency. I'll return it the next time I come to Washington unless you need it now, in which case I'll get someone to drive it down."

The DDO said, "Consider it a going away present. You incurred a lot of expense beyond the three million ransom, so the car is part repayment."

Doc said to Bill, "I have an idea. Let's you and I go to Scranton for a couple of days. We can meet with our new employees, Grant, and Stanley, and relax a bit with Sean. Then you can go out to the coast with the new guys, help find us a Silicon Valley office and visit with your folks. I'll have the plane drop you off, and I'll head over to Lion's Pride to check on things and to bring Shannon home. As we get closer to being done with the renovations, I'd like to take you, Grant and Stanley, over there to see for yourselves what Lion's Pride is all about."

Bill said, "That sounds terrific, it'll be good to see my folks for a bit after all I put them through over the past couple of weeks."

When they landed at Wilkes Barrie/Scranton Airport, they took a taxi to O'Leary's and checked Bill in. Sean was not in, and Grant and Stanley hadn't yet arrived so Doc and Bill went to the pub, said hi to Brian and ordered a pair of Laphroaigs, one on the rocks one neat.

Bill asked, "So what's the plan for tomorrow with the new guys?"

Doc said, "I've lined up the executive conference room for the day, although I suspect the meeting won't take all day. So you guys can head out west after we're done or relax, maybe a game of golf. You call that shot. I don't have a formal agenda, so I plan just to fill everyone in on what the company is all about, each person's role, stuff like that. I want to set the tone for future meetings as being relaxed and casual. After all this time working for a large bureaucracy, I want our company to be a place where, sure we work hard, but we also take the time to enjoy life. And we hold meetings as seldom as possible."

Sean came into the room like a hurricane in Florida, larger than life and threatening to do property damage. He ran over and hugged Doc and shook Bill's hand making them both feel at home right away. The bartender, without being asked rushed over with a large Jameson's for the boss and fresh drinks for Bill and Doc.

Doc said, "What do you hear from Lion's Pride Sean?"

"I spoke to them all this morning and everything is just fine. Oh, they have had some minor issues, mostly with obtaining the right building and decorating materials but all in all they're doing well."

Doc said, "I'm pleased to announce that Bill has joined us as executive vice president so you'll be seeing a lot of him from now on. He'll be taking over my use of the Emerald Isle Suite now that I'm staying at my own place, so put the word out that he's a VIP would you?"

"You bet I will. You always have a room here Bill, no, more than a room, you have a home here. You don't drive a Mustang by any chance do ya?"

"No. I have a BMW somewhere, but I hardly ever use it."

"Well, that's good then, as it'll fetch a good trade-in value on your new Mustang."

Just then, Grant approached the table, and Doc jumped up to shake his hand and welcome him on board. He said, "Gents this is Grant Thomas, our new director of recruiting. Grant this is Bill Wong our executive vice president and this handsome gentleman is Sean O'Leary, the owner of this fine establishment. What'll you have to drink?"

"A Bud would be great." Sean signaled to the bartender, mouthed the word "Bud" and one was delivered with a frosted mug.

They made the usual small talk about the flight and the weather. Grant was taken with the beauty of O'Leary's Arms, and it's park-like location.

A short while later Stanley came along and once again introductions were made and his drink, a rare Bourbon, was ordered. Once every- one had a drink and was relaxed. Doc said, "Just a little business then we can get on with our evening. Tomorrow morning we'll meet at nine o'clock in the Executive Board Room in the

Business Center just down the hall from the front desk. Dress is casual as it will be for all of our infrequent meetings. In the morning we'll go over a few things; I have asked Sean to join us, I'll explain why at the meeting. Sean, have you got any idea where a guy can get a good steak in this town?"

"As you know the best beef available anywhere in the US is right here at O'Leary's. If anyone of you has a steak that isn't one of the best you've ever had, then it's on me. Which reminds me of the old story about the Englishman, the American and the Irishman, who are having a jar in a pub together. The Englishman says, "In my local in Liverpool if you pay for four pints, you get the fifth one free." "That's not as good as my pub in Boston where if you buy two pints you get the third one free." The Yank said. The Irishman, never one to be outdone said. "Well in my pub in Dublin, you gets to drink all the pints you want and then go upstairs and have all the sex you want free."

"Wow, you've actually done that?" the American says. The Irishman says, "Well no, not me, but me sister has many times."

They dined at O'Leary's and got to know each other better. Following dinner they went back to the pub for an after dinner brandy, and Doc immediately thought about Shannon as he sipped his St. Agnes. Due to the time change he would put off calling her until breakfast in the morning.

The alarm went off in Doc's bedroom at seven o'clock. He set it early because he wanted to talk to Shannon without having to rush, and he wanted some time to rough out his plan for the morning. He called Shannon and said, "Hi love sorry I didn't call yesterday. But I had a lot going on and the time change is so different between here and Asia that it's best for me to call early my time. Are you ok? Anything new?"

"Hello sweetheart, all is going well here, at least for Anne and I. The building materials suppliers are driving Bev crazy; between being slow, poor quality on some things and unavailability of some things, the lady, is going nuts. She even jumped in a big truck and drove it to Harare herself to get stuff she desperately needed. She is one determined person when she puts her mind to it."

"That's the main reason we made such good partners at University and will now, she is strong, smart and determined, a formidable combination. Some people push the envelope; Bev pushes the whole stationary store."

"How is Bill?"

"He's doing fine. He's agreed to join us and is here for the meeting with the two new guys I've hired. What do things look like now?"

"Well, there is still a lot of hammering and sawing, so it is both noisy and dusty. Bev has stationed a full-time room attendant in each of our four suites to dust, wash and vacuum all day long. There is so much dust we are having our meals at poolside. Bev says this part will be over in three weeks and then it's just painting and decorating, so much cleaner and quieter. I think I'll go home in a few days and come back in three weeks or a month to oversee the decorating. That should take a week or two and then were done. So I'd say eight weeks from now to the grand opening day."

"That's good work, way faster than we initially thought."

"Yes, but there was considerably less construction work involved than we first anticipated."

"I was thinking that I would come over in a few days and see how things are going then fly home with you. How does that sound?"

"Oh, Doc it sounds grand but aren't you tired from all the travel lately?"

"It's been ok with the private plane and the bedroom on board. It makes the time fly if you'll pardon the pun. What about the wedding plans, how is your mother doing on that front?"

"It's all set, they've arranged: the ballroom at the hotel, guestrooms, the menu, the cake, and all the other details."

"Maybe we should time it, so we come back over for you to oversee the decorating for two weeks then go straight from Lion's Pride to Ireland in time for the wedding."

"That could work, let's see how it's going in a few weeks."

"If I have the time, I might call that realtor you

have lined up just to let her know we haven't forgotten about her. What's her name again?"

"That's a good idea; her name is Brenda Sopel with Scranton Realty. If you have time, get her to show you the three best lots she would suggest. She's sent me photos by email, but it's so hard to tell much that way."

"I'm also going to Ottawa to pick up the Mustang then drive it to the cottage and leave it in the garage there. The deputy director of the Drug Enforcement Agency gave me that Mustang Cobra that I have in O'Leary's garage. I paid for some expenses in connection with getting Bill out and the DDO figures that will make a contribution towards them. "Hey, I just remembered something, we haven't discussed a honeymoon yet. Where do you want to go?"

"You know, it's never even occurred to me to plan a honeymoon. Where do you want to go?"

"Oh no you don't, it's up to you to decide. Think of somewhere you have always wanted to go but haven't and we'll go there. By the way did you ever change that setting for your diamond?"

"Ok, I'll think about the honeymoon. I decided that I like the ring just as it is. Bev checked with her jeweler because she'd told him just to put in a temporary setting. But he figured it was just as easy to do a permanent one, and there'd be less chance of losing it."

"Ok love I'll let you get back to work, I love you and can hardly wait to see you with St. Agnes in hand. Can you transfer me to Bev?"

"Ok love you too, here she is."

"Hi Bev, how's the frustrated general contractor?"

"Hi wise guy, don't even go there. What's new?"

"Bill has joined us as executive vice president. I've hired Grant Thomas and Stanley Maxwell as I had said I would, and they'll report to him. They're all here at O'Leary's for a meeting in about an hour. As we get closer to being ready, like just before the grand opening party, I want to schedule a meeting at Lion's Pride with everyone together. The new guys can tour the property and get a full understanding of what we're doing. I'm going to have them open an office in Silicon Valley; so they'll be out there beating the bushes for developers in the next few weeks.

I have a research project for them first. Thanks for sending me that DVD tour of Lion's Pride. What about the agriculture study?"

"It's underway; we've been lucky to find just the right guy. He's a retired prof from the agriculture faculty at Zimbabwe University. He's very well connected with government, academia and every aspect of food production and distribution, so I'm looking forward to his report. His first reaction, when he did some soil tests and flew over the land, was that it looked to have potential. One problem might be water, but he'll look into that. On another front, I have looked into the idea of a private jet, and the numbers work so go ahead and buy one, just make sure it has a private bedroom with en suite including a shower. I'll send you a package with all the info I've gathered and the numbers."

"Any particular brand you prefer?"

"No, you decide. You'll be practically living in it for a while."

"Ok, I'd better run. My meeting starts shortly and being late for the first meeting I called is not setting the right example."

CHAPTER THIRTY-ONE

Doc said, "Good morning gentlemen and welcome to the first of what I hope will be rare meetings. I'd like to start off by saying that Bev and I want this company to be successful of course, but we also believe that people who work with us should enjoy their job. We want to create a stress-free or at least stress minimalized environment.

I invited Sean here this morning because, as the owner of the management company for Lion's Pride, it's essential that he fully understand our vision for the enterprise. It's good for you all to know each other because, over the years, your paths are going to cross a great deal.

Just to make sure that everyone is clear, Bev and I have created Software Conceptions Inc. to team up with software developers creating joint ventures with him or her to our mutual benefit. We are in the final stages of renovating a grand mansion in Zimbabwe to be the "campus" or home base for software developers who wish to participate in our joint ventures. Those that join up with us will move to Lion's Pride and live in a luxurious resort environment, complete with all the trappings of a millionaire's lifestyle. They will work on creating new software offerings, which the company will then take to market in a joint venture firm, half-owned by the software developer and half owned by Software

Conceptions. I'm going to show you a very well done DVD produced recently about the overall Lion's Pride property."

Doc then pushed a button, which dimmed the lights and started the DVD projector. Bill, Stanley, and Grant were amazed at what a beautiful place it was. When the DVD was over Stanley said, "I can see where developers are going to be highly motivated to produce to continue to live in this paradise. It's like a Four Seasons resort in the Caribbean."

Doc said, "Exactly, and this was shot just before the renovation started; it'll be even nicer when Shannon gets through with it. The idea is to create an environment where the developer is king or queen, treated like royalty as long as they produce. After all, the end result is to make a profit. Now that you have seen the DVD, and there are copies in the packet in front of you, let's discuss everyone's role in this.

I want to start with Sean's part because he may have to leave the meeting, and I want to give you all time to ask him questions. Sean's company holds the management contract to operate the resort side of this business. His employee, the general manager of the resort whom you will all meet, is Anne Watson. Together they are charged with running the operations just like they run this hotel; that is to say, better than five-star level. Do you have any questions about this aspect of things?"

Grant said, "If I wanted to arrange something

special at Lion's Pride, say a Christmas dinner dance or a special lecture for the developers, who would I contact?"

Sean said, "It's probably most efficient if you deal directly with Anne when it comes to special requests. We are going to be well geared up to provide whatever you want so just let her know. Try to give her as much lead time as you can, because given the relatively remote location, it could take some time for her to arrange any special equipment if necessary. We are self-sufficient and most special requests that require equipment we don't have on hand can be satisfied in Harare."

Stanley said, "On occasion I may want to send over potential clients, will there be accommodation available at Lion's Pride?"

Sean said, " Yes we'll have guest suites to accommodate visitors. Just let Anne know the details and she'll make all the arrangements including flights, side tours and anything else you want to provide your guests. Her secretary, Mona, you'll find is the epitome of efficiency."

Doc said, "Anything else for Sean?" There was a pause while Doc waited to see if anyone had any more questions then he said, "I'm glad that you've all had a chance to meet. O'Leary's here will be our unofficial eastern office for now so Sean will see that you are all logged into the computer as VIP guests. I'd urge you to try out various rooms and once you have found one that you particularly like, let Sean know and the room will be tagged as your first choice when you visit. You may also sign your bill when checking out and the charges will go to the Software Conceptions' company account."

Sean said, "You have complimentary use of the business center 24 hours a day, which includes the use of this conference room. A hotel limo will pick you up and deliver you back to the airport and will be available to take you wherever you wish to go while in Scranton, again all complimentary. We can also arrange a helicopter shuttle to and from the American Express Tower in New York City. There is a charge for this, however."

Doc said, "Thanks, Sean, you are welcome to stay for the rest of the meeting if you wish, suit yourself."

Sean said, "I'll stick around for a bit, and then I have a lunch meeting I have to run off to."

Doc said, "Ok let's stand up and stretch, refill coffees, get muffins and handle bathroom breaks. Say ten minutes?

When they reconvened, Doc said, "Stanley, let's start with you. For openers please tell us about your background and a bit about yourself."

Stanley said, "I received a bachelor's degree in business administration with a major in marketing from the University of Chicago. Then I did a Masters in Science in software engineering at California State University at Fullerton. I worked in software development at Microsoft for three years and Amazon for two years before joining my last firm, Software Associates, as sales and marketing manager. I worked there for six years. My specialty has been in sales, marketing, advertising and business promotion. My accounts have included some of the largest software consumers in the world."

"Thanks, Stanley," Doc said. "Where I see you fitting in would be almost a direct continuation of your activities at Software Associates. Calling on major software consumers, selling the programs written by our developers but with an added duty. Grant's job, which we'll get into in a moment, is to identify potential developers and to recruit them to join us. Once Grant has identified a candidate, I want you, Stanley, to vet him or her from a marketing perspective and assess their probability of producing marketable software. Any new developer has to also be cleared by Bill. So all three of you must interview and approve all newly recruited developers before we send them to Lion's Pride. To reiterate, we want talented, creative software developers who have strong entrepreneurial tendencies. They must want to become wealthy and understand that we have the skills and resources necessary to get them there as long as they do their part and produce. It's the function of the three of you to find these people, qualify them and recruit the qualified ones. We will give anyone put forward by you three, a year to demonstrate that they are a valuable team member. Anyone who fails to do that will be let go. Any questions at this stage?"

Grant said, "Yes, just so I'm clear on the organization structure, Stanley, and I report to Bill and Bill reports to you, is that right?"

"Almost, Stanley and you report to Bill and Bill reports to both Bev and I as equal partners in Software Conceptions."

"So will Bill be based in Silicon Valley with Stanley and me?"

"You got it. When you three get back out West, your first task will be to hire a secretary and find appropriate office space. Bill will make all decisions on that. There're a couple of projects that I want to see done right off. Stanley, I want you to build a database of potential customers for our software. Build it by country and make it global. I want to be able to punch in say, 'Brazil' and have a list appear of the top potential software consumers with all contact details. This database will be the foundation of your other task, which is to work with Grant on developing a business plan for the company. I don't want to get into the details of the plan today. Bill, I'd like you to oversee it and let's target three months from today for completion. Does that make sense?"

All three indicated that three months would be sufficient time to get the plan done.

"Just to be clear, I'd expect that you would start now with your daily activities. Stanley, you making sales-calls on prospective software buyers and Grant, you getting started with all the right schools to recruit graduating students. We'll be able to move people into Lion's Pride in about three months. Should you come up with any hot prospects prior to that, we can get them started right here rather than lose them. Grant, tell us your story."

Grant said, "I had a pretty strict upbringing, my father was a career soldier, retired as a Brigadier General. We lived in Europe, Asia and all over the US. I ended up in military boarding school, then West Point and served a term as a Lieutenant, mostly in a recruiting capacity. I completed a Masters in Human Resource Management at UCLA and went to work as a recruiter at Carnegie Mellon University specializing on recruiting students into the Computer Engineering Program. I served a four-year term as chair of the US Council of University Recruiters and have published a book on recruiting for universities, not exactly a best seller. I am a keen sailor, a mediocre golfer, and a big Vancouver Canucks fan. So I'm looking forward to recruiting in the Vancouver market, particularly during hockey season." Doc said, "Thanks, Grant, I have, no problem with you hiring in Vancouver during hockey season as long as you also get up there the rest of the year as well. Your individual project will be to build a database of potential recruiting targets including not only academia, although I suspect that'll be the big one, but also corporations, government and anywhere else you see fit. Your database plus Stanley's will become the backbone of the business plan. I also want both of you to work with Bill in overseeing the installation of the technical production aspect of Lion's Pride. Start with a meeting with Brian White, get some leads, then find us an audio/visual production guru. In light of our schedule, this part of the work should be given top priority. When you recruit and when you do marketing, you'll want to be able to emphasize the physical beauty of Lion's Pride, the quality of the leading edge AV equipment and computer equipment but also the pedigree of the guru."

The meeting ended at noon, and the guys had lunch at O'Leary's then Bill, Grant and Stanley headed out to the airport to fly to San Francisco on the private plane. They were full of that enthusiasm that usually follows a business meeting where plans are properly laid out.

Doc called Brenda Sopel, the agent from Scranton Realty and made arrangements for her to show him the three lots she had identified for Shannon. The first lot was good in that it was closest to a school with an excellent reputation. On top of that, it went all the way from kinder-garten to grade twelve. The drawback was that the lot wasn't quite large enough in terms of usable space. It had quite a large gully that went the length of the property. The lot was divided into two pieces, one piece being about a quarter acre and the other piece about an acre and a quarter. Not impossible, but probably difficult and, therefore, expensive to build on. The second lot was suitable from a building perspective, but it was closer to a lower priced housing area with the challenges that this could entail. The third lot was the best of the three. It was well into the best neighborhood, a reasonable walking distance to the top school and backed on to a small lake that was stocked with trout. Doc loved it immediately. Brenda told him that she was expecting an offer on it tomorrow. Doc liked Brenda and trusted her judgment, he knew that she was also a friend of Shannon's and had been for years.

Doc said, "What do you think? If I was your brother what one would you recommend?"

Brenda said, "I would recommend this one right here."

"What about price, is it over, under or about right on the market?"

"I'd say slightly over between five and ten percent."

"If we draw up an offer at twenty percent below asking, no subjects, what are our chances?"

"The owner knows there is an offer coming probably tomorrow, so I think he might counter at full asking."

"Let's try it and see. Make the offer valid until midnight."

"Ok, all he can say is no or make a counter."

"Go ahead and draw it up, I'll sign it and you deliver it right now. He must be aware that he is five to seven percent over market value. He'll want to take the sure thing and act now, maybe not."

"Ok I'll get on it now, can you swing by the office in about a half hour to sign it?"

"I'll do one better than that, I'll go with you."

"At the risk of losing a sale, what if Shannon doesn't like it? Won't she be upset that she didn't even have a say in it?"

"No, she won't be upset because we, meaning you and me, aren't going to tell her that she owns it. When she gets back and has a chance to look the market over, she'll make a decision. If it's this one, we'll surprise her with the deed. If it isn't this one, we'll buy the one she wants and keep this as a long-term investment. If I buy it anywhere below your market value estimate, I can't go far wrong keeping it as a future college tuition source."

"You must be planning on having a lot of kids."

"Five."

The offer was presented at six thirty and countered by seven fifteen at full asking less five percent. Doc went back at seven thirty at full asking less ten percent, final offer. The owner blinked first and accepted this offer.

By seven forty-five, Doc and Brenda were in the coffee shop next to her office. They toasted the deal with clinking latte cups and Doc said, "Remember, don't say anything to Shannon about this. I want it to be a total surprise. I'm not going to influence her in any way. It has to be her decision. If she selects this one by herself, keep track of her second choice then quietly buy it. I want to give it to her as part of her wedding present and as an investment for our kids college funds. I'm going to tell her that we looked at these and that I thought they were all great. We'll be back towards the end of next week and you can show them to her then, I may not even attend the tour so that I make sure not to exert any undue influence."

"Wow, she is one lucky girl, that is quite the wedding present!"

Doc had dinner with Sean. After a few games of darts he said, "I've been craving your corned beef and cabbage for the last two weeks, topped off with a creamy Guinness. It just doesn't get any better than this."

Sean said," When I hired the chef I surprised him by having a brisket of corned beef in the walk-in cooler and had him prepare this as an interview dinner. Not bad for an Englishman!"

Doc said, "I bought a surprise wedding present for Shannon today, a building lot over in Pinewoods. It backs onto a small lake stocked with trout."

"But don't ya think she may get a wee bit upset since she has her heart set on doing this house herself from scratch as you promised?"

"I'm keeping the purchase secret and letting her pick out any lot she wants. If she doesn't choose this one, I buy her the one she chooses and give her this one as a wedding gift."

"Now that's an idea but you're going to drive me crazy waiting to see what she does."

The next morning, Doc drove the Cobra up to Brockville to see how things were going with the cottage renovation. He had a tour of it with Gary and the contractor and was very pleased with the quality of the workmanship. Gary said the progress hadn't been as fast as he'd hoped given the extra crew they put on the job. The contractor explained that the progress had been slowed down somewhat when they discovered a termite infestation in the sub floor which necessitated a good deal of extra work to rectify. Doc understood that the work was required if the cottage was to be a stable structure. He told Gary and the contractor," Shannon and I are planning to spend a lot of time here over the years; we want the job emphasis to be on quality rather than speed."

Gary said, "That's exactly what I told him on several occasions, but you know these contractors, they only listen when the guy who writes the checks talks. Come on down to the boathouse, I've got something to show you."

CHAPTER THIRTY-TWO

When they got to the boathouse, Gary opened the door, motioned for Doc to go ahead in and said, "Well what do you think?" Tied to the dock in the boathouse was a brand new eighteen-foot fishing boat with all the right equipment.

Doc said, "I love it! You did a super job picking this one and getting it set up properly. I can almost feel the largemouth bass on the line. Thank you, Gary, I think you and I are going to get a lot of pleasure and a lot of fish with this baby."

Gary was eager to show all the features to Doc, so he got to see the down riggers, the electric bait tank, the under-seat cooler, the fish finder and the steering and control mechanism. Gary had installed the new motor that Doc had bought recently as well as a small, five horse-power "kicker" motor.

Gary said, "Have you got time to try her out? We could go out for an hour or so."

"Not today, Gary but next visit for sure. I think Shannon and I'll come up in a couple of weeks to see how things are shaping up and we'll go out and terrorize the perch then." Doc knew that once out there, they would forget all about time and the "hour or so" would consume the rest of the afternoon.

Doc asked Gary to drive him to the bus terminal so he could get a bus to Ottawa to retrieve the Mustang. Gary said he and Barb would go and get it if he liked. Barb could drive one car home, and Gary would drive the other. Gary said, "You just leave it to us. We'll go up there next week maybe spend a few days at the condo to check it out. Barb can go to the hot air factory and listen to the politicians."

"Are you sure you want to do that?"

"Once the condo sells we'll probably go to Ottawa a lot less so we'll do it, get in some shopping, visit our favorite restaurant and relax a bit. Besides, I know you want to get back to business so hit the road, and we'll see you in a couple of weeks. I'll keep an eye on these construction guys."

Doc said goodbye and pointed the Cobra south. He had thought about leaving the Cobra at the cottage and driving his much loved '06 Mustang down to Scranton. But the hassle involved in transferring the cars from one country to another were too much to deal with right now with everything else that's on his plate.

When he got back to Scranton, he went to Starbucks, got a coffee to go and drove to his new lot. He got out of his car and sat against a tree trunk, enjoyed his coffee and mentally planned the new home that might soon sit here.

He called the jet charter service, set up his flight and requested his usual pilot, co-pilot and flight attendant. The flight planner said that the flight crew Doc requested was already scheduled on another flight tomorrow but since Doc was such a good customer he'd switch them over to his flight.

Doc went to O'Leary's and had a quick visit with Sean and said, "I'm going to head over to Lion's Pride tomorrow to pick up Shannon. Is there anything you want me to take over?"

"Yes there is, I'll have chef bake a chocolate cheesecake for Anne. She loves chef's cheese-cake. And I'll have some flowers for her sent over to your place this afternoon. I really miss that woman around here. Donald's a nice guy, but he isn't the GM that Anne is, it'll be good to have Shannon back in the saddle here."

Doc's cell phone rang and the call display said, "Software Conceptions Inc." Doc answered, and the caller was Bill sounding quite excited. He said, "Good news Doc, Grant made a presen-tation to the graduating class at Stanford this morning. We have three interested parties coming in for interviews."

"Wow, that is great news but coming in for interviews where?"

"I forgot to tell you; we've located suitable office space for us in the building next to Brian's. It has five offices, a reception area, and a confer-ence room. Stanly is out right now buying office furniture and supplies, so we'll move in tomor-row. The interviews start the next day. Brian has loaned us his conference room for a few days. Oh, and Brian's executive assistant has a close friend, Kea, who is a qualified executive assistant, joining us tomorrow."

"Good going, you guys aren't wasting time. If any of these candidates are suitable to the three of you, we can get them started either at O'Leary's or in our new offices, whatever works best for them. I'll leave that with you but let me know as soon as the interviews are over, particularly if any work qualify and wish to join us. I'll be waiting anxiously by the phone."

"Ok, Doc is anything else happening?"

"I'm going over to Lion's Pride tomorrow to check up on things and to get Shannon. We'll be back in a few days. Don't forget to call me when you have any news re the candidates."

Doc had a quiet dinner by himself at Carmella's, thought about Shannon and how much he missed her.

The next morning Doc, with cheesecake and flowers for Anne, boarded the jet and said to the two pilots and the flight attendant, "Can we have a coffee and chat before we depart?"

"Yes sir, Mr. O'Connell, that's one of the joys of flying private, we can leave whenever you want."

Rosemary, the flight attendant, served up a pot of coffee and croissants, and they all sat at the conference/dining table. Doc said, "I am going to buy a plane, mostly for my use, but it will also be available for other people in our company from time to time. I've been very happy with the service provided by the three of you and would like you all to consider joining my company. I'd also like your advice on what plane to buy, something around this size, maybe slightly larger to accommodate a sleeping area for the crew. Think about what plane you would choose if you were going to be flying it all the time. I wanted to put this on the table now so you could think about it and talk it over while we head for Harare. Since a lot of my trips will be long haul, we'll need another pilot, preferably one with training as a meteorologist because I don't want to fly anywhere near storms as you know.

Also, think about how much runway we'll need to do a private strip.

In terms of compensation, I'll pay you your present wage plus fifty percent and match your benefits package. You can live where you are now or move to Scranton, your choice. If you elect to move, we'll cover your moving expenses. Any questions?"

"Doug, the senior pilot said, "Mr. O'Connell, I take it you will be based out of Scranton, right?"

"Before we go any further, my name is Donovan. My friends and that includes you three call me Doc. Yes, I'll be based out of Scranton."

"Where do you three live?"

Doug said, "We're based out of Newark and live in that area."

"Well discuss it among yourselves and let me know what you think is best should you join my company. If you come up with any questions while we are on the way, let me know. I don't want to rush you, but I would like an answer by the time we land back here."

Randy, the co-pilot said, "Does this have to be a package deal or could one or two of us accept your offer without the third?"

"Good point Randy. I'll accept any of you who are interested in joining me. Anything else?"

Rosemary said, "I can tell you right now, I'm in. I'm a single mom and need the money. But quite frankly, Doc, I like working with you and think my future prospects will be good with your company."

"You're hired. Have you ever thought of becoming a pilot?"

"I am a pilot, at least for pleasure flying."

"If you want to upgrade to jet certification, we'll pay the costs. Then we don't have to find a third pilot. Speaking of paying the costs, the company will cover your childcare costs as well since we'll be keeping you away from home sometimes for long stretches. Ok, let's head for Harare."

During the flight, Doc learned that Rosemary was a qualified nurse who had taken her now four-year-old girl, Patty and escaped an abusive relationship with her ex-husband. She has friends in Scranton and looked forward to moving there. Doc said, "Do you rent or own in Newark?"

"I rent a two bedroom apartment."

"I think you should have a bungalow with a nice yard for Patty. Why not buy something?"

"I don't have the down payment, my ex left me with practically nothing after the divorce."

"I'll lend you the down payment. Hand me a pad and pen, please. "Doc wrote down the contact details for Brenda Sopel.

"Call Brenda, tell her you work for me and what you would like in terms of a house. Specify that it has to be near a great school. Brenda has kids of her own and will know what you mean."

"Doc, I'm having trouble calling you Doc, but I'll get used to it. I don't know how to thank you for your kindness."

"You can start by getting me a coffee. Which reminds me, on the new plane three things I want never to run out of are Jamaican Blue Mountain Roast coffee, Laphroaig 18-year-old Scotch, and St. Agnes Brandy."

"I got it and here's your coffee, sorry it isn't Jamaican Blue Mountain."

"Give some thought to the interior for the new plane. I want a crew berth with shower and toilet forward, a bedroom aft with shower and toilet much like this one and your idea of a perfect galley. We'll need a dining/conference table to sit six, seating for six and sleeping arrangements for four in the main cabin. "

"Ok, I'll think about it and do some online searching for ideas."

She went to the flight deck in response to a call from the pilots. Doc finished his coffee and went into the bedroom for a shower. He felt good about his new hire and hoped the pilots would also come on board. He got into bed and fell asleep after reading two chapters from "Mr. Mercedes" written by his favorite author, Stephen King.

When he awoke, it was morning, so he pushed the intercom and told Rosemary to work her magic on breakfast as he's starving.

He showered again and dressed casually then entered the main cabin.

Rosemary said, "Good morning Doc, did you sleep ok?" She handed him a coffee.

"I did thank you. A senior executive of a five-star cruise line told me once that their staff is warned not to ask passengers if they slept well. If they did sleep well, it had nothing to do with the staff, and if they didn't sleep well, there was nothing you could do about it."

"I never thought of that, but it's a good point. I'll avoid the topic from now on."

Doc was sipping on his coffee when Doug called Rosemary to see if Doc was awake and, if so would he like to visit the cockpit for a chat. She advised Doug that yes, Doc was awake and hungry. His breakfast was about to be served so how about if he comes to the cockpit after he has eaten. Doug agreed and signed off.

Doc's breakfast included a fruit bowl with yogurt, an omelet made with egg whites, three turkey sausages, whole-wheat toast and hash browns. He ate heartily and complimented Rosemary on her cooking, not realizing that she had put together as healthy a breakfast as she could under the circumstances.

After breakfast, Rosemary told him of Doug's invitation to the flight deck. He armed himself with coffee, took one for Doug and Randy and headed to the cockpit.

As he entered the flight deck he said, "Good morning gentlemen, what's our ETA?"

Doug said, "We'll be on the ground in one hour and twenty minutes. I alerted Lion's Pride and they're sending a car for you."

Doc sat in the jump seat, took a sip of coffee and said, "So what's up?"

Doug said, "Randy and I have talked it over and agreed that we'll accept your offer."

"That's great news! I'm very pleased to hear this. I feel very comfortable with you both on the flight deck."

"We'll also move to Scranton so we can be available to take care of our new plane. We feel that the ideal plane from our perspective is the Boeing BBJ."

"Ok call Boeing and set up a meeting with their sales and interior design people for the week after next. I'd like for all three of you plus my fiancé, Shannon to attend the meeting with me, so everyone has input to the design of the interior. Let me know when you have the meeting arranged. I suppose we'll have to go to Seattle, which is fine. Once the meeting is over we can go to San Francisco for a day, Shannon can fly home commercial, and we'll go on to Hong Kong."

Doug said, "What would you think about us having Rosemary on the flight deck when she is not needed in the cabin?"

Doc said, "So she can get some experience towards her jet engine certification?"

"Yes. Randy and I were thinking that she could sit in the cockpit when not needed in the cabin. Initially, we could explain everything to her. Eventually, she could sit in the right seat for part of the flight. Randy has agreed to take care of routine cabin duties while she does this. Of course, she'd still handle cabin duties as well and prepare all meals. You would understand why if you ever had the misfortune of tasting Randy's cooking. He could screw up a peanut butter sandwich! We could help prepare her for her jet certification exams and coach her through the process. She is a good friend, and we'd do anything for her."

"I'm a hundred percent on board with this plan. Doug, as Captain, you oversee her training and balance it with her cabin duties. Randy you better learn how to make a great cup of coffee. I hate peanut butter sandwiches. For most of the flight, particularly when I'm alone, I'm able to take care of myself. I think it would be best for Randy to sit in the jump seat when Rosemary is in the right seat as his default position. If I need him, I can simply push the button. If it is not ok for him to leave the cockpit at that point, Doug, you say so, and this overrides the call attendant button. Those of us in the cabin will wait until it is safe for Randy or Rosemary to come to the main cabin. Does this work with you guys?"

Randy said, "That'll work, we'll make a jet jockey out of her. One other thing, I've been thinking about what you said regarding the need for a meteorologist. If the company pays for it, I'd like to take the course."

"That's a deal; enroll as soon as possible. Try for an online program, so you can study while you travel. Rosemary is very fortunate to have friends like you. I've got an idea. Why don't you three come out to Lion's Pride for dinner? I'll send a car for you at six tomorrow. That'll give you time to get some rest around the pool. You can meet Shannon, my fiancé, Anne, the GM of Lion's Pride and Bev, my partner. These are primarily the people you will be flying around. We can celebrate you're joining the team."

Shannon was at the airport, and as soon as Doc cleared customs she ran over to him, took a small liquor flask, opened it, took a swig and planted a big kiss.

Coming up for air Doc said, "You wouldn't believe how often I've thought of this moment. How thoughtful of you to remember the St. Agnes."

The flight crew came into the passenger area, and Doc introduced Shannon and cautioned them all to take special care of her because she is the most precious thing in his life.

Doc took Doug aside and said, "We haven't had a chance to discuss arrangements for you folks when on the ground. What are your present company's policies?"

Doug said, "We stay in 3-star hotels and have a meal allowance of fifty dollars US per day."

Doc said, "From now on you stay in 5-star hotels and have a meal allowance of one hundred dollars US a day. Plus you may charge a reasonable amount to the company for such things as entertainment, transportation and so forth. You as captain will approve any such expenditures. My only thoughts are that you all get the opportunity to enjoy the places we visit and to learn what you can about different cultures. Trust me, over the years you are all going to be exposed to a lot of different cultures. I want you to benefit from this opportunity."

Doc reached into his wallet and extracted three one thousand dollar bills. He slipped them to Doug and said, "See that they have a good time here, and this will tide you over until we get the company credit cards sorted out. Once you've checked into the best hotel in town, give me a call, so I know where to send the car tomorrow. Take them out to a great dinner and once again, welcome aboard."

As they sat in the back seat of the Bentley, Doc said, "On the way over I hired those three. They are the best flying team I have ever seen. The week after next they're going to fly us out to Boeing in Seattle where we are all going to design the interior of our new plane, under your supervision of course."

Shannon snuggled up to him and said, "I'm glad you hired them, you've always felt safe with them, and that makes me worry less about your travels. I've got a big surprise for you when we get to Lion's Pride."

CHAPTER THIRTY-THREE

As they headed towards Lion's Pride, Doc's phone rang and the screen showed, "Software Conceptions Inc." Doc answered, "Hi Bill, what's new?"

"You are not going to believe this. Of the three developers that originally expressed interest, we have decided to admit two of them. The other one just didn't impress us with his ambition or lack of ambition. One of them is already about halfway through writing a new video game that both Grant and Stanley feel could be a winner, and the other one has some good ideas. They both want to start right away, and we feel that we should allow them to do so. One is happy to work here until Lion's Pride is ready; the other feels a change of scenery would help her be creative, so she has asked to go to Scranton. They're both about to graduate, but their courses are online so they can finish anywhere."

"Ok send the one who wants to come to Scranton on her way as soon as she's ready to go."

"The developer's name is Hilda Anderson."

"Ok. Send her along first class and advise Sean of her arrival. He'll take it from there. See if she needs any special computer equipment and, if so, advise Sean as well so he can have it ready."

"That's not all the news. Grant and Stanley,

encouraged by the results of the Stanford presentation have developed a "dog and pony show" to take on the road for a recruiting blitz. Grant is going to handle targets in the west while Stanley deals with potential clients back east.

As part of their road trip presentation development, they put on a presentation at University of California, Berkley. Brian White and three of his top people and I sat in the audience to observe the pitch. We also had the presentation professionally videotaped. The net result is that we four observers were able to make suggestions for changes that both Stanley and Grant appreciated. So they're polishing up the presentation as we speak, and our secretary....excuse me, our administrative assistant is busy scheduling two road trips, one a western trip, and one an eastern trip. Our guys are going to be on the road for a few weeks."

"Fantastic, at this rate we're going to be up and running full blast in no time."

"You don't know the half of it. We've had four other developer candidates call us from the Stanford presentation. We're not sure yet if it's word of mouth between students or if some simply need longer to make a decision. We'll find out pretty quick. They're coming in for interviews on Friday of next week. While the guys are on the road, we have set aside Fridays and Saturdays if necessary for interviews, so both road warriors will return to the office here each Friday. They will interview interested candidates immediately after their presentation and decide which ones get invited to the office for a second interview with myself and whichever recruiter they have not yet met. We will then compare notes and decide which ones to admit into the program."

"I'm going to come out next Friday for the interviews to see the process in action."

"Sounds good, I'll have Kea book you a room."

"We'll come in Thursday afternoon so book a double for Shannon and I and three singles for the flight crew for Thursday and Friday nights. See if Brian and Kristen are available for dinner with you, Shannon and I on either night."

"Do you want the flight crew staying at the Four Seasons?"

"You bet. I've hired them to fly our new corporate jet so like all our employees; they go, first class."

"What happens if we end up with more qualified candidates than we have room for?"

"We should be so lucky! Meet with the GM at the Four Seasons and get a corporate account established. We can put some of them there. It's near the office isn't it?"

"Right across the street."

"Call Sean and ask him how many he can handle at O'Leary's until Lion's Pride is finished. We might as well give him a few months of one hundred percent occupancy and keep the business in the family so to speak."

"Good idea, I'll get right on that because I have a feeling that this thing has a great deal more potential than you and Bev anticipated,"

"That's no problem; we can handle as many qualified candidates as you can generate. We just need to be creative in our approach. You've got me worked up, keep in touch."

When they got to the mansion, Bev and Anne greeted him with a big welcoming hug and led him inside and directly to the elevator.

"What's this, where are we all going?"

Shannon said, "Remember I told you that I had a surprise for you, well close your eyes."

Doc closed his eyes, and they lead him down the hall then stopped. Bev said, "Ok open your eyes."

Doc opened his eyes and saw twenty open suite doors. Before he could ask, Anne explained, "The hotelier in me couldn't stand to think of all these rooms standing empty for visitors. So the three of us decided to keep only ten rooms for visitors and to add these suites to the inventory giving us a total of eighty suites for developers. We've closed off the end of the hallway with a door leading into a concierge lobby and the entrances to all our private quarters. This is accessible only by entry code, and a concierge will be stationed in this lobby twenty-four hours a day, so we are assured of total privacy."

Doc said, "If things continue as they have started off, we're going to need a whole lot more rooms. Has anybody got any bright ideas?

Bev thought for a minute and then said, "Come with me." She lead them back to the elevator, pressed the button for the main floor and lead them down the main hall and out the exit. They walked along the garden path, past the pool and came to a stop in front of the garage.

Bev said, "Behold the Lion's Pride Annex" as she waved her hand towards the garage.

They all went inside and looked at the building from this new angle. Anne was the first to speak, "How many suites could we put in here?"

Doc said, "Call Johnnie and ask him to come over with a few guys and the biggest tape measure he has."

Bev hit her phone button for Johnnie and asked him to come over as Doc requested.

Johnnie said. "What do you need to be measured?"

Bev said, "The size of the garage building."

"I've got the original architect's drawings for all the buildings on the property. Why don't you come over to my office and we can look at them? It's a quicker and more accurate way to get the building's dimensions."

"Good idea, we'll be right there."

By the time they got to Johnnie's office he had a fresh pot of coffee going and some muffins that he'd had his administrative assistant run over to the kitchen to pick up. They looked at the plans and Doc said, "I wonder how easy it would be to add floors to this structure?"

Johnnie looked at Bev and said, "When all these buildings were built, your uncle had them built to the same standard. So the garage here is built as solid as the main house. I'm no architect but I think some floors could be added."

Doc said, "Johnnie if you were going to add living space for guests on this property, how would you do it?"

"I think you've got the right idea. I'd take a hard look at expanding the garage if you need the rooms quickly. If the garage expansion doesn't prove feasible, then I guess you are into a new building with all that entails in terms of time to build and construction costs."

Doc said, "Thanks, Johnnie, we'll think about this."

The group moved back to the mansion and Anne suggested lunch by the pool since there was still so much noise and dust happening inside.

As they got comfortable, Fred, the bartender from the Zulu Pub approached the table and said," Welcome back Mr. O'Connell, it's good to see you again. Can I take drink orders?"

Doc said, "Thank you, Fred, it's good to be back. Well, ladies what would you like?"

They placed orders, and the group looked over the menu and made their selections when Fred came back with the drinks.

Doc said, "What do you think Bev, should we do a feasibility study to see if the Annex makes sense?"

"Sure, we can do that easily, but we want to keep in mind that the idea is to get our capital out of here, so we need to look at the overall project cost in relation to that objective. At some point, our investment here will reach a state of diminishing returns if we put more money into Lion's Pride than we are getting out of it."

"I couldn't agree more. Why don't we get the architect and contractor to do a feasibility study and let us know if an expansion of the garage makes financial sense as opposed to a new build situation? And how many suites, similar to the ones in the mansion, could they possibly add? They could also tell us how much investment we are looking at on a per suite basis. Then we can estimate the demand for suites, which we should have a pretty good handle on by next month. We can then crunch the numbers and see if any addition at all looks feasible and if so, how many suites we should build."

Bev picked up her phone and asked Mona to invite the architect and building contractor to a meeting at lunch tomorrow to go over the progress to date and to discuss the feasibility of adding suites.

After lunch, Doc and Shannon went to their apartment. Doc noticed that the entrance to the suite adjacent to his had been closed off and inside, the wall between the suite and the apartment had been opened up. The effect was that the apartment was now much larger and had three bedrooms, four bathrooms, two kitchens and two living rooms. Shannon explained, " Bev wanted us to have lots of space for when we start having a family and figured it was just as easy to do the work now."

"The way you're talking about the number of kids we're going to have, we might need to add a couple of more suites down the road."

"Do you want to practice? I can get a sip of St. Agnes."

"You get a sip and meet me in the shower, I need to clean up after the flight."

Afterward, Doc was spent and fell into a deep sleep nestled in Shannon's arms. When she was sure he was sleeping soundly, she unwrapped herself and slipped quietly out of the bed, She went into the new addition suite and took a shower there so as not to wake Doc. Then it was back to work.

Bill met with the GM of the Four Seasons and opened a corporate account at a favorable room rate. He then called Sean and said, "Hi Sean have you got a minute?"

"Always for you Bill what's up?"

"Well, it's looking like we may have underestimated the demand for our business arrangement. Grant and Stanley are pounding the pavement and getting a tremendous reception wherever they go. It's certain that based on the reaction so far, we are going to have close to a full compliment of developers lined up as soon as Lion's Pride is ready. In fact I'm going to ask Doc to meet with the contractor and see if they can't move quicker. In the meantime, we were thinking of putting some developers up at your place until Lion's Pride is ready. How many can you accommodate for say two months?"

"Let me look into that and I'll get back to you shortly."

"Ok, I have the first one on her way, her name is Hilda Anderson and she'll be arriving on the United flight at one forty-five tomorrow. I told her there would be a car to pick her up. She's bringing her own Mac laptop but needs a large Mac computer screen and a color printer in the room."

"It'll be done."

Sean hung up and went to look at the bookings for the next two months and to confer with Donald, the assistant general manager, about the number of rooms they can make available to Software Conceptions.

There's a fine line between maximizing occupancy and making sure that regular guests are accommodated. They decided that they would want to hold back twenty rooms for regulars and thus could let Software Conceptions have up to forty. He called Bill back and said, "We can let you have up to forty rooms over the next two months. Do you think you'll need that many?"

"The way it's looking we may need all of them and more. We can put some up at the Four Seasons across from our office and some may elect to stay at home until Lion's Pride is ready, but we want to be prepared for every eventuality. The last thing we want is to start off as a company that makes promises that it can't keep."

Sean said, "When are Doc and Shannon coming back, do you know?"

"I'm not sure. I know they plan to be out here next Friday, and then Doc is headed for Hong Kong for a week or so."

When Bill hung up, Kea handed him a message to call Grant. Kea gave Bill a coffee and went to call Grant.

She said, "Grant on line one."

Bill said, "Hi Grant how is it going?"

Good, almost too good, I've qualified six more candidates for next Friday's meeting, so that's ten so far. It looks like we'll have to meet Saturday as well."

"We'll have to see what Stanley comes up with, but if this interview list keeps growing we may have to reschedule presentations planned for the week after next and keep both you guys in the office just interviewing all week."

"That's probably a good idea, let's have Kea reschedule all presentations by a week."

Bill said, "FYI Doc is coming out next Friday for the interviews. He wants to see the process in action."

"That's good, maybe he can handle some of

the interviews himself."

"I don't like that idea. We'll stick to the original plan of having you, Stanley, and I do the interviewing and candidate acceptance. Doc has enough on his plate to worry about without these details and besides, I want the acceptance procedure tightly controlled by the three of us."

At that point, Kea leaned through the office door and handed Bill a note saying Stanley was on line two.

Bill took the call saying, "Stanley, how are you, any news?"

"Yes, I've just finished interviewing twenty-two candidates and have extended second interview appointments to sixteen of them."

"Pass their contact details on to Kea. We are going to have to start scheduling appointments for the full week after next. Kea is going to reschedule the presentations by a week. We now have twenty-six candidates for second and third interviews and the week is not over. Keep presenting but have the ones you want to go forward contact Kea for an appointment time. I'm telling Grant the same thing."

After he woke up to find Shannon gone, Doc went for a walk around the mansion looking at the work that had been done and what was left to do. He was satisfied that the quality of the workmanship was top notch so the finished product will be in keeping with the rest of the mansion. He met the interior decorators that Shannon contracted and was pleased with their progress. Shannon's touches were apparent everywhere. He sat down with Bev and said, "I'm amazed at what a good general contractor you've become. I never in my wildest dreams thought I 'd be walking around a construction site with you in a hard hat giving everyone orders. I think we're at a point now where we need to finalize a completion date so we can move developers in. Let's push the architect and contractor tomorrow. Bill tells me they're now up to twenty-six confirmed candidates for second and third interviews starting next Friday. Prospective candidates are signing up so fast that they're suspending presentations for the week after next to accommodate what he is forecasting to be between forty to fifty potential candidate interviews. We already have one moving into O'Leary's tomorrow and two others starting in our San Francisco office and staying at the Four Seasons. At this rate, we'll have an overflow before we are even open for business."

"That's a nice problem to have."

"If Shannon's ready, I'm going to suggest that we head for home the day after tomorrow. I need to stay on top of this recruitment frenzy. By the way, I've invited our new flight crew for dinner tomorrow if that's ok."

"Of course, I'd like to meet them, you hold them in such high regard."

"Between you and me, I've got a bit of a surprise for Shannon when we get back. I'll have her call you to tell you about it."

CHAPTER THIRTY-FOUR

Doc said, "Shannon, I think we should head home as soon as we can. When do you think you can get away?"

"How about the day after tomorrow, would that work?"

"Perfect, if you're sure it's ok with your interior design crew."

"Yeah, I'll meet with their lead designer, Karen, tomorrow. I've already done the design part with her, so all they have to do is follow my drawings and get it done. So far, they've been very professional and very conscientious about following my plans. If they get stuck, they have Bev here to make decisions, and they can always Skype me."

"Ok, I'll let the aircrew know that we are leaving at noon, the day after tomorrow. I think I'm going to goof off by the pool tomorrow."

Doc's phone went off in his ear, and he almost jumped out of bed thinking it was a fire alarm, but no fire, just Bill.

Doc said, "Do you have any idea of the time zone change between here and San Francisco?"

"Sorry, did I wake you?"

"No. I'm usually awake at four forty in the morning but normally only when I'm going fishing with Gary."

"Ok I'll watch it next time but I think you'll want to hear this, are you sitting down?"

"No to tell you the truth I am laying down."

"Well, you better sit up, so you don't choke. We now have seventy-five candidates that have passed the initial interview and are signing up for the second and third interviews. We will have the forty rooms at O'Leary's full and the best part of a floor in the Four Seasons occupied. The phone has been ringing non-stop between students who saw the presentations at a University to word-of-mouth referrals. Starting Friday when you're here and for the next week, our interview schedule is full. I may have to put off any more presentations until these are dealt with."

"It's up to you, but I'd suggest that you don't do that. I'd keep Grant on the road presenting, and you and Stanley do the second interviews. Arrange the schedule so that third interviews by Grant are handled when he is in between presentations. Keep building the developer group. When O'Leary's is full, put them into the Four Seasons or other five-star hotels in the area of the office. We can't let any of these people go."

"I hear you, but there is another issue. Hilda Anderson feels her video game is ready to go."

"Great, so make it go. Check with Brian and find an A/V studio and get them on it. Tell Stanley to make sales calls in between presentations and sell the program. Let's get some cash flow coming in for a change. Tell Hilda to email me a copy of her program and I'll get the copyright registered in the US, Canada, Europe, and Asia. I'll get a JV company set up between her and us, complete with all the trimmings, like accounting, legal, etc. She has nothing to worry about except her next software creation. We are leaving for Scranton tomorrow and will be there a few days before going to Seattle to buy a plane and then to see you and our new offices in San Francisco. Knowing Shannon, she'll probably want to make suggestions about the office décor. If you're smart just take note of the ideas and incorporate at least some of them into the décor."

"Ok I hear you, I'll call tomorrow, later in the day than I did just now and fill you in on what's happening. Do what you can to move the construction along. We need rooms now."

"I don't think we can move these guys on construction much faster and maintain the quality level we want. We'd better plan on two months before moving in any people so make whatever arrangements you need with hoteliers, but keep these geniuses on the hook. I don't want to lose even one of them."

Shannon spent the day going over last minute details with the interior decorators. Doc had a coffee with Johnnie and went with him to look at the progress being made on the sports fields. Johnnie was a very impressive guy. He had already found a supplier of portable buildings to house the car collection in case it was decided to proceed with the renovation of the garage into suites.

Doc sat by the pool and went over the consulting reports on the agricultural potential for Lion's Pride. He then found Bev, and they sat under a poolside umbrella and had an iced tea. Doc said, "I spoke to Johnnie about the sports fields and possible garage conversion. I think we should leave the sports fields up to him; they don't involve a lot of money or much of our time. I think the agricultural project while the consultant's report is positive, will require some money and our time. My suggestion is that we put this on the back burner for now and let's focus on getting Lion's Pride finished, and developers checked in."

"It's interesting that you should come to this conclusion because I have been thinking the same way. Let's consolidate our efforts on the developers and get the incubator off the ground."

"Is there anything else we need to cover before I go?"

"No, I don't think so. I am going to miss Shannon around here. You sure picked a classy lady there."

"I know, I feel very lucky, she's one in a million."

"Don't forget dinner with the flight crew. I think Anne has something planned for out here to escape the dust."

Doc went for a swim, and then did one more walk around the renovation project before going into the Zulu Pub for some dart practice and a

Laphroaig.

Anne and Bev turned the dinner into a bit of a farewell party for Shannon. She had an impact on the staff at Lion's Pride, and many of them came by to give her little going away presents that they had made themselves based on many generations of Zimbabwean tradition. The flight crew was amazed to see the nature of the company they had joined and were made to feel at home with everyone. They left early as they had preparations to make in the morning for the noon departure.

Anne was invited to join Doc and Shannon on the flight home but declined as she felt she needed a few more weeks with her training project. Besides there was nothing for her to do in Scranton except to say goodbye to Sean and the staff and pack for her move to Lion's Pride.

On the flight home, Doc and Shannon had lots of time to get caught up on what each was doing. Shannon said, "I'm anxious to get back home. Lion's Pride is a beautiful place, but I guess I'm still a bit of a homebody. I'm looking forward to getting together with Brenda and seeing those properties that she has lined up. It's going to be fun to build our dream home from the ground up just the way we want it. Besides the man cave, multiple car garage, tennis court and swimming pool have you had any other bright ideas or have you even had time to think about it?"

"Oh I've thought about it but I've intentionally

avoided doing any planning in my head because I still want this to be your creation."

"Ok I get that, and I appreciate it, but don't be shy about giving me ideas when you get them. Let's call them suggestions, that I may or may not incorporate into the design."

"Well since you ask, what if we were to make the house as environmentally friendly as possible? I'm thinking of things like solar panel roofing, geothermal heat, air conditioning and hot water, a rainwater capture and storage system for irrigation, maybe a waste treatment plant, hi-tech insulation, and windows. There are a lot of new technologies out there to help make our house more 'green', why not look into it?"

"I think that's a superb idea. It'll drive up the cost of the house because a lot of this technology is still in its infancy."

"I don't care. In the long term, the increase in building cost will be mostly offset by savings on things like electricity, heat, and air conditioning. Plus we'll have the satisfaction of knowing that our home is as efficient as possible from an environmental perspective."

"You know, we could incorporate some of these ideas into the cottage while we are at it. I'm going to do some research and find out what I can and maybe identify an architect who is on the leading edge of this."

"Speaking of the cottage, we should drive up there for a couple of days and see how things are going, maybe try out the new boat."

"Give me a few days to get over some of the jet lag and get up to speed on what's happening at O'Leary's, and then I'd love to go. Once that cottage is done, I want us to go there and hide out for at least two weeks."

"Two weeks! Now that caught me by surprise; it never occurred to me to take two weeks and hide out in a cottage."

"Well, you had better get used to it. Because, it's all well and good for us to work hard to build our future together, but we're going to take the time along the way to maintain our health and sanity. Remember what you and Bev decided back when she asked you to be her business partner; you would balance work with having fun. My mission is to hold you both to that commitment."

Rosemary somehow managed to create a dinner that would have done chef Griff proud while still getting a lot of cockpit time in the jump seat. She was real keen to get her jet engine certification and earn her way into the right seat some day. For Doc and Shannon, it worked well because they could fend for themselves for most of their requirements and enjoyed this opportunity for some rare one-on-one time together.

Shannon suggested that they renew their membership in the mile high club, and Doc was in the bed before she finished the sentence.

Shannon wanted to check out O'Leary's and say hi to Sean, so they had the limo stop at the hotel on the way home. Sean, of course, was happy to see them and gave them each a big hug. While Shannon went to her office, Doc and Sean went to the bar for a coffee. Even for Sean, ten a.m. was a bit too early for cocktail hour. They talked about the progress at Lion's Pride; Sean had spoken with Anne while Doc and Shannon were in the air, so he was up to speed.

Doc said, "How is it going with our first developer?"

"She's terrific, I've had a chance to have a coffee with her and she loves it here. She usually comes down early and goes for a five-mile run then disappears into her room all day just coming out for meals.

She explained that she has to force herself to stop working long enough to eat. So she makes a routine of having her meals in the dining room then going for a walk along the river trail that you enjoy, then back to her computer. I've never seen her in the pub, I don't think she has time for that sort of thing."

"Most of the people we team up with will be similar in that they will have a clear vision to become wealthy through their software development. If they don't, they won't be productive and, therefore, will not be with us for long."

"Bill tells me to expect some developers over the next few weeks. It's great that the response has been so good."

"Yes, I'm afraid that the response level has caught us all by surprise. Bill has to adjust his planning on a daily basis to deal with the high degree of interest. Grant and Stanley are learning on the fly and having to be flexible in their planning as well. Poor Kea is run off her feet rearranging appointments with developers, rescheduling presentations and dealing with all the travel arrangements. At this stage, I'm trying to keep everyone focused but I'd have to describe the situation as mildly chaotic."

"Why don't you go out there and help out?"

"Because, it would be seen, and rightly so, that I'm trying to take over from Bill. That's the last image I want to portray at this point. I need to let Bill run with it and make the decisions. He knows I'm here to back him up, and he'll call on me if it gets to be too much for him to handle. I've known Bill and worked closely with him for a long time. He can deal with a hell of a lot."

"Anne was saying that Shannon was quite the fireball at Lion's Pride; she had those interior designers jumping. They still are. I guess Shannon was able to motivate them and convinced them of the need for both quality and speed. Anne says there is a general understanding by all involved that there is a deadline, and it's drawing close."

Shannon came along and said," Ok you two, break it up, I need a nap in my own bed for a change and not one hanging at 40,000 feet."

Doc and Shannon had a long nap, a proper backwashing shower and went to Carmella's for a quiet dinner. By mutual consent, it was agreed that business talk was off the table for the evening.

The following morning Shannon was up early partially due to jet lag and partly due to her desire to look at the building lots with Brenda. She had to wait for about an hour before she could call Brenda, so she put on her running gear and left a note for Doc, who was still asleep. She took

her familiar route and maintained a good pace until she got to her usual coffee bar. Equipped with a copy of the morning edition of the Scranton Times-Tribune and a tall, non-fat, half sweet, latte, she found a window seat and read, sipped and ate her croissant. She chose a different route back to her apartment, one that took her to O'Leary's. She went in, said hi to Donald, and asked if anything was happening, found out that all was good and left. Time to call Brenda.

Arriving home, she found Doc awake and having coffee on the balcony.

"I'm about to call Brenda so get ready."

"I don't think I'll go, I don't want to be an influence on this decision, it's your baby."

"Oh come on, you should see them all and if I want your input, I'll ask for it. It's a big decision for us and two heads….. you know?"

"Ok I'll go but I am not speaking unless spoken to."

"Hi Brenda, this is Shannon, let's go look at lots, shall we meet at your office?"

Brenda said, "If you like I'll swing by your place and pick you up. I always find that if I drive, the client has a better chance of sizing up the surroundings. You're not only buying a building lot; you're buying into a neighborhood. How about ten minutes?"

"We'll be downstairs waiting."

When they met Brenda, Doc said," I'm just along for the ride. I'll sit in the back and won't say a thing, forget I'm here."

As soon as the SUV started Doc said, "Can we stop at Starbucks for a coffee to go?"

Shannon, smiling, turned to Doc and said, "I thought you weren't going to say a thing. We're not even out of the parking space, and you are already asking for stuff."

"Ok, let's get a coffee, I'll buy and then I'll shut up."

First Brenda took them to the two properties that Doc didn't own and then finally to Doc's lot. Shannon got out of the car and walked the lot from side to side taking in everything.

Doc could see the wheels turning as she visualized this site. She went down to the small lake and stood on the shore fantasizing about a fire pit by the water, a glass of wine, maybe some steaks on the grill. She was sold, Doc could tell.

Brenda said, "I don't want you to rush; there is no need to decide today. What you should do is list the three lots in order of preference on this pad and then go home, sit with a glass of wine and list in detail the pros and cons of each lot.

Come back and revisit them if you want, walk the lots again, walk the neighborhoods and talk it through. Doc, don't talk, just listen, and then go home and sleep on it. Tomorrow when you wake up you may have some questions for me. If so give me a call and I'll buy the coffee while we chat about your concerns."

Shannon said, "Well take it."

Brenda said, "You'll take what?"

"This lot."

"Are you sure?"

"Yes, write up the offer, we'll come with you to your office and sign it. Offer full asking price less fifteen percent and let's see what happens."

"Ok, but for my curiosity why this one?"

"The neighborhood, proximity to a great school, the size of the lot will permit us to build what we want without feeling that we're on top of the neighbors. Then there's the lake. I can see Doc floating out there in a fishing Kayak with a six-pack of cold Buds. The place has a relaxed, homey feel about it without even having the house. I don't think we could find a better lot for the family house I have in mind."

"How would you rate the other two lots?"

"Both pale by comparison, but I guess if I had to choose a second choice, it would be the first one we saw without the gulley running through it. The gulley lot wouldn't even make the list."

"Shall I phone the owner and see how he responds to your offer?"

"Sure, go ahead, let's see how keen he is to sell."

CHAPTER THIRTY-FIVE

Brenda punched a speed dial number into her phone and Doc's cell rang. He looked at the screen and excused himself saying he had to take it. He walked away a few yards and turned to get some privacy. He answered and heard Brenda say, "Hi, good news I have an offer on your lot!" Doc, speaking low so Shannon couldn't hear said, "Tell her it's been sold." Brenda turned to Shannon and said, "It's been sold." Just then, Doc came over and handed her a paper. With obvious disappointment on her face, she accepted the document and said, "What's this?"

Doc said, "Read it."

Shannon opened it to find that it was a deed for the property with the owner listed as Miss Shannon O'Sullivan.

She looked at Doc and said, "If this is a joke, I don't think it's amusing!"

Brenda stepped in quickly and said, "Shannon it's no joke, Doc bought this lot for you last week, you're standing on your own property."

Shannon looked at Brenda and then at Doc with a stare of amazement. Her beautiful green eyes, usually large and sparkling seemed to be even larger; her mouth fell open as she yelled and threw her arms around Doc."

Shannon said, "How did you know I'd choose his lot?"

"I think I know you pretty well by now Shannon O'Sullivan. Besides, if you didn't want this one I would have bought you the one you wanted and kept this as an investment or sold it down the road."

"Let's go to O'Leary's, get a picnic basket and come back here for lunch at the lakeside."

"You've got it. Brenda, thanks for being such a good sport and playing along with this. I wanted it to be a day Shannon will always remember."

Brenda dropped them off at the apartment so they could get the Cobra and go to O'Leary's. Shannon called ahead, and chef prepared a picnic basket fit for a royal banquet. Sean came out of his office and gave them both a big congratulatory hug. He then led them into the pub and cracked open a bottle of Cristal for a toast to the new homestead. Sean said, "I never could understand that tradition of smashing a perfectly good bottle of champagne on the bow of a ship that's about to be launched. It's much better to drink the champagne first then smash the empty if you've got a notion to smash something."

Shannon said, "Sean I'm going to need a good architect, one that has experience with environmentally friendly residential buildings. Any ideas?"

"Let me make a few inquiries. I know a few architects but the green kind you may have to import from a larger market, maybe New York. I'll check it out and let you know."

The picnic was exciting and relaxing. After

the picnic, they spent time talking, walking the land and sitting on the lakeshore planning their house.

Shannon said," I should go into the office and get a few things caught up so we can drive up to the cottage tomorrow."

Doc asked, "How is Donald doing? You'd mentioned that he had a minor meltdown when Sean and you were at Lion's Pride."

"I talked to Sean about him and it looks like he's ok as long as he has someone senior on hand to make the tough decisions. We doubt that he'll ever make a full GM, probably he'll stay an assistant forever."

"I've been thinking of an idea. What if Sean hires someone else to be GM and leaves Donald as assistant general manager, at least for now?"

"Where does that leave me?"

"It leaves you free to travel with me, to do some interior design work when you get bored traveling, build our family home and then build our family. We don't need your income, and I like hanging out with you."

"I don't know, I've been a part of O'Leary's since it started, I think I'd miss being out of it altogether."

"Maybe we could buy a half interest in O'Leary's and you could keep your hand in as an owner."

"Let me think about that. If we were to buy a half of O'Leary's would Bev want in?"

"I'd feel obligated to offer it to her; we're business partners, and I think it's only fair that I give her the opportunity to invest in whatever we do business wise."

"Let's talk about it while we go up to the cottage. By the way when do you want to leave?"

"Let's get an early start. I'd like to spend some time there getting the feel of the place. It's strange not to have it waiting there all comfortable and ready to help me relax. When you talk to Sean, ask him if it's ok for you to accompany me to Asia. We'd be back next weekend."

On the way to the cottage Doc said," Did you mention anything to Sean about us possibly buying in?"

"No, I didn't want to bring it up until we're sure we want to do it. There is no sense in getting him worked up over nothing."

"Do you think he'll go for the idea?"

"It's hard to say with Sean. It's his baby; he built it from scratch, and I doubt he would be willing to sell it to just anyone. As you know, he treats me more like a daughter so he might consider it more of a family thing than a business transaction. It's easy enough to find out, we can ask him once we're sure that we want to do it."

Doc said, "What was his reaction when you told him I want you to come with me to San Francisco and Asia for a week?"

"He just said that it was fine with him, I'd put a lot of time into Lion's Pride and that we should spend some time together. They'll be alright while I'm gone as long as Sean is at the helm but we'll soon have to replace Donald."

"I want to introduce you to a few people but particularly Andrew Chang. Andrew is GM of the Mandarin Oriental in Bangkok, and I think he'd make a good GM at O'Leary's if we can lure him away."

"It's a long way from Bangkok to Scranton. Do you think he would give up the excitement of Asia for the relative peace and quiet of Pennsylvania?"

"He's American born and grew up in some smaller towns on the west coast, so he's not a stranger to the American way of life. We'd have to craft an offer that he can't refuse as they say in the gangster movies, but I think I might be able to get him interested. For now, let's just have dinner with him, and you can judge for yourself if you think he'd be suitable. I can tell you that the hotel he runs is as good as or better than any other that I've stayed at."

They stopped at the duty-free shop at the border, and Doc bought a bottle of St, Agnes for later on. He said, "I'm an old Boy Scout and the Boy Scout motto is 'Be Prepared.' Although I doubt that many Boy Scouts would have much of an idea what a bottle of St. Agnes prepares one for!"

Shannon said, "Why don't you find a quiet little place we can pull into, and we can crack open the bottle. I'm no Boy Scout, but I can tell you I'm so prepared that I put a blanket in the trunk for just such an emergency."

Arriving at the cottage, they were amazed at the progress. Gary was beaming as he showed them around. He said," By the end of next week you'll be able to move in furniture and use the place properly."

Shannon said, "Doc, let's go into town and look at some furniture."

Gary said, "Barb has a list of antique places in the area if you'd like to shop for some antiques."

Shannon said, "That would be great, I'd love a copy of it."

Gary left to go to his house to get the list of antique places. Doc took Shannon down to inspect the new boathouse and the new boat. Shannon said, "They've built the boathouse to the same standard and design as the cottage, it's beautiful workmanship."

"Yeah, when Gary sets out to do something he does it right. I knew when he took on this job that it would be done as if it was his own place."

They drove into town, and Doc was surprised at the number of furniture stores and the quality of their offerings. Shannon got a bedroom suite and mattress for the master bedroom, and leather, cottage-looking sofa, and chair. They went to five antique stores; one was an antique barn and Shannon picked up some occasional tables and a grand old roll top desk.

She said, "All in all, I'd say we had a pretty good day finding all this furniture so quickly. This will get us started. We can occupy the place as soon as it's finished and then I'll slowly tour the other antique outlets and stores in Kingston and Ottawa to fill in whatever else we need."

"Why don't we get a hotel and spend some time just enjoying Brockville. I'd like to take my other Mustang into a carwash and get her a good scrubbing inside and out before putting her back in the garage."

"Sounds like a plan. Let's walk the main street and the waterfront and find a restaurant for dinner."

After supper they returned to their hotel, it was clean and comfortable but not exactly a Relais & Chateaux. Doc said, "So what do you think of my little hide-a-way town on the river?"

"I love it. I can see why your family wanted their cottage here. It's the perfect size community, not too big, and yet has everything you need. It has a unique rural/urban hybrid feeling to it. I think our family is going to enjoy the time we spend here."

"I'm so glad you like it; I relax here more than I do anywhere else. Mind you I get the feeling I'm also going to be pretty relaxed at our Scranton place."

"Does Brockville have an airport capable of handling our corporate jet?"

"I'm pretty sure it does, but I'll get our pilot to look into it. It would be real convenient to be able to land here from time to time."

After breakfast Doc's phone rang and it was Bill, "Doc I can't believe the reaction we're getting. By the end of next week, we're going to have all the qualified developers that Lion's

Pride can accommodate and then some. Stanley has licensed Hilda's program to a major gaming company that's introducing it in a new game format they've developed. The company is worldwide so if it takes off it will take off big time. In the meantime, Quincy, one of the developers working out of our office and staying at the Four Seasons has got something market ready, so Stanley has that in front of a few large companies. We've got four more developers on the way to O'Leary's and next week Sean's going to have a full house. One of the developers, Sarah has an app ready to go that looks like a winner. I know you hate meetings, but I think you, Grant, Stanley and I need to do a little strategizing, so I've called a meeting here in the conference room for one o'clock on Sunday. Can you make that?"

"You bet. We'll get a new course plotted to account for the overwhelming response we have had from developers.

We're departing for Boeing tomorrow to finalize the purchase of the plane. As soon as that meeting is over, we'll head down to San Francisco." Doc and Shannon swung by the cottage for one last look around and to say goodbye to Gary and Barb and then pointed the Cobra south.

When they got home, Shannon went to O'Leary's to do a few office things while Doc went home to prepare some paperwork for his upcoming trip to Asia. Doc then went to O'Leary's and met up with Sean and Shannon for dinner. When Sean went to deal with a phone call, Shannon said," What about asking Sean what his thoughts would be about our desire to buy a half share?"

Doc said, "Why not? It would give him a chance to think it over while we're away. You ask him."

"Ok, I will."

When Sean returned, Shannon said, "Sean, Doc and I have an idea to run by you. We thought it best to put it on the table now and let you digest it while we're away. I want you to understand that this is just an idea, if you don't like it we won't be offended, we'll just forget about it. What would you think about us buying half of O'Leary's? I want to spend more time with Doc, for now on the road and later, at our home and cottage as we start to raise a family. But I love O'Leary's and hanging out with you, so I'd not want just to quit and walk away. If you were interested, I would help identify a capable GM to replace me, as we both know that Donald just won't cut it. You don't have to say anything tonight, just think it over and we can discuss it some more when we get back."

Sean said, "I'd better get a fresh drink, it appears this bottle has evaporated."

He looked at the bartender and held up the empty bottle of Jameson's; magically a fresh one arrived, and Sean poured two fat fingers. He said, "Coincidently, I have been thinking along similar lines. I realize that I'm going to lose you

and I guess it's part of the natural order of things but it's very difficult, you are my only family. Let me think about it but we will do something. Start keeping an eye out for a five-star level GM. I want to spend less time on the day-to-day operations part of O'Leary's and more time on the management contract side. I think there is a future in management contracts at the grand luxe level.

We'll make some arrangement when you get back. Bring me one of those things that the Chinese use to stamp on an inkpad and put on documents. I forget what they're called."

Doc said, "A chop and I'll get one made for you in Hong Kong."

Sean said, "Are you going to Hong Kong this trip?"

"Yes, I have some things to organize there such as joint venture companies with several of our developers, some accounting and legal details to do with these joint ventures and a few other things. Shannon will get a chance to see and no doubt fuss with the décor of the Hong Kong apartment. I don't want to spend a lot of money on it because at some point once things settle down; I want to buy a boat to live aboard at the Aberdeen Marina Club."

Sean said, "A boat! Where am I supposed to sleep on a boat?"

"The one I have in mind has five or six large

guest bedrooms; we won't have any trouble putting you up."

"By the way Shannon, I have a line on an architect for you. I'm checking out his credentials, particularly on the environmental side and should have some news on your return."

Doc said, "Have you heard from Bill about the four students that are on their way?"

"Yeah, that's great. He warned me that the floodgates might open next week."

"That's right, our team has been going like crazy and are spending all next week interviewing and qualifying potential developers. Bill says to expect to fill up between next week and the week after, so it should be jumping around here for a few months, maybe longer."

Doc and Shannon went home to get ready for tomorrow's flight to Seattle and San Francisco. They Skyped Bev and caught her in her office. She said, "Wait one minute and I'll try to get Anne in here." A few minutes later, Anne, short of breath from running down the hall, entered the room.

Shannon said, "All is well with us. We've bought a lot to build our house on and are quite excited about that. Our cottage renovations are progressing satisfactorily. We are off to Seattle, San Francisco, and Hong Kong for just over a week and all is well with Sean and O'Leary's."

"We know about the Sean and O'Leary's part, we hear from him every day. We taught him how to use Skype, and now we wish we hadn't.

He has poor Anne walking down the halls with her laptop showing him the renovation progress in real time. He even yells at the tradesmen!"

Doc said, "Let me give you a business update. Bill reports that the response is overwhelming. They are now scheduling interviews for the week after next because next week is full. We'll have more than enough developers to fill Lion's Pride within two weeks. And these are the cream of the crop having been interviewed by all three, Bill, Stanley, and Grant. This is working somewhat differently than we had planned. For instance, we are getting interview requests from as far back as our original presentation at Stanford. Word is out in the software development community, and the phones are ringing off the hook. We're meeting Sunday in the San Francisco office to refine our business plan to incorporate the higher than expected flow of demand from developers. I have some ideas, but I want to run them by Bill and the team before putting them on the table. So I'll get back to you after we meet."

Bev said, "One idea that Anne and I have been kicking around is to move all our tradesmen to one floor at a time starting with level two, the first floor of developer rooms. Finish that floor, then move all the tradespeople up to level three and move in developers to floor two and so forth. That way we can start bringing in floor two developers by next week."

Doc said, "I love it. Bill and the guys will be pleased to hear this. I'll also have more to report on the licensing agreements Stanley has got going for the software that the developers have already produced."

CHAPTER THIRTY-SIX

On the way to Seattle, Doc and Shannon had some time to talk in private as Rosemary continued her education on the flight deck. Doug said that she was a quick learner and that they are going to let her start flying right seat when they are flying without passengers. That way both Doug and Randy could devote their attention to giving her training while flying the plane without the distraction of having to provide cabin service.

Doc said to Shannon, "I have the seeds of a plan in my head that I want your opinion on before we meet with the guys on Sunday."

Shannon said, "Ok give me a few minutes to finish off the cabin design for the new plane, I'm just about done."

"I'll go take a shower and read for a while. Let me know when you're ready."

Shannon had been working on a computer template that Boeing had provided which was essentially a CAD or computer assisted design program. The program allowed her to allocate the available square feet, about the size of a one-bedroom apartment, into various configurations. She could change the layout until she was comfortable that she had the optimum use of the space for their needs. Doc, bowing to her impressive interior design capability, was staying out of it until she was done so he wouldn't disrupt her train of thought. Since a lot of their travel would be long haul, she wanted a crew space with a double bunk, a toilet, and a shower as part of an extended flight deck. This way one crew-member could be sleeping while the other two flew the plane allowing for them to be fully rested even on long trips.

Shannon had gone over the plan, particularly for the crew area, with the crew and had incorporated their suggestions. She was feeling pretty good about it and took it into the bedroom to go over it with Doc.

Shannon said, "Ok finally ready for your critique oh great one."

Doc took her offered laptop and sitting up on the bed carefully looked at every detail before he said," I think it looks great. The dining/conference table for six, sleeping arrangements for four in the main cabin and the bedroom for two works for me. There's only one thing that's missing."

"What's that?"

"If I were you, I'd relocate the forward washroom to the main cabin end instead of the flight deck end of the crew bunk room. And incorporate a double door system, so the bathroom is accessible to the main cabin as well as to the crew bunkroom. Otherwise, you're going to have passengers coming into our bedroom or disrupting the flight deck to use the head!"

"Oops, I never thought of that. It's a good thing you caught it. Back to the drawing board,

I'd better redo the drawing before the Boeing meeting. What idea did you want to run by me, put it on the table so I can think about it?"

"Since the demand for developer joint ventures is so much greater than we thought, why don't we either buy or build another resort/campus elsewhere. Maybe Silicon Valley or Vancouver to act as an entry-level facility with Lion's Pride as a reward for producers. Under this scenario, new developers would start out at the new facility and be eligible for a move to Lion's Pride as a reward once they produce a marketable product."

"Or we could expand Lion's Pride as we talked about."

"Sure or we could do both, expand Lion's Pride and get a start up facility elsewhere."

"Or we could expand the existing Lion's Pride and develop new Lion's Pride level resort/campus accommodations elsewhere."

"Or don't enlarge Lion's Pride, just build another Lion's Pride in a different luxury location like say the Caribbean or the South of France."

"All right, that's enough alternatives. They all could work, some maybe better than others. Let me get back to the plane designs."

"We'll continue this discussion at Sunday's meeting, get everyone's first reactions then let the idea ferment in their brains. You and I will have the long flight to Hong Kong to continue to discuss it."

They landed at Boeing Field and were directed

to taxi right up to the commercial aircraft sales building. They went inside and were taken into an executive boardroom that was fitted out with all the latest A/V equipment. The conference table probably used up a good portion of the Washington State harvest of red cedar for the year. The plush leather executive chairs would be the envy of any Fortune 500 boardroom. The overall impression achieved its intended effect of wowing the visitor with high-tech luxury. Carl Lowden greeted them, his friends called him "the Big C" due to his reputation as a master closer. He was the image of the classic senior executive marketing VP. A retired pilot, of course, he was a gracious host as well as a knowledgeable guide through the process of buying a $95 million dollar airplane. Doc got the impression that Carl could sell watches to the Swiss.

Once introductions were out of the way and refreshments had been served Doc said, "Our flight crew has selected your BBJ executive jet, so there is no need on your part to try to sell us. We're sold. We are here today to finalize the design and get the order going so we can take delivery as soon as possible."

Carl said, "That's great, of course, we are delighted that you have selected Boeing and assure you of our continued support. I have here the specifications that Doug, Randy and Rosemary have sent along and there is no problem with anything on this list. Let's focus on the cabin layout that Shannon has been working on. If you could bring it up on your laptop for me, I'll plug it into the system so we can all look at it."

Once the layout was on the screen, all of the meeting attendees could look at it and offer any suggestions. Sheila McDougall, the Boeing cabin designer, offered a few minor suggestions, mostly relating to the galley layout. She said, "Shannon if you ever want to change careers let me know. This design is unique, to the say the least, but very practical and efficient for the type of flying you are going to be doing."

Shannon said, "Thank you, Sheila, we've all put a lot of thought into it."

Doc said, "Where do we go from here?"

Carl said," Ken Halton, our Finance VP has all the paperwork ready for your signature. Ken will deal with the financing for you."

"Not necessary. Ken, contact Phillip Waters at Hong Kong Shanghai Bank in Hong Kong, here are his contact details and let him have your bank transfer details. The deposit will be transferred immediately."

Carl Said, "Well all right then, that's the second fastest financing we've ever done. The only one faster was a certain billionaire who put a new 747 on his Amex."

Doc said, "What are we looking at delivery wise?"

Carl said, " You're in luck, we have one just finished. All it needs is the interior so we can have it ready in a month."

"Ok let me know the exact date when you

have it and we'll come get it."

They said their goodbyes and were wheels up for San Francisco in fifteen minutes. Doug said to Randy," Don't you just love these manufacturer's airports, you spend a paltry $95 million, and they give you a cup of Starbuck's and a priority take off."

When they arrived in San Francisco, they went directly to the Four Seasons. Doc called Bill from the car and asked if he'd like to meet them in the bar around five o'clock. Bill agreed and said dinner was on with Brian and Kristen White at seven o'clock tomorrow, the reservation was made. Shannon and Doc went down to the health club, did a half hour on the treadmill and a half hour on the bike then jumped in the pool for a mixture of laps and goofing off. They returned to their suite, broke open the St. Agnes then satiated, fell into a deep sleep until the alarm went off at four-thirty. Another quick sip of St, Agnes, and a fast backwash shower and they were down at the bar by ten after five.

After big hugs all around Bill said, "It's unbelievable the response we're getting to our developer joint venture package. Grant made a presentation to the American Society of University Career Advisors and the calls are coming in from students and advisors from all over the US. We have had some calls from Asia and Europe.

In fact, a group based in Hong Kong, want to

meet with you about representing us in Asia. I've got their contact details in my office. I sent an email to Dr. Lau and Sir Anthony to ask if they would check this group out; we'll probably have an answer before you take off for Hong Kong.

Sorry about the Sunday meeting, I know you were hoping to leave Sunday for Hong Kong, but things are moving so fast that I want to make sure we're not going off the rails anywhere. I thought we'd have presentations from Stanley, Grant and myself then hear what you wish to put on the table. I guess three to four hours should do it. I'd like to see some decisions come out of it. I was waiting to get your agreement, but maybe we should patch in Bev on Skype, what do you think?"

"Bev and I are equal partners Bill, you never need my permission to include her or to pick up the phone and call her if you wish. There are no secrets between us, and there will never be any politics in this company. So good idea, why don't you call her and see if she' s available?"

Shannon had heard some good things about a restaurant called the Crazy Crustacean not far from the hotel so they went there and were pleasantly surprised. Despite the whimsical name, the restaurant served some of the best local seafood in the Bay area.

The next morning Shannon and Doc went to the office early to get a tour before the interviews started. Their first reaction was that the offices were adequate but could use a little of Shannon's magic. She said she would come back soon and do some touching up. In the meantime, she took a lot of photos of the space to take away with her. They both felt that Kea was a great person and that she would be a strong asset in the long term.

The conference room was on the small side and rather sparsely furnished in Doc's opinion, but would do for their interviews.

Doc had asked that the Friday meetings be with developer candidates who had already been vetted by both Grant and Stanley following their presentations. He was interested in watching the final interview process that determined if an offer would be extended to the candidate.

Doc said, "Shannon would you like to sit in on the interviews? I have agreed to be a fly on the wall observing only while the interview was in progress and only offering input if I had any, after the interview but prior to the offer. If you sit in it'll increase your understanding of the process that would be beneficial to us both."

"Sure, I'll sit in if it won't bother anyone. It would be useful for me to get a better understanding of the candidates from a couple of perspectives. The more I know about them, the better I can design living and working environments for them."

The interviews went well all morning with Doc having very little to contribute and accepting Bill's decisions on which ones to bring on board. Bill had a great way with interviews, a natural human resources kind of guy who made the candidates comfortable and ready to reveal their innermost thoughts.

He even had a nice way of turning down candidates that didn't fit. He told them that they didn't quite qualify now but perhaps, with some more field experience, they might qualify at a later date. In the interim, they should do some software development on their own and re-apply when they have something that they think is near market ready. There could be no promises; however he told them that he would look at their future development submission as a basis for another application. By noon, Doc felt that they had seen enough and he and Shannon headed back to the hotel.

Doc said, "Well what are your thoughts?"

"I think Bill is a super interviewer; he has a style that I always liked when I was being interviewed. I think even those candidates who weren't accepted today left the meeting thinking that they would try hard to qualify to come back for another shot at it. The DVD presentation on Lion's Pride impressed all who saw it. They recognize that here is a developer's dream and a good shot at having their work turn into a very profitable career."

"You see, that's why I like it when you take an active role in our business. You inspire fresh ideas. Just now for instance what you said about the developer's dream and Lion's Pride gave me an idea. We're going to shoot a DVD of several of our early success's that have software they have developed now bringing in steady profits. We can tell their stories while they are in Africa showing them on a photo safari, visiting Victoria Falls, enjoying the recreational facilities at Lion's Pride and working in their deluxe suites. Having the successful developers tell their own story will drive home to potential recruits that it can be done when they work with us.

In the afternoon, Shannon called O'Leary's to see how Sean was doing and got an earful from him about how well things were going. The four new developers joined Hilda and were quickly settling in. Kea had called to reserve ten more suites for people who would arrive next week, so O'Leary's was filling up fast. Donald hadn't had any more problems with the workload, so Sean said to keep 'em coming.

Dinner with Brian and Kristen was a very nice evening. Doc wanted to treat them to a memorable dinner to thank them for the help that they had given to them thus far. Brian's connections into the high-tech world were invaluable and saved Doc and Bill lot's of time getting set up. Doc invited them to visit Lion's Pride for a holiday once the opening was completed and things settled down.

The Sunday meeting was hosted by Bill, who started off by saying, "Thank you all for coming and hi to Bev in Africa. I'm sorry to drag you away from your friends and families on a Sunday afternoon and I'll try to move this along as fast as I can. I felt it was an ideal time for us to meet while we have the visiting royalty with us," he gestured towards Doc and Shannon. "As you all know, the recruiting program has generated far more potential candidates than any of us expected. Frankly, we are the victims of our own success right now with more people to deal with than we have room for. I believe Doc has some ideas in this regard so I won't dwell on it at this point. I think that Grant, Kea, and Stanley are to be congratulated on their professional handling of this tsunami of business. While it has been chaotic around here, to say the least, I am pretty sure that this chaos has been contained and not been evident to the developers. Grant, let's hear from you first."

Grant put up a PowerPoint presentation and said, "Since we all know where we are at right now, I wanted to focus on where I think we should be going in terms of recruiting in the future. So far we have only scratched the surface, we haven't even reached out to ten percent of the universities and colleges offering computer software related credentials in the USA. These slides will show you, based on our original success rate, that we could probably recruit thousands of candidates in the States never mind other markets worldwide.

We have many options, but the easiest thing would be to bump up our selection criteria. For instance, only accepting developers that have had software make it to market. Or we could keep on the way we are going, recruiting potential developers and expanding facilities to accommodate them as fast as we can. I'm offering these ideas for consideration by the group as we look to the future rather than anything I expect we'll resolve today."

Bill thanked Grant and asked for questions.

Doc said, "Thanks for both a tremendous recruiting effort and a great presentation. Please email me a copy of the PowerPoint presentation so I can look at it more closely on our way to Hong Kong."

Bev said, "I would like to add my thanks to Doc's for all the hard work done so far, you are quite a team!"

Bill said, "Ok Stanley, you're up."

Stanley said, "Thus far our efforts, rightly so, have been focused on recruiting, and I have been working closely with Grant. I see the future for me being more devoted to the sales side and, in fact, I propose that we hire another sales rep to be based on the east coast, preferably New York City, we have four products now on the market, and sales are exceeding expectations. Doc, these are the developers that you will be creating joint venture companies for while you're in Hong Kong. The point is that we'll soon be generating product much faster than I can sell by myself. So I'd like to get ahead of the curve and be prepared for the flow of product that our people will generate."

Bill said, "Thanks, Stanley, comments?"

Doc said, "I have a comment. Stanley, if Bill agrees, hire an east coast rep and a west coast rep as soon as you identify the ones you want. I want you in the role of Sales Manager overseeing the sales force because I agree; we need to get on the leading edge of this company and not be constantly playing catch up. I have a couple of ideas that I want to put on the table, not for decision purposes but consideration purposes. I have your business plan to read on the plane and you'll have the ideas that Shannon and I have for you which are detailed in this memo we have prepared for you. Bev, Kea will email you a copy after the meeting. The discussion Shannon and I had on the way out here centered on alternatives for the future of the company.

Given that we have determined that there is a high demand for what we have to offer we could expand Lion's Pride by adding suites perhaps to the garage foundation. The architect and builder are considering this alternative, and we should have their thoughts by the end of next week. Right Bev?"

"Yes, they said they'd be back to me with a preliminary feasibility study and estimate of costs and timing no later than next Friday. They have already had engineers and other technical types crawling around the site."

Doc said, "Another alternative is to expand O'Leary's and add more suites there. Another is to build new facilities here in Silicon Valley and/or maybe in the Vancouver, Canada market, perhaps at Whistler.

Another idea is to reproduce resort/campus facilities similar to Lion's Pride in exotic destinations like Bali, the Caribbean, maybe the south of France.

We could also look at creating a two-staged process for the developers. Under this scenario, they all start off in whatever facilities we decide on here in the US and Canada, then only the ones who produce at least one marketable product get to go to Lion's Pride. So lots of ideas on the table, everyone should think about them, discuss amongst you here in the San Francisco office. Let's do a conference call in a month to kick it around some more and hopefully, come to some decisions. For now Shannon and I have a plane to catch so unless there is anything else, we'll say our goodbyes to all."

CHAPTER THIRTY-SEVEN

Landing in Hong Kong was always exciting for Doc. He had heard that Hong Kong meant, "Fragrant Harbor" and the city certainly had a unique odor, not entirely unpleasant. A frequent visitor, even with their eyes closed, always knew as soon as they left the air-conditioned airport terminal, they were in Hong Kong.

As it was Shannon's first visit to Asia, she was overwhelmed by the combination of sensual elements that were comprised of sight, odor, and sounds. The boat traffic in the harbor, the car traffic and the movement of millions of active people in such close quarters, mostly engaged in some form of commerce, all combined to over-whelm the uninitiated.

Doc said, "You're going to love it here. The people of Hong Kong live to make money. I am sure the first expression all Chinese babies born in Hong Kong learn is, 'Yeng-Lei' or profit."

Doc had ordered a stretch limo to pick them up at the airport. He asked Shannon, "What do you feel like, dinner at the club or straight home to bed?"

"I'm not too tired; the bedroom on that jet is a real asset on these long haul flights. I probably slept half the way."

"A little better than half the way actually. So the club then?"

"Sure let's have a look at this place you have

been talking so much about."

To Shannon, The Aberdeen Marina Club was incredible, just as Doc had said it was.

They had their choice of five dining alternatives, and Shannon chose the Horizon Chinese Restaurant, determined to get right into the local ambiance. Doc had phoned ahead from the car and reserved a window table overlooking the swimming pool with waterfall and the marina full of luxurious yachts. Off to their left, the Jumbo Floating Restaurant was aglow with thousands of colorful lights bringing an exciting life to the harbor at night.

After dinner, Doc gave Shannon a quick tour of the rest of the facility and said she should come back tomorrow for a swim and get her membership card.

When they arrived home, the driver carried in their luggage, and the doorman welcomed Doc back. They went to their suite and Shannon wanted a glass of wine and a tour of the "flat" in that order. Doc fixed them each a drink and showed her around. As they looked at the various rooms, Doc said, "You can imprint your style on the place. I purposely left it pretty plain and devoid of clutter so that you could have some fun with it. As I mentioned to you, once things settle down, we might move aboard a boat. But we can talk about that some more once you have had a better look at the club and have seen some of the live-a-board vessels."

"I don't even want to think about moving

anywhere tonight. I feel like I haven't stood still in a week, actually I haven't now that I think about it."

Shannon went out on their large patio to watch the passing boats and Doc went to the kitchen to refill their drinks.

When he came out, he said, "I've left the card for the limo service on the counter beside your key to the suite. There is also a card with a few things on it in English and Cantonese. I've listed our address and phone number here. Also listed is the address for the Aberdeen Marina Club, same for the Hong Kong Club, which is downtown. My lawyer and accountant's offices have been told to take care of you if you should call and need anything whatsoever. When you call for a car, they don't speak very much English so if you say 'Doc home one' they'll send a standard Mercedes here to pick you up. If you say, 'Doc home two', they'll send a stretch limo here. If you go out with the car service, when you get where you are going just say 'wait' and the car will stay around where you are, watching for you. If you don't want him to wait just say, 'go' and he'll leave.

If you get stuck, call my temporary secretary, Winnie, at the accounting firm listed on the card. She's Chinese and has been told to expect the odd call from you when you need to deal with some Chinese people who don't speak English. She is a great lady and will take excellent care of you."

"I think I'll be in good hands as long as I have the card full of numbers. Tomorrow I think I'll sleep in then test this card by ordering a car and going to the Marina Club for a workout, swim, and lunch. I was thinking of booking a tennis lesson but don't want to push it too hard given the jet lag."

"Good idea, you could toss in a spa visit for a massage while you are at it then home for a nap. I've been thinking about a spot of St. Agnes tomorrow night."

"I could go for that, what time will you be home?"

"No idea. I've got a breakfast meeting at the Hong Kong Club with Sir Anthony, our lawyer and Dr. Lau, our accountant to set up the joint venture companies we need. Then I'm off to see office space with my realtor friend Art Chandler. Then an interview with our potential administrative assistant, and back to the Hong Kong Club for a drink with the Managing Director of the firm that wants to represent us in Asia. To end the day I have a reception at the Canadian Embassy. So where do you wish to have dinner?"

"Since you are going to have a day like that, I know what I'm going to do. I'm going to go to that grocery store you showed me at the Marina Club; I'm going to buy some ingredients and come back here to fix you a home-cooked dinner."

"Now that'll be the best part of my day!"

The next morning Doc had already left for his

breakfast meeting at the Hong Kong Club when Shannon woke and fixed herself a cup of tea. In a way, it seemed strange to her to be far away from Scranton and not in a plane or a hotel. As she sipped her tea on the patio gazing out over the South China Sea, she felt that Hong Kong and she were going to get along just fine. She was determined to get Doc to teach her some 'market Cantonese'. That's enough of the language to get by in most day-to-day transactions like shopping, traveling by cab, bus or the famous subway system, the MTR.

Doc arrived at the Hong Kong Club for his meeting with Sir Anthony and Dr. Tom Lau. They discussed the formation of the new companies that would be required to handle the affairs of the joint venture arrangements between the developers and Doc and Bev's company, Software Conceptions Inc., (SCI). They met, sat down, made small talk and ordered breakfast. Sir Anthony, or Anton as he preferred to be called, said, "The accountants Tom has assigned to your file and the lawyers that I assigned have met. They've developed a template for you to look at. It's designed for your particular situation. As long as all the companies are to be fifty-fifty joint ventures and your fifty percent is to be always held by SCI, all we need is the full legal name and address for your joint venture partners. As of this morning, we have ten joint venture companies to create and…"

Doc interrupted and said, "No we have four

to create."

Anton said, "That was as of yesterday; there are six more as of today."

Doc said, "Sorry, I forgot to check my email this morning. I guess I'd better start staying on top of that now that things are happening so quickly."

Tom said, "Our SCI team, as Anton and I call it, have put the template up on a secure website. I'll email the URL to you. Each time you want to do a joint venture, simply have the JV partner read the agreement online. If they are happy, have them download, sign and send us the two pages agreeing to our appointment as the lawyers and accountants for the JV.

Doc said, "It's slick. I like it. We can handle the whole thing online. I'm sure some of them will have lawyers and accountants that will have questions, so they can direct them to your SCI team. Can all the software products developed by one JV partner be handled by the original JV company?"

Anton said, "We've designed the template so that all you need is one JV company per developer, provided that the partners remain the same. When a developer produces a second software product, you just have to advise us by email and we'll put it into the JV."

"Great, please copy Bill and Bev on this. You may have to walk Bill and his team through this process for these first ones until they get the hang of it." Looking at Tom, Doc said, "I'm using one of your visiting client's offices to interview a possible executive assistant this afternoon so I may see you later."

Doc noticed his realtor friend, Art, coming into the restaurant, so he excused himself, said his goodbyes and signed the chit to pay for the breakfasts. Doc and Art shook hands and went out to Art's car, which the driver had parked in the circular driveway and was dusting with a large feather duster. The car took them through Central District, which was bustling as usual at eleven o'clock on a weekday morning.

Art said, "I think you'll like this space. The building is a classic piece of Hong Kong historical architecture. It was renovated about twenty years ago. The best thing about this office and why it will go quickly is that the previous tenant was an Aussie billionaire who maintained it as a base for dealing with his diversified interests in the region. He completely gutted it and built an amazing space to impress his visitors, and I'm sure they were impressed. Although up until his death last month he had only conducted business here on a few occasions according to the lady he had as an executive assistant. You'll see, the work was done six years ago, but it looks like it was completed last week." When they arrived, Doc took one look at the building and said, "I'll take it."

Art said, "Well let's at least take a walk through before you go signing any leases."

Doc said, "Let's do it."

The lobby and elevator doors were all redone in their original classic finishes. The original art on the lobby walls depicted scenes of early Hong Kong, many featuring Tea Clippers in the harbor, antique looking wall sconces added to the overall feeling of going back in time. The elevators themselves had been replaced recently with new ones that had also been finished to fit in with the theme of originality. Art pushed the button for the eighth floor. The space, Art said had been built to impress and it sure did. Doc's mouth dropped open when he saw the interior. There were four good size offices, three of which had never been used. The entry lobby featured an antique desk elaborately hand carved in rosewood. The seating was all brown suede that was also the wall covering.

The executive office featured another elaborately carved rosewood desk the size of an aircraft carrier, albeit one from a small country. There was a private washroom with a shower and closet for fresh clothes and a built in wet bar and audiovisual center complete with video conferencing equipment. Art said, "You know when you're in Hong Kong by yourself and you go to an evening function and don't want to go all the way to Repulse Bay after? Or you have a late night meeting here and just don't want to go home to an empty flat? Just push this button. Go ahead, push it."

Doc pushed it, and a queen-size Murphy bed glided quietly down. It had been fitted so well that there was no way anyone could tell there was a bed in the wall.

Doc said, "Amazing I sure never expected that. If you've got the paperwork on you, I'll sign now."

Art opened his briefcase and produced the lease and the keys. Doc signed the lease, gave Art a company check and the deal was done. He called Vivian, the executive assistant candidate and told her the meeting site has been changed from the offices of Lau and Porter to the offices of Software Conceptions Inc. She asked for the address, and it occurred to Doc that he didn't know so he asked Art who said, "88 Ice House Street, Eighth Floor, Suite 8."

The interview went well. Vivian had come as a referral by Winnie, Doc's part-time executive assistant at Lau and Porter. Doc went over her resume, told her about the business of SCI talked about the duties that he expected her to perform and asked her when she could start. She said, "When would you like me to start?"

Doc said, "How about tomorrow morning?"

"Sure, why not?"

"Here is a key for the office. Tomorrow get it set up with all the necessities like phones, photocopiers and everything we'll need to do business from here. Get Winnie to set us up with an account at the office supply places that she uses. Her boss can make the necessary account arrangements through HKSB. Can you go to our San Francisco office next week, once you have this office ready? I'd like you to get to know our people in that office and to work with Kea to develop office systems for doing things that are standardized between the two offices.

At least at the beginning you will be working here mostly alone, coordinating things with our lawyers, accountants and the people in San Francisco. Ask Winnie to introduce you to the teams of lawyers and accountants that have been assembled to deal with our business. Get one of those notice boards that you see in office building lobbies and have it mounted on the wall beside the front door. Put up the names of each new business that we create and let the lawyers and accountants know that the new address for all our businesses is 88 Ice House Street, Eighth Floor, Suite 8. Any questions?"

Doc met with the company interested in representing them in Asia. He got along well with the Managing Director, a very business like individual and a Chartered Accountant, Wing-See Lo. Doc felt that there could be a potential business relationship with her company at some point. For now, however, he said he wanted to wait until they got a little further down the line and consolidated the work that they already had underway. He said that he'd get back to her in a few months.

The reception at the Canadian Embassy was uneventful. Doc did get the opportunity to renew acquaintances with a few old contacts, but his heart wasn't in it. He wanted to get home to

Shannon and relax a bit.

For her part, Shannon had a wonderful day. She worked out, swam and had lunch at the Aberdeen Marina Club with a lovely lady, Eileen, who lived aboard a fifty-five-foot sailboat at the club. Eileen gave her the inside scoop on life aboard. After lunch, Eileen took her on a tour of the docks pointing out the various boats that people lived aboard. They finished the tour with an iced tea in the cockpit of Eileen's boat 'Passing Wind' and she was off to the grocery store.

When Doc got home, he was ready for some conversation that didn't involve work. Shannon had managed to find some corned beef and made Doc a delicious corned beef and cabbage dinner using the O'Leary's recipe.

On the way to the plane the next morning, Doc took Shannon for a drive around the Island then to see the Hong Kong office. He wasn't surprised to see Vivian already working away on her cell phone ordering all the essentials they would need. Shannon was very impressed with Vivian and the offices and picked out one for her own.

Doc promised that the next time they come to Hong Kong they would stay for at least a week. Shannon could do her thing with the office space if she wanted to, although there didn't seem to be much left to do at least from Doc's perspective. They made quick video conference calls to Bev and Anne at Lion's Pride, Sean at O'Leary's and Bill in San Francisco. Bev reported that they were checking in twenty developers on Friday, so there was a lot of excitement about this event. Sean said all was well at O'Leary's and he had a deal to discuss with them on their return. Bill reported six more software products ready for market. Today Stanley and Grant were interviewing several sales rep candidates to work for Stanley selling the developer's software for the west coast region. Stanley was heading for New York for interviews with sales rep candidates the following day. Doc gave them all an update and said to expect Vivian to call Kea to set up a trip to work with her for a few weeks.

They arrived at the airport and were greeted by the crew then took off for Bangkok not suspecting what this trip would do to the rest of their lives.

CHAPTER THIRTY-EIGHT

Doc arrived in Bangkok in time for a reception at the US Embassy arranged by Bill via the DDO's office. He met several interesting contacts, one of which had a rather large software project for SCI to bid on. Now that he was genuinely looking for these opportunities, he was glad to have kept communications open with Jim and the DDO.

Shannon had met Andrew's wife Cathy, and they'd taken a Mandarin Hotel limo to do some shopping. Cathy was an expert shopper and knew all the places for deals. Among other things, Shannon wanted to buy silk for her wedding party dresses. She was also looking in antique shops wherever she traveled trying to find different and exotic pieces for the cottage and the Scranton house. She decided not to buy anything for their Hong Kong flat until they decided what they were going to do about the idea of living aboard a boat. Shannon had dinner with Cathy and Doc with Andrew because time was short, and Doc wanted to talk business with Andrew in private. Andrew took Doc to his business club, the Pacific City Club, where he had arranged for a private room. The organization was similar to the most expensive business clubs in the world's major cities. It had all the trappings of the Hong Kong Club, and the private room Andrew had reserved was both posh and comfortable with the requisite over-stuffed leather club chairs and many beautiful pieces of English antique furniture. Doc had explained in a phone call to Andrew at his home that he wanted to speak with him away from the Mandarin.

Their butler delivered the drinks and asked if they would like a cigar. They both said that perhaps after dinner they might have one with their brandy. One should no longer mention the word "brandy" around Doc as it automatically conjures up thoughts best left for when the business is done.

Andrew took a drink of his gin and tonic, Doc sipped his Laphroaig and opened the discussion, "Andrew, I'm sorry about the all the melodrama. But I have some business to discuss with you that requires absolute confidentiality, and I didn't want us to meet at the Mandarin for fear of someone hearing our conversation. I'll just lay everything out on the table then answer your questions, OK?"

"Yes, I've found that to be the most efficient way to deal with business."

"Shannon and I are about to purchase a half interest in O'Leary's Arms, a Relais & Chateaux property in Scranton Pennsylvania. Sean O'Leary, the owner of the hotel, is like a father to Shannon. She has worked for him since the day she arrived from Ireland, and he treats her like a daughter. O'Leary Management, which we will also acquire a half interest in if all goes as planned, holds a management contract on a property we own in Zimbabwe called Lion's Pride. This is a grand old mansion on 1,900 acres, which we are renovating into a Relais & Chateaux style property. It will become a resort/campus for eighty software developers who will be in residence there and creating software. I would like to see this operation grow, and there are several ways to accomplish this, all of which are under study now by our senior staff. We have taken the GM from O'Leary's to manage Lion's Pride leaving the management of the Scranton property up to Sean and an assistant GM. For now this is working; however, Sean wants to focus on management contracts, so we're going to need a strong GM with extensive international hotel management experience to run the Scranton property. Our long-term plan is to open more resort/campus style properties and to look for management contracts at other Grand Luxe hotels. Ultimately we would want you to become President of the resort/campus chain and management company."

"I'm a bit confused, you refer to it as a resort/campus chain and also as a residence for software developers. Which is it?"

"It's both. For now O'Leary's Arms is a pure hotel, although we are using part of it temporarily to house developers until the renovations to the Zimbabwe property are finished. We are moving twenty developers into Lion's Pride this Friday and another twenty on each of the following three Fridays. Within a month, we will be fully operational at Lion's Pride.

"I'm certainly intrigued by the idea of running a chain of five-star plus hotels where demand is practically guaranteed."

"Can you get away for a week?"

"Do you mean now?"

"Yes. I thought that you, Cathy, Shannon and I could go over to Zimbabwe the day after tomorrow. You and Cathy can see what we're up to, and Shannon needs to do some last minute interior design oversight. Then we could carry on to Scranton so you could see O'Leary's and meet Sean. All expenses paid and no commitment required on your part until after you've visited the places and talked it through as a couple."

"I'll talk to Cathy to see if she can get away right now. I don't think she has too much on her calendar that can't be moved to accommodate an all expense paid trip around the world. Any chance we can see some wild animals?"

"I'll go you one better than that; we'll charter a helicopter to show you the property then fly over to Victoria Falls. We'll then go to a big game safari place I know where we can be driven out into the wild to see some big stuff first hand. How does that sound?"

"Sounds like Cathy better be free to join me because I'm going."

"Shannon and I are going down to Jakarta this evening, I have two meetings there in the morning, then three in Kuala Lumpur. Then we will be back tomorrow afternoon, stay at the Mandarin overnight and the four of us can take off for Zimbabwe the next morning.

The flight will give us lots of time to explain everything to Cathy and to answer any other questions you might have."

"Where are you meeting Shannon for your flight to Jakarta?"

"At your hotel. We can drive back together."

Doc had arranged a late check-out at the Mandarin Jakarta and a car to take Shannon on a quick city tour while he held his meetings in a private conference room in the hotel.

In between meetings he called Bill and was told that the software production was now up to twenty-two sales with a dozen more likely to close in a few days. If this rate continues, the $450 million in Zimbabwe will have been repatriated to their Hong Kong account in under two years. Bill said that Stanley had several great sales rep candidates for the east coast territory, and Grant had narrowed it down to two candidates for the west coast. Bill said he might hire both of the west coast reps and base one in Vancouver and one in their Silicon Valley office. He might also get Stanley to hire two, one for New York, and one for Chicago to deal with the Midwest. Doc agreed with this strategy and suggested the Vancouver person be fluent in Cantonese and Mandarin so they can also cover Asia for now.

In Kuala Lumpur, Doc took a suite at the Mandarin and arranged a quick city tour for Shannon. His meetings generated some SCI potential contracts and some intelligence that might be useful to Jim and the DDO. After his meetings, they boarded the plane to return to Bangkok and Shannon immediately went to bed. Doc put through a call to Jim on his secure cell.

Jim answered, "Hi Doc, the DDO and I were just talking about you guys. How are you doing?"

"We're doing fine, our new business is screaming busy. Bill hardly gets out of the office, and I am hardly ever on the ground."

"How is Shannon holding up, is she ready for the wedding?"

"She's doing fine. We are on a whirlwind tour of Asia, and she's sleeping in the bedroom as we head to Bangkok to pick up two passengers and continue to Zimbabwe. I wish I were getting air miles. The wedding plans are proceeding quite well under the direction of Shannon's mom. We'd be in deep trouble without her calling the shots.

Basically, I gave her an unlimited Amex and all we have to do is fly in on the big day."

"Well I'm looking forward to the wedding, I love Ireland and will probably stay on an extra few days to play some golf."

"Well stay as long as you like as our guest. The hotel has guaranteed to hold the rooms for as long as the guests want them. Getting down to a little business now. I heard from a fellow in Kuala Lumpur, a highly placed official that there is a significant shipment planning to be loaded in containers headed for Vancouver and Seattle on a ship called Sea Voyager registered in Panama. The street value is rumored to be in the order of $150 million USD."

"Wow. Thanks, Doc we'll start tracking that ship right now. Any idea of where she'll be loaded with the materials and when?"

"My contact mentioned that it would be loaded at Krong Preah Sihanoukville sometime in the last week of this month."

"We'll have them on satellite from the time they load and have a welcoming party waiting for them in Vancouver once we determine who the receiver is. We owe you big time for this one."

"Ok boss, see you in Killarney."

Doc's phone rang and it was his friend from Hong Kong Shanghai Bank so Doc said, "Hi Phillip, what's up?"

"Hi Doc, the money is starting to roll into the SCI account and the accounts for the developers. We've discussed with Bev how she wants the SCI funds invested but so far we haven't talked about the developer's money."

"What do you suggest?"

"I could prepare a standard agreement offering them the option to have their funds placed into the same investments that SCI funds go into. Or they could instruct us to move the funds into their personal banks. They could just leave the money here in an interest bearing account, although I wouldn't recommend that alternative because the interest is so low."

"Ok. Prepare the offering letter and run it by Bev and Bill. If they don't have any problems with it, then send it out to the developers. Automatically send one to the JV developer partner as each one get's their company set up by Anton and Tom. We should get this process as automated as possible."

"All right I'll get something to Bev and Bill by tomorrow and copy you."

The next morning the group was wheels up at six a.m. and on their way to Zimbabwe. Cathy, an avid reader, and researcher, hardly ever went anywhere without as much information as possible on the destination. She was full of questions on Lion's Pride so Shannon played the DVD on the giant screen. Both Cathy and Andrew were amazed by the beauty and facilities at the property.

Cathy said, "When you explained what you were doing, I was having trouble getting my head around why all these geniuses would want to team up with you and go live in Africa, now I see why."

Shannon said, "Wait until you get there. The place will be run to five star standards, the service will be superb. The food without equal under the care of chef Griff, who came to us from La Bristol in Paris. The accommodations are as luxurious as your Mandarin and an array of recreational alternatives that make it the best resort style property in Africa. Probably one of the top in the world. Our objective was to create an environment so luxurious, that once a resident moves in they wouldn't want to leave. To stay, they have to produce. As part of their recruitment, they told us that their goal was to become a multi-millionaire. So at Lion's Pride they will live like one while they produce the software that will allow this objective to be a reality."

Doc said, "We thought it would take anywhere from a year to three years for us to recruit enough developers to fill Lion's Pride. Here we are two weeks from having our renovations finished and we've enough developers to fill Lion's Pride waiting. We are forced to use other facilities like O'Leary's Arms and the Four Seasons, Silicon Valley to take care of our overload. Our developers are not even in Lion's Pride yet, and they're cranking out a marketable product from their temporary quarters. You can see why we are going to need someone of your caliber…… no, we are going to need you, to see our growth ambitions fulfilled."

On arrival at Lion's Pride, Bev and Anne welcomed Cathy and Andrew as if they were already members of the family. Anne could hardly wait to show off her hotel to a GM with credentials and experience like Andrew but suggested that the new arrivals have a spa massage and swim to shake off some of the jet lag.

She personally led them to their suite, which, of course, featured the welcoming gifts of wine, flowers and chocolate dipped strawberries. In the suite, Andrew said to Anne, "I'll pass on the spa if you are ready for a tour."

"I'm ready, what about you Cathy, do you want to join us or rest a bit?"

"I think I'll relax and do the pool and spa with Shannon and Doc."

"I'm not sure that Shannon will be there, last I saw her she was off to inspect the interior décor work. Maybe Doc will be there but if not, make yourself at home and enjoy the spa."

Anne showed Andrew all around, introduced him to the senior staff and chef Griff, who answered all his questions. They looked at the guest floor that would be ready in a few days, and Andrew was most impressed with the quality of the rooms. They took Robert's golf cart drive around the property for a quick look at the stables and the garage full of antique cars. Andrew was most interested in seeing the staff quarters, so they went over to the staff village. He could see children and their parents playing in the swimming pool, mothers pushing infants on swings in the park and kids everywhere riding bicycles. He went into the small store and ordered a coke while he talked to the shopkeeper about life at Lion's Pride. The storeowner said that the people working here understood that they are way better off than any other group of employees in Africa, and no one would leave of their own accord.

Anne said, "If you have seen enough for now, we should head back to the group who are no doubt at poolside near the Zulu Bar, Doc's favorite place."

"Sure let's go, it's about time for something cool to offset this heat."

At poolside, Fred approached Andrew and said, "Welcome to Lion's Pride Mr. Chang, my name is Fred, may I get you something from the bar?"

"Hello Fred, what do you suggest?"

"Something tells me this will do it." He lifted the lid off a silver bowl full of ice and set it in front of Andrew. In the center of the ice was a new creation of Fred's he called the Lioness's Pride. It was a mixture of local fruit juices dark rum, light rum and a liqueur that Andrew couldn't identify. It was served in a tall frosted glass that was kept chilled by the ice in the silver bowl, the lid kept the sun off it."

"This is a fantastic drink Fred and an incredible presentation, thank you."

To permit her guests to enjoy the pleasant African evening, Anne had planned a poolside dinner. Chef Griff pulled out all the stops with his signature dish, a whole lamb roasting on a spit turning over hot coals served with four vegetables, all local and an amazing potato concoction of his own design.

Andrew said, "What's the plan for tomorrow?"

Anne said, "Doc told me that you wanted to see Victoria Falls, so we have a helicopter scheduled to arrive at nine o'clock in the morning to take you to Victoria Falls. After a look at the world's largest waterfall and a picnic lunch, you'll be delivered to Tom's Safaris for an afternoon of animal photography in the wild. You'll return here for drinks at six o'clock and dinner at seven o'clock. How is that for a plan?"

Cathy said, "It sounds wonderful, is there anyone else coming along?"

"Unfortunately no, Doc's busy with Bev, Shannon is driving the decorators as hard as she can. I'm sure you can imagine what my days are like Andrew, with the first guests arriving in a few days. Fred has volunteered to accompany you so, you are in good hands."

CHAPTER THIRTY-NINE

Shannon decided to stay on at Lion's Pride to oversee the completion of the first floor of rooms and to move things along on the other floors. The plane would return to pick her up after flying the Changs to Bangkok. Doc had to go now, as he wanted to introduce Andrew to Sean and the O'Leary's brand. Also, his Ottawa condo had sold, and they needed him for closing details. Typically he would have dealt with this by email and courier; however, he also wanted to check out the cottage. Gary had sent an email to say the work was done and awaiting his final approval.

On the flight home, Doc could tell that Andrew was warming to the idea of joining up with them. He had spent a long time talking to Bev, and it was obvious from the way he spoke about her today that he was most impressed with her, both as an individual and as a businesswoman. Cathy too was asking the right questions if one was considering a move to O'Leary's. The Mandarin Oriental organization was an old, well-established part of the world's five-star hotel industry and Andrew no doubt had a bright future there. To leave Mandarin for a new start-up like SCI required a leap of faith normally beyond Cathy's leaping ability. However in this case she recognized the strength of this new company in terms of assets and quality people.

She was slowly becoming enthusiastic about her husband's possible change of careers.

Andrew had called into his hotel and spoken to the assistant general manager who reported that all was under control and told Andrew to relax if he needed him he knew how to find him. After the call, Andrew stretched out on one of the couches and took a long nap. The previous day had been memorable to say the least but tiring as well. Doc used the small office set up in the bedroom to deal with email and to make a few phone calls. He called Vivian on her cell at the new Hong Kong office and said," So how are you doing, any problems?"

"No sir, the phone system is coming in this afternoon, the photocopier tomorrow, the computers arrived today and the computer technicians are setting them up as we speak. By the next time you come into the office, you'll think we have been here for years. I had to order another notice board for the wall outside the office door. We are getting so many new companies that it is taking us several hours a day just to set up the new files. I am planning to visit San Francisco, probably by next Tuesday or Wednesday. I wanted to mention something; Kea said she was booking me on Cathay Pacific first class. Should I be traveling first class, it is so expensive?"

"You are worth it Vivian, besides all our employees travel first class. We've found that the extra cost is worth it because often our people meet contacts as they fly, sometimes resulting in revenue for the company. Also, we've determined that when you travel first class you arrive well rested and more efficient in doing whatever work awaits you. One other thing, don't call me sir, call me Doc."

"Alright sir, I am certainly not complaining, I just wanted you to know."

"You are still calling me sir."

"Oops, sorry sir."

"Don't be surprised if Kea books you into a suite at the Four Seasons across from our offices, just enjoy your visit and get to know the people, that's the main idea. Once things settle down at Lion's Pride, probably in two months or so, I want you to go there for a week to get to know the people and the property. Ok bye, Vivian, call me if you need me."

"Goodbye, sir."

Doc figured that Vivian's last boss must have been a tyrant because she was always calling him sir and appeared frightened or in awe of him.

He felt that over time, as she got to know him she'd become more relaxed and that they would make a good team.

He pushed the buzzer for Rosemary and got her to bring him a coffee and cookies. She was on full-time cabin service duty this flight as there were guests aboard, so she was relegated to the jump seat as an observer and frequently called into the main cabin.

As Doc was going through his email his cell phone rang, it was Bill calling. Doc answered,

"Hi Bill what's new?"

Excitedly Bill responded, "What's new?...... What's new? I'll tell you what's new. Somehow you have lit a fire under the Deputy Director of Operations of the US Drug Enforcement Agency and the President of the United States, that's what's new!"

"Whoa, slow down big fella, how come you're so excited?"

"The DDO called me to tell me that the intelligence you gave them through Jim has resulted in the single largest drug bust in history. Apparently you didn't think this intelligence was a big enough deal to share with me?"

"Hang on Bill, I was going to tell you about it but I just haven't had the time. Besides the deal wasn't supposed to go down for a few weeks yet."

"Well they either moved it up or were always intending to do it now, but let it slip that it wouldn't be for a couple of weeks as a subterfuge."

"So how come all the noise from the DDO and the President."

"Actually it's noise from the whole group, Congress, the Senate, anybody who's anybody in Foggy Bottom. They aren't releasing the dollar value of the bust; they only will say that it involved the largest bust ever in the history of the drug wars. Confidentially, the DDO feels that it could be in the billion-dollar range at street prices. The whole ship was full of it. The President wants to give us another medal and the DDO hit him up with a more practical idea. Are you sitting down?"

"Yes."

"The President has had the government procurement office put us on their preferred supplier list for software. By itself, this has the potential for us to develop a new division that could make us serious players in the software development business and make the company incredibly profitable."

"You had better talk to Brian White about some recommendations for an executive to head up this division when things start to happen, they'll happen fast. I'm heading for Scranton with Andrew Chang and need a day and night there. Then we'll fly to Brockville and Ottawa and on to San Francisco. I'll send the plane on to take Andrew and Cathy home and I'll spend a few days with you so we can digest this latest development. You'd better start thinking about more office space, probably twice or three times the space you already have."

"I'm on it, there is a great space coming up on the floor above where we are now. The landlord is willing to put in a stairway connecting the two spaces. I'll show you when you get here."

Doc said goodbye and went out to talk to the Changs and be sociable for a bit. He said, "A few things have come up that I need to take care of.

So after we leave Scranton, I need a brief one-hour stopover in Brockville, then an hour in Ottawa and then we're off to San Francisco for a half-day with Bill. The plane will take you to Bangkok and carry on to pick up Shannon and return for me."

"Boy, your pilots are kept busy," Andrew said.

"Yes, we're getting our own plane. Here I'll show you the DVD of it. As you see Shannon designed the interior to provide a double bunk cabin with a toilet and shower that the crew can access from the flight deck. Rosemary is a pilot and working on her jet engine certification. On long haul flights, one of them can sleep and shower then take the place of another, so they all get some rest and shower time. Theoretically we could fly around the clock. We wouldn't, however."

Cathy said, "That's interesting that Rosemary is in training to fly jets, good for her."

Doc said, "Yes she's quite a lady. She also has paramedic training. Randy, our co-pilot is studying meteorology online. So we're going to be pretty well self-contained."

Rosemary served a fantastic beef Wellington prepared by chef Griff and poured a bottle of Chateau Margaux that Bev had donated to the flight home.

They watched the movie 'Patton', one of Doc's favorites, then turned in for the night. Doc went into the bedroom and just sat in the easy chair thinking about all he had to do.

The next morning they touched down at Scranton airport and took the limo Sean had dispatched back to O'Leary's. After meeting Sean, Cathy went to their suite to freshen up; Sean collared Andrew and took him on a tour of the property. Doc took the opportunity to speak on the phone with the architect that Sean had identified for their house and satisfied himself that he was the right guy and had substantial environmentally friendly building design experience. Doc pointed out that it was Shannon's project, and he would have to be interviewed by her before being retained. Doc ran over his wish list, and the architect made copious notes. Doc said, "Shannon will be back next week so she'll give you a call. We're both most anxious to get this house built, but we want it done right. Be forewarned, Shannon is an interior designer so working for her will present some challenges that you might otherwise not have to endure. It's kind of like when a nurse has to go to the doctor for some complaint. Get my drift?"

Sean and Andrew hit it off immediately, both from separate cultural backgrounds, but both united in the world of five-star hotel management. Andrew loved everything about O'Leary's Arms and marveled at the suites that were every bit as good as his Mandarin Oriental Suites in Bangkok. They had dinner together at O'Leary's then the Changs excused themselves to head for their suite. It had been a long flight and an exciting day, and they were exhausted.

Doc and Sean went to the pub for a drink or two. Doc said, "In case we do the purchase of the half interest in O'Leary's, I took the initiative of speaking to Andrew about the possibility of joining us as GM here for now with possible promotion to President when we expand into a chain. I realize that was presumptuous of me but things are moving fast with Software Conceptions Inc., and I can't afford to waste a lot of time."

"We'll do a deal on O'Leary's. I'd rather discuss it with you and Shannon together but rest assured a deal will be done. So go ahead and offer Andrew the position. I spoke to Anne after you guys were airborne, and all three of the ladies agree that we should hire Andrew."

"Ok, I'll talk to him tomorrow on our way to San Francisco."

Doc went home to their apartment to get some fresh clothes and check the mail. He called Shannon and then spoke to Bev, filling them in on the new developments with the US government. He explained the tremendous potential for new business for their company by being listed as a preferred supplier for software. He realized that he was exhausted and fell into a deep sleep.

The next morning he had breakfast with Sean, Andrew and Cathy then had the O'Leary's limo take them to the plane. They stopped in Brockville, and Doc took them to his cottage where he conducted a whirlwind inspection and signed off on the work. He was extremely pleased and knew Shannon would feel the same. When they landed at Ottawa, Doc went into the private aircraft terminal lounge and met his realtor, signed the paperwork to sell his condo and they were wheels up in a total of 40 minutes.

They arrived at the San Francisco office in time for a meeting with all the staff. Bill had been friends with the Changs for years and was thrilled to hear that Andrew had decided to join them. Bill and Doc took the Changs for dinner at the Four Seasons and talked about old times and the exciting future that was developing with Software Conceptions Inc. and O'Leary's.

The next morning after breakfast, they said goodbye until the wedding and the Four Seasons limo took Andrew and Cathy to the plane. Bill had called an impromptu meeting since both Stanley and Grant were in the office.

Bill said, "Doc, I want to update you on events here and have the guys available to answer any questions. We've hired four representatives; one based in New York City, one in Chicago, one for here and one for Vancouver. As per your request, Syrus Yu, our Vancouver rep, is fluent in Cantonese and Mandarin and is eager to cover Asia as well as Western Canada. All the new reps are in town for training. We have organized a group lunch at the Four Seasons for you to meet them all. Stanley and Grant are actively recruiting a rep to handle government contracts; we'll base him or her in Washington. We now have 20 developers about to land in Lion's Pride with another 20 packing to go next week. We are awaiting word from Bev on the completion of the third floor but if all goes as planned the next group will check in two weeks from today. We now have forty-three developers that have produced marketable software, and all of these will go to Lion's Pride. If any of the others produce in the interim, which I am sure they will, they'll also go. So within three weeks we expect to have sixty rooms filled with another twenty available as developers qualify.

The developers who haven't produced yet will be kept here at the Four Seasons once our allocation of rooms at O'Leary's is used up. They will be on standby for when suites become available at Lion's Pride. That is, of course if they start to produce.

We're still getting applications in and will schedule a new series of interviews as soon as our new reps are trained. We have them spend time with Stanley and Grant on the road to see how it's done. They're learning how to market the software and how to recruit developers with lectures from experts in the field including people from Brian's company. So we have the foundation here for an excellent network. It'll be interesting to see how the government contracts work out. Doc, would you like to say a few words?"

Doc said, "First I want to thank all of you for your hard work in getting this company off the ground. As one of you said, we have almost become victims of our own success. We never in our wildest dreams could have foreseen the level of demand there would be for developers wanting to join us. In a very large part, it's because of your hard work that these developers came to us. Bev and I had a long meeting the day before yesterday and agreed that we need to expand quickly as soon as Lion's Pride is full and operating. The bottom line is that we are going to grow this company, so there is going to be lots of opportunity for advancement over the years. When Lion's Pride is in operation, Bev is going to work out a profit sharing program so that you will all participate financially in the success of the company."

With the meeting over, Doc called Boeing in Seattle and found out that their plane would be ready for pick up in three days. They would provide a day of training for Doug and Randy including some time in the air with a Boeing, flight instructor. Doc asked if Rosemary could sit in on the training as well, and they agreed.

Doc worked with Bill over the next three days, meeting the new people and giving them his views on the future of the company. He met with Syrus Yu and said that he wanted him to spend about half his time in the Hong Kong office. He wants him to meet Vivian, who should be arriving tomorrow and get to know her. Vivian can help him find accommodation in Hong Kong and get him started on his job there.

Having delivered the Changs to Bangkok, the

plane went on to Zimbabwe to pick up Shannon.

The plane came back from Lion's Pride with Shannon to get Doc and immediately headed for

Scranton. The flight crew had to drop off the aircraft and fly commercial back to Seattle for training.

Back in their apartment, Doc said, "Break out the St. Agnes, I need a backwash and he headed for the shower."

"Shannon said, yes it seems that it has been so long since we've made love. Our travel schedules have been so hectic."

Afterward, they went for a drink with Sean, and he took them into his private office. He handed Shannon a glass of Cristal, Doc a double Laphroaig on the rocks and he picked up his two fat fingers of Jameson's. He raised his glass and said, "First a toast to the bride and to the groom. May you have as many children as there are sands on Inch Strand Beach."

After they drank, Doc said, "Is that an old Irish toast?"

"It must be as its been made by an old Irishman about an old Irish beach in County Kerry. Now down to business. I have thought about your idea of buying a half interest in O'Leary's Arms and my answer is no." Looking at the smile fade from Shannon's pretty face he quickly added, "I have decided to give you a half interest as a wedding present. I had planned to leave it to you in my will Shannon, but this way is more fun as I get to see your smiles. I'll leave you the other half in my will."

Shannon put her glass down and gave Sean a long hug of appreciation. Doc also hugged Sean and thanked him for his generosity and said, "You said you were going to give us our wedding as a wedding present, but we'd much rather have this."

"Oh you'll get both, I like giving presents to those I love."

Doc told Sean that Andrew had accepted their offer and would start in a month. Cathy will come over to look for a place with Brenda in two weeks.

Shannon had a meeting with the architect and retained him to do the design of the new house. She went over the basic structure that she had in mind, the number and types of rooms and all the other details that she and Doc had assembled on their wish list.

Over dinner at Carmela's she said, "It's difficult to believe that we've accomplished so much in so little time. It's even harder to believe that our wedding is next week. Which reminds me, where are we going for our honeymoon?"

"It's a surprise."

CHAPTER FORTY

The new plane was terrific. Much more space than the previous one and, of course, the layout was custom designed by Shannon for their needs. On the flight to Ireland, they took a bottle of St. Agnes with them into the bedroom for their first-mile high club adventure in the new surroundings. They were arriving in Ireland a week before the event so Shannon could give her mom a hand with the final details. And Doc could get in some male bonding time golfing and fishing with Kevin O'Sullivan his new father-in-law to be. Doc had leased a cottage just outside Killarney and rented a Land Rover. They had lucked out on the weather, as it could be quite rainy this time of year. Guests started arriving three days before the big day, so the pre-wedding parties got underway. The Castle Dunloe was a grand hotel, and the guests were treated like royalty particularly as they were the guests of Sean O'Leary, a cousin of one of the owners. There was a private lounge reserved for the guests where they could congregate to meet one another, have drinks and hors d 'oeuvres. Sean took no time sourcing out a local pub and by the second day of his arrival in Ireland he was a regular there and knew at least half the patrons by name. He would drag Doc off for a few jars and a game of darts whenever he could.

Shannon's mom, Mary, had been very well

organized with side trips arranged for those interested in seeing a bit of the area. Kevin organized a golf tournament and a fishing derby, and Doc chartered a helicopter to take guests who were interested, to see various sights in the region. By the wedding day, the festivities had been well underway for at least three days. The wedding itself was almost anti-climatic, but they had a beautiful service in an absolutely gorgeous old church with a thatched roof. It was located on a lakeside in a green valley just outside of Killarney and could have come right out of a painting by Frank O'Meara.

The reception was first class with a great band, several bars and a dinner that would be talked about for years. Sean, the self-appointed and enthusiastic master of ceremonies told several of his famous jokes. He made a speech, toasted the bride, then the groom, then the maid of honor, the best man and himself as master of ceremonies. Shannon was glad she didn't have a lot of bridesmaids or Sean would have created a drinking binge that would have gone on to sunrise. Everyone danced, laughed, wished Doc and Shannon well and had a good time.

The following day many of the guests headed home or off on side trips, a few lingered on, playing golf, fishing or sightseeing. Doc and Shannon left a few days later on their undis-closed honeymoon. When they were airborne, Doc said, "Ok where do you want to go, it's time for you to make a decision?"

"I didn't even think of a place since you said it was a surprise; I figured you had a place in mind."

"I do have a place in mind and we'll go there unless you have somewhere you'd like to go."

"No, I'll go for the surprise."

"Excuse me a minute while I go and speak to the pilot, he doesn't know where we're going."

When he got back from the flight deck, they had dinner, watched a movie and went to sleep. They were so physically exhausted that they went to sleep without the St. Agnes. The next day they touched down in San Diego. Doc had ordered a limo, and he gave the driver an address. When they got to the building, Shannon could see that it was a condo building of about thirty stories. They went in; the doorman greeted them and by pre-arrangement, let them into a condo on the top floor. The condo was empty of furniture but had stunning views over the ocean with floor to ceiling windows everywhere. It had six bedrooms, seven bathrooms, two offices, a kitchen, living and dining room. The deck was huge and ran around all four sides of the building. The condo consumed the entire thirtieth floor of the building.

"What is this? Shannon asked.

Doc said, "I figured we needed a place in the sun for vacations with our five kids, so decorate away, the building is your wedding present."

He handed her a sales brochure for the building. It was called St. Agnes Towers.

"What are we to do with this building, shall we rent out suites, sell off condos or what do you have in mind?"

"I've been thinking of diversifying into other business areas and maybe using this building as both a U.S. head office and a starting point for new software developers. We can easily accommodate over two hundred suites here. New developers would come here first and graduate to luxury Lion's Pride campuses as they prove their development capability. As we've discussed, I want to develop more Lion's Pride luxury campuses in highly desirable locations. I'm thinking of the South of France, the Caribbean, Whistler, Thailand, and maybe Hainan Island in South China.

We could get involved in the educational side, graduating our own developers in countries where software education is lagging ours. I'd also like to start our own production studio. I'm thinking of a world-class studio to take the software produced by our partners to the market ready level.

We'll provide education to graduate our developers. Also we will provide the workplaces for them to create their software such as Lion's Pride. We'll have the studio for the final production of their work and the infrastructure to take it to market. It will be a fully integrated company where we control all the steps from developer education through marketing the final products.

We also need to think about a campus in the

vicinity of Washington, DC to handle our new government software business.

I'd like to turn the day-to-day operations of Software Conceptions Inc. over to Bill as President. I'll retain the title of CEO and use my time to look into other opportunities for Bev and us around the world. I've been thinking a lot lately about China. I have a feeling that there is serious money to be made there."